– Liverpool –
MMXXIV

Lost in the Garden

dead ink

Copyright © Adam S. Leslie, 2024

The right of Adam S. Leslie to be identified as the author of this work has been asserted by them in accordance with the Copyright, Designs and Patents Act 1988.

First published in Great Britain in 2024 by Dead Ink, an imprint of Cinder House Publishing Limited.

Print ISBN 9781915368485
eBook ISBN 9781915368492

Cover design by Luke Bird / lukebird.co.uk
Typeset by Steve J Shaw / white-space.uk
Edited by Dan Coxon

Printed and bound in Great Britain by Clays Ltd, Elcograf S.p.A.

www.deadinkbooks.com

 Supported using public funding by
ARTS COUNCIL ENGLAND

 Funded by UK Government

MIX
Paper | Supporting responsible forestry
FSC® C018072

Lost in the Garden

Adam S. Leslie

dead ink

Dedicated to the memory of
Sonya Chenery

I always assumed we'd end up on a park bench somewhere having weird conversations about snails, unusual musical instruments and Doctor Who well into our 90s, but fate bonked you on the noggin and now I have to do all this without you. You were one of the very best of all people – deeply creative, endlessly curious and fiercely moral right down to your atoms. An artist, singer, songwriter and musician (as folk singer Nya Shelley, or a saw-playing Marlene Dietrich); an advocate for mental health and the queer community; and someone with whom I was always sure of a fascinating conversation about everything and anything. I miss you tons, Sonya. Anyway, here's a book, I think you'd have liked it. Millie Molly Hooray!

On meadow green live oak and snail
No plough to toil of furrow
The shepherd sits 'neath starry sky
He'll rise again tomorrow

1

Ice-cream van chimes elicit a synaesthetic Pavlovian response. The sound tastes of vanilla; it tastes of chocolate flake and neon-red spirals of strawberry sauce. It tastes of all the myriad possibilities illustrated in lurid colour beside the serving hatch. A miniature church cast in pinks and yellows and powder-blues, its oversaturated bells calling the children of the parish to worship. The communion wafer, the communion soft-whip ice cream, the blessed chocolate flake rearing from its icy white hillock like the pole of the holy crucifix, waiting for the cross-beam, waiting in giddy anticipation to receive the condemned Christ in His martyrdom. And the swirl of strawberry sauce, right at the very end, representing the blood of Our Lord swirling down the hill of Golgotha.

It was six years at least since Heather had last heard the chimes of an ice-cream van. Six years since the rattly metallic music had drifted across the foot of her street, *half a pound of tuppenny rice, half a pound of treacle*, then turned the corner onto Catswort Drive, the way it always did, parking up across the road from the post box, engine thrumbling. And then – after the momentary shock had subsided and before delight had fully set in – the race against time: pulling on shoes, collecting stray coins, corralling family members. Herding everyone outside before the van hoisted its skirts and wended its inscrutable way to a more remote part of the village.

You had to be quick. The ice cream van was not a patient creature.

2

Six years ago, a different kind of pollen drifted in on the summer winds.

Up till then, Heather had been training to become an astronaut. Or at least, that's what she liked to tell people. No one ever believed her, of course, but that was the joy of it – their scepticism as she doggedly stuck to her story, adding ever more unlikely details onto the creaking, swaying stack of unlikely details.

'They make us sleep in our spacesuits,' she would say, 'even when we're at home. It's difficult for married couples, so the government supplies them with special double spacesuits they can wear at the same time.' Or, 'An important part of astronaut training is wrestling, to see how strong we are. Only the very strongest and most agile can become astronauts. But anyone caught biting is expelled.' Or, 'When you go to space, they give you freeze-dried water to drink. You add water, and you get more water. The only problem is, this water is twice as heavy as it has twice the amount of water in it. So astronauts spend a lot of time weeing.'

People her own age usually called bullshit pretty quickly, but older adults – the grown-ups – were always too polite, even as Heather watched their eyes cloud over. Their questions tailed off and they were reduced to repeating 'oh' and 'that sounds fascinating' as her yarn grew increasingly colourful and far-fetched.

In reality, Heather had no idea what she wanted to do. She'd toyed with the idea of becoming an author. The writer's lifestyle really appealed to her, which was odd for someone who found it impossible to sit still. But in the end, despite sitting behind a laptop all afternoon and staring at the blinking cursor, she couldn't think of a single thing to write.

She took jobs in shops and call centres, but was just too restless, too fond of pranks, and was fired from every single one, usually for frogs or insects or swearing or face paint or weird smells or inappropriate clothing or too much running around; or even, on one occasion, fireworks. Four years, thirteen jobs, thirteen dismissals, no regrets.

'What do you want to be when you grow up?' adults asked her when she was little.

'I'm not going to grow up,' she'd always said; and true to her word, she never did. If only 'an enthusiastic pursuit of mischief' was a viable career option. Or even plain old 'farting around'. Why grow up and become all boring and old when there were yet more hijinks to be had? She hoped beyond hope that *something* would happen to derail the adult world's obsession with Settling Down, Finding a Career and Fitting In.

Over the coming months, Heather wondered if she'd wished too hard.

3

After the strangers came, nothing was the same again.

Voices on the radio told the people to stay inside, and the people did. Voices on the radio promised the army would come and make things right, but the army never arrived, and soon most of the voices on the radio stopped speaking too.

It took the people a while to figure out where this sudden influx of strangers had come from, exactly who they were. Immigrants who'd been sedated or hypnotised, perhaps, wandering blank-eyed across the countryside, loitering in public byways, utterly passive, arms by their sides, twitching mouths agape. Maybe refugees, mute from shock, fleeing some unknown catastrophe in one of the big cities.

Before long, though, people began to recognise relatives they'd recently buried. There was Uncle Frank, lost to cancer a month ago, roaming the village streets. And there too was Grandma, gone after a tumble in her hallway, now blithely meandering across Headingham football pitch as if she'd never been away, as if she'd never been lowered into a hole in the churchyard in front of her sobbing relatives.

They were all dead.

At first it was assumed they'd risen from their graves like zombies or vampires – but they were neither rotten nor bloodied, nor had any aversion to daylight. Besides, the topsoil at the church was intact: those who hadn't been cremated were still safely interred.

These were ghosts.

At least, that was all anyone could think to call them. If they *were* ghosts, they were corporeal ghosts, mostly clad in dusty black formalwear, pressed white shirts and shiny black shoes. Strong, clumsy, bad-tempered, stripped of personality. They would break fences, clatter into each other, bring down garden walls and hedges, smash windows – lash out at anyone who came within reach. Mostly, though, they just stood around with an air of mournful detachment, speaking wordlessly, mouthing along to a long-forgotten script. And when they weren't standing still, they wandered. They migrated in sluggish, dejected flocks, trudging across fields, ambling along country lanes, or milling in paddocks and meadows.

Heather spent hours of her life sitting on the deep windowsill of her bedroom, gazing over her garden and the fields beyond, just to watch the dead wander to and fro. She'd bring a pillow for her back, and a cup of tea or a glass of lemonade to tuck beneath the triangular crook of her knees, and she'd peer out like a cat surveying local birds. This was the aspect of the writer's lifestyle she'd secretly longed for: the endless afternoons of contemplation. The silence of her house and the silence of the world beyond the double-glazing. And there she was in between the two spaces, content to float in her own liminal void, safe in her nook, just being and thinking.

Sometimes the dead did nothing, and that was fine. Sometimes the garden was empty and there was barely anyone in the fields either, and that was fine too. And for someone who found it impossible to sit still, she really took to this new vocation. It was oddly peaceful, oddly calming, even as her back twitched and tingled at the thought of the ghouls finding a way inside and wreaking havoc in her little home.

Heather didn't recognise most of the ghosts. She guessed they came from long ago. Maybe even hundreds of years, though it was hard to tell from their clothing. But occasionally she saw ones she knew. There was Mrs Kelway, who taught her to play the recorder; and there was her father, as young as the day he died.

Mrs Kelway lingered in the garden. She stayed there a whole week, gazing around as if she'd forgotten something, like a woman searching for a lost cat. But to Heather's disappointment, her father drifted right through, gone by nightfall. She always hoped he'd return, but he never did. She imagined him wandering lonely over hillsides, trying to find his way home, unaware he'd already been and gone.

The ghosts never looked angry or fierce, but always perfectly serene even as they clamoured to get inside. Like magpies, they collected weapons – they'd find cudgels and they'd strike if they got close enough. No one knew why.

Despite the tranquillity of her days, Heather found it difficult to sleep. Often the dead would bang their hands on her windows. They'd broken into other houses and killed the occupants. Most had been old people who couldn't escape in time, but it still worried her. What if she somehow slept through the whole thing? No matter how many doors she locked behind her on her way to bed, how well fortified her house was, how many bookcases and chairs she stacked against her bedroom door, Heather only dreamt of ghosts. Ghosts in her house, ghosts in her room, ghosts while she took a bath or sat on the toilet, ghosts looming over her as she lay paralysed with fear.

But during the day she enjoyed watching their strange minimalist existence, like experimental theatre, their skin greenish-white and translucent in the sunlight. She found it hard to look away. The sad bespectacled girl who stood barefoot on her lawn for three days, motionless except for an occasional turn of her head. The man in the peaked cap who lingered by the fence and gestured backwards, then wandered off with rounded shoulders. The family of ghosts who went everywhere in a cluster, two adults and three children, carving an aimless trajectory across the fields and her neighbours' gardens. Heather wondered whether they'd been a family in life, or if they'd found each other after they'd died and formed a unit out of instinct.

Sometimes the ghosts' heads would tilt suddenly upwards and they'd stare straight at Heather, eyes wide. Sometimes they'd point. Heather always ducked away from the window whenever this happened, receding into her house till her back stopped twitching and her skin lost its goosebumps. Most of the time, though, the ghosts kept on the move. Or they'd gather at the top of the field by the hedgerows and long-abandoned water troughs, and just lurk for no readily apparent reason.

Besides the sudden reappearance of the dead, other things were wrong too. Just little things. Front doors changed colour overnight, their locks fit different keys, they opened outward instead of inward. Pets changed colour, or were slightly larger or smaller than before, or they changed sex. Light switches inverted, windscreen wipers swapped sides, fridge magnets demagnetised, televisions detuned, piano keyboards swapped ends with the high notes on the left and the low notes on the right. Beyond the rash of wild conspiracy theories, nobody had a good suggestion, either for the changes or the ghosts. The best anyone could come up with was that reality itself had become sick.

One particularly stark and humid Thursday afternoon, Heather's boyfriend Gabriel came to visit. But he was dead too, and she hadn't even known. He peered through her window for a while, but soon meandered away again, a stout branch clutched in his fist.

They found Gabriel's body in his flat, slumped in front of his burbling television. He'd taken an overdose.

Heather cried for three days.

Eventually, the people grew bored of waiting and ventured back outside. The ghosts were slow – it was possible to avoid them and they were easy to outrun. But they killed the complacent, they killed the picnickers and the sunbathers and the outdoor lovers. They could band together, cut off escape routes, and that would be that.

They themselves were, however, impossible to kill. People tried fighting them, hitting them with cars, beating them with rocks and clubs, dismembering them, setting them on fire... but they always remained stubbornly unscathed. The only way to dispose of them was to trap them – push them into pits and bury them, or herd them into concrete bunkers and seal them inside. But this proved to be too inefficient, and so many people died trying that eventually it was considered safest just to leave them roaming and stay out of their way.

Heather formed the Chicken Club with five of her friends. Tall and charismatic Steven, Rachel with her cynical smirk, Sandy's big smile and freckles, muscular John's wild bushy beard like an Edwardian strongman, and Paulette's amazing brain always thinking of new ideas. They were the six closest friends that had ever been for those precious few weeks.

They set each other challenges. Dares to keep life exciting, now that everything else had ground to a halt: walking blindfolded along the footpath between the High Street and School Lane; affixing stickers to the backs of ghosts; playing games of hopscotch on the old disused playground while the dead closed in. John liked to wrestle the ghosts – he was good at disarming them and laughed at their blank-eyed struggling. Heather's favourite was the one where she and Steven stood in the woodland to see how long they could kiss with their eyes closed. Two minutes. Now three minutes. After three and a half minutes, they raced back to Heather's house all hot and damp, and had sex in the hallway by the wellington boots.

Bystanders winced whenever the Chicken Club convened, watching between fingers and from behind curtains, but none of the gang was ever seriously hurt. They were always too wily – their antics had made them alert, and each of them survived to fight another day.

By August, Sandy, John and Paulette had all disappeared.

4

Six years of summer.

Six years without grey skies or snowdrifts or icy northerly blasts. Six years of sweltering in the same gelatinous humidity. Very occasionally it was a dry heat, a soily heat smelling of bug carcasses and stones, but usually the air sweated as much as the people. When it rained, it rained hot, and the villagers gathered outside, splashing and dancing, or lingering under the skies with their mouths wide like baby birds.

Paulette wondered if a good stout winter might clear away the dead – she'd look out of her window one frosty morning to see the fields sparkling and normality restored. But soon Paulette was gone, and so was John and so was Sandy. And soon afterwards, Paul Atkinson and Lizzie Wells and Simon Hunter and Paul Howard had all disappeared too.

People enjoyed the perpetual summer for the first year. 'I don't miss all that horrid cold,' they would say, licking their ice-cream cones with a happy chuckle. But by the second year, resentment began to set in. They grumbled more and more. They prayed for cold, they prayed for an end to this – they just wanted *something* to change. By the third year, the elderly had grown so tired of it all that they began to pass away, joining the ranks of the ghosts to wander blank-faced across the countryside. *There's Sue Jones from the library; there are Irene and Pearl and Katie from the knitting club; there's Bill, the allotment treasurer.* The middle-aged, meanwhile, became sluggish and indolent and careless. They fell foul of accidents or were hammered to death by their own departed parents and neighbours. Many refused to take even the most basic precautions, and simply went about their day as if nothing had changed. Nearly all of them were killed within a few weeks.

Only the young survived. They thrived, climbing trees, scavenging food and building fortifications. Childhood called them back; it had prepared them for this moment.

On meadow green live oak and snail
No plough to spoil the furrow
This shepherd now 'neath starry skies
Shall ride again tomorrow

5

Steven Cook was bad at hide-and-seek. He was so tall and always wore such bright colours. Heather found a chunk of bark the size of her arm and hurled it into the tree, where it caught him square on the side of the head. She bounced and giggled.

'Hey!' said Steven.

'Three and a half minutes!'

'Well, maybe I wanted to be found, have you considered that?'

Heather raised her arms towards him, stretching and straining and jumping. 'Pull me up!'

But Steven scuttled down from the tree and raced past her, zigzagging deliriously out into the meadow, where the heat haze threatened to swallow him up.

'I want to play in the trees!' Heather called after him. 'Hey, let's have sex. I've never had sex in a tree!'

'You wouldn't like it,' Steven told her, looping around her and laughing at nothing.

'Who says I wouldn't like it?'

'I says you wouldn't like it. It's not your thing.'

'How do you know it's not my thing?'

Steven slumped down into the long grass with a happy grunt. 'Because I know what your thing is. Tree sex is uncomfortable. Branches poke into you. You always feel like you're going to fall out.'

'Wait – you've had sex in a tree?' Heather kicked him in the side.

He grinned up at her, one eye scrunched up from the glare. 'Of course.'

'Who with?'

'A lady.'

'I don't believe you.' She sat down next to him, halfway along the length of his torso, and pressed her hands on his belly.

'Suit yourself.'

'Who? Come on, tell me who with. Is it someone I know?'

'I never reveal my sources. I'm the model of discretion. Anyway, it was ages ago.'

'I don't care anyway. Do I seem like someone who cares? You can do what you like. None of my business.' Heather shrugged and lay her curls on Steven's belly, squinting up at the baking blue void. Something flashed and sparkled overhead.

'I hear, with my little ear,' said Heather later as they strolled back the way they'd come, kicking their feet in the dust of adjacent summers, 'something beginning with C.'

'The sea?'

Heather dug her hands deep into her pockets, hunched her shoulders, and walked around Steven in a loping figure of eight. Steven bounced from foot to foot.

The sun had edged closer to the horizon by now and was hot and gold and swollen. The grass smelled of evening;

Steven and Heather's shadows stretched out along the track in front of them, stupid and elongated.

'I really miss Sandy,' said Heather.

'Sandy, Sandy, Sandy, she always came in handy.'

'Do you think she's dead?'

'Maybe.' Steven shrugged.

'Doesn't that bother you?'

'Yeah.'

'If they're dead,' said Heather, 'how come they don't have ghosts?'

As if summoned directly from the underworld, a ghost emerged from the bushes immediately to the left of Heather. It was Mr Jankowski, who used to run the newsagent before he died of cancer. He wasn't carrying a weapon, but he did seem keen to wrestle. He wrapped his arms around her in a clumsy bear hug and the two of them tumbled to the grass, Heather wriggling in alarm.

'Get him off me!' she cried, as Mr Jankowski tried to squeeze and bite and gouge her.

Steven folded his arms and chortled.

'Steven, I mean it! Get him off me!'

Steven glanced languidly around till he located a sturdy branch – and then proceeded to beat Mr Jankowski with it till he lay still. Heather extracted herself from the tangle of limbs.

'What the fuck, Steven?'

'He just wanted to play.'

Heather aimed a kick at Steven but he stumbled out of the way, laughing.

'He could've killed me, you fucking fuck! Jesus, Steven!'

Steven bent to examine Mr Jankowski, then placed a foot on the ghost's shoulder and rolled him over onto his back. Mr Jankowski was motionless, his limbs floppy and his face neutral, almost serene – but his eyes still moved, darting this way and that without focusing on anything in particular. He seemed unaware of Steven and Heather's presence now.

'Come on,' said Steven, 'he'll be getting back up soon.'

'Your turn to hide,' said Steven.

'But I already found you.'

'Exactly. Now it's your turn.'

'I don't want to play this anymore,' said Heather.

'Come on, I hid for you. Now it's your turn.'

'Fine, okay. But this is the last one.'

Heather retreated to her favourite shady dell. She sat on the ground with her back against a tree and waited. She'd made sure to choose a hiding place obscure enough to seem convincing, but obvious enough that she'd be easily found and they could get back to something more fun like naked bedtime wrestling.

She waited. She daydreamed about Steven in various stages of undress. She drummed her palms on the ground, improvising a complicated tattoo. She watched a shield bug clamber across the dirt and stones, and wondered how it made its decisions and whether it knew it was making decisions. She constructed a list of crisp flavours in her head, from favourite to least favourite (prawn cocktail top; roast chicken bottom). And the shadows of the trees grew ever taller, stretching their crooked fingers out across the dell.

How long have I been here? She glanced at her watch, but had forgotten to remember what time she'd arrived. Steven was taking too long, though, she knew that much. And now she could see black and white specks at the far end of the dell, shuffling to and fro. The ghosts were becoming aware of her presence.

Heather stood.

'Steven?' she called.

She scrambled up the side of the dell and back into the meadow. She'd half expected to see Steven's lanky frame darting through the tall grass, half frantic with worry. But no – Steven was nowhere to be seen. The meadow was deserted except for ghosts.

Heather walked back to Headingham, worry gnawing at her belly. The outskirts were thick with the dead, so she took a long route down a side street past the abandoned Shellycoat Arms pub, its sightless windows boarded up. A pink clown face leered out of the chipboard, spray-painted by Rachel two years earlier. Someone more recently had added the word 'COCK' emanating from the clown's mouth. 'If you're going to mess with a person's artwork,' Rachel had raged to the universe at large, 'at least make it clever.'

Heather was fortunate she'd come back when she did. She risked getting cut off if she left it much later. Spending the night in the fields with no torch and no provisions – and no toilet – wasn't her idea of a fun time.

There was a light on at Steven's house. She cupped her face to the kitchen window. The living room glowed amber through the open kitchen door. She could see the living room curtains and the top of Steven's green armchair, and his drawing of a cat framed on the far wall. But no sign of Steven.

'Are you here?' she called, banging on the front door.

She trudged around the back of the house. Steven's bedroom light was on too, and his curtains drawn.

The back door was unlocked.

There was movement in Steven's bedroom. The squeaking of bed springs. She expected to find him halfway through some clandestine fuckery with another woman – her bottom and legs a mirror image of his bottom and legs like some grotesque wobbly playing card, the Jack of Sex – but was instead greeted by the sight of two large suitcases open on his bed. Steven was packing.

'Where *were* you?' he said, badly feigning surprise.

'Where were *you*?' said Heather.

'I couldn't find you. I looked all over.'

'Not very hard. I didn't hide very hard. What's all this?'

'It's just for a couple of weeks.'

'When were you going to tell me?'

'I didn't want you to be upset,' said Steven.

'Why would I be upset?'

'I'll be back before you know it.'

'Why would I be upset?'

Steven continued to pack in silence, stacking folded shirts on top of folded shirts.

'Steven, why would I be upset? Where are you going?'

'Almanby.'

Heather felt as if someone had taken a big swing and thumped her hard in the stomach. '*Almanby?* You're serious?'

'I told you you'd be upset.'

'What are you going there for?'

'Because I want to.'

'But… it's dangerous. Everyone knows it's dangerous. You're not supposed to go to Almanby. That's just… that's just one of the basics.'

'Have you ever been to Almanby?'

'Of course not.'

'Then how do you know?'

'*Everyone* knows.'

'Everyone knows because people tell them. But if they never go, how do they really know?'

'Because. I don't need to go into space to know there's no oxygen.'

'I'll be fine.'

'I'm never going to see you again.'

'Don't be silly.' Steven shifted uncomfortably, refused to meet her gaze while he packed.

'No one comes back from Almanby. You know that.'

'No one comes back because no one ever goes.' He kissed her on the forehead. 'Where do you like to eat?'

Heather shrugged. It was like someone had removed a cork and all the energy had drained out of her.

This would be the last time she ever saw Steven. She knew it and he knew it.

'Why? Why Almanby?'

'I want to help.'

'How?'

'I don't know yet.'

'You help here. You look after people, you bring food to people. You help people build walls and make their houses strong.'

Steven was indeed something of a local hero – oozing charisma, he'd fortified the homes of the few remaining old people, helped them move safely around the village, organised grocery deliveries. He'd even built barricades across some of Headingham's streets and the villagers had a little street party, till the ghosts knocked the barricades back down. But it was fun while it lasted, and everyone appreciated the gesture. People loved Steven.

'Remember what it used to be like?' he said. 'Before all this? Back when there used to be change and progress and… life. When stuff actually happened. When there were new buildings and new inventions and things to do. When people actually worked towards something. Everyone had their own little dreams and ambitions and wanted to make something of their lives.'

'So?'

'So, I want to help.'

'So help here.'

'I have helped here. I want to help somewhere else.'

'So help somewhere else. Why does it have to be Almanby?'

'I want to help in Almanby.'

'Mrs Gibson.'

'What about Mrs Gibson?'

'She never came back.'

'That was three years ago.'

'She only went for the weekend.'

'Heather, people disappear all the time. We know that better than anyone else. John and Paulette and Sandy. Prithpal and Paul and Lizzie. All the others. You don't need to be in Almanby to vanish off the face of the Earth.'

'Steven, listen to me. This is crazy. It's just so obvious I don't even know how to say it. *Don't walk on the quicksand, don't touch the powerlines, don't go off with strangers, don't play on the farm, don't go to Almanby*. How hard can that be?'

'Look, I'm just going to scope it out, see what I can do. I'll be fine. Hand on heart.'

'Right.'

'Where do you like to eat?'

'I dunno.'

'You like Badoer's?'

'The Italian place?'

'Yeah.'

'It's all right.'

'I'll book a table for two, Badoer's Italian Restaurant, three weeks from today, okay? I promise. In three weeks, I'll be sitting across from you chowing down on ciabatta and stuffed mushrooms.'

'No you won't.'

'Heather. I swear.'

'I'm going to miss you, Steven.'

On meadow green lives Oaken Snail
No doubt to spoil his burrow
The shepherdess 'neath starry skies
Shall hide her face tomorrow

6

Six minutes late.

Six minutes late.

Rachel Harrison and her bicycle lean against the red telephone box on Wainford Green – Rachel on one side and her bicycle on the other.

Six minutes late.

Rachel's arms are folded. She's still, patient, waiting.

He's never been six minutes late before.

With each passing second, the fact that he's late at all seems ever more ludicrous.

Six minutes late.

Six minutes late.

Suddenly, the telephone rings. Its shrill scream arcs like lightning through the stillness of dusk.

Rachel opens the door and lifts the receiver.

'Yeah?'

She listens to the voice on the other end. And then, with dismay, she closes her eyes and leans her forehead against the glass. It feels cool against her skin.

'Are you sure? I need you to be absolutely certain.'

Rachel nods at the sound of his voice, even though he cannot see her.

'*Okay,*' *she says at last, and hangs up the phone.*

She kicks her way out of the telephone box, grabs her bicycle, and throws it at the hefty trunk of the Wainford Green oak tree. The bike clatters into a heap a few feet short.

'*Bollocks!*' *Rachel yells.* '*Bollocks, fuck and bollocks!*'

7

Dusk was Rachel's favourite time of day. The heady stink of night-time plants, still hot from the day's glare, filling the atmosphere now with their aromas. Everything red and purple and lavender, at once insubstantial and supremely solid. Nothing was quite real at twilight. Her friends looked like ghosts, and ghosts looked like faceless department store mannequins. This was the most dangerous time: it was more than possible to stumble into an ambush, but Rachel enjoyed the frisson. She loved swerving out of the reach of grabbing fingers, her tyres crackling in the dust, safe in the knowledge that the ghosts could never match her speed.

There were only a couple of surviving members of the Chicken Club now. Three when Steven had been here. But they hadn't seen him in months, and there was every possibility it was just Rachel and Heather left.

At the height of their fame, they were the six biggest celebrities in the area – the Three Musketeers x2. There was a Chicken Club fan club – a club for a club – and Paulette wrote a column in the weekly gazette in which she outlined each of their antics in full. Steven and Sandy were the fan favourites – Steven was pure charisma and Sandy was just so sweet. But the others had their admirers too, and traded off their popularity to varying degrees. Rachel (the dark, mysterious one) basked in the attention – no, she basked in the *admiration* – but never really interacted with the fans. Heather (the zany one), meanwhile, fully exploited the situation, exploring all the strange and cobwebby corners of her sexuality with a variety of willing gentlemen, even though everyone knew she was 'secretly' in love with Steven.

More than a year after the Chicken Club had officially disbanded – following the disappearance of Sandy, the first to go – Rachel would still be approached by tentative strangers. 'Excuse me, are you Rachel Harrison…?' She missed the thrill of it all. She missed the anticipation and the adrenaline spikes and the feeling of being alive. It was a shame it had to end when it did. There wasn't much these days which could replicate it.

Well, there was one thing. But it was costly.

The Triscutine Picture Palace was Headingham's very own one-screen art deco cinema, a marble-white slab in the gloom nestled among a bed of nettles and thistles grown wild. The Triscutine's owner, Rob Hartley, had died almost two years ago, and even now could still be seen glumly roaming the playing field behind the cricket pavilion. A small army of volunteers had kept the cinema afloat ever since – and by Rachel's reckoning, tonight would be Heather's shift.

This was the first job Heather was actually good at, let alone interested in… and of course, it was unpaid. That pretty much summed Heather up. Still, it kept her out of mischief, apart from occasional farting noises from the back row during some of the more torpid films.

Rachel dismounted while she was still in motion, unhooked the pizza box from between the handlebars, and deftly nudged the bike to a standstill against the side of the cinema. It slid a few feet, the handlebars twisted round like a snapped neck, and neatly parked itself. Feigning nonchalance, Rachel shouldered the door open and pushed through into darkness.

The auditorium contained a solitary figure two rows from the front, mop of curls distinct against the throbbing screen. Rachel sauntered down the outside aisle, shuffled along row C, and slotted in next to Heather. She dumped the pizza box onto Heather's lap.

'Ooh, my favourite – food!' said Heather. She flipped open the lid, and together they tucked into the glistening pizza. Mushrooms and artichoke hearts. Heather was a vegetarian, bless her little artichoke heart.

'No customers?' said Rachel.

'Nope.'

They chewed in silence, watching colours and shapes flicker across the screen. Rachel squinted. The film seemed to consist mostly of pulsating blobs, arcs of red, orange and yellow, with green threads wriggling in between. Occasional glimpses of human faces. A cat lying on floorboards convulsing, or maybe dancing. A lingering close-up on woodgrain. Fluid in a jar or vase... murky, dirty, something floating in it. Two women in silhouette, holding hands, walking down an avenue of tall trees. Or... no, there's something between them, something large and dark and organic, like a huge internal organ, and they're carrying it, straining under the weight. A field, a figure in the distance – a young man, partially hidden behind a hedge, apparently watching. Watching the viewer? Or watching someone just off frame, behind the camera. A dog. A tracking shot through a garden overgrown with tall grass, hollyhocks, foxgloves and gooseberry bushes, the picture almost too orange to see. A wooden gate, a child sitting on the gate holding an ice cream. Black beetles, a billion of them, swarming across a field. And that cat again, still writhing but as if to music. Was it injured or just happy? Then the sea, frothing and bubbling… coins sparkling in a rock pool. A row of toy soldiers in a gloomy attic, all decked out in bottle-green uniforms, bayonets glistening with blood. A little girl, lying on her back in the long grass, her bright red shoes jutting skywards. And a hole in the ground with something big and dark and alive down down down inside towards the bottom.

'What is this anyway?' said Rachel.

'It's called *The Something Wheel*. It's slightly different every time I watch it.'

'How's that even possible?'

'I don't know. They've all been like this recently. The last four or five.' Heather pointed at the screen. 'That tree has never been in it before.'

'How many times have you sat through this one film?'

'Six. This is the seventh. No one else ever comes.'

'Right.'

The soundtrack largely consisted of a low hum, like a loose electrical connection, and something which sounded like turning pages or an object being swished vigorously through the air.

'I got a phone call,' said Rachel.

Heather sat up and looked at her. 'Seriously?'

'Yeah.'

'I didn't know you even had a phone.'

'Phone box.'

'You lucky bastard. You were just walking past and it was for you?'

'No, I already knew when he'd call.'

'Still, that's jammy. Who was it?'

'Remember Oscar?'

'Which Oscar?'

'There is only Oscar.'

'Oh. No, then.'

Rachel took a big bite of pizza and chewed thoughtfully.

'And?' said Heather.

'He wants me to deliver a package to him.'

Rachel took another big bite of pizza.

'And?' said Heather.

'Thing is,' Rachel told her, 'it's secret.'

'Secret? Why's it secret?'

'Because of what's in the package.'

'What's in the package?'

'I just told you. It's secret.'

Heather's eyes grew big and round. She sat up straight. 'But it's illegal, right?'

'Terribly illegal.'

'Drugs?'

'Better than that.'

'Guns?'

'Nope. I told you, it's secret.'

'So what's my role?'

'You don't have a role. I'm just bringing tasty pizza for my best pal Heather.'

'Come on, Rachel – you tell me there's an illegal package, and then—'

'It's dangerous. Too dangerous for you.'

'How can it be too dangerous for me? I was in the Chicken Club. I'm the zany one, I'll do anything. How can it be too dangerous for Heather McLagan?'

Rachel gave Heather the most extravagant wink she could muster, tweaked her friend's nose, then headed for the exit, hands thrust deep in pockets.

'Anyway, better get on,' she said.

'Rachel!'

'See ya next time!'

'*Rachel!*'

By the time Heather had followed her to the front door, Rachel was already cycling round and round in tight circles, her face almost invisible in the half-light.

'Where is this Oscar of yours anyway?' said Heather, pizza box clasped awkwardly under one arm. She took a bite of pizza. It tasted different outside – earthier, more wholesome. She had a sudden craving for ginger beer.

'Almanby,' said Rachel.

'*Almanby?*'

'What?'

'You're going to Almanby?'

'So?'

Heather gestured broadly, as if hoping to conjure the all-too-obvious answer in the air in front of her.

'Oh, Steven,' said Rachel. 'I forgot.'

'How could you forget? *Steven. Almanby.*'

'Right.'

'That does it, I'm definitely coming, and you can't say no.'

'He can look after himself.'

'He only went for three weeks. That was six months ago.'

'He's hooked up with some girl. Forget about him.'

'It's not that…'

'Don't kid yourself, Heth, it really is that.'

'No, Rachel, listen. There's something I need to show you.'

'What is it?'

'It's secret.'

'Very funny.'

'I'm not joking, Rach.'

'All right.' Rachel rolled to a halt. Heather climbed on the back, one arm wrapped around Rachel's middle, the other still clutching the pizza box.

'Where are we going?' said Rachel.

'My house.'

Pedalling hard to account for the extra load, Rachel set off back along the lane.

8

When Heather was a child, she would hide from her mother
for hours at a time in the loft. 'How stupid she must be,'
Heather would think. 'I always hide in the same place, but
still she can never find me.' Only later, when she was an
adult, did Heather realise that her mother had simply taken
the opportunity for a break. An afternoon gin and tonic
while her daughter crouched in the loft rubbing her hands
with devilish glee.

Now her mother was gone, and the loft was full of all
her old belongings. Her hats, her notebooks, those eerie
watercolour paintings she always brought home from charity
shops. But Heather still hid up here sometimes – when she
couldn't settle in her own bed, when the thought of ghosts
breaking in through the windows made her too jumpy to
sleep, she would lie up here on the floorboards and gaze at
the stars through the skylight.

A few weeks ago, she'd found a shortwave radio in one of
the boxes, red and dusty and battered, and small enough to
fit in her pocket. Silver plastic lettering spelled out the word
'ORBITRAN'. She had no memory of ever seeing it before,
but written on a piece of tape on the back was the name
'ALICE McLAGAN'. It'd belonged to her grandmother.

Heather found a fresh pair of batteries in her odds-and-ends drawer, popped them in – and to her joy, the old thing worked! It mostly emitted swirling, fizzing white noise, but at least she was getting something.

That evening, she'd sat up in the loft and carefully turned the little plastic dial on the side, hoping to find music, or even someone telling stories before bed. Foreign voices skittered past through the interference – French, Dutch, Spanish, and other languages she couldn't identify. A flash of opera. What seemed to be a road safety song sung by German children. A brass band rendition of a song she remembered from long ago.

Each little flower that opens, each little bird that sings
He made their glowing colours, he made their tiny wings

And then a familiar voice. Speaking very calmly and very evenly.

She'd stopped here, barely breathing, and listened to the voice. For hours. Till the sun came up and the loft was flooded with grainy grey light that seemed to sit inside her lungs. And the voice never paused, it never seemed to grow tired or slow. Heather wondered if it was a recording, but something told her this was happening live. He was speaking now.

'I've been listening for the last few nights,' Heather told Rachel as she fine-tuned the dial. The man was never quite in the same place twice, as if he was drifting, blowing on the wind. Even though Heather knew he wasn't.

'And?' said Rachel.

'Ssh.'

A blip, a fraction-second of a voice. *That was it!*

She backtracked by half a millimetre, then a quarter of a millimetre.

And there he was. Right on the edge of hearing, barely audible above the sea wash of interference. His voice was as relentless as ever, though it sounded a little more unsteady today. Wavery.

'What's he saying?' said Rachel.

'Ssh.'

A microscopic nudge of the dial, and suddenly the man was there at the forefront.

I often feel warm sometimes. He's shamed by the grass he's in. And they knew Brazil, in spite of the fact that...

But it didn't last for long. After only a few seconds, the signal disintegrated back into noise again.

'It's drifting.'

'Heather, what is it?'

...So curious. I want to come with you. That's probably all that matters...

'He doesn't sound familiar to you?'

...Existence in all clarity. Groups fought across the globe. You can take over and dance once the column is safe. And they're tough to take good care of. A mixture of geohouse and fluterhosen. You're going to get your tail bodied off...

'No.'

'It's Steven.'

'It could be anyone,' said Rachel.

'It's Steven.'

'It's spy code. It's a numbers station.'

'Sometimes he calls for help. *Help me, please help me*. Over and over. The rest of the time it's this.'

'Where's it coming from?'

'Almanby.'

A chill rippled Jacob's ladder down Rachel's back. It couldn't be Steven... could it? The timbre sounded a little like him, but it was so frail, so hesitant. It had none of his brio, none of his verve and charisma. It was like Steven with all the Steven removed.

The voice disappeared once more and static rattled on for a few seconds, weaving, twining, kaleidoscoping, painting inscrutable patterns inside the electric void. Then a noise, like the voices of tormented souls, reared up behind it. A howling, cacophonous roar. Like nothing human, nothing earthly.

'Is that Almanby?' said Rachel, at last.

'Yeah. I worked out the range and the position.'

'What are we hearing?'

'I don't know. Just Almanby.'

The cacophony dipped, tuned out, faded once more beneath the wash of shortwave static and a brief burst of brass band music. Then:

...And, not surprisingly, the heart chambers are full. When she heard the rumours each time, she didn't say anything. She had a good reason to it. Cost him a good pound a week to keep shabbing up his clothes. You will be broke, and no one will give you the fare home.

And now the voice was gone. Heather turned the dial, but there was no sign of it. She clicked the radio off, and they were left in a pool of settling silence.

'We'll need a car,' said Rachel at last.

'We'll need a driver.'

'Leigh.'

'Leigh can't drive.'

'All right, Christie McNamara.'

'She disappeared, remember?'

'Paul Doolan.'

'He disappeared too,' said Heather. 'Paul and his sister went at the same time.'

'How about Simon?'

'He's gone too.'

'Seriously? Simon Thorpe?'

'About three weeks ago.'

'Nobody told me. Shit.'

'Simon's gone, Paul's gone, Jess is gone. Greg Hargreaves, Prithpal Gala, Helen Moore, Lucy Warren, Jack Peterson, April Pennymonger. Even Marcy Ziegler. All gone. Fuck, Rachel, that's a lot of people.'

'I know who we can ask.'

'Who?'

9

In other schools, in biology class, they dissected frogs and mice and crickets. I went to a Catholic school, so we just dissected bread.

The worst part about living in the countryside is all the nay-sayers. Or horses, as they're more commonly called.

I went through the library tearing out the final page from all the murder mystery books, so that readers would never find out where the author grew up.

On the weekend, I like to fly vintage planes – mostly Spitfires and Hurricanes, but I'm also bi-curious.

The later Jeeves and Wooster novels had more sex and violence. They were by 12A Wodehouse.

I remember the days when you could buy two altos and a soprano, and still have change from a tenor.

Bromine. It's the chemical element men can enjoy. Right, lads?

A goldfish is a great prize to win at the fair, isn't it? You win at the coconut shy, and you get a new pet. I was never good enough to win top prize, though, I only ever got second place. That's why my bedroom was always full of silverfish.

A pun that doesn't quite work is called a punnet. That was one.

Invisible ghost in the streets, visible ghost in the sheets.

If the singular of feet is foot and the singular of teeth is tooth, why isn't the singular of sheep, shoop? 'I'm the black shoop of the family.' I'd go with that.

What's a mountaineer's favourite music? Drum and basecamp. Thank you. I'm here all week.

The problem I have when I'm making pancakes is that I always get the milk and the flour mixed up.

When a statue becomes famous, do other statues erect a person to it?

My friend's cat scratched my face – bloody cheek!

How can you tell Angkor Wat is getting old? It's greying round the temples.

I found out why all that noise was coming from the lake. The local geese were having a gander reveal party.

You know how children in horror films are always, 'Mummy, the lady in the corner with no face talks to me when you're not here. She's nice, she tells me to do things, she's my friend.' Meanwhile, real children are howling and won't go to bed because they've seen a washing-up glove.

Shall I compare thee to a summer's day? You're a bit sticky and only tolerable in small doses.

I wonder if Chubby Checker ever twisted his ankle?

That most generously forgiving of all Greek singers – Magnanamouskouri. Don't leave yet, I have more where that came from.

I'm not superstitious and never will be, touch wood.

Irrespective of whether she has Bette Davis eyes – if all *the boys think she's a spy, independently of each other, there should at least be some sort of investigation.*

Don't you think that cartoon show Thundercats *should've just been about some cats hiding under the table with their ears flat?*

The best way to scotch a rumour is to cover it in pork and roll it in breadcrumbs.

Antonia Coleridge was crushingly shy. Excruciatingly shy. She hated being the centre of attention, she hated anyone looking at her. She had little self-confidence, not much in the way of charisma, and wanted nothing more than to blend into the background. She was embarrassed by her height and her stooping shoulders, she was embarrassed by her sexuality, she was embarrassed by her mixed-race heritage (when most people around her were white), she was embarrassed by the utter temerity of her own existence.

Naturally, Antonia Coleridge became a stand-up comedian.

And she hated every moment of it, every single millisecond that she stood up on stage and recited her sequence of increasingly desperate puns, but something drew her back, drew her back, drew her back, even as she played to audiences of twenty, then fifteen, then twelve, as more and more people died or vanished off the face of the Earth. She kept writing those crappy one-liners, she kept climbing up on stage, microphone gripped in her sweaty paw, to deliver them in her now-trademark wobbly monotone.

She did get laughs. Well, she got sympathetic chuckles. But even the chuckles made it worthwhile somehow, at least till the next joke fell flat. Then, at the end of the set, she'd leave the stage feeling wretched and hollow, and vow never to do it again.

She always did it again.

A large part of her drive, Antonia suspected, was simply the hope that one day Heather McLagan would show up. Heather McLagan would watch her set, Heather McLagan would laugh at her jokes, Heather McLagan would become a fan, and maybe even want to sleep with her.

Antonia was desperately, stupidly, achingly, pathetically in love with Heather McLagan.

Heather McLagan was everything Antonia wasn't. Small, charismatic, outgoing, universally popular, cute-as-a-pixie and naturally funny. And also straight. Heather went everywhere with the tall, charismatic, outgoing, universally popular, handsome-as-a-movie-star and naturally funny Steven. 'Forget it, mate,' Rachel would tell her. 'They're fucking.' But that didn't change the way Antonia felt.

Antonia existed on the periphery of Heather's friendship group, but suspected that Heather was barely even aware of her existence. Even in a village the size of Headingham, with its rapidly dwindling population, she somehow hadn't made it into Heather's sphere of consciousness. They'd interacted a few times, hung out as part of a larger group, but she doubted Heather could name her or pick her out of a line-up.

Tonight's gig initially felt like any other – a disappointingly-attended show held in the less-than-starry venue of Headingham village hall. Antonia was second on the bill to a floppy-haired ten-year-old boy whose jokes were even worse than hers, but who nonetheless seemed to have twice the confidence and received twice the laughs.

But, after such an inauspicious start, it turned out to be the gig she'd been working towards this whole time. As she squinted out into the audience, surveying her adversaries for the evening, she spotted an all-too-familiar bobble of curly hair on the back row.

Heather.

Heather is here!

* * *

Somehow, Antonia managed to get through her set without forgetting any of the jokes or blushing so hard her face exploded or simply fainting dead away. In fact, the extra little spike of adrenaline seemed to boost her comic timing, give her that little bit more edge and a little bit more punch. Jokes which had never got laughs before got laughs tonight. Even the Angkor Wat gag, which no one ever understood because no one in Headingham knew what Angkor Wat was. Even the fucking godawful Magnanamouskouri gag.

She fucking nailed it.

Heather and Rachel were waiting for her at the side doors when she left the village hall. Antonia's head throbbed and her whole body seemed to be trembling with a combination of adrenaline come-down, excitement and nerves. She tried her best to look nonchalant, like this wasn't the most significant night of her life, but instead felt stiff and awkward and weird.

So, no different to normal then.

'Hey, Ant, great show,' Rachel said, as she hopped down off the wheelie bins.

'Antonia,' said Antonia.

'How are you, buddy?'

'Tired. Hi, Heather.' She hoped that sounded sufficiently casual.

'Hi, Antonia,' said Heather, and Antonia almost dissolved there and then. *Heather knows my name.* Even if Antonia herself had only that moment said it out loud for all the world to hear, just that one stupid little thing still meant the world to her.

My god, I'm pathetic.

'I've got neighbours on one side with this bloody dog barking all hours. Bloke on the other side drilling into my bloody bedroom wall. I can't sleep, I can't think. All my friends are disappearing. How come *they* don't disappear?'

In her effort not to seem like an eager puppy, she instead ended up sounding grumpy and a little incoherent. She hoped beyond hopes that Heather found this charming rather than off-putting.

'Listen, Toni. How would you like the honour of doing me a favour?' said Rachel.

'I'll sleep on it.'

'That might not be possible. It's one of those now-or-never things.'

'Well, never then.'

'I lied about the never part.'

'Rachel, it's almost midnight. What could possibly be so urgent?'

'An illegal package drop,' said Heather, with a huge beaming grin. 'Like, serious spy shit.'

'Oh Jesus.' Antonia knew she should dial down the grumpiness, but it was the only thing right now which was preventing her from crumbling to powder there and then. She couldn't do neutral – she'd only be able to manage nauseatingly overeager or sour and surly.

And anyway, she *was* tired and she had a headache, for all her Heather-based excitement. Grumpy seemed apposite.

'Heather's coming,' said Rachel.

'I'm coming.'

'No,' said Antonia. 'I'm not getting involved in whatever this is. Where are you taking it, anyway?' Even the presence of Heather wasn't quite enough incentive to get her mixed up in one of Rachel's schemes.

'Almanby,' said Rachel.

'*Almanby?*'

'You've been saying how you've wanted to get out of the village for ages.'

'Almanby isn't what I had in mind. I thought it was supposed to be dangerous?'

'You don't believe that crap, do you?' said Heather.

'Come on, Tonia, what else are you going to be doing?'

'Sleeping,' said Antonia.

'So you'll do it, then?' said Rachel.

Antonia opened her car door and stepped inside.

'Nope,' she said.

'I'll give you fifty quid.'

'Seventy.'

'All right, seventy.'

'Nope.' Antonia gave Heather what she hoped was an endearing smile and not an awkward grimace. 'Nice to see you, Heather,' she said.

'You too,' said Heather.

Antonia shut the door, started the engine, and set off down the apron of the car park, the gravel popping like popcorn beneath her tyres.

'That went well,' said Heather.

'She'll be back.'

'How do you know?'

'She's a comedian. She'll take the money.'

10

Eight years.

Eight years Antonia had daydreamed about spending the evening with Heather McLagan, going on an adventure with her, having the opportunity to really make an impression. Even now, she couldn't quite believe she'd said no and driven away. That was the power of Rachel Harrison.

Rachel was Antonia's oldest friend. But also her worst friend. But also her best friend. They'd played together when they were two tiny tots in kindergarten. By the time they started primary school, Antonia was one of the larger kids, broad-shouldered and with a permanent anxiety frown, and nobody knew yet not to be afraid of her. Rachel took her everywhere, on all her shady wheeler-dealing and her forays into outright extortion. It began to dawn on Antonia that she may well be Rachel's henchman.

When Antonia's natural moral compass began to assert itself, she stepped away from Rachel's more dubious activities – but they were still mates. It was Rachel that the other kids soon realised they were really afraid of, not that lumbering misfit Antonia, and so it was Rachel who stood in the way of Antonia being more severely bullied than she already was.

Rachel was the only person Antonia ever confided in that she was a lesbian, and Rachel for her part didn't spread it around.

Yes, Rachel was a pal. But she was a harsh pal. She knew how Antonia felt about Heather, but consistently refused to introduce her. 'Do it yourself,' she'd say, or, 'It's not going to happen, mate, forget it.' Rachel and Heather were close, but Rachel never invited Antonia along whenever Heather had a party or a barbecue or a late-night camping trip. Antonia only ever found out about it days later. 'I didn't think it'd be your thing,' Rachel would shrug, knowing full well it was exactly Antonia's thing.

But tonight, Rachel had suddenly reversed her usual policy and brought Heather along to Antonia's gig – *and Antonia had simply gone home.* She had a policy of her own, though, which overrode all other policies: she would never ever knowingly become embroiled in one of Rachel's schemes. They were often illegal, always immoral, and usually involved a selection of seedy characters with whom Antonia didn't want to become acquainted. Antonia wanted nothing to do with any of it – Heather or no Heather.

She had only been lying on her bed and staring at her ceiling for a measly ten minutes before next door's dog began its high-pitched shrieking.

Yip yip yip yip yip yip yip yip yip
yip yip yip yip yip yip yip yip
yip yip yip yip yip yip yip yip yip yip yip yip yip

'Shut up!' howled Antonia, banging her fists on the adjoining wall. 'Shut the fuck up!'

That fucking dog was driving her out of her fucking mind. She was seriously considering taking a cricket bat to it, or to her neighbours, or both. It wasn't the dog's fault, of course – she'd often see her neighbours from her bedroom window, obliviously playing in their garden while that poor shitty fucking piece of shit dog bounced around, craving attention and receiving none. *Yip yip yip yip yip yip yip*, said the dog as its owners ignored it.

Yip yip yip yip yip yip yip, said the dog at 6.15 in the morning.

Yip yip yip yip yip yip yip, said the dog all day.

Yip yip yip yip yip yip yip, said the dog till ten at night. Or eleven. Or midnight. Or one.

Sometimes Antonia felt like suiciding herself, but that wasn't the answer. Maybe she'd break down the fence so the ghosts got in. She wished she had the guts to go round and angrily confront them, threaten them with all sorts of physical sanctions till they got the message, but she didn't have it in her. So she continued to yell impotently at the wall and wish she was dead.

Yip yip yip yip yip yip yip, said the dog.

In the house on the other side lived the white-bearded man whose hobby seemed to be drilling. Drilling in the morning, drilling in the evening, drilling at suppertime. He was quiet now, but only because the mangy old bastard was probably blissfully asleep. Once, when her mother was ill and they'd called an ambulance, and then had to manoeuvre her wheelchair awkwardly between parked cars to get to it, he'd yelled out of his window at them to *shut that noise up*. And then the next morning, at eight a.m., when Antonia and her mother were recovering from a stressful night spent in A&E, he cheerfully resumed his drilling.

She felt like getting a drill of her own and boring him to death.

There was a ghost in her bathroom, like a spider in the bath – big and solid and dusty and unwelcome. A man in his fifties she didn't recognise, dressed in that familiar black suit which all the male ghosts seemed somehow to wear, and with her snapped-off brass showerhead clutched in his fist.

At once, he lunged for Antonia.

Luckily, the bathroom door opened outwards, and she was able to slam it shut and press her full weight against it before he reached her. The ghost pounded on the other side with the showerhead. The wood throbbed from the force of it.

All the exterior doors were locked. There was no sign of a forced entry. Were they materialising out of thin air now? Was this a new skill they'd learned – a dash of dandelion and burdock, and suddenly they were teleporting ghosts?

Well, this is just the icing on the fucking cake, isn't it.

11

Heather squinted at the package. It was about the size of a bottle of wine, but much, much lighter, and wrapped in brown paper and haphazard sellotape.

'Is this it?'

'Yeah,' said Rachel.

'Small, isn't it.'

'It's exactly the right size.'

Heather scooped the box up and shook it firmly. Rachel threw her hands up in horror.

'Don't shake it!'

'Are you sure there's anything even in here?'

'It's not too late to revoke your invitation.'

But Heather continued to rotate the parcel in her hands, peering intently at it as if hoping to develop X-ray vision.

Without warning, the big grey rectangle of Rachel's television spontaneously flickered into life, then began to cycle through the channels, before settling upon a strange, angular animation.

Heather grimaced with sudden revulsion, stumbling away from the television as if it contained spiders.

'Rachel!'

Rachel made a flamboyant gesture, grinning with mischief – then slid several feet across her own living room carpet, from one side of the room to the other, apparently unaided.

'*Rachel!*' Heather cried.

'It just pisses you off because you don't know how I do it,' said Rachel.

'It pisses me off because it gives me the creeps.'

'So behave yourself.'

Heather glumly returned the package to the coffee table.

A knock at the front door. Rachel winked at Heather.

'Told you,' she said, and headed off to the hallway.

Heather grabbed the package, shook it some more and held it up to the light. She squeezed it and poked it.

'What is this?' she said to herself.

Rachel returned to the living room, a glum Antonia in tow.

'I know exactly what you were just doing,' said Rachel as Heather attempted to slip the package back onto the coffee table unnoticed.

Antonia sprawled on the sofa, her long legs dangling over the arm.

'All right?' said Heather.

'Hello,' said Antonia, somehow making it sound like a word she'd never said before.

'Right, you pair of ugly fuckers,' said Rachel. 'Are we going to do this or not?'

12

This was getting silly. He'd always been so punctual.

Rachel completed her fifth circuit of the telephone box. It'd once been a lighter shade of red until it changed, overnight, six years ago, to a deep burgundy.

Eight minutes late.

Come on!

Heather and Antonia stood together in strained silence. Eight years Antonia had daydreamed of this moment – when she'd finally be alone with Heather, when she could engage her in proper conversation. She'd run it over in her head a billion times, acting out Heather's part, each of them hanging off the other's every word, and falling more in love with every passing syllable.

But now it actually came down to it, everything she'd pretend-discussed with Heather over the years escaped her. Every topic, all the witty one-liners – all gone, flown from her brain like migrating birds. Her arms were stiff and her fists clenched. A couple of times she nearly spoke, almost, almost, almost, till she realised no words were coming out because she had no words to say.

Heather glanced around into the darkness of Wainford Green, her arms folded across her chest.

Say something. Anything. Say anything.
This is your chance to show you have chemistry.
You do have chemistry, don't you?
You have *to have chemistry.*
So say something!
Come on!
'My bathroom's haunted,' Antonia said.
'Where are you going to pee?' said Heather.
Antonia shrugged. 'I don't know.'

Heather wandered over to Rachel, arms still folded tight.
'What are we waiting for?'
'Directions.'
'I thought you knew the way.'
'No.'
'You couldn't have got them before we set off?'
'I have to get them after midnight.'
'Why?'
'Because I do.'
'Thanks, Rach, that's really helpful.'

Suddenly, the telephone rang. Its shrill scream arced like lightning through the stillness of night.

13

Rachel cleans her teeth at her bathroom sink.

Bottom left, bottom right, front, top right, top left.

But now there's a taste in her mouth. Bitter like basil seeds. Except it's not only in her mouth, it's also inside her head, inside her skull. There's a bitterness all around her brain, and—

The light in the ceiling flares extra bright. Extra white. Like it's going to burn out, like it's straining at the leash to pop and fizzle into oblivion.

Rachel stops cleaning. She blinks hard. It takes effort, as if someone has put her into slow motion.

'No, not now,' she says. 'Not now.'

Sound stretches, elongates. The noise from the tap becomes the noise of a great waterfall, filling Rachel's skull, flooding her body, sluicing down through her veins and her arteries and her capillaries, into her eyeballs and out through her fingertips. And suddenly she's oh-so-very heavy. Unbearably heavy, like all the stars of the Milky Way pressing down on her at once with their caustic basil seed taste.

She's on the linoleum. Her dropped toothbrush lies a few feet from her head, orange blood on the bristles. She hears the sound

of someone screaming, grunting, howling through clenched teeth
– and realises that it's her.

Distant somehow.

Or very close, far too close.

Her whole body shakes.

She tastes blood now too.

Her throat is numb from the screaming.

'Not now,' she says. 'Not now.'

14

Rachel seemed to live her life entirely below the surface. There were always a dozen schemes on the go at once, a dozen secrets – whatever Rachel said she was intending to do was never the full story. And nothing was ever done for the joy of it. There were no simple pleasures. If Antonia and Rachel visited the fairground, Rachel would invariably disappear for long periods, then turn up looking red and flustered but oddly satisfied, her face one big smirk; or perhaps Antonia would spot her between the legs of the Ferris wheel, locked in clandestine discussion with various rascals. Last time they went swimming, Rachel didn't get any further than the changing rooms before she disappeared altogether and left Antonia to churn out lengths miserably on her own – before finally turning up three days later and refusing to say where she'd been. Even something as simple as cleaning her teeth, it turned out, could end up taking the best part of thirty minutes.

Rachel was Antonia's best friend, but Antonia wasn't Rachel's. This was something Antonia had come to terms with a long time ago. Antonia needed Rachel more than Rachel needed her. The one thing Antonia brought to the table in their friendship was *friendship*. Real, straightforward, actual friendship. They did things together because they wanted to, and for no other reason or ulterior motive, and they notionally enjoyed each other's company. The trouble was, Antonia couldn't help feeling that straightforward fun ranked pretty low on Rachel's priority list, and that she rarely had more than seventy-five per cent of Rachel's attention at any one time.

Antonia perched in the driver's seat of her car, gripping the steering wheel and staring glumly ahead. Behind her, Heather slouched in the back, her big eyes half-focused on the shadows outside. Antonia's brain whirled like a tombola as it tried to think of something to say, *anything*, but it was going too fast now, spinning out of control.

Why is she so quiet?

Heather was supposed to be the talkative one – the over-excitable one, like a toddler who'd ingested too much yellow food dye. Why not now? What was so uninspiring about Antonia's company that it'd knocked Heather into her lowest gear? Heather in power-saving mode. Antonia felt invisible and miserable.

At last, after many long, achingly quiet minutes, she stretched her arms and said, in her most nonchalant tone, 'Rachel, eh?'

Heather looked up.

'Crazy,' said Antonia.

'Yeah.'

'So, what do you reckon this is all about?'

'A package or something.'

'Do you know what's in it?'

'No. Rachel didn't say.'

'A nice night for it, I suppose.'

'Yeah. It's warm.'

'Don't get to see you much,' said Antonia, as if they had any kind of relationship at all. 'How are you these days?'

'Me? Oh, I'm good. I'm good. You?'

'Yeah. I'm good too.'

Antonia scratched her head. She could tell jokes to a room full of people but couldn't hold a simple conversation with one solitary person.

'The reason sea captains are nicknamed skippers,' she told Heather, 'is because they're always so happy.'

'I'm not sure what you just said,' said Heather.

When Rachel finally reappeared, she was grinning hard and seemed almost giddy.

'Right, you couple of hideous wankers,' she said, 'ready to rock'n'roll?'

And now they were moving, threading through narrow country lanes, spooling out from Headingham, the grey-white patch of illumination from their headlamps feeling the way, rising and falling with the undulation of the tarmac. Occasionally, it'd pick out an itinerant ghost which had wandered into the road, and Antonia would have to slam her brakes on. Once, they came within a few feet of smashing into Rachel's late Aunt Jennifer, who gazed at them blankly for a moment, then hobbled on her way into a neighbouring cow field.

Rachel wound her window down and pelted Aunt Jennifer with pennies.

'That's for buying me socks for Christmas!' she called after her.

15

Heather leaned forward between the seats. 'Do you guys remember a kids' show called *Sock Draw*? It was about these sock puppets who lived in a house. But the gag was, it was all hand-drawn animation. So, it was funny, because they were sock puppets, like really simple sock puppets, but someone went to all the trouble of drawing them, rather than just using socks with eyes stuck on.'

'Straight on here,' said Rachel. 'Take a left.'

'You remember it, right, Rach?' Heather hummed to herself. '*Sock Draw, Sock Draw, remember what a sock's for,*' she sang. '*Sock Draw, Sock Draw, playing all day long. There's Posy and Peter and Piglet and Sue. Watch the Sock Draw, they'll show you what to do. Sock Draw, Sock Draw, Sock Draw, Sock Draw, Sock Draw, Sock Draw days.* You remember that, Rach?'

'Swing a left after the bus shelter.'

'I thought we're going to Almanby?'

'We are. I just need to collect someone first. Here.'

'Wait, hang on. We're going to *collect* someone?'

'Yeah.'

'To go where?'

'Almanby, of course.'

'I didn't agree to this. Who?'

'Just a friend.'

'Rachel, who?'

'Here. Don't miss it.'

A black hump against a near-black sky, Wood Farm sat isolated amid the big swoop of fields around Headingham: a child lost in the supermarket, or a heathen excommunicated from the village. It'd been the home of the Hine family for centuries, but had lain empty ever since the whole lot of them were wiped out by an influx of ghosts two or three years back. The sign declaring 'WOOD FARM – NO TRESPASSERS' had long been dislodged from the gatepost, and now lay impotent in the ditch like the punchline to a bad comedy sketch.

With an ever-deepening scowl, Antonia manoeuvred onto a long track which snaked out into the darkness towards the farmhouse.

'Steven would love this,' said Heather, grinning and bouncing. 'He'd get such a kick out of it.' She pointed at something random in her exuberance, a passing piece of air.

'Seriously,' said Antonia, 'what are we doing here?'

'I told you,' Rachel said.

'No one lives here.'

'My friend does.'

Halfway up the track, they arrived upon a horizontal tree. It'd blown over, or been deliberately felled, and now blocked the way. Antonia pulled up and switched off the engine, and the car wheezed into silence.

* * *

'Wait here,' Rachel told Heather, unbuckling her seat belt. 'Don't go anywhere, we might need to leave in a hurry.'

'What if they come over?' Antonia nodded at a collection of pale ghosts on the far side of the hedgerow, a little way out into the field. It was so dark, they seemed to be hovering.

'They won't.'

'Rachel, you didn't say anything about a friend.'

'He's cool. Maybe stay in the car till he comes, though. He's quite… shy.'

'*Shy?*' Antonia threw her hands up in exasperation.

Rachel opened her door, winked at Antonia, then began to scramble under the trunk of the tree. A grinning Heather exploded from the car after her.

The night air was thick and humid, as if carved from a block of jelly. Everything seemed to be sweating – the trees and the hedgerows and the tarmac of the track. Heather's shirt stuck to her belly and across her shoulder blades, and salty drips trickled down her forehead. Undeterred, she skipped and darted around Rachel in her usual mandalas of over-excitement. Giddy just to be out of the house and on an adventure – giddy just to be alive. Giddy for giddiness's sake.

'Hey, Rachel, it's cold tonight.' Heather mimed blowing into her hands and patting her arms.

'Go wait with Toni.'

'That's not the right answer. Hey, Rachel, it's cold tonight.'

'No, it's not. What are you talking about?'

'It's a joke. Ask me why I didn't bring my coat. Hey, Rachel, it's cold tonight.'

'But it's not cold.'

'I'm going to keep saying it till you do it properly. Hey, Rachel, it's cold tonight.'

'Fine. Why didn't you bring your coat?'

'I burnt it. To keep warm.'

'Right.'

'Because the coat would've kept me warm if I'd worn it. I didn't need to burn it.'

'Yeah, I get it. Don't give up the day job.'

'I don't have a day job.'

Without warning, Heather veered off. Like a magpie, she'd spotted the glint of an abandoned shopping trolley among the nettles. She swooped in, pulled it free, attached herself to the back and ran at full tilt towards Rachel. Rachel deftly stepped to one side and hooked her fingers onto the front as it passed, swinging Heather round on a wide parabola. Heather whooped loudly.

In the field, half a dozen ghosts rotated in their direction – blank-eyed but craning like meerkats.

'Ssh,' said Rachel, then climbed into the trolley. 'You're my lackey now, you have to push me.'

'Everyone's your lackey.'

'This is true. Faster, serf, faster!'

Heather pushed her at a run for a few yards. Rachel stretched her arms out wide. Heather leapt on the back and let the momentum carry them along the track.

'I'm the king of the world!' Rachel announced.

Then, abruptly, Heather yanked her to a stop.

'Time's up! That's enough lackeying for one evening.'

'Watch this,' said Rachel. 'Stand back.'

'What?'

'Just stand back, you'll see.'

Heather shrugged and stepped away from the trolley. Fingers pressed to her temples, Rachel closed her eyes in concentration.

The trolley shifted an inch. Then two inches. Then, apparently unaided, it began to roll gently along the track.

'Jesus Christ, Rachel! Stop it!'

'I love getting a reaction.'

Heather looked appalled. 'Stop it, Rachel. Stop it! Fuck!' She picked up a crumpled soft drink can and hurled it at Rachel's head.

With a wicked chortle, Rachel hopped out of the trolley and – after suspending in mid-air for the smallest fraction of a second – dropped to earth and carried on walking as if nothing had happened.

'How do you do that?' Heather said with a grimace.

'It's all in the wrist, I told you.'

'But seriously, how do you do it?'

Rachel tapped her nose.

'I sometimes wonder,' said Heather, 'if you might be evil.'

Rachel arched her shoulders. 'Never really thought about it,' she said. 'Yeah, maybe.'

'Like, a missionary of the Devil or something.'

'An emissary?'

'Yeah, that's the one.'

'Don't you think I'm too nice to be an emissary of the Devil?'

'Not really. I wouldn't say you were nice. You're *personable*, I'll give you that. 'Nice' is a stretch.'

'Maybe I'm Jesus.'

'Jesus isn't evil.'

'No, but I'm presenting an alternate possibility. It doesn't have to be something evil. I could be the second coming, you don't know that. Besides, I'd know if I was evil.'

'You'd know if you were Jesus.'

'Who says I don't?'

Heather skipped and hopped and hummed a tune. Rachel wasn't sure whether this was just Heather entertaining herself, or whether it was designed to annoy her personally. Just in case, Rachel opted to be annoyed by it.

'My uncle was a magician,' Heather said at last.

'What did he do?' Rachel said.

'Magic tricks.'

'Yeah. I mean, what magic tricks?'

'Sawing the lady in half. It's done with extra feet.'

'Well, yeah, obviously.'

'So I know a thing or two about magic tricks.'

'And yet you can't work out how mine are done.'

'No. It pisses me off.'

'It's more fun not knowing.'

'It really isn't. It really, really, seriously fucks me off.'

'You're a tough crowd, Heather.'

When they reached the farmhouse, they found it half caved-in like an Iron Age skull. Filthy polythene like flayed skin hung over the missing front door. It fluttered and swished and rustled.

'Stay here,' said Rachel.

'Aw, Rach...'

'I mean it. Stay here.'

16

Antonia jumped as a body fell against her car bonnet with a little curtsey of the suspension. She glanced up from where she'd been leaning her forehead against the steering wheel – to be confronted by the sight of Heather beaming in through the windscreen. Heather darted around to the driver's-side door and motioned for Antonia to roll down her window while shouting something which sounded like, 'Do you dare me to take my shoes and socks off for the next ten minutes?'

Antonia wound the window down. 'What did you just say?'

'Do you dare me to take my shoes and socks off for the next ten minutes?'

'Do you want me to?'

'It's up to you. So, do you?'

'I don't know.'

'Yes or no?'

'Which is the right answer?'

'It's up to you.'

Antonia looked pained. 'I normally like longer to think about things like that. I don't have an opinion. I'm sorry.'

'Well, I shall.'

Heather proceeded to strip off her shoes and socks, then walked in circles in an exaggerated fashion, lifting her knees and grimacing in apparent discomfort as she moved further from the car. Then she tucked her hands behind her back and strolled casually back and forth, kicking her feet up in front of her.

'La la la, what a nice night for a simple stroll. Sure you won't join me, Ant?'

Antonia's frown deepened. There was nothing she'd have loved to do more in that moment than pull off her own shoes and join Heather in her hijinks. This was exactly what she'd been hoping for all these years: Heather cut loose, dragging her away on adventures. But, with deepening gloom, Antonia now realised that this wasn't who she was. She wasn't spontaneous, she wasn't impulsive. A great wall of shyness held her back, a thick screen of her own smoked-glass timidity. She remained where she was, buckled into her seat, something large and leaden and insurmountably heavy lying in the pit of her stomach.

'You'll feel alive,' said Heather.

Antonia knew that she would. She knew she'd love every second of it. And every second that she stayed stubbornly inside the car, she hated herself that little bit more.

'But it has to be a dare,' Heather continued, wagging a finger. 'Otherwise it doesn't work.'

'Well,' said Antonia.

'So, I dare you to take your shoes and socks off for the next twenty minutes.'

'But you're doing it for ten minutes.'

'That's the rule of daring. Each dare has to be bigger than the last. You're getting off lightly.'

'Well,' said Antonia, feeling a little sick.

'Well?'

'Um,' said Antonia's front-brain, 'I'm not sure it's my thing.'

'Fair enough,' said Heather, giving up disappointingly easily. She was studying the dirt and grit on the bottom of her foot.

If only she'd asked once more, Antonia lied to herself, *I'd have done it for sure.*

Now Heather was scampering this way and that, jumping onto the trunk of the tree and racing up and down the track.

Just go and fucking do it. It's not a big deal. You don't even have to take your shoes off. Just go out there and join in. For fuck's sake.

Heather hopped and skipped and grinned with delight.

Antonia remained buckled into the driver's seat of her car.

A bat careened through the sky, too fast to register as movement, just a series of three or four animation cels, and then gone.

Antonia knocked on her windscreen and pointed past Heather to where a ghost had now emerged, apparently out of nowhere – a tall, willowy woman with blonde hair tumbling over her shoulders. She looked like she might've been a model, or maybe an actress from the Victorian era or the 1920s. Antonia thought she was very beautiful – though it was difficult to ever find the dead genuinely attractive, the same way it was impossible to become aroused by statues or drawings or any other simulacra. There needed to be something behind the eyes, some trace of a human soul, otherwise it was just aesthetics. She'd tried to wank off to a photo of an erotic sculpture before, just as an experiment, and it didn't work, not even close.

The ghost had what seemed to be a silver candlestick clutched in its fist. Miss Scarlett made flesh. It was lurching in Heather's direction, edging between the bank and the car, and dangerously close.

'Uh-oh,' said Heather.

'Come back to the car!'

'I'm going for a pee.'

'Now?'

'Yeah. It's pee-time!'

'But…' Antonia gestured towards the ghost.

'It's an old Chicken Club game. Can you finish peeing before the ghost catches up with you? They're so fucking slow, it's a doddle.'

'But…'

'See you in three minutes!'

And with that, Heather darted through a gap in the hedgerow and out into the darkness, her shoes still clasped in her hand.

'Heather, wait!' called Antonia. 'Whereabouts where will you be?' She opened her car door to follow, but Heather was already gone.

'Fuck,' said Antonia.

17

'Sam? Sam, it's me. Are you ready?'

Sam's dismal squat in the back of the Hine farmhouse was more fucked up than the last time Rachel had seen it, just over a month ago. Sam was a friend of a friend, which was Rachel's favourite kind of friend. They were the type of friend you didn't have to grow too attached to or like too much. They were the type of friend which could come in handy. Like her, Sam had a finger in every pie – or, as he liked to say, 'a penis in every vagina', guffawing delightedly each time as if he'd just thought of it. There was always something shady going on with Sam Washington, and Rachel wanted in on all of it – even if she didn't know what it was.

Not that things were working out too well for good ol' Sam these days. He'd lost his little cottage in Litswood to some frightening-looking men with polyester jackets and buzz cuts, for reasons upon which he refused to elaborate, and now lived in the increasingly raddled shell of a house in the middle of a field, like an old-fashioned vagrant. He'd set up a bed (a stained mattress and a sleeping bag) and a meagre living area (some magazines, a portable television with no plug, and a tiny gas stove) in one corner of the large bathroom on the first floor, the only room remaining which wasn't open to the elements.

* * *

Sam must've taken a turn for the worse since the last time Rachel had seen him – the place had descended further into degradation. The sleeping bag was filthy and torn. There were countless half-eaten tins of food dotted around the floor, many overflowing with mould or teeming with flies in the sticky summer air. The washbasin was half-full of dirty water and dark floating things.

'Sam?' said Rachel. 'Hey, Sam boy.'

On the floor by the door was a torch. Rachel scooped it up, flicked it on, and scanned the earwax-yellow circle of light around the hovel. She wiped her sleeve across her face – as much to dispel the reek of festering whatever-it-was as to clear away the layer of sweat. Even this late at night, it was still hot.

Towards the far end of the space, half-obscured by shelving units, was a black office chair – a new addition. In the chair sat a man, slumped backwards, his legs trailing out before him. His face was so pale and sunken and waxy that it took her a moment to recognise him.

'Sam?'

She walked towards him, stepping over cans and food-encrusted cutlery. He looked twenty years older and fifty years deader, like someone had exhumed him for the occasion. His skin sagged and his hair was thin and wispy. He barely seemed to be breathing at all. His open eyes stared right through her.

She bent to examine him. If he was aware of her presence, he didn't react.

'Shit.' She blew on his face. 'Can you hear me, Sam?'

Nothing.

'You're dying, aren't you, you silly sod. I told you this would happen. You always leave this to me, you never do anything for yourself, and now look at you.'

She straightened and placed her hands on her hips like a disappointed schoolmistress.

Imagine that, she thought. *Imagine living all that life, all thirty-two years of it, only to end up here. Alone and half-dead in a pit of your own filth.* The big bloody drama of his birth. The proud parents. The baby photos displayed on the mantelpieces of countless grandmothers and aunties. The first day at school. The first school disco. The first kiss. The hours of homework, the thousand-billion dinnertimes, the half-eternity spent cross-legged on the carpet watching television. His favourite cartoons. The baths, the birthdays, the haircuts, the parents' evenings, the holidays, the swimming lessons, the sports days, the Christmases, the football matches, the new shoes, the favourite records, the girlfriends, the mornings, the myriad of dreams played out nightly inside his brain. All for this.

She reached out and ruffled what was left of his hair.

'Oh well,' she said. 'All the more for me.'

18

Heather didn't quite make it to the ten-minute mark. Seven and a half minutes, then she decided there were too many sharp stones and pieces of broken glass, and too many eager-looking ghosts. First rule of the Chicken Club: it stops being fun when you get yourself killed. It stops being fun, in fact, once you end up with a shard of glass through the foot, in the manner of the boy on the beach, who cropped up periodically in those grainy films they used to show before the main feature at the Triscutine Picture Palace. No one knew where they came from, but the projectionist showed them anyway. Heather's favourite was the one where the man slipped on a rug on a polished floor – she laughed and laughed.

She finished peeing, reinstated her shoes, then wandered further out into the deep-space blackness of the field, tracing an insolent corkscrew across its bumps and ridges, all the while imagining Rachel and Antonia's growing irritation at her absence. 'Where *has* she got to?' Rachel would likely be grumbling at this very moment. 'I can't take her anywhere.'

Heather gave a husky chortle.

There were bodies here, she realised. In the scrub of dried-out bushes, the remains of what looked like a small cluster of partygoers lay in a dejected heap, silently mouldering, their blood glinting in the moonlight. Even at this distance, Heather could make out some of their fancy dress costumes – Fred Flintstone, Princess Leia, an orange traffic cone, a penguin. They must've been on their way to a bonfire party, a late-night dance, and been caught out by ghosts.

Feeling suddenly strange in her chest, Heather hunched her shoulders and hurried in what she hoped was the right direction for the car.

Up ahead, a knot of ghosts blocked her way, half a dozen young people – maybe the souls of the deceased partygoers, dressed now for their dour afterlife, or maybe their killers. Another ghost emerged crawling from the darkness to her left and made a grab for her. Its fingers twined around her trouser cuff.

'No you don't, you ugly bastard,' said Heather as she pulled away. But she was unbalanced now, and as the ghost kept coming she tumbled to the hard, dry earth.

'Fuck off, will you.' She kicked out at the ghost, but didn't have space to right herself. And now one or two of the party ghosts had taken note, their interest piqued by the commotion, and they began to head purposefully in her direction.

'What are you going to do?'

'What do you mean?'

'You know what I mean. You have to do something, this is perfect.'

'She's not interested.'

'You don't know that.'

'You're always telling me she's not interested.'

'Never say never, Toni, never say never. Look, she'll do anything. I swear to God! I've known her for years, this woman has no boundaries at all.'

'She's straight.'

'She's not anything. She's just like...' Rachel gestured broadly. 'The world is her oyster. Her sexy, sexy oyster.'

Antonia grimaced.

'Come on, mate, don't waste this.'

'Has she ever shown an interest in women?'

'I don't keep track of these things.'

'You're supposed to know everything.'

'It's none of my business.'

'That's the stupidest thing you've ever said, Rachel! Other people's business is the whole reason you exist. You just told me you've known her for years and she'll do anything.'

'She'll *clearly* do anything, but I haven't been keeping a record. Look, when's something like this going to happen again?'

'I don't want to talk about it.'

'Don't take this the wrong way, Toni, but you're a fucking idiot.'

Antonia shrugged awkwardly and they fell into silence.

Rachel inflated her cheeks then deflated them slowly.

Antonia drummed her hands on the steering wheel.

'How long does it take one person to have a piss anyway?' Rachel said at last. 'Like, a minute tops. What the fuck is she doing?'

Antonia and Rachel glanced at each other – 'Fuck' – then burst from the car. They ran back along the track a little way.

'Heather!' Rachel called. 'Heather, where are you?'

'Heather!' yelled Antonia, surprising herself with the volume.

From the void of an adjacent field, Heather cried out, sounding distant and panicked.

The pair scrambled across the ditch, through a gap in the hedgerow and – like astronauts cut adrift – out into the field, feet pounding on invisible clods and hummocks.

'Heather!' Antonia called again.

Another shout, closer but away to the right. They veered off, aiming themselves in the approximate direction of Heather's voice, hoping not to run headlong into a tree or hollow.

Rachel stopped, and Antonia came up sharp beside her. Up ahead, a small figure lay on the dirt, curled like a prawn. Three ghosts were gathered around her, one of them raining blows with a thick wooden staff. Her right arm was up over her head, shielding her face.

Antonia reached her a little ahead of Rachel, pulling a burst of speed from the last of her reserves. She threw her not inconsiderable bodyweight into two of the ghosts. The three of them tumbled to the hard, dry earth, Antonia grazing her palms and elbows.

Rachel was on the scene next. She grabbed Heather by the hand and pulled her to her feet, all the while aiming kicks at her remaining assailant. Heather wriggled free from Rachel and joined her in angrily kicking out at the ghosts.

'Not so big now there's three of us, are you? Let's see it, then! Come on, shitbaron! Let's see what you've got!'

'Heather, come *on*!'

Rachel and Antonia grabbed an arm each and ushered her back the way they'd come. After a few hundred yards, Antonia stopped and bent double, hands on her knees and ribcage heaving. 'I'm a comedian. I'm not used to all this running.'

'You must be,' said Rachel, 'I've seen your act.'

Antonia straightened once more. 'Is this how you normally spend your evenings?'

Actually, these days, many of Rachel's evenings seemed to involve lying on her bed, screaming, shaking uncontrollably and watching inanimate objects twitch and judder. Her limbs too long, her hands too big, her duvet too small to grip, her wallpaper too far away and at the same time too close, right up against her face and howling with despair. Or was that her own voice?

She shrugged. 'I prefer something a little quieter,' she said.

If only I wasn't such a fucking pushover, Antonia seethed miserably. *If I could just say no once in a while.*

Antonia wasn't a fan of cardiovascular activity. She'd much rather read a book than go jogging. In fact, she should by rights be sound asleep by now – dog/drill permitting – and having unsettling psychosexual dreams about Heather. Last night she'd dreamed of drawing a wobbly picture of her childhood home in felt tip marker on Heather's naked back while Heather giggled and squirmed and Antonia felt very strange in her lower belly. She woke up all sweaty and disconcerted.

On meadow green lives Oaken Snail
No doubt to spoil his burrow
The shepherdess 'neath starry skies
Shall hide her face tomorrow

19

The king's horsemen pursue Heather deeper into the forest.

She can't remember exactly why the King of France has sent a battalion of his best musketeers to hunt her down, but she knows she must stay ahead of them. If they catch her, they'll surely kill her.

Oh yes – it's because her right arm is made of gold. Even now, here in the back of the carriage, it feels numb and heavy as it lies across her lap. Cold, despite the heat. The king wants the gold for himself, but it's her arm and she needs it. The last thing she wants is for it to end up in the treasure hoard of some greedy monarch.

Shadows flicker across Heather's face. She must be travelling quickly now, hurtling between the trees, but she can't open her eyes. It's as if her eyelids are made of gold too, like the gold in the top corner of the field where her grandmother grew rhubarb in leathery clumps beneath rusted-out buckets.

What made me think of that?

'It was a wrong number,' *a woman's voice says. It's her friend Rachel. Rachel is sitting in the back of Heather's skull, driving her like a dodgem. Did she shrink herself down and climb in through her ear?*

'But she wouldn't stop talking long enough for me to say anything,' *Rachel's voice continues.* 'So I had to sit there and listen to her go on and on about how sorry she was. Y'know, like, if we can put this behind us, we can move on with our lives, all that sort of thing. Really grovelling.'

Up ahead, in a clearing, a large mansion wrapped in ivy lies like a slumbering marble giant. The building seems to be deserted – abandoned for a hundred years probably, given over to the moths and dust mites. No one else knows it's here. Heather hopes she can hide in the kaleidoscoping rooms till the soldiers give up and go home.

The mansion is a maze of interconnected rooms which stretch out in all directions and worm into the soil. It used to be a school or a hospital. Aquamarine paint peels off the walls like big coppery eyelids.

'What did you do?' *a different woman's voice asks.*
   'What could I do?'
   'Tell her you're Rachel and not this other person?'
   'Nah, I was enjoying the grovelling too much.'

A battered wooden door stands open. Heather makes her way towards the door. The dust, plaster and paint chips crunch beneath her feet and dig into the skin. Through the door is a wide, elliptical room. A ballroom. Ornate, panelled in dark wood, with gold filigree roses and cherubic faces. It feels like the most familiar place in the world, as if she's finally home.
   In the centre of the room is a wooden chair.

* * *

'So what did you do?'

'I waited till she'd finished, then I hung up the phone.'

'That's it?'

'If I'd said anything, she'd have realised it was a wrong number.'

'You're actually evil.'

'I have my moments.'

'You realise you probably ruined her life?'

'Almost certainly.'

Someone is tied to the chair by the wrists. As Heather looks closer, she realises that it's her – she's in the chair and she can't move, no matter how hard she strains against the leather bindings.

A girl stands where she was standing moments before. A little girl, ten or eleven years old. Her eyes are window blue and stare right through Heather. She wears bright red shoes, almost too bright to look at, like the strawberry sauce on the ice cream cone clasped in Heather's right hand.

Heather can't tell if the girl is a ghost. Maybe she's ill, or cold. But Heather is warm. Uncomfortably warm. Her ice cream has already started to melt, and trickles down the cone, making the wafer soft. She feels the liquid dribble over her knuckles and along the length of her forearm, before dripping off her elbow. It's so cold against her hot skin it hurts, tracing the route of her veins.

(Her arm doesn't seem to be made of gold after all. Maybe it was just a rumour?)

'It makes a better story, though, doesn't it? There's Gedby. I used to work at the old weather station at Gedby. I spent a summer killing chickens for the farmer. I've still got the scars on my hands and all up my arms.'

'You would wilfully ruin someone's life for the sake of an anecdote, wouldn't you.'

The strap holding Heather's right arm against the chair is too tight. It cuts off the blood supply and makes her arm feel numb and heavy. Sore. She wiggles her fingers. The girl notices and bends to look. She produces a stick of bright red lipstick from her pocket, as bright as the strawberry sauce on Heather's ice cream, now spiralling down her forearm like milky blood.

Heather tries to pull away, but the girl grabs her tightly. It feels as if she'll crush the bone.

'I couldn't believe how vicious the little shits could be.'
    'Be fair. You were killing them. Sky.'
    'No.'
    'Signpost.'
    'No.'
    'Sticks.'
    'No.'

Slowly, the girl twists the lipstick till the tip emerges, wet and raw like an exposed wound.

'Steering wheel.'
    'No.'

Very carefully, she begins to draw a spiral pattern on Heather's bare forearm.

* * *

'Speedometer.'

'No.'

The touch of the lipstick is painful. Hot. As if it's transferring its rawness to her. The patterns spread now, like a disease, up Heather's arm and onto her neck. Concentric loop after concentric loop.

'Side door.'

'No.'

The lipstick snags and breaks. Heather jolts with pain. She winces, tries to pull away, but the girl screws the metal tube with all her strength into the flesh of Heather's arm. Heather rocks and judders, desperately trying to free herself from her bonds, to flee this chair and this room and this pain. She'll take her chance with the king's guards, anything to escape this girl with her beard and her eyes on backwards and her ha'penny of judgement and her small voice telegraph and—

The rocking of the car jolted Heather awake.

Blinking, confused a moment. Lying half stretched out, knees up, travelling sideways. The rumble of the car engine snaking up through her spine and into her skull, making a nest there.

It was daylight already. The harsh perma-summer sun stung her eyes, dazzling her as it flashed through the glass of the side window like laser fire.

* * *

'Seat,' Antonia said in the front of the car.

'Warm,' replied Rachel.

'Seats,' said Antonia.

'Warmer.'

'Seat belt.'

'Freezing cold.'

And then, an inrush of pain. Twisted, knotted pain, like muscles pulled taut all down Heather's right arm. She popped her cuff buttons and rolled up her sleeve. Her arm was bruised green and yellow from the beating she'd taken from the ghosts, with four purpling fingernail marks running the length of her forearm. One must've grabbed her on the way past. She'd been too startled by their sudden appearance to notice.

Heather rolled her sleeve back down. There was nothing she could do about it for the moment, and the pain was normalising, flattening out to a dull throb. She blearily pivoted upright. They were deep in open countryside. It was still early, but already the heat haze had risen from the earth like an invading army, like the skeletons from *Jason and the Argonauts*, and the sun had baked the sky cobalt blue and naked, burnt all its clothes off. Now just a tortoiseshell of fields lay ahead of them, as flat as the ocean or an alien world, and impossibly green. Woodland, misted blue by the distance, stretched out to their left – and even against its furthest flank, Heather could make out the pinprick-small presence of ghosts. Tiny moments of black and white.

* * *

'I don't know,' Antonia said. 'Sand.'

'Where do you see sand?'

'I'm running out of things to guess.'

Heather glued on a smile and ruffled Rachel's and Antonia's hair from behind. 'Morning, chumps! Chump Alpha and Chump Beta. Pillock One and Pillock Two.'

Antonia beamed into the rear-view mirror. She looked slightly too happy, her smile a little too wide, a little manic – almost like an entirely different person, a passing simulacrum.

Heather didn't know what to make of Antonia. She could read most people, but this one was beyond her. She was a conveyor belt of different emotions, none of them quite willing to stick, like someone window-shopping emotions. Or one of those big clicky wheels from TV gameshows, with the sparkly hostess spinning it and spinning it and unwilling to allow it to rest on any one thing for more than a few seconds. Sometimes Heather would catch Antonia scowling from beneath her brows – then she'd break out into a wobbly lopsided grin, before folding up awkwardly and descending into a quiet gloom. All within the space of a minute.

Still, she seemed all right. Docile enough. Rachel was friends with some proper lunatics: the kind of fidgety weirdos who gave the impression that they'd stab you as soon as laugh at one of your jokes, and even they wouldn't know which till they did it. Antonia at least wasn't one of those. She was no worse than harmlessly peculiar.

'Morning, Heather!' Antonia said. The word 'Heather' seemed to catch in her throat a little, as if her oesophagus had momentarily contracted to prevent its escape.

'Have we been driving all this time?' said Heather.

Rachel glanced back and nodded at her.

'Soil,' said Antonia.

'Still cold.'

'Soils. Plural. Different kinds of soils.'

'No.'

'How long was I asleep?' said Heather.

Heather's arm hurt, but she was sure it'd pass. As a former Chicken Club member, she was a past master of incurring minor injuries. She'd fallen from a tyre swing, fallen from a hump-backed bridge, tripped over her own feet, tripped over John's feet, cracked her head on a kerb, been hit by a bicycle, been hit by a tandem, received a bite from a dog and slashed her thigh on a barbed-wire fence, the latter of which involved a triumphant trip to the hospital for stitches and a tetanus jab. It was all in a day's work for Heather McLagan, and a bop and a scratch on the arm from a couple of ghosts wasn't enough to faze her.

Anyway, today was a good day. She was going to be reunited with Steven, have the best hug in the world ever, plus maybe a sex or two, and everything would be right again.

Right?

Rachel's mysterious brown-paper package lay in the footwell of the back seat. Heather scooped it up, shook it, and held it to her ear. There was something in there, but it was almost insubstantially light. What could possibly be worth going all this way to deliver?

She shook it again, more vigorously this time. 'I hear with my little ear…'

'No!' said Rachel.

'Just a corner.'

'No.'

'Then give me a clue.'

'No.'

'Sun,' said Antonia.

'No.'

'Shadows.'

'No.'

'Shallow dip in road.'

'No.'

'She hasn't thought of anything,' Heather said, leaning between the seats. 'She just likes to say no till she gets bored, then she'll say yes and pretend you won. She's a sociopath.'

'Stones,' said Antonia.

'No.'

'Sun visor.'

'No.'

'Subliminal radio sounds.'

'Yes! Yes, that's exactly what I was thinking of! Well done! You're the best at I-spy!'

20

At around three a.m., Antonia had closed her eyes. Just for a moment, just for one small, solitary moment. Just to rest them. Heather was sound asleep in the back, and Rachel's chin was resting on her chest. And the road rumbled along beneath the soles of the tyres, the throbbing undulation in the tarmac, the soft vibration of engine through the steering wheel, the hug of night. The snooziness was catching.

But Antonia isn't driving a car at all, she's tucked up in bed, listening to the sound of a car on an old-fashioned gramophone in the corner of her room, balanced on the small white table where her television normally stands. The gramophone's gaping funnel-shaped speaker looks like the maw of a triffid. It glistens with saliva.

She snapped awake a second later. The car already had two wheels on the grass verge, and the hedgerow loomed in from the left-hand side.

After that, she pulled up for a five-minute nap which lasted three hours, but neither Rachel nor Heather appeared to notice.

She felt better now. Less crabby. In fact, actually quite alert. Heather was in the back seat of her car and Antonia had nothing to rush home for – this was exactly the sort of situation she'd daydreamed about for the last eight years. Just her and Heather, plus Rachel to help keep the conversation flowing. Antonia could be herself around Rachel, they had a rapport, and Heather would witness her as she really was, instead of the stumbling, mumbling buffoon she so often became in her presence.

There was a chance she might actually enjoy today.

Except.

Except they were going to Almanby. And that was a bad thing. Definitely, positively, unambiguously a bad thing.

Antonia had read a book at school when she was small. It was called *One Two Three & Away*, and it was about a river that you could only cross via a line of white stepping-stones. But you mustn't ever step on the black stepping-stone, everyone said, otherwise something terrible would happen.

And Almanby was a bit like that. All the other villages were fine to visit, but Almanby was the black stepping-stone. Even before all this, even before the end of society and the arrival of the ghosts – back when Antonia was little. Don't talk to strangers, don't step out into the road without looking, don't eat wild berries or mushrooms, don't play in the farmyard, *don't go to Almanby*. They didn't even live near Almanby, but grown-ups impressed upon them how important it was to avoid the place nonetheless. Like an old wives' tale, like a piece of wisdom passed down through generations which no one questioned or even thought too hard about. Like folklore. It was just something everyone knew, a rule everyone followed.

Don't go to Almanby.

And Antonia was going to Almanby.

They should've made a grainy information film warning about it, like the ones they'd sometimes show at The Triscutine Picture Palace... the man slipping on the rug, the woman leaving her pram unattended on a busy high street, the boy reaching for his frisbee wedged in the insulator of an electricity sub-station. There should've been another: three friends driving through blazing sunshine, enjoying their innocent day out – but wait, what's this? We suddenly realise they're heading towards Almanby.

And then—

And then what?

No one knew.

Well, Heather's sweetheart Steven Cook knew. Steven Cook had gone and never come back.

That's a great sign...

Steven Cook: the fly in Antonia's Heather-shaped ointment.

When it came down to it, it didn't matter how impressive Antonia was or how much of a rapport she built with Heather over the course of today. Heather was straight and in love with Steven – which, Antonia felt, may prove something of a hurdle.

Caller on line two. Hello, caller?

Hello, Brian.

What's your name?

Mary. Mary Harris. I'm from Fulingham.

Hello, Mary. We're talking about childhood recipes. Food that only your family ever seemed to make. What have you got for us?

Well, Brian. When I was small, my mother would cook shepherd's pie…

Shepherd's pie, good. A family favourite right there.

But she'd grate radishes into it.

Radishes? As in supermarket radishes?

The round red ones, that's right.

That's definitely unusual, Mary, never heard that one before. Into the potatoes, or into the filling?

Both. Into the filling, into the mash, and then on top of the pie with the cheese.

The hour rolled on, and so did the road, and so did Antonia's shimmering silver car, burnished champagne-gold by the low early-morning rays. Its shadow was a blue-black clown car, stretched out and ridiculous, wobbling with every undulation of the road, going everywhere the car went like a mocking parody. Her hands pressed to the glass, Heather waved at her own shadow, barely visible in the corner of the window, and it waved back.

She sat back and allowed her head to loll. Sunlight flickered through the branches of the trees and into her eyes like a faulty projector, like the frantic flashing of a signal lamp, its operator lost at sea. Lost amid an ocean of fields and meadows and sprawling gold-tipped woodland, heading inexorably out into the void, forever and ever maybe.

Maybe they'd never return. Maybe they'd never see Headingham and their little homes again. Maybe they'd die out here – maybe they'd die in Almanby if they didn't die on the way, or they'd forget their own identities and just roam in bewildered circles forever, flashing their signal lamps and hoping some kind soul would rescue them.

And the sunlight was ever so bright.

Heather stretched her arms.

'It's going to be a beautiful day,' she said.

21

Once, when she was eighteen, Heather slept at a random old man's house. He came out to complain about the noise when she and some of her rowdier friends were staggering home from the pub. Heather immediately bade her pals goodnight, told the man she'd be sleeping at his house that night, then followed him indoors.

The man was so startled by her bravado – and possibly so intrigued by this strange young woman inviting herself into his bungalow – that he never questioned it, not even for a moment. He made her a cup of tea, prepared the spare room, and cooked her breakfast the following morning. She thanked him profusely and tucked a twenty-pound note under his teapot.

Every year she would send him a Christmas card.

She only ever received one back, which read: *To my mysterious lodger. Did I dream you? Christopher.*

After a few years, she went round to visit him, but there was a woman living in the house now with a brace of children. She didn't know what had happened to Christopher – the house was empty when she moved in – but she remembered receiving a couple of Heather's Christmas cards. She rummaged around in a drawer for a bit, then returned them to Heather, unopened.

That afternoon, Heather drove to the animal shelter, picked up an elderly grey cat with cloudy eyes and bits of ear missing, named it Christopher, and lived with it till it died. She buried the cat in her garden, stuck a bamboo pole in the grave, and attached Christopher's laminated Christmas card to the pole. She had no idea why she did any of this, but it made her feel better.

'I think I love you,' said Steven, when she told him.

22

White birds rode the thermals in big looping circles, too high to properly make out. Crop fields rustled and swayed in sympathy, painting in Van Gogh swirls – the dry rattle of yellowing corn, the silver-backed grass. Even the little plasticky green leaves and shoots of the underground vegetables shuddered and twitched in the hot air. Higher still, a satellite turned, caught the sun, flashed. Antonia's car sparkled in reply.

I'm here at the beautiful Edwardian cottage of Mr and Mrs Bletso in the heart of rural Feringthorpe. Susan Bletso has been collecting toys since she was fourteen, and has during the last forty years amassed over ten thousand items, from the mass-produced trinket to the ultra-rare teddy bear. Susan, what first attracted you to the idea of collecting toys?

Rachel sat in the long grass by the side of the road, one eye screwed up against the reflection from the tarmac, pale and bright as a projector screen. Antonia leaned against the bonnet of the car, map open, face cracked with concentration.

'It won't do any good,' said Rachel.

'What?'

'That map. There's no point trying to use it.'

'I can read maps.'

'It doesn't matter. It's not accurate.'

'It's Ordnance Survey. I've had this map for years.'

'We're going to Almanby. Your map won't take us there. The route changes every day. Trust me. I've got today's directions.'

'I don't believe you.'

'Why not?'

Antonia shrugged. 'Directions don't change.'

'They don't out here. But it'll be different when we start to get close to Almanby. Lots of things will be different. We have to be careful.'

Antonia folded up her map. 'I never know when you're being serious.'

'Do I look like I'm not being serious?'

'No. But like I say, I never know. You have an excellent poker face. If there's one thing I've always admired about you, it's your poker face.'

'Let's just use my directions, okay?'

'Fine, you're the boss. Speaking of which, I still get that seventy quid, right?'

'Of course.'

This is quite a unique item. Here. If you look closely, you'll see she has marbles for eyes.

Oh yes. My word, that's quite remarkable. Two regular glass marbles, exactly the type you'd expect to find children playing with in the playground, with light blue filaments. Have you ever come across another doll like this before?

No. It probably wasn't manufactured like this. We think it may have been modified by a previous owner. A little girl with a particularly ghoulish imagination.

And I love her red shoes. Look at them.

They're rather magnificent, aren't they.

'Hey, Rach,' said Antonia. 'Remember that time all those bugs swarmed onto the playground?' She sauntered over and sat on the grass verge a few feet from Rachel, pulled off her shoe, rattled it and peered inside. Then she put her shoe back on, entwined her fingers behind her head and lay back on the grass. 'We thought they were, like, a farmer burning straw or something and it was all burnt bits. Smuts. But the first few started hitting the glass, and we saw they were beetles. Big blister beetles. Like, a plague of them. Remember? We had to run around and close all the windows, stop them getting in. Some of the girls were screaming, and Mrs Howbrook was yelling. I remember brushing them off my page. They were all on the floor. In our shoes and going down our tops. In our hair. Tracy had an allergic reaction to them. Her hands got all red and blistered and weepy. The teachers had to take her to hospital. Remember?'

'No,' said Rachel.

'You were there.'

'I don't remember it.'

'You were sat right next to me.'

'I don't think that was me.'

'We always sat together in class.'

'I must've been off that day.'

'You were laughing. You thought it was the best thing ever.'

'That does sound like me. Funny, I don't remember it at all. I wish I did, it sounds great.'

Look at this beautiful drummer boy. Where did you find this?
This belonged to my grandfather. I think he received it from an aunt or a grandparent for Christmas when he was maybe ten or eleven. We don't really know the origins of the item or where it was bought, but we think it could be French or Belgian.
It looks turn of the century.
It does, although we estimate it's newer – maybe 1930s, early 1940s.

'How far till Almanby?' said Antonia.
'Don't start asking that already.'
'I'm the driver, I think I ought to know.'
'Still another few hours.'
'Like, how many?'
'I don't know. Five or six?'
'*Five or six?*'
'What?'
'Five or six. I can't begin to tell you how much I hate you.'
'That's because you actually love me. Just think of the material you'll get out of this.'
'That's not how comedy works.'
'Observational comedy.'
'Have you seen my set?'
'I've *seen* it. I wasn't necessarily listening. Anyway, five or six hours ought to be plenty to actually build up the courage to talk to your fellow human being.'
'We have been talking.'

'Actually talking. Flirting. Making a move on her.'

'I'm bad at flirting.'

'Mate, you're *so* bad at flirting. But do it anyway. Dare her. Dare her to kiss you. Seriously, she can't resist a dare. I promise she'll do it. Say, *I dare you to kiss me on the mouth for ten minutes. With tongues.*'

'I'm pretty sure that's sexual assault.'

'It's not, because she doesn't have to do it.'

'It's obtaining tongue under false pretences.'

'The fact that you say things like that, Antonia Coleridge, is exactly why you're single.'

Heather felt strange, as if there was something in her belly which didn't belong there. No, not a *thing*, a *feeling* – like waiting outside the headmaster's office for punishment, but there was no headmaster and no real notion of the punishment either, so it didn't make any sense. She *never* felt like this, even before her most dangerous Chicken Club stunts... she'd get that familiar excited, nervy adrenaline tingle, yes, but not this dull sensation. Heavy. A nagging unease growing embryo-like inside her.

Her arm hurt, she was on her way towards the dreaded Almanby, and Steven was all *wrong*. But Heather was blasé, right? Blasé was her MO. Life was just one big domino-topple of hijinks for Heather McLagan, yes sir. So this anxiety shouldn't be happening, it wasn't who she was. She was life's great adventurer.

And as the daylight blazed down with magnesium intensity and cast shadows blacker than tar, Heather thought of the dream she'd had in the back of the car, and the ice cream she'd held. She could still feel its cold wetness all down her right arm where the pain now lived; she could still smell its strawberry vanilla aroma. Like a shark, Heather could sniff out ice cream from twenty miles away, or so she liked to imagine. But could sharks smell blood in their dreams? Heather could smell ice cream in hers.

She really wanted an ice cream.

Really *really*.

Really really fucking *really*. Vanilla ice cream. Chocolate ice cream. The weird yellow banana ice cream that tasted of plastic and chemicals. She'd even go for a couple of scoops of that excessively sour berry sorbet from the back of her freezer which looked like the red parts of run-over rabbits. At this stage, she didn't care. But what she did know was that ice cream in her belly would dissolve the hard, smooth thing which currently resided there.

She had to have ice cream.

She'd smuggled her ORBITRAN radio along with her on the trip. She didn't know why she'd kept it secret from the others, just as she didn't know why she'd excused herself to a secluded patch of countryside in the guise of 'going for another piss, guys, my bladder, honestly'. But she had.

Sitting cross-legged on a tuffet of grass, she extended the aerial and flicked the radio on.

A swirl of shortwave noise, darker and denser than before. Almanby. With her tongue set at a jaunty angle, she carefully tuned the dial in, millimetre by millimetre. There was less music now – a snatch of rattly, jangly folk music, accordion and tambourine, just for a second, but mostly noise.

'Where are you?' whispered Heather.

The degrees of rotation became ever more microscopic, a fraction of a fraction of a fraction. Still the sounds whooshed and whirled past.

'Come on, come on.'

And then a voice.

…I think part of the fun of it will be that it frees itself. That's not a council, that's two singers clamouring in voice. Because it's probably at breaking-knees point in trip-up-falgary. Can you find that little broken man? Can my parents shoot him? I'm six foot high and more than mandible mouth. Sorry if I don't… Thirty years ago. Now that job's got changed back into medicine…

Was that even him? His voice sounded so strange, even less like Steven than when she'd listened from her attic.

…Suppose I barge in when you were seventeen. I might have to dance with you again, breaking the barrier. Cashew bugs are for people who are afraid of worms. Go-easy nightmare, go-easy nightmare, go-easy nightmare, go-easy nightmare, go-easy nightmare, go-easy nightmare…

No, it had to be him. It had to be.

'Hold on,' she said. 'I'm coming to get you.'

'I thought he was a real policeman,' said Rachel. 'They said he was a real policeman.'

'No, he just turned up at school and told them he was a policeman,' Antonia said. 'I heard my mum telling my dad about it. They didn't check, they didn't ask to look at his ID, they didn't ring the police station to see if they'd sent anyone, they just believed him. So there's this complete stranger telling us things, how to stay safe over the summer holidays, be careful when riding our bikes, not to talk to strangers. Not to talk to strangers, can you believe it? He's up there doing this ten-minute bit about making sure you know exactly who someone is, not trusting them if you're not sure. The teachers all sitting there, smiling happily, nodding along.'

'I remember the talk. I had no idea about any of this other stuff going on.'

They're beautiful, aren't they? I honestly don't remember where they came from, though. We've had them for years.

That was something I wanted to ask – with over ten thousand items, do you ever completely forget about things? Find toys you don't recognise?

Not often, but occasionally. Those tin soldiers over there, with the green uniforms. I have no memory of buying them. My husband doesn't know how they got here. Like they moved in of their own accord. But I suppose sometimes you just forget.

'The talk was fine. I mean, how hard can it be to make up a bunch of advice to give to nine-year-olds? Look both ways, close gates behind you, cycle on the left, don't drink poison, don't play on the farm, don't go to Almanby. Afterwards, Mr Durkin called the police station to thank them for sending someone over, and they had no idea what he was talking about.'

'He wasn't wearing a uniform.'

'Exactly. I guess the teachers thought he was CID.'

'So who was he?'

'I don't know. Some pervert. Mr Durkin gave his description to the police, but they never caught him.'

This is probably the oldest item in my collection. We think around eighteen forty-two, maybe earlier.

Well, isn't this wonderful. I love the inlay here. Is that abalone?

Yes. Abalone shell and mahogany. And these pegs are ivory. Not something you'd make today.

The detail on this is amazing. Look at her eyelashes. And her little fingernails. Are they glass?

That's right, we're pretty sure the fingernails are glass.

A tramp of footsteps, and a small, curly-headed figure emerged from the rippling bands of heat.

'Nice pee?' Rachel said.

'Great thanks,' said Heather. 'Hey, Rach, I want to show you something.'

'Heather...'

Heather gestured with a sideways nod of her head, then set off back the way she came. Rachel glanced at Antonia, who shrugged.

Rachel jogged to catch up with Heather, her brow prickling with sweat from even that small exertion. It was so hot out here. 'This had better not be your urine.'

They reached a scrubby patch of nettles, gorse bushes and dried-out cow parsley, hemmed off behind an unhappy-looking rectangle of barbed wire. On the wire was a hand-painted wooden sign which read: I BET YOU'RE GLAD YOU WON'T HAVE THAT STRAWBERRY IN YOUR MOUTH MUCH LONGER.

'Huh,' said Rachel.

'What do you reckon it means?'

'It's just junk. It probably used to say 'No Trespassing' or something. We're getting closer to Almanby.'

As if expecting to be shocked or bitten, Heather reached out a forefinger and gingerly touched the sign – then, when nothing happened, attempted to remove it from the fence.

'What's going to happen when you reach Almanby?' said Rachel. 'With you and Steven, I mean.'

Heather shrugged.

'You know, he probably won't be Steven anymore.'

Heather glanced at her but didn't reply.

'I wouldn't pin all my hopes on just one guy, that's all,' Rachel continued. 'Who knows how long any of us has left these days?'

'What are you trying to say?'

'Live while you still have the chance. Any love is good love. Male or female.'

Heather gave up on the sign and marched back towards the car, high-stepping through the long grass.

'Are you hitting on me?' she said as she passed Rachel.

'Of course not.' Rachel strode to catch her up. 'I just want you to be happy. In ways that don't necessarily involve Steven.'

As the road and the car hove back into view, they could see Antonia sitting in the driver's seat, staring straight ahead.

'Think about it, yeah?' said Rachel.

Heather pulled a face. 'I'll bear whatever you just said in mind.'

Antonia popped her door open a crack and waved them over.

'What is it?' said Rachel.

Antonia gestured at the now-silent car radio. 'They said they were going to repeat it.'

'What?'

'Wait.'

Three seven alpha three, roaming. Three seven alpha three, roaming. We interrupt this programme to bring you an emergency broadcast from Bembrook East Weather Station.

An unknown meteorological event has been detected emanating from Almanby village. RS coordinates zero one by zero one. Logged and traced. The properties of this event are as yet unknown. Repeat, the properties of this event are as yet unknown.

The public are advised to take all reasonable precautions and to remain indoors until such time as the event passes.

Next scheduled update at oh seven twenty-three.

Operator Blackbeard, three seven alpha three.

End broadcast.

—highlight of your collection, Susan. It really has been wonderful to see, thank you so much.

It's been a pleasure.

'Huh,' said Antonia.

'Unknown meteorological event, eh?' Heather wandered away from the car, out into the field, till she was a tiny stick-figure among the expanse of grass and dirt. They saw her gaze up into the inscrutable blue bowl of the sky as she walked. Puffs of powdery soil caught the sunlight wherever she placed her feet and trailed behind her, tinting the heavy air yellow-brown.

'What do you think it is?' she called back to Rachel and Antonia.

Antonia grimaced. 'They said we should wait inside. It sounded serious. They interrupted a programme!'

'It's just precautionary. It's probably perfectly safe.'

'Then let's go,' Rachel called. 'Heather, please, I want to get there today.'

'But it's an unknown meteorological event! My favourite type of meteorological event!'

Rachel walked out into the field to where Heather now stood. Antonia watched as they debated with lots of hand gestures, just out of earshot, soundless mannequins. Out along the rim of the field, ghosts milled.

I'm standing now outside the beautiful three-bedroom cottage of Laura Jones. Laura has lived here in Far Thineborough for eighteen months. And in all that time, Laura, you haven't looked in your new attic. Why not?

I suppose there wasn't really the time when I first moved in. And then, as time went by, I still didn't look and I still didn't look, and it became too much of a big thing, if that makes sense?

Heather walked back towards the car with Rachel. Every so often she would jump on a particularly inviting clod of earth. But, a good few metres from the car, she stopped once again and tilted her head to the sky.

'My money's on snow,' she said. 'Or maybe a dust storm. A dust storm – can you imagine!'

'Come on,' said Rachel.

'Have some patience, Rach! I want to experience this. I want to know what an unknown meteorological event feels like.'

'Nothing's happening.'

'It has to come all the way from Almanby. Give it a few minutes.'

'You can experience it from inside the car.'

Heather rolled her eyes.

So we're going to open your new attic for the first time and take a look at what previous occupants left behind, if anything. It could be empty, it could be full of lost treasure. This is what I really love about making this programme. All right, Laura, lead the way.

Heather suddenly hugged herself, took a step back and whispered, 'I can feel it coming.'

But the air was still impossibly still, the sky was still impossibly blue. Not a trace of weather in it. The silence weighed heavily, pressing down more and more with every passing second – only the insolent chatter of birdsong, the rustle of warm air passing through the treetops, and the endless burble of Antonia's car radio, occasionally obscured in a breaker of shortwave noise, reminded them that they weren't deaf.

Okay, well, there are some plain cardboard boxes. So we do have something to look through. Maybe three large boxes at the far end of the space. A couple of smaller ones. There's an exercise bike to my left. These look like drapes. An oil painting here in a frame – it's a young girl in a field with grass and poppies up to her midriff, and she's wearing a big hat. Look how blue her eyes are. I don't think this is a lost Monet or anything, but we'll take it down later for a proper examination. I love her red shoes. All right – I'm moving across the floor now towards these boxes. The ceiling is very low here, I'm having to bend double.

'Heather,' said Rachel.

But Heather continued to gaze fixedly upwards. Rachel put her hands in her pockets and trudged back to the car.

They're sealed with packing tape. Just a moment while I cut this one open. It seems like it's been sealed for a good few years.

Rachel climbed into the passenger side and closed the door. Antonia pulled her door shut.

They glumly watched Heather through the windscreen as she paced in random zigzags, hopped, circled, and occasionally threw in a pirouette.

'I don't know what you see in her,' Rachel said.

'But you're straight.'

'You don't think she's a bit… annoying?'

'No, I think she has verve,' said Antonia.

'Verve?'

'Yeah. She's sparky.'

'Honestly, mate, she'd get on your nerves. Seriously, think about it. Imagine sharing a house with that for a year and not wanting to strangle her.'

'I reckon it'd be fun.'

'Jesus, you're a sucker for punishment.'

'Yeah, I'm friends with you.'

It looks like books in this first one. Some published books – here's a copy of Anne of Green Gables *– and some writing books, exercise books.*

'What should we do?' said Antonia.

'Just leave her out there.'

'She might get hurt.'

'What by?'

'Weather.'

'Weather. Right.'

'What, you don't think weather can hurt anyone?'

'You reckon she might get sucked up into a tornado and transported to Oz? Come back with a pair of shiny red shoes?'

Aha. And here we have a photo album. It's black, a textured satin finish, with a repeated bicycle pattern on the front. You can just make out, someone's written on the front in black marker, 'PROPERTY OF ANNE GREEN'. This is wonderful. Let's take a look. It's very dusty, it looks like it hasn't been opened in years. Flicking through, a lot of the pages are empty, but there are some Polaroids towards the middle.

'You should go out there,' said Rachel, nudging Antonia. 'Go on,' she said. 'Stand next to her. Talk to her.'

There seems to be a family. I'm guessing it's the Green family. I don't know which one might be Anne, if any, but there are a few of the same people repeating across several photographs. A boy in a hat. These two are probably the grandparents. Here they are again. Grandpa looks rather stern, but grandma seems jolly. Judging by the clothes and hairstyles, it's the 1970s, maybe early '80s. The same couple again. This looks like a conservatory or a summer house. What I love about this is how happy everyone looks. There's a lovely photograph here of a child with a mop of curly hair enjoying an ice cream. I love her blue cardigan. She looks like the happiest child in the world in that moment.

'Tonia, will you just go. She's just a human being, go talk to her, Jesus.'

'I'm shy.'

'You tell jokes to a room full of people two nights a week.'

'It's my active compensatory factor.'

'I know you, Coley. If you fuck up this trip and don't even try to chat her up, you'll be stabbing yourself in the legs with pencils and whining to me for the next year. And so, on behalf of your deeply irritating and pathetic future self, I'm telling you to go out there and talk to her.'

With a loud emptying of her lungs, Antonia seemed to deflate a moment, then immediately re-inflated slightly larger than before. She opened her driver's-side door and unhappily levered herself out of the car.

She picked her way across the field to Heather.

'Hey,' she said.

'Hey,' said Heather, without taking her eyes off the sky.

'Weather,' said Antonia.

'Yeah.'

'It's…' Antonia gestured broadly.

'Yeah,' Heather replied with a baffled shrug.

'Shall we…?'

'Yeah,' said Heather, and then: 'What?'

'Shall we go wait in the car? Where it's safer.'

'No,' said Heather. She cupped her flattened hands over her eyes to shield them from the sun. 'Can't you feel it?' she said.

'I don't know.'

'I think it's rain.'

'I can't see any rainclouds.'

Antonia scrutinised Heather's small, pretty face as she watched the sky: so intently, so seriously, like a little hamster.

'Come back to the car,' she said.

Heather shook her head.

Antonia squeezed her hands together. She paced around in circles a few times, hopped awkwardly from foot to foot, and then, eventually, trudged back to the car.

She found Rachel with her forehead against the dashboard.

'When I said you should go out there,' said Rachel, 'that's not what I meant.'

Antonia slumped in her driver's seat and looked glummer than anyone might've imagined possible.

So, you had no idea any of this was up here?

No, none at all.

This is interesting. Notice this figure in the background of many of the photos? Not just here at the beach, but look, here at this park. And he's here in the garden too. A tall, slim young man, dark hair. He's never in the foreground, he never seems to want to be part of the photograph but, look, he's there so often. Do you think he's a member of the family? Maybe a shy uncle. Or a sulking teenage brother.

By now, Heather's eyes were closed, her arms were splayed wide, and her face was turned to the heavens.

'You'd remember it for the rest of your life,' said Rachel.

Antonia gazed miserably from the window. 'I don't know why you're so invested in this anyway,' she said.

'Because you're my friends.'

Antonia looked at her with genuine surprise. 'That's the closest I've ever heard you come to admitting you care about anyone. Most of all, me!'

'I care about people. I want you to be happy. We're mates, aren't we?'

'Yeah, I guess so.'

'Well then.'

This one looks like a funeral. And this whole next page is the same funeral. That's a strange thing to put into a photo album. Especially so many pictures of the same event. I wonder whose funeral this is.

Who's missing?

That's a good question. Both the grandparents are in this shot.

Maybe it's one of the younger people.

Could be. Or it could be another friend or relative who isn't pictured. Maybe the man. The shy boy.

No, there he is.

Where?

Just there, in the back of frame. See?

Good. I'm glad he's okay.

'Look, if you go out there, I'll give you eighty pounds.'

'Is that eighty on top of the seventy you're already giving me?'

'No, that's eighty total.'

'You'd pay me ten pounds to go and stand next to Heather?'

'Yeah.'

'What's the catch?'

'Who says there's a catch?'

'Because it's you.'

'I'm offering you ten pounds to go outside and stand next to Heather for the duration of whatever the fuck's going on. Take it or leave it.'

'All right. I'll take it.'

At that moment, in a roar of static, the car radio signal was gone, pulled like toffee, until it became a high-pitched banshee howl, rattling, cackling, stretching, throbbing.

Antonia groaned. 'Oh, what now?'

A half-moment later, a wall of white exploded against the car windscreen. Rachel and Antonia jumped, imagining at first that the glass had spontaneously shattered and they were about to be peppered with sharp little green squares.

But it was hailstones.

A hundred trillion hailstones, as fervent as God's own Old Testament wrath, or the combined wrath of all the lost souls who hopelessly wandered the streets and fields. A hundred trillion hailstones out of nowhere, out of the bluest of blue watercolour skies. The clouds hadn't blown there, like normal clouds – they'd materialised, boiled from out of the humidity, magicked into being by *something*.

'Jesus,' murmured Rachel. She and Antonia stared blindly at the deluge, at the overpowering onslaught. 'I hope your windscreen holds out.'

'I hope my roof holds out,' said Antonia.

And then, as quickly as it had started, the hailstorm ceased, halving and halving and halving in moments till there were just a few solitary pellets striking the window...

...and then silence.

Rachel and Antonia's ears rang.

...in the middle of eating lunch. I love their old-fashioned toys here. Look at that plastic trumpet! And this girl has a tiny military drum, it's extremely cute.

Look at this girl here. I love her bright red shoes.

'Where the fuck did that come from?' said Rachel.

'Heather!' In a sudden flurry of activity, Antonia opened her door and stumbled from the car. Rachel followed.

The world had turned white, like a sketchbook version of itself, already melting into tracing paper under the glare of the sun. A small figure now lay motionless on its side, curled armadillo-small. At first – just for a moment – they thought Heather was dead. But then her legs moved, and she rolled over. Even at that distance they heard her emit a light groan. Hail crunched beneath Antonia's and Rachel's feet as they raced across the field towards her.

'Heather!'

Heather moaned again as they brushed the pellets off her and helped her sit up, like a defrosted ice mummy. Her right arm had been clasped over her head to protect her face, and she flexed her fingers now.

'Are you all right?' said Antonia.

Heather looked at them sleepily and said, 'It felt like an orgasm.'

23

The road unfurled like a tape measure before them, straight and relentless and oddly purposeful. A Roman road, maybe. Or maybe this was all an enormous drum with scenery glued onto the outside, and someone was turning a big handle, round and round, round and round, round and round – and the scenery was all so similar that maybe none of them had noticed they'd been driving past the same tree, the same field, the same turn-off, the same lonely farmhouse, the same straggle of ghosts, the same uppity horse, the same barn, and the same tree again, for the last five or six hours. Or seven hours. Shouldn't they be at the sea by now? Or right off the edge of the world, and blissfully floating through the cool, refreshing vacuum of space?

Almanby was a long way distant, it seemed – yet when people spoke of it, when teachers warned their pupils not to venture near it, when parents evoked it as a spooky bedtime story, it always sounded so local. Such a looming, imminent threat. The undefined beast just beyond the horizon. Just past the next village over.

But they were still only out near Eddingham and Earbury Fen and Elyingsham. Still so far to go.

* * *

And we've also recently seen an increase in unseasonal meteorological activity. There have been widespread dust storms which have reached speeds of up to two hundred miles an hour. Last week, astronomers at the Edge Green Observatory witnessed a localised dust storm in the region of Hale and Bond, around four hundred miles wide and one hundred miles high, and some signs of electromagnetic activity. And in April, a series of carbon dioxide geysers were observed in Utopia by several amateur astronomers, lasting almost a week. These geysers were so active and so dense that they totally obscured many of the surrounding geographical features.

It was still morning, but already the heat was a heavy thing with tendrils. A big bulbous kraken. It writhed soggily, making everything worse and more difficult. Even breathing was starting to become a chore. No one wanted this hot air in their lungs – neither the stale, dead air which clung to the inside of the car, nor the boisterous hairdryer wind which blew in whenever they wound down the windows.

Heather counted ghosts till it made her sleepy. Drowsing on the back seat, she pictured Steven turning into a crab, or some kind of crustacean, his big blue eyes and kind face disappearing behind a hard orange shell. The creature had two enormous pincers and more legs than it needed, and it rampaged across the countryside, pinching the heads off children and cattle.

She blinked and yanked herself out of her hypnagogic reverie. She didn't want that horrible image in her head anymore. Where on earth had it come from?

Cydonia seems to be a hotspot for unusual meteorological activity. At approximately forty degrees north and nine degrees west, we've witnessed seismic activity, we've witnessed eruptions of carbon dioxide, we've witnessed unusually high winds, all within the last eighteen months.

Heather thought happy thoughts about Steven. Her birthday, when he surprised her with a huge party in the village hall, and all her friends were there, even people she didn't know, and there was an old-fashioned disco with records by Wham! and Bucks Fizz and Fuzzbox and The Bangles. The time she got the flu, and he spent nine days living at her house, fetching her glasses of cola, mopping her brow and helping keep her temperature down. The impromptu holiday to France they took together, just on a whim, back when it was still possible to go abroad. They'd had the best time anyone could have. Heather hadn't realised it was possible to be that happy.

Surely that kind of spirit was immutable? Surely Steven couldn't be hardened, changed, turned into something alien and unrecognisable? Surely Steven was just too... just too *Steven* to be corrupted.

We've also seen an increase in radioactivity – an overall increase in the background noise emanating from Mars. Whether this is connected with the weather, or the two are being exacerbated by the same root cause, or whether it's pure coincidence, we've yet to determine. But there's certainly a sense of... I mean, this is a gross anthropomorphisation, but there's a sense that Mars is agitated.

'Edethorpe. We went to that birthday party in Edethorpe once,' said Antonia. 'When we were ten or something. Remember the man?'

'Which man?'

'The man who was there. The one at the birthday party.'

Rachel tapped her feet in the footwell and thought, *Cars have carpets. Like houses have carpets.* She'd never really thought before about cars having carpets, like it was a piece of living room on wheels. It's a shame they were never a nice thick shag pile, or a patterned rug. 'Which man?' she said.

'I think it was Alice Loeb's party. She had a swimming pool, remember? We were all in our bathing costumes. And there was a man standing... like, over towards the back of the garden. A young thin guy. Just standing there.'

'That was her brother, wasn't it?'

'Was it?'

'I don't know. I think her brother was there.'

'I felt really uncomfortable. I could feel him watching us the whole time, over behind the hedge. I couldn't enjoy myself.'

'You could never enjoy yourself anyway.'

'You know what I mean. It was creepy, I didn't like it. I always tried not to think about it, but it's just popped back into my head, I don't know why.'

'I guess I didn't notice him.'

'I feel like he was always there.'

'Where?'

'Alice's house. Or... we went on that big picnic with her family, and he was there too.'

'It was her brother, then.'

'No, he was like… over there. Not with the rest of us. He was watching.'

Rachel shrugged. 'You have a better memory than I do.'

'I want an ice cream,' said Heather a little later.

'Great. Of course, Your Majesty. I'll reach into my fridge and fetch you one,' Rachel said.

'Don't be like that, Rach. I just want an ice cream.'

'I know, you just said. What do you want me to do about it?'

'I was hoping you might buy me one.'

'Great plan, Einstein. Let's stop at one of these many hundreds of shops we keep passing, and I'll be sure to pick you up a Strawberry Split.'

'Rachel,' said Antonia.

'There's bound to be a shop eventually,' Heather said.

'Don't hold your breath,' said Rachel.

'Toni – if you see a shop, will you buy me an ice cream?'

'Of course,' said Antonia. 'My treat.'

'See, that's what a real pal is like.'

'There aren't any shops out here!' cried Rachel. 'If there are no shops, how can she buy you an ice cream?'

'Because if she sees one, she'll stop.'

'But there *are* no shops!'

'Fine. But if there is one, she'll stop.'

'But she won't stop because she won't see one.'

'I know. But if she does.'

'Fuck!' said Rachel.

* * *

'How's your arm?' Antonia said.

Heather flexed her fingers, a perplexed expression on her face. 'Sore,' she said.

24

'Stop the car!' cried Heather, banging on the side window.

'What?'

'That was my dad! Stop the car!'

Antonia pulled up. Heather opened the near-side door and spilled out onto the grass verge, running back along the road to where a ghost ambled morosely in a nearby paddock.

'There you are, you daft old bugger,' said Heather. She sat on the bank and folded her arms around her knees. 'Where have you been? I haven't seen you in ages.'

The ghost rotated to face her, all the time mouthing silent words.

'What are you saying?' said Heather.

The ghost began to trudge in her direction – slowly, almost painfully, till it came to the paddock fence. Even at this distance, she could smell his musty smell. That same aroma all the ghosts seemed to have – earthy, prehistoric, like some long-forgotten ancient embalming ointment, or the sap of a tree that had become extinct a hundred thousand years ago. When all this passed and the dead were finally gone, back to whichever afterlife they belonged to, there'd be no smell more nostalgic.

The ghost was so familiar – her dear beloved father, standing right there before her, after all these years. She'd adored her dad. She'd adored their in-jokes, their shared secret language, their long bike rides, their giggly candlelit dinnertimes, their spontaneous weekend discos in the living room: scratchy old vinyl records, tiny Heather jumping and jumping and jumping, her father chuckling at her antics. He was so tall, his face was so kind. Yet his eyes, blue as butterflies, looked right through her now, just as she knew they would.

'You're looking well. I mean... sort of. Better than I thought you would. I'm doing okay. I'm on an adventure with my friends. They're in that car. Rachel and Antonia. You know Rachel. I reckon you'd like Antonia, she's nice. She seems really sound. We're going to Almanby to find Steven. You remember Steven, right? I'm sure you met.'

She picked up a pebble and tossed it at him. It bounced off his face.

'I miss you. I'm glad you're all right, though. You seem to be doing okay. Have you made any friends out here? Met a nice lady-ghost?'

He gazed somewhere beyond her into the middle distance. His mouth moved, said all those mysterious ghost words that no one had ever quite managed to decipher. But Heather knew he wasn't talking to her. He was barely aware of her at all, except as another fleshy skittle to be knocked down if she wandered too close. He'd use the tightly gripped half-brick against his own daughter as quickly as he'd use it on anyone else.

'Remember when I was little and I used to climb up on your knee, and we'd do pat-a-cakes? I loved the pat-a-cakes.

Adam S. Leslie

'Pat-a-cake, pat-a-cake baker's man.
Bake me a cake as fast as you can.
Prick it and pat it and mark it with B.
Put it in the oven for baby and me.'

25

Clouds sailed on the upper atmosphere like the underside of orbiting spacecraft, almost too high and distant to contemplate.

Meanwhile, down below, the countryside rolled on into eternity, green upon green upon green. Great banks of white poplar fluff billowed across the road on the soupy air currents, obscuring Antonia's view every now and then. And butterflies – white and yellow and orange and robin's-egg blue – flitted around the ghosts, round and round and round, incredulous at their sluggishness.

How long had they been driving now? The day stretched back as far as Heather could remember. Antonia's comedy show felt like a parallel lifetime; Heather's shift at the cinema and Rachel's pizza delivery. She could barely even bring to mind waking up that previous morning in her damp little bed, stretching her calf muscles while wondering what to do with the hours ahead. Did she have any inkling, any tickle of ESP, that she might end the day on her way to Almanby to root out Steven like a truffle?

No, like an Easter egg. Wrapped in shiny foil, nestled somewhere in this expanse of countryside. She would find him.

We're the equivalent of five floors under the earth now. That doesn't sound much when you're standing with your feet on the ground and the sun on your face, but you can certainly feel it when you're down here. The air is noticeably thinner, it's very dry, it takes a little more effort to breathe. Ah, now. Here we are. This is interesting. We're in some kind of lower chamber, probably dating from the mid-to-late sixteenth century. I only just managed to squeeze through the gap. It's set back from the main tunnel. I'm in a cylindrical room, maybe seven feet by fifteen feet. Five feet from floor to ceiling. I have to bend double. The brickwork's remarkably well preserved, it's hard to believe this has been here well over four hundred years.

'I'd sell both of you right now for ice cream,' Heather muttered lazily, though she didn't know if Rachel or Antonia heard her. The more she tried to shoo the notion of ice cream from her head, the more it clung on, barnacle-like. The more she tried to think about other things, the more it tugged her sleeve. Strawberry ice cream, bubblegum ice cream, pistachio ice cream, mint choc-chip. Anything.

There was a photograph of Heather aged seven or eight – she hadn't seen it in years, yet she could still picture it vividly. Standing in the middle of a park in her favourite sky-blue cardigan, a towering soft-whip cone clutched tightly in her two little paws. Two chocolate flakes, victorious. The ice cream van was visible in the background, half out of frame, a line of children snaking away from it.

And on her face was the broadest grin imaginable.

Her father had bought the ice cream. Or at least, he'd given her the money for it, the bright constellation of coins in her palm, but she was the one who'd gone over and spoken to the woman in the van, specified what she'd wanted. She didn't have enough for the large cone with two flakes, but she couldn't quite comprehend this, and the woman took pity on her and waived the missing pennies. Heather was an adorable child, and difficult to refuse. She usually got her way.

That was the first time she'd bought something all by herself. She queued up on her own, she asked on her own, and she handed over the money on her own. It was a big deal, and she felt like a grown-up – a properly sophisticated little miss around town.

But now, her abiding memory of the whole thing was: *My father bought me that ice cream.*

Here we see a similar engraving to the one we found carved into the wall of the church. The figure of a woman, barefoot and broad-shouldered. She's shown here as a giant, looming ominously over trees and houses. In some depictions she's human-sized, often a witch or a mage of some description. But this time she's literally supernatural, above nature, above everything. Physically powerful.

She is the Egesgrime, the Green Woman of local lore. Sometimes known as Anne or Ennis or Annis. Legend has it, she lives under the soil, emerging at night and roaming the countryside to steal unwary children from their beds. You can see how fearsome she looks in this illustration. There's a real monstrous quality to her. She's simultaneously beyond human and less than human. A personification of the natural world. A personification of the unpredictable nature of mortality, when many children were not expected to survive past their fifth birthday.

'If you could have any flavour ice cream at all,' she said to Antonia and Rachel, 'what would it be?'

Rachel pretended she didn't hear. She gazed out the side window at a line of ghosts following each other along a streambed in a glum conga.

'I don't know,' said Antonia. 'I haven't really thought about it. Maybe Neapolitan? Or... mint choc-chip. What about you?'

'I was thinking mint choc-chip too,' Heather said. 'But if I could have any flavour at all, I'd go for vanilla.'

'Really? Out of all the flavours in the world?'

'I love all the different flavours, but... ice cream *is* vanilla, you know? You can have bubblegum or pistachio or strawberry, but – if you want to really *have* ice cream, it's got to be vanilla. You know?'

'Yeah.'

'But I'll take anything right now. A nice lemon sorbet. A grapefruit sorbet. Ever had a grapefruit sorbet?'

Rachel turned and glared into the back seat, her eyes flashing suddenly black with anger. 'Heather, will you just stop,' she shouted.

'What? We're just having a conversation,' said Heather.

'There are no shops out here. None at all. You're not going to get ice cream. You're not going to get gelato, you're not going to get sorbet, you're not going to get low fat cholesterol-free frozen yoghurt. Thinking about it isn't going to help, talking about it isn't going to help – all it'll do is annoy me. Fuck. Change the subject and think about something else, all right?'

'Yes, Mum. Jesus.'

Green Ennis, it's said, would take the children out to the woodland, where they'd forget about their families and their village community. Under her influence, they'd even forget about their own humanity – in essence, they'd become feral, they'd become animals, and spend the rest of their days roaming the woods. In other versions of the story, Ennis would eat the children, gulp them down whole, or bite their heads off and consume them bit by bit. A fairytale witch in all but name.

And we can read accounts of human sacrifice to appease the goddess, to assuage her appetite, stretching on for centuries. One or two or three adult victims in exchange for countless infants. To our modern eyes, it seems unthinkable, barbaric, but at the time these inscriptions were made, it would've been considered a case of simple mathematics.

A dot of colour up ahead, red against green, as if someone had pricked the scenery. The bloodspot swelled and transformed into a car, parked up by the side of the road and exhaling steam from more than one place. A figure was bent under the flap of the bonnet.

As they approached, the figure straightened and waved them down. He was small, wiry, dressed in dark-coloured clothes that looked as if he'd shrunk inside them. His crown and the lower half of his face was covered in thick black hair he'd clearly hacked at himself without any notion of style or aesthetics. He looked for all the world like a caveman who'd wandered off from his prehistoric diorama, found some discarded clothes under a hedge, and commandeered a car from somewhere.

He didn't smile as Antonia slowed to a halt and cranked down her window.

'Car trouble?' she said, aware even as she was speaking that this was the world's dumbest question.

'Yeah,' replied the man. 'It was okay until twenty minutes ago. I don't know what's going on.'

Antonia switched off her engine.

'What happened?' said Rachel, as the three of them climbed from their car.

'I was going along fine, and then it just stopped. No warning, nothing.'

Heather wandered over and peered under the bonnet. 'Any smoke?' she said.

'No. It just seemed to give up.'

'Could be the transmission,' said Antonia.

Rachel said, 'It's Almanby.'

Heather squinted sceptically at her. 'What do you mean, it's Almanby? How can a village break a car?'

'You got too close.'

'That's fucked that, then,' said the man, kicking his front left tyre.

'Where were you going?' said Antonia.

'I was going to Almanby. Bollocks.'

'We're heading that way, if you'd like a lift.'

Antonia expected the man to look pleased or relieved, or to show at least some kind of gratitude that a trio of passing strangers had offered to rescue him. But his expression didn't change, his scowl didn't relent. 'All right,' he said, flatly. 'Just a moment.'

Antonia glanced across at Rachel, who was equally unreadable.

The man wandered over to his open driver's-side door, leaned across into the footwell of the passenger side—

And emerged holding what appeared to be a homemade gun: a short length of copper pipe attached to a wooden backboard sawn or carved into a gun shape, and wired up to a large blue battery and various other crudely soldered-together components.

He pointed the contraption at Antonia.

'*What the hell's that?*' she cried.

'I'm carjacking you.'

'I offered you a lift!'

'This way, I'm in charge. Get in the car.'

'Asking nicely would've done it. Jesus Christ.'

'This *is* me asking nicely. Get in the fucking car. Now.'

Heather beamed. 'Did you make that yourself?'

'Come on, let's go.'

'Let me see it.'

'In. Now.'

'Hey, you get to sit in the back with me. We're going to have so much fun! Come on, let's get going. Antonia's going to buy me an ice cream.'

Heather grabbed the man by the hand and pulled him into the car.

'Perfect,' said Rachel. 'Absolutely bloody perfect.'

'What's going on?' said Antonia. 'What's all this about?'

'That isn't something you need to know,' said the man. 'The only thing that's important is that you get me to Almanby by three.'

'What happens at three?' Rachel said.

'If we're not in Almanby, I shoot your driver.'

'Why me?' cried Antonia.

Heather chortled. 'Because you're the driver, of course! This is so much fun.'

'Hey,' said the man suddenly, leaning forward between the seats. 'Aren't you Antonia Coleridge?'

'Yeah.'

'Oh, fantastic. I love your stuff. I have your DVD, it's hilarious.'

Antonia rubbed the back of her neck. 'Thank you.'

'Tell me a joke.'

'I don't really...'

'Go on, tell me a joke.'

'Better tell him a joke, Toni,' said Rachel.

Antonia leaned her forehead against the hot black plastic of the steering wheel. 'Um. I read that Jimi Hendrix wrote 'Foxy Lady' about a woman he caught on a killing spree in his chicken coop. I mean, I don't really do jokes in the traditional sense...'

'No, it was good,' the man said.

'Yeah, that's funny, Toni,' Heather chuckled.

Antonia turned the key in the ignition and started the engine.

'I haven't even made a DVD,' she said miserably.

26

Knowing Antonia's luck, she'd probably just picked up a serial killer, and they'd all soon end up as dismembered body parts in some grotty patch of woodland cordoned off with police tape.

She'd gone through a misguided serial killer phase when she was sixteen. She'd read endless leering books about Ed Kent and Chuck Spiers and Ellis Warren and Frank & Phil Donnelly. She'd tried to imagine what it'd be like to drive around and select random people to slaughter. Much to her relief, she never could, not really, not convincingly. But even now, when it came to identifying potential serial killers, she still knew what signs to look out for.

Carjacking was pretty high on the list.

Either way, this wasn't the trip Antonia had been promised. It wasn't the trip she'd been settling in to enjoy. She was still coaxing the real Heather, like a squirrel, out into the open – peeling away those layers of manic extroversion, teasing out a more thoughtful and authentic Heather. One you could actually have a conversation with.

All that was gone, now. The shutters had been pulled back down, and Wild Heather was back. Insane Toddler Heather. True, this was the Heather that Antonia had initially fallen for, the unstoppable force-of-nature Heather – but Antonia was more mature now, she preferred the lucid Heather, the human Heather, the smart and funny Heather.

Now, though, Heather was joyously monologuing at the probable serial killer in the back of Antonia's car, whose name, it turned out, was Daniel. Even if Daniel wasn't a serial killer, he'd still openly threatened to murder Antonia, and she could see nothing to suggest that he wasn't serious. And if, at one minute past three, he did place his gun against her head and pull the trigger, would Heather even care? Was this really all just hijinks to her, all just a hilarious lark?

'See, what gets me is that someone thought, what we really need are special bags to store our feet in,' Heather was saying. 'Like, I get up in the morning and put these bags on my feet. Don't you think that's weird? I mean, like, why? I don't put my hands in bags. Not unless it's winter. Which it isn't. Why not make shoes more comfortable, then do away with socks altogether? Yeah? Rather than all hard and crap. Don't get me wrong, I like socks. Thick, woolly socks on a cold morning. That was bliss, wasn't it? Dan? When it used to be winter. Like, when your feet are all cold. Right? But think about it. You have this drawer full of little bags, and you have to keep washing them, and then when you've washed them and dried them, you have to chase them round till you've matched up all the pairs. All the Tuesday socks with the Tuesday socks and all the Wednesday socks with the Wednesday socks. Because it's important for your feet to know the days of the week, right? What's that all about? And if you mix the days up, there's going to be some kind of cosmic disaster. So, they should stop making socks. Though, I suppose, if they made shoes more comfortable and did away with socks, you'd have to keep taking out the linings of your shoes and washing them. And we'd be right back to square one. And I'm sure you'll agree, Daniel, that it's much easier just to put elasticated bags on your feet than it would be to have to keep inserting them back inside your shoes every time you wash them. Then you'd still end up with a drawer full of these ridiculous bags. And imagine how crunkled up they'd get. It'd be so frustrating. You'd keep putting your foot in and they'd keep going down to the front of the shoe, you'd get so irritated, and then someone would have to say, hey, I've got this great idea, why don't we invent something where we put the lining on our feet before we put our foot into the shoe? And then after that all they'd have to do would be—'

Daniel finally snapped. '*Will you shut the fuck up about socks! Jesus fucking Christ! Do you ever fucking stop talking?*'

'*Sock Draw, Sock Draw, living in a sock drawer,*' Heather sang. '*Sock Draw, Sock Draw, living in a sock drawer.* This is the second series theme tune, this is the best theme tune. It's slightly different from the first series, but only slightly. *There's Pete and Posy and Peppermint too. There's Sam and Sandy and Bobby and Sue. Sock Draw, Sock Draw, socks are clever. Sock Draw, Sock Draw, friends forever. Join us, join us, we all love socks.*'

27

Eastyarm Weather Station eleven hundred hours bulletin.
Wind speed: seven miles per hour, six point zero eight knots.
Temperature: twenty-seven degrees Celsius, eighty-one degrees Fahrenheit.
Cloud cover: one per cent.
Air pressure: one thousand and twenty millibars.
Humidity: sixty-four per cent.

Eighty-one degrees. And the day was still cool – it'd get hotter than this.

Antonia daydreamed of snow. She daydreamed of wet woollen gloves and chapped lips and chilblains and earache and lying in bed, too cold to sleep. How wonderful all those things were, how she missed each and every one of them. She dreamed of building a snowman and naming him Jack, and watching him age with the thaw, shrinking and folding like an old man, till he was gone to water in the roots of the grass. She dreamed of tobogganing, of slipping on ice and picking grit from her grazed palms, of getting a chill and needing to pee so often it became embarrassing. She dreamed of hot cocoa and snowball fights and of wrapping a scarf around her face, sore from the wind.

Six years. Maybe more now, it was hard to keep track.

'It was big and red and round, and everyone thought it was a planet,' said Heather. 'This big red planet with a ring around it. But, like, months later I realised it was actually a cherry. We thought we'd been sucking on a planet all that time, and we'd actually been sucking on a big cherry. The ring wasn't the ring at all, it was the stalk! And when you ate it, it'd turn your mouth red – *for hours!* My mum used to have such a problem with it, it drove her nuts – *why do you have to eat those awful things, Heather? Look at your mouth, that can't be good for you* – but I loved them. What were they called? Cherry Blast? Was that it?'

'Heather, would you shut up for five minutes?' said Rachel.

'Why five minutes?'

'That's the minimum. Five minutes minimum. I don't want to hear about socks, I don't want to hear about bogies, I don't want to hear about ice lollies. I don't want to hear anything.'

'Fine. Your loss,' said Heather.

'I'll live with it.'

Daniel sat bolt upright. 'Here!' he cried, suddenly energised, jabbing an index finger towards a towering stack of bales to the right of the road, as big as the straw king's palace. 'Stop the car! Stop the car!' He poked the barrel of his homemade gun into the back of Antonia's skull. 'Stop the car or I'll shoot.'

'I'm stopping the car, Jesus,' Antonia said.

* * *

'Out!' Daniel said. 'Get out! Out of the car!'

Daniel was already halfway across the field to the bales, stubble crunching underfoot like stubby pencils. He was agitated, excited, so full of conflicting impulses that it seemed as if his body wanted to go in seven directions at once. As the trio exited the car, he gestured vaguely towards them with his gun, still walking backwards.

'Stand in a line. Right there. In a line. Any one of you tries to get back in the car, any one of you moves, I'll kill her. In fact, I'll kill all three of you. How's that? I don't need you.'

'Then why don't you just leave us here and take the car?' said Antonia.

'You're insurance.'

'What for?'

'Look, for a start, I'm taking you with me so I don't *have* to kill you. If I leave you, I'll kill you, okay? I'm not having anyone knowing where I am or where I'm going. So this is me being nice, because you're really annoying. But believe me, I will kill you if I have to. And maybe if I don't, because me being as nice as this is quite rare. I might change my mind.'

'This is great, this is really fantastic,' Antonia said, as they watched Daniel traipse the rest of the way to the bales.

Now they were out of the car and in the vicinity of the bale stack, they realised just how big it was – much bigger than it'd appeared from the road. It had a *presence*. It loomed as high as a town hall, as long and broad as a chapel, spun from gold in the sunlight. Maybe it was centuries old, new bales stacked on top of old ones as they rotted down and grew smaller. The structure sighed and crackled in the heat.

Flying insects of every description buzzed around and over and in and out of the thing, delighting at their adventure playground. A kingfisher-blue dragonfly, half a foot long, whirred past Daniel's head and off around the corner.

Carefully, Daniel began to count the rows of bales.

'Fucking hell,' added Antonia, for good measure.

'I like him,' Heather said.

'Do you remember Rachel?'

'I'm Rachel.'

'Rachel in our class,' said Antonia.

'I was in our class.'

'No, the other one. There were two. She used to have fainting fits. We'd come in from play and she'd still be out on the grass. The teachers would have to go out and carry her in.'

'Doesn't ring a bell.'

'She was really nice. She had these really pale blue eyes. Like, really pale blue. I used to talk to her all the time. But then sometimes this thing happened, these fainting fits or epileptic fits or whatever they were, and I got scared of her. I was scared to see her falling down and lying on the ground, and I didn't want to talk to her after it'd happened. It always took me a few days to get over it. She tried to talk to me, and I was awkward, I ran away from her and wouldn't look at her. I haven't thought about her in years, but... I can still see those bright red shoes of hers. You must remember those shoes she wore all the time? Like Dorothy. That's what the headmaster called her: Dorothy. But her name was Rachel. She was the other Rachel. I wish

I knew where she was so I could apologise. Such a shitty way to behave. But I was just a child, I didn't mean it. She knows that, right?'

'What's he looking for?' said Heather.

Daniel had counted the bales along the length of the stack. Now he was counting the width.

Heather plunged her hands nonchalantly into her pockets and, grinning like a poltergeist, set off towards Daniel.

'Oh no,' said Rachel. 'Heather…'

Heather sauntered up to Daniel and leaned her head against his shoulder.

'What are you looking for, Dan?'

He shrugged her off.

'You still haven't told us why you're going to Almanby,' she said. When he didn't reply, she continued, 'We're taking a secret package.'

'Jesus, Heather!' said Rachel.

'And we're looking for my friend Steven. He's gone missing. I guess you don't know Steven? About this tall. Very handsome. Charismatic. Like a young… actually, he's pretty unique. You'd know him if you'd met him. About this tall.'

Daniel finished counting the width and then began all over again, double-checking his first count.

'You must be doing something pretty cool, right? I mean, to have a homemade gun. Does that thing even work? What does it do?'

'Heather!' said Rachel.

'You like ice cream, yeah? I'd kill for an ice cream. I'd take that gun, I'd point it right into somebody's face, and I'd…'

'For Christ's sake, Heather!' said Rachel.

'I once had apple ripple. Steven bought it for me. Like raspberry ripple, but apple. It blew my fucking mind. There was a cinnamon undertow, just subtly, like...' She gestured, too enraptured by the memory of it to verbalise her passion. 'It was amazing. Here's a riddle for you: when I was going to St Ives...'

Daniel thrust his arm into the gap between bales, and pulled out a small, red cash tin.

'Hey, what's that?' said Heather.

He took a key from his pocket, unlocked and opened the tin, then removed a small cloth parcel, little bigger than a matchbox or a custard cream biscuit, and tied up with string. It looked so wholesome.

'What's that?'

He unwrapped the parcel. Inside was an electronic component – a thin Perspex rectangle glued to a green wafer of circuit board, with various candy-coloured resistors and diodes and capacitors soldered around it. Silver filaments sparkled in the sunlight.

'What's that, Dan?'

He slipped the whatever-it-was into his pocket.

A collection of ghosts, which had been eyeing them for a while from the far side of the field, were now marching in their direction. Their footfalls crackled against the stubble, slow and ominous.

Daniel set off back towards the car.

'Hey, Dan,' said Heather. 'What was that?'

28

As the road wound on, long and straight and dusty, they began to pass more and more vehicles abandoned along the verge. Cars like empty snail shells painted bright colours by children. And now a double-decker bus; and a little later a big blue lorry with the word 'PELICAN' along the side; and later still two cars crumpled and upside down in the ditch.

HD 34445. Yellow dwarf. Distance: 150 light-years. Galacto-centric distance: 25,303 light-years. Magnitude 4. Right ascension: 5 hours 36 minutes 12.81. Known planets: 6.

And all the while, ghosts threaded between the gusts of poplar cotton, sometimes in pairs or groups, often alone. Once or twice, a whole flock of them surged onto the road, forcing Antonia to slow as they crossed into a field of tall grass. She half-expected to see a collie dog bringing up the rear, barking commands. Some of the ghosts glanced over towards the car and made eye contact with Antonia. She felt queasy, like she always did when they looked at her.

Come three o'clock, would she be joining their ranks?

Why did no one else seem to be taking this seriously?

HD 33636A. Yellow dwarf. Distance: 94 light-years. Galacto-centric distance: 24,221 light-years. Magnitude 4.7. Right ascension: 5 hours 11 minutes 46.34. Binary system.

Something lay at the bottom of Antonia's stomach, heavy as a crystal ball. A big glass egg of panic, waiting to hatch into something shrieking and kicking. Heather flirted in the back seat with the man who'd threatened to execute her. Heather's voice was quiet now; Antonia couldn't hear what she was saying over the thrumble of the engine – but in the mirror, she could see her, up on her knees, leaning in to Daniel and whispering enthusiastically. Daniel no longer looked annoyed or frustrated: he nodded often, and occasionally even smiled. 'Yes,' Antonia heard him say, 'I think so too. That's ridiculous.'

They both laughed.

HD 37903. Blue dwarf. Distance: 970 light-years. Galacto-centric distance: 25,108 light-years. Magnitude 0. Right ascension: 5 hours 41 minutes 38.39. Companions unknown.

A sign appeared on the road ahead of them: ANNE GREEN CAFÉ 2 MILES.

'Please can we stop?' said Heather, bouncing on her knees. 'Please. Tonio. They might have ice cream. Please. You promised.'

'In case you hadn't noticed,' Rachel said, 'there's something of an imperative for us to reach Almanby. Unless you want to see Antonia get shot?'

'But they might have ice cream!'

'Heather, no, for Christ's sake.'

'It's fine, we can stop,' said Daniel. 'We have time.'

The crystal ball in Antonia's stomach grew that little bit heavier.

Gliese 205. Red dwarf. Distance: 18 light-years. Galacto-centric distance: 24,152 light-years. Magnitude 9.2. Right ascension: 5 hours 31 minutes 26.95. Companions unknown.

'Are you sure?' she said, keeping her voice as level as she could. 'Perhaps we should make sure we get to Almanby?'

'I think you'd better stop,' said Daniel, pointing his gun towards the back of her head. 'Heather wants ice cream. We can stop for ten minutes.'

'I want ice cream, Toni!'

'I think you'd better stop,' Rachel said to Antonia.

Alnilam. Blue supergiant. Distance: 1,976 light-years. Galacto-centric distance: 25,303 light-years. Magnitude -7. Right ascension: 5 hours 36 minutes 12.81. Companions unknown.

Anne Green Café lay across a wide concrete forecourt. Trailing plastic tape, striped orange and white, flapped and fluttered, tied at one end around a pebbled bollard.

The place was an American-style diner with a jaunty concrete atomic-era fin swooping across its sloped concrete roof: once upon a time, it had aspired to a clientele of silver-suited astronauts, trilby-wearing salesmen, short-sleeved cops and pink girls on roller-skates – but now, although the glare from the sky and the bright apron of the forecourt rendered the interior dark, it was clear the place was long abandoned, despite the 'OPEN' sign which hung limply in the door.

Nonetheless, Heather skipped excitedly across the concrete and cupped her face to the window. Just inside, propped up on a stand, was an illustrated chart of the ice creams on sale, all its colours long-since bleached off by the sun except for stubborn blue.

As if reciting an incantation, Heather read the list aloud.

'"Two-Ball Screwball, Strawberry Shockwave, Pineapple Shockwave, Lime Guzzle, Mister Blister, Berry Blue, Vanilla Twist, Lime Twist, Burnt Cola Firebomb, Bubblegum Avalanche, Lord Richardson, Caramel Dunker, Strawberry Dunker Deluxe, Cherry Belly, Vanilla Sandwich, Happy Face Sally, Head of the Family, The Banana Box, Vanilla Killer, Chocolate Lobster, Rosalind the Robot, Raspberry Blastberry, Betelgeuse Orange Treat, The Colosseum, The Big White, Mr Jones the Janitor, Applecadabra, Bananacadabra, Ugly-Wugly, Apple & Blackberry Utopia, Blue Versus Green, Apricot Dracula, Alberto Frog, Mint Choc de Milo, The Raspberry Dilemma, Gregory the Gorilla, Rose Opus, The Violet Fancy, Equestrian Carousel, Frankenstein's Mummy, Ganymede, Peg Leg Pauline, Roman Holiday, Strawberries and Cream, The Kensington Pear, Angry Green Goblin, Vanilla Ghost, Strawberry Foot, Mr Happiness, Cherry Rhapsody."'

'Don't get your hopes up,' said Rachel at her shoulder, and pushed through the door into the café.

'I want a Vanilla Twist,' said Heather.

* * *

The café interior smelled of congealed sugar and old grease. Chairs and tables still sat like country dancers in their little teams across the checkerboard floor, and there was a coffee machine and a soda dispenser lurking resentfully behind the counter – but otherwise the place had been abandoned long ago.

'Actually, I want Bubblegum Avalanche,' said Heather. 'Or a Caramel Dunker.'

'There's no one here,' said Daniel. 'You can have as many as you want.'

'*Coooool.*'

'Hello?' Rachel called, just in case.

While the others fanned out to explore the café, Daniel retreated to a table in the far corner of the room and slumped down, head in hands.

On the wall, a chalkboard read: TODAY'S SPECIAL. Heather found a nub of yellow chalk and wrote underneath: IT CERTAINLY IS, then set off in pursuit of ice cream and/or mischief.

Antonia and Rachel found themselves in the kitchen to the rear of the café. It was larger than they'd expected, and had been left spotlessly clean. On the far side of the kitchen lay a bundle about six feet long – possibly a corpse, though neither Antonia nor Rachel felt inclined to look too closely. The smell could just as easily be coming from spoiled food… couldn't it?

Antonia sat against the aluminium work surface, leaned close to Rachel, and whispered, 'We could kill him.'

'What?'

'There must be something in here we could use…' Antonia was now rummaging through drawers and cupboards and feeling up on the shelves above her head.

'Toni! You're insane!'

'It's not you he's threatened to shoot!'

From one of the drawers, Antonia produced a broad-bladed chopping knife. She gripped it hard and held it in front of her face.

'You don't have it in you,' said Rachel.

'Don't I?'

'You're really going to go in there, walk up to him, and stick that into him?'

'I could at least threaten him, get the gun off him.'

'Right.'

'Why not?'

'You're hardly an imposing character.'

'I'm bigger than he is.'

'And?'

'Look, if it's me or him, then I choose him. Why should I just passively go along with this and wait to get shot? Who says he's not going to shoot all three of us anyway, as soon as he gets there?'

'Who says he will?'

'I'm not going to take that chance.'

'So instead of passively waiting to die, you're going to actively get yourself killed?'

'Nope,' said Antonia, and turned to go. Rachel caught her by the crook of the elbow and dragged her back, grabbing the wrist of her knife hand. 'Get a hold on yourself.'

'Let go of me, Rachel. Let me deal with this.

'Just stop. Breathe.'

'I don't want to die!'

'I don't want you to die either. But are you really going to be the idiot who takes a knife to a gun fight?'

'Then what do you suggest?!'

'We'll do what he says, we'll get through this, no one will get hurt. Okay? Toni? I know guys like him, I'm friends with guys like him, he's all talk. It'll be fine. Yes? Yes?'

'You'd better be sure about this.'

'Trust me.'

Rachel prised the knife from Antonia's fingers and laid it down on the side.

'It's going to be okay,' she said.

'I hope so.'

Rachel picked up a plastic beaker from a rack, filled it from a tap, took a swig – and promptly spat it into the sink.

'No good?' said Antonia.

'No, I just enjoy spitting out water.'

Heather staggered into the kitchen, looking like someone who had just suffered a bereavement.

'There's no ice cream!' she said in an appalled whisper.

'You've checked the freezer?' said Antonia.

'I've checked everywhere! There's no ice cream. There's the big list out front, but there's no ice cream anywhere in the whole building. Not even... not even *one*.'

'I told you,' Rachel said.

'It should be illegal. Causing me emotional distress. There should be a law against it.' Heather glanced over at the bundle on the far side of the room. 'Ew,' she said.

* * *

'It's me. Yeah. Just outside Edbury Fen. Of course. The package is all present and correct. Yes, of course. Hold on.'

Rachel placed the receiver on the desk and walked to the door of the secluded back office. The corridor outside was empty apart from a dried-up mop and bucket standing sentry by the far door back into the café. Rachel silently closed the office door, returned to the mouldy red executive chair, and picked the receiver back up.

'There's something else, too,' she said. 'We seem to have picked up a hitchhiker.'

Antonia found herself alone in the kitchen.

Just her and the knife.

Heather had wandered off, still on her hopeless quest for ice cream, rechecking all the empty storerooms and freezers she'd checked only three minutes before. Rachel promised to be 'back in a mo' but didn't elaborate.

Just Antonia and the knife.

With the blade hidden behind her back, Antonia edged back into the café. Her heartbeat thumped in sync with the sparkly pink throbbing around her eyeballs. Her fist hurt from the tightness of her grip on the handle of the knife, and she could feel sweat begin to accumulate between her fingers.

Daniel had his back to her. He sat upright now, gazing out over the forecourt, over the flatness of the emerald fields swaying silently. Pylons marched like Japanese spirit gods across the far distance, woozy and blue from the heat haze. And beyond those, close to the horizon, a family of wind turbines waved their giant arms in eternal semaphore.

She could do this. Her life depended on it. She could kill a man, sure she could. Or at least maim him to the extent that he'd no longer be a danger. Aim for the neck, a hard jab with the blade, point first. If she went for his torso, she might not do sufficient damage. Bounce off a rib or stab into a soft area padded with fat, and he'd just be sore and vengeful. He wasn't a fat man, but there was probably enough around his midriff to cushion him from serious injury. And even if she did hurt him badly around the middle, he might still fire his gun at her. He might even be able to grab the knife, and that would be that. That was one thing her serial killer books had taught her – people could fight back, even when seriously injured. You had to make sure you incapacitated them on the first or second blow. If she lashed out at his face or his neck – or, indeed, anywhere around his head – he'd be too startled to react any way other than defensively. She could paralyse him or blind him. Or at least get the gun away from him so she could turn it on him. She was always frustrated by characters in movies who knocked out their captors to escape from perilous situations, but never took the time to incapacitate them while they were unconscious – and so, of course, they'd end up being chased through the woods by the very foe from whom they'd just escaped.

She wouldn't make that mistake with Daniel. If she got the gun off him, she'd shoot. She wouldn't think, she wouldn't give him the chance to gloatingly talk her out of it – another movie frustration – she'd just point the gun and pull the trigger. As many times as necessary till he stopped moving. Rachel would be cross and Heather would be distraught and probably never talk to her again – but she'd be alive. They'd all be alive.

So. She could do this. One action. One swift, sudden movement. Wham! Straight into the windpipe or the jugular. Take him by surprise.

Still she edged towards him, step by step, almost trancelike, knife hidden behind her back.

Just one step closer.

Just one step closer.

Just one step closer.

At last, Daniel turned and fixed her with a dark, unreadable glare. He looked older than before, more haggard. More dangerous.

Antonia came to a halt. She was still a good ten or twelve feet away. Far from striking distance. But she could rush him. Couldn't she? She could still take him by surprise. He wouldn't be expecting it – even at this distance, he wouldn't have time to go for his gun. Would he? If that thing even worked. It looked pretty ropy. Of course, if it didn't work, she'd be committing outright murder. Killing an unarmed man. But maybe that was a chance she'd have to take.

So she'd do it.

She'd have to do it.

For her own sake. Her own sake and safety, she'd do it.

'If Chubby Checker was so into the twist,' she said at last, 'why did he only do it annually?'

Daniel turned back, continued his reverie.

After a moment to gather herself, Antonia continued to creep forwards.

Just one step closer.

Just one step closer.

Now within striking distance, she moved the knife out from behind her back.

She jumped as something came crashing to the floor.

Daniel spun around and Antonia hid the knife again.

Heather appeared from behind the counter, her face flushed with annoyance, her teeth bared.

'There aren't even any crisps, you guys!' she said. 'No fucking crisps! Not even plain!' Then she clocked the fraught atmosphere. 'What's going on?'

'Nothing,' Antonia replied, a little too quickly.

That was that, then. The nest of metal mixing bowls which Heather had knocked onto the floor had squandered the element of surprise. Heather had possibly done it on purpose, just for the sake of causing a racket.

Antonia exhaled her own bodyweight in carbon dioxide, then stumped off to sit on the floor by the cigarette dispenser.

'Aren't you going to ask me what's wrong?' said Heather, slipping into the seat opposite Daniel, her curls eclipsing his view of the fields.

'No.'

'Well, I'll tell you, Danny Boy. I'm worried. I'm worried I'll forget what he looks like. Steven, I mean. I can't picture his face anymore. I used to look at him all the time. Like, in person or just in my head. I'd see him when I closed my eyes. When I was asleep. Now I have to think of something specific just to remember what he looked like. A moment when I made him laugh. Or his reading face. When he was really concentrating. He looked different when he was concentrating. Very serious. What do you reckon that means? That I can't remember him, I mean. Dan. Dan, are you listening?' She folded her arms and scrutinised his impassive face. 'You're serious, too. Always so serious. You don't have to be. It's not as bad as you think it is. Whatever it is that's bothering you. Nothing's ever as bad as you think. We're all just people, after all. It doesn't matter what we do or where we go, or all the weird ideas we have about ourselves and our own importance. We're all just people. And you know what? I like you, Dan.'

'Then you're an idiot,' said Daniel.

'I think you're lonely.'

'You don't know anything about me. I'm some dick with a gun who's hijacked your car. What do you care how I feel?'

'You were once somebody's baby. Somebody's precious baby boy. You once meant the whole world to two people who did everything to keep you alive and smiling and happy. Their hearts melted the first time you smiled. The first time you spoke and your first steps from one to the other. They counted your toes and sang songs to you and told you bedtime stories. What happened, Dan? Where did all that go?'

'Jesus Christ,' said Daniel. 'Can you at least do me the courtesy of being afraid of me?'

Heather looked mystified. 'Why?' she said. 'Why is that something you want?'

Rachel emerged from the back offices and crossed the floor of the café.

'Because I'm going to shoot you in the fucking face!' Daniel yelled.

'Play nicely, children,' said Rachel, as she pushed her way out onto the forecourt, screwing up her face and shielding her eyes from the glare.

Leaving the knife where she'd sat, Antonia stood and followed on behind. As she passed Daniel's table, he jabbed a finger at her and said, 'Three o'clock.'

Antonia threw her hands up in dismay as she exited.

'Are you really going to kill Toni?' said Heather.

'Of course. If we're late.'

'But if we are late, what difference will it make? We'll already be late. Shooting Toni won't make us not late.'

'Because what's the point of a threat if you don't carry it out?'

'Hm.'

As Heather pondered this, she flexed the fingers on her right arm.

'Are you all right?' said Daniel.

'Yeah.'

'Let's see.'

Heather unbuttoned her cuff and rolled her sleeve up. The flesh of her arm was marbled and mottled in purple. It looked as if it went down to the bone.

'That's not good,' said Daniel. 'It looks infected.'

'It's nothing.'

'You should get someone to look at it.'

'You're looking at it now, aren't you?'

'I mean a doctor.'

'Out here?'

'I don't know. I'm just saying, it looks infected.'

Outside, the car horn sounded. Heather rolled her sleeve back down.

'Come on. The car's getting impatient.'

She beamed and linked arms with Daniel. Together they headed for the door.

29

Antonia watched Heather and Daniel in the rear-view mirror. Their voices were still too quiet to hear, and were drowned out by the weird swirling folk music which had somehow made its way onto her car radio like a viral infection.

> *Did you ever see a lassie,*
> *A lassie, a lassie?*
> *Did you ever see a lassie,*
> *Go this way and that?*

Heather said something, and she and Daniel laughed. He tipped his bushy head back with sheer mirth. She brushed a fingertip lightly across his lips. Daniel leaned close, cupped his hand to her ear and whispered. She smiled and nodded. Her eyes sparkled.

> *Go this way and that way,*
> *Go this way and that way.*
> *Did you ever see a lassie,*
> *Go this way and that?*

Somewhere, deep in Antonia's subconscious, a memory wormed its way to the surface. One Christmas she'd built a snowman and named it Jack. She made him a crown of pinecones painted gold. After Jack melted, she collected together the pinecones and put them in an empty biscuit tin.

But there was something else, something she'd pushed right to the very back of her brain. A dark edge to the memory, like the edge of a razorblade. A sadness or… something frightening. There'd been a reason why she'd kept it buried for so long. It wasn't just that Jack had melted. She knew that he would, she was prepared for that. There was another thing.

A body. Someone found a body at the edge of the field where she built Jack. The same day he melted and she collected the cones. In the thaw, a dog-walker discovered a man in the ditch. Antonia remembered the police tape and the serious-looking officers. She watched them dumbly while placing the pinecones in the tin, carefully, one by one.

Why had she remembered this now? After all these years. Even while she was reading about Ed Kent's and Chuck Spiers's lurid crimes, the memory had lain dormant. Why now? Because she might, in the next few hours, end up dumped in a ditch herself, put there by Heather's new boyfriend?

Or had it even happened at all? The more she thought about it, the more it felt like a scene from a movie, the more she could picture herself in 16:9 widescreen, with chilly blue cinematography and a tense score. She tried to dredge up a sense memory, some notion of what it'd *felt like* to stand in that thawing calico field, solemnly watching the police go about their duties.

Nothing. She had nothing.

Oh dear, what can the matter be?
Oh dear, what can the matter be?
Oh dear, what can the matter be?
Johnny's so long at the fair.

The real Heather had disappeared. She was only Cartoon Heather now. Grinning, clowning, flirting for all she was worth. Showing off like an over-excited child. The long-standing crush that Antonia had had on Heather somehow fooled her into thinking that Heather was as near to perfect as it was possible to be. A magical woman. And she'd somehow fooled herself into imagining that her own life would be perfect if only she could somehow couple it up to Heather's: a train carriage waiting to be pulled along by a particularly sparky locomotive.

But Heather was as flawed as anyone else. She was more than spontaneous; she was more even than wild. She was reckless. She was out of control. She could vanish inside herself, nowhere to be seen. Her eyes would film over, taking on a slightly panicked look, as if Heather was trapped inside her own body, unable to make it follow her commands, like one of those ants whose brain gets possessed by fungus spores. And all the while, hijinks would ensue. The highest of hijinks. The most irresponsible, untempered, unruly of all hijinks.

He promised he'd bring me a carful of people,
He promised he'd bring me a piece of green circuitry,
He promised he'd buy me a Head of the Family,
Nobody knew he was there.

* * *

'We're being followed,' said Heather a little while later, after shooing a fly out through her open window.

'What?' Daniel craned around, tried to see from the back window. 'Stop the car!' he cried. 'Stop the car!'

Antonia was so startled by his sudden exclamation that she stamped on the brakes and they thudded to a halt.

'There,' said Heather, pointing back along the road for all she was worth.

'Where?'

'There!'

'Where?'

'There! Where I'm pointing! There!'

Daniel clambered from the car to peer back along the road. The air stank of grass and apple blossom and petrol fumes. Heather, Antonia and Rachel emerged behind him and followed his gaze.

'There's nothing there,' said Daniel, shielding his eyes from the sun.

'There! Look!' Heather was practically hopping. Dandelion seeds and thistle cotton billowed around her.

'There's nothing there!'

Heather walked further back along the road, back the way they'd just come. 'No, there! There!'

'I can't see anything!'

She paused. 'It's gone now.'

'What was it?'

'A car.'

'What car? What did it look like?'

'Red.'

'Red? Are you sure red?'

'It was following us for, like, an hour.'

'Why didn't you say something?'

'I just did.'

'Why didn't you say something sooner?' Without warning, Daniel ran back along the road, receding till he was just a small black stick-figure rippling in the heat.

Rachel said, 'Are you fucking with him?'

Heather shook her head.

As they watched, Daniel came to a halt, his feet set wide apart.

'It stopped whenever we stopped. Always the same distance.'

'You're hallucinating.'

'I swear!'

'Guys,' said Antonia.

'So where is it now, then?' Rachel said to Heather.

'I don't know,' Heather said.

'I swear, you're fucking with him.'

'I'm really not.'

'Guys,' said Antonia. She nodded towards Daniel.

He was a long way from the car now, his back turned to them.

'Let's go,' Antonia whispered, and took a couple of paces towards the car. 'Come on, let's run for it.'

'We can't,' said Rachel.

'This is our chance. Come on!'

Antonia began to walk back quickly. Rachel watched Daniel intently for a few moments, breathing hard, but he didn't move. Then she turned and followed Antonia.

'Heather, we're going,' Rachel said, in as urgent yet unobtrusive a voice as possible.

'We can't leave Dan behind,' Heather said.

'Will you shut up and run!'

'Run? Why?'

Antonia waved urgently at her. 'Heather! Come on!'

'Why are you whispering?'

'Fucking hell, Heather, we're going!' Rachel jogged back, grabbed Heather by the wrist and yanked her towards the car. Antonia winced, hoping she wouldn't start yelling or shrieking or loudly singing or something else designed to alert Daniel to their escape plan. Just for a lark. Just for the hell of it. Just to send them all to hell.

But no, somehow Heather kept quiet, and they arrived safely at the car.

Antonia and Rachel opened their doors as carefully and quietly as they could.

Along the road, alerted by the soft clunk of the doors, Daniel turned.

Heather waved.

'Heather!' Rachel cried.

Antonia leapt into the driver's seat and turned her key in the ignition. The engine juddered and growled like a bear shaking off the last vestiges of hibernation. Rachel opened the back door and pushed Heather inside, falling on top of her – just as Daniel raised his gun.

'Go go go!' yelled Rachel from where she lay atop the giggling Heather on the back seat.

Antonia stamped on the accelerator. With painful reluctance, the car began to pull away. A popping sound behind them like firecrackers or popcorn. They expected the back windscreen to shatter inwards at any moment; or maybe the fuel tank to take a hit and the whole car to go up in flames, incinerating them where they sat and adding to the net heat of this already scorching day.

But the car was picking up speed now, and as Rachel tucked Heather's flailing legs inside and pulled the door shut behind them, Daniel shrank to a small sinister point of black in the rear-view mirror...

...then was gone.

30

The landscape was made of gold. An optical illusion. Lenticular. Hologrammatic, reflecting greens and browns and the billion colours of nature.

Asylosaurus, melanorosaurus, riojasaurus, herrerasaurus, eoraptor, ceolophysis, thecondontosaurus, staurikosaurus, plateosaurus...

chanted the voice on the radio, barely audible through the kaleidoscoping shortwave noise, hesitantly sounding out the consonants as if fumbling in the dark.

And still more abandoned cars. And crashes – three, four, five, six cars concertinaed together, their doors hanging open and their occupants long since gone. And here now was a farmhouse, its farmyard strewn with bodies and soaked in blood and swarming with ghosts. Smoke gushed from the windows, thick and black.

...pisanosaurus, mussaurus, alwalkeria, vulcanodon, kotasaurus, fulengia, emausaurus, lophostropheus, ohmdenosaurus, tachiraptor...

As if reading Antonia's mind, which rolled over and over like a bingo hopper, Rachel said, 'So, Heather, are you missing Daniel now he's left us?'

Heather looked up sleepily from the back seat. 'Who?'

'Daniel. *Daniel.* The man who was in the car.'

'Oh, him. Has he gone?'

'Of course he's gone,' Rachel snapped. 'Can you see him anywhere? We left him a few miles back.'

'Good. I didn't like him, he was always shouting.'

'You seemed to be getting along well with him,' said Antonia.

Heather shrugged. 'Did I? No, he was horrible. He was always so angry, and he had that gun. He scared me. I'm glad he's gone.'

…leyesaurus, seitaad, dilophosaurus, dracovenator, pegomastax, gryponyx, fabrosaurus, gigantoscelus, lycorhinus, abrictosaurus, heterodontosaurus, komlosaurus…

'You seemed pretty keen on him,' Antonia said, with a strained chuckle. She was aiming for nonchalance but achieved the opposite. Rachel glanced across at her. 'Like you fancied him or something silly like that.'

'Me? No, I'm in love with Steven, remember? I'm going to see him in a couple of hours. Why would I…?' She drifted off, distracted by a group of ghosts in long, flowery dresses. They looked so pretty, like girls on their way to a summer party, that Heather was momentarily caught off guard. But they were all dead, every one of them.

* * *

Heather held the piece of circuitry to her eye. She screwed up her other eye and rotated her head towards the sun till her entire field of vision was the most vivid, vibrant green.

She didn't even really want Daniel's piece of circuit board – she was just curious why *he* wanted it so badly... so she took it. No one ever expected her to be a skilled pickpocket, which made her extra-double-good at it. She'd learnt the skill for a Chicken Club dare, rummaging through the pockets of ghosts without them noticing. To her disappointment, they didn't keep anything interesting in there, just grubby stubs of pencils and folded sheets of paper, as if intending to take notes but never getting around to it, plus the occasional waxy pre-decimalisation coin.

A later Heather-prank involved swapping over people's belongings – they'd discover they had someone else's wallet and house keys and handkerchief, and they'd have to track down their counterpart to swap back. Heather sometimes made it more difficult by throwing a second swap into the mix... so people would track down the person whose possessions they had, only to find *that* person had someone else's.

The Chicken Club didn't do points, but she awarded herself 100 points for that one.

So lifting Daniel's piece of circuit board was a doddle. A doddle and a half, really. She might never know why he wanted it or what it was for, but she took quiet satisfaction from the fact that she had it and he didn't.

And then after that she spent thirty minutes daydreaming about quite how furious he would be when he discovered the thing was no longer in his pocket, chortling occasionally as she imagined his funny face all red and screwed up like a raisin. Clutching his chest, lying down on the grass verge and expiring, toes to the sky.

A-he-he-he, she chuckled.

In the front, Rachel flipped open the glove compartment and rummaged through.

'What are you looking for?' said Antonia.

'I'm thirsty.'

'I haven't got anything.'

'I only want water.'

'I haven't got any water. I haven't got anything. You know that. You've looked in there already. I didn't bring anything.'

'You didn't bring *water*?'

'Yeah, I didn't bring water on a journey I didn't plan and wasn't expecting. Shocking, isn't it.'

Rachel gazed vacantly into the glove compartment till Antonia leaned across and snapped it shut.

…hesperosaurus, euhelopus, torvosaurus, stegosaurus, kentrosaurus, yingshanosaurus, apatosaurus, dacentrurus, allosaurus, ornitholestes, brachiosaurus…

Antonia pointed down a side road. 'Dunthorpe Wastes,' she said.

'What's out there?' said Rachel.

'Nothing, that's why it's called Dunthorpe Wastes.'

Heather leaned forward between the seats. 'My grandma used to live in Dunthorpe Village,' she said. 'On Rectory Street, near the pond.'

'I thought she lived in your house,' said Rachel.

'Nah, that was my other one. Everyone's entitled to two. This was Granny Green. She kept things preserved in jars. She had cupboards full of pickling jars. And all in the cellar, too.'

'What sort of things?'

'Fungus. Bits of animals. She had this rabbit foetus. She didn't tell us it was a rabbit foetus, though. Do you know what she said it was?'

'What?'

'My grandpa. She said that after he died, she'd pickled him till he shrank. I screamed the house down. I couldn't sleep for weeks, stupid cow.'

'You know,' said Heather, a little later, flexing her fingers, 'an ice cream would take my mind off my arm. All white and milky and making the rim of the cone wet. Sitting on the grass, licking around the outside, catching the drips as they come down. If that's heaven, then I don't want to go to hell. Antonia – if we see a shop, will you buy me one?'

'Of course.'

'Thanks, Tonio.'

Rachel popped open the glove compartment and began to rummage through.

'What are you doing?' said Antonia.

'I'm thirsty.'

'I know. I don't have anything. You already looked.' Antonia reached across and snapped the glove compartment shut.

...dryosaurus, mamenchisaurus, othnielia, saurophaganx, guanlong, archaeopteryx, barosaurus...

Heather thrust her arm between the seats and shook the package in Rachel's face. 'What's in this thing, anyway? Can we open it yet?'

'You can't open it at all,' Rachel told her. She sounded very far away.

...pelorosaurus, shamosaurus, iguanodon, erketu, gastonia, irritator, neovenator, sauropelta, valdosaurus, zephryosaurus, sinosauropteryx, nodosaurus, ouranosaurus, harpymimus...

Antonia pointed across the fields to where a blue stiletto spire poked above the horizon. 'Daughborough,' she said. 'And Daughling-on-Daugh.'

'We're too far east for Daughborough,' said Rachel.

'I swear, it's Daughborough.'

'Nah. That's Denbrooke. That's Denbrooke church, where the cannibal lived. It was in the news. The Denbrooke Church Cannibal. He ate those parishioners.'

'He was the vicar?' asked Heather, leaning forward between the seats.

'No, he was the cannibal.'

...caudipteryx, jobaria, liaoceratops, muttaburrasaurus, minmi, microraptor, austrosaurus, baryonyx, archaeoceratops, hylaeosaurus...

The blackened skeleton of a tractor flamed in the middle of the field, vomiting gutfuls of grey smoke into the atmosphere.

'If we see a shop, we can stop, right?' said Heather.

* * *

A little later, they passed an orange Ford Escort conked out by the side of the road.

'That's Steven's car,' said Heather.

They pulled over. Heather and Rachel climbed out to examine the car. With a sudden burst of panic, Heather realised she may be about to find Steven's corpse, still strapped into the driver's seat. But the car was as empty as it was kaput. Steven was long gone.

'I guess we know he made it this far at least,' said Heather, scratching her curls.

There was a scrap of paper tucked under one of the windscreen wipers, folded in half. Rachel carefully removed the note, but before she could read it, Heather snatched it from her fingers.

The note said:

Heather,
I told you not to follow me, but I know you'll come anyway.
The car's knackered, so I've continued on foot.
If you want to find me, I'm staying at 7 Penfold Lane.
Stay safe.
Love,
Steven
xxxx

31

'Heather. Heather my floating feather!' Steven whispers, leaning close. 'You're aware that I love you. We'll run away together, and then we can—'

Heather woke with a start. Foggy and confused, she glanced around the car. It was still moving. For some reason, she'd expected it to be parked in Almanby by now, and they'd be just about to venture forth into the mysterious village to track down 7 Penfold Lane. But no, they were still in motion.

'How long was I asleep?' she said.

Rachel looked at her watch but didn't reply.

'You okay?' said Antonia.

'I'm not sure.'

'Not far now. We just passed Cudburn.'

'What's Cudburn?'

'It's a village.'

...archelosaurus, graciliceratops, nedoceratops, tyrannosaurus rex, parasaurolophus, styracosaurus, lophorhothon, mapusaurus, triceratops, gallimimus, daspletosaurus...

Heather felt lighter, as if the thing in her stomach had shrunk just a little. They had a location for Steven now, and she knew he was expecting her. Maybe things weren't so bad after all, maybe she wasn't waiting outside the headmaster's office for punishments but for rewards. Sweets for good behaviour, a penny for work well done. Steven, intact and in one piece, beaming from ear to ear at the sight of her. Twist ending: maybe the headmaster *was* Steven, and he'd chortle with mischievous delight as he cast off the gown and mortar board and wrapped her in the squeeziest hug ever.

…tyrannoraptora, lithostrotia, orodrominae, troodon, wannanosaurus, velociraptor, iguanadon, protoceratops, maiasaurus, euoplocephalus, tyrannotitan, spinosaurus, chubutisaurus…

Heather thrust her arm between the seats and shook the package in Rachel's face. 'What's in this thing, Rach? Can we open it yet?'

'You can't open it at all,' Rachel told her. 'It's not for you.'

…dromaeosaurus, carnotaurus, ankylosaurus, khaan, pachyrhinosaurus…

Rachel flipped open the glove compartment and began to rummage around.

'Did you bring water?' she said.

32

Deadly mono-secret: sounds like a pendulum inside her towel

said the voice on the car radio, close to being entirely obscured by the fizzing static.

This is a piece of carpet shock… it's a theatre of nonsense, we all gain something from it. I've had your breakfast, I've scared your teeth out. The other thing we worry about is the petalments. And anyway, if it had been a few dancing elements in the reign of heaven.

None of them spoke. Each of them pretended they didn't know exactly who they were listening to. Heather stared fixedly out of a side window, watching cornfields and straw bales and ghosts and car wrecks and poplar trees and pylons and butterflies parade past the car.

Bouncing the baby bomb! She's no miniature-cruncher, is she? The air is almost caged with liquid shouts of freedom. It's the bizarre silence fund: a lot of customers are de-stretched-out now. It's a terrible school, but it has seen some beautiful bright blue jeans, hasn't it, Binks? Is it about keeping things warm to fit in with Egypt? He's twenty per cent more than happy…

Then the voice faded, overwhelmed, and was gone, and all that was left were the howling, phasing Catherine wheels of shortwave interference.

Antonia reached across and clicked the radio off.

Up ahead, a sign pointing along a winding track read:

COLLINGSHURST 2
CALVERTON 1½
CARLTON BRANSWORTH 1
CAVERSHAW EAST 1
CAVERSHAW WEST ½

'We're getting close,' said Rachel.

And then,

Just like that,

The engine coughed,

The engine sputtered,

And the car rolled to a halt.

'No!' cried Antonia.

'Uh-oh,' Heather said.

Antonia cranked and cranked and cranked the ignition, desperation spiralling around her insides, but nothing happened. She hammered her fists on the steering wheel.

'No no no!' she howled. 'Don't do this to me!'

She tried the ignition one more time, cranking it till she nearly wept, but still nothing. Bursting from the car, with Heather and Rachel following gingerly behind, she prised open the bonnet. The engine was as heavy and lifeless as a hunk of raw meat, fresh from the butcher. Wisps of steam emanated from the pistons.

'I don't believe you!' she sobbed. 'I trusted you! I thought you were my friend! How could you do this to me? You fucking traitor! You fucking traitor!' She slammed the bonnet and collapsed against the tarmac, her arms wrapped over her head.

'Now we're screwed,' said Heather with a shrug.

A team of ghosts was meandering across a nearby potato field in their direction. Heather chortled and pointed to the one closest to them. She had untidy reddish hair and a familiar oval face.

'Hey, Rachel,' she said, 'that one looks like you.'

'Where?'

'There. Look.'

'Oh yeah. That looks like me all right. Must be a distant relative,' said Rachel.

'Well, it's getting closer all the time.' Heather took a step backwards. 'We'd better get out of here.'

Rachel tugged Antonia to her feet. 'Come on, Tone, we're going.'

'What? Wait a minute! We can't just leave my car in the middle of nowhere!'

'Why not?'

'It's my car!'

'It's dead. There's nothing we can do about it. It's Almanby. Same as Daniel's car. Same as all the other cars.'

'When is a car not a car?' said Heather, chuckling mysteriously to herself.

'I've only had it three months!' said Antonia. 'I paid good money for this!'

'No, you didn't,' said Rachel. 'You paid evil money for it because money is the root of all evil.'

'Fuck you, Rachel! Fuck you! I've had enough. I didn't even want to come. I've been dragged through the middle of God knows where, I've been insulted, I've been ignored, I've been threatened, my car's fucking dead now, and I still haven't had a full night's sleep! I'd have been better off taking my chances with my idiot neighbours and their fucking racket. And all you can do is stand there and tell me that money is the root of all evil? You, Rachel – *you* are the root of all evil.'

The ghosts were beginning to draw dangerously close by now. Heather leant into the car and fished out the package. 'Better not forget this,' she said.

'Ah, thanks Heth!'

'Can we open it yet?'

'No, but you can carry it if you like.'

'Thanks Rachel!' Heather beamed and shook the box. 'There's *something* in here,' she said.

Hands thrust into pockets, Rachel sauntered out into the field, away from the ghost and off towards the yawning, stretching horizon.

'Where are you going?' said Heather.

'Almanby.'

Heather pointed along the road. 'This way.'

'This way,' said Rachel. 'Can't you feel it? It's over there. Over the horizon. It's waiting for us.'

Heather hugged herself as a sudden chill passed over her, despite the cloying humidity. She *could* feel Almanby – a dark, heavy presence, brooding, lurking, festering, *alive...* simultaneously pushing her away and calling her on from beyond the curvature of the Earth.

And Steven was there. Right at the heart of it. Part of it, but distinct too.

Heather jogged to catch up to Rachel as she strode out over the grassland. But Antonia didn't budge. She remained beside her car, its silver sheen already growing as grey and faded as the cars they'd left behind them. As the first of the ghosts came within striking distance, she shoved them away.

'Get away from it!' she yelled. 'Don't you dare touch it!'

One of the ghosts carried a hammer with a wicked-looking claw, another had a sturdy length of branch, and a third, dressed in a black ballgown, seemed to be clutching some kind of ornate silver candlestick like an errant Cluedo pawn. Others crowded in behind, pressing closer, threatening to overwhelm Antonia. But she was blind with rage and pushed them hard in the chest whenever they came too close.

'I said, don't touch it!' she howled. 'Get your fucking hands off it! Leave it alone!'

By now, the hammer ghost had put its weapon right through Antonia's windscreen. Antonia launched herself at it, grappling with it, punching it as it tried to land a second blow, and the pair toppled to the ground. The other ghosts crowded round, one of them aiming at Antonia with its hunk of brick but hitting the hammer ghost on the side of the head.

Heather raced back across the field and dived right into the fray, shoving ghosts this way and that as she battled to reach Antonia. With the hammer ghost now raising its weapon to take a swing at Antonia's face, and the candlestick ghost also sidling in for a go, Heather grabbed Antonia under the arms, hauled her upright, somehow managed to extricate her from the melee, and hurried her away across the fields.

33

Antonia daydreamed of snow. She daydreamed of wet woollen gloves and runny noses; sleet-lashed cheeks and disgusting wet trouser-cuffs that chafed her ankles; and she daydreamed of lying in bed too cold to sleep, wishing desperately, hopelessly for another body to keep her warm, nestling its wild curls in the crook of her shoulder. Tucked up beside her, almost half her length under the covers, its cold heels pressed against Antonia's shins, loose fingers idly caressing her side.

What would it be like? She'd imagined it so often now that the real experience was almost inconceivable. It could only exist in a parallel dimension. It's not that it could never live up to expectations – it probably would, Antonia's expectations were exceptionally modest... lying in a semi-naked romantic clinch with Heather was satisfaction enough, frankly. Anything beyond that was a bonus. It was the *fact* of it happening, that was the hard part to wrap her head around. The moment they climbed into bed together, the universe would wink out of existence, or simply shake the pair of them off like a disgruntled horse.

Heather was straight, but – like Rachel said – probably *would* do anything. Antonia could dare her to go to bed with her, or bribe Rachel to dare her, but Antonia could never live with herself. That wasn't how Antonia wanted it to pan out. Heather had to do it because she wanted to do it.

Was Antonia even Heather's type?

When Heather rescued her from the ghosts, Antonia forgot all about her car in that moment. Heather's arms under her arms, her surprising turn of strength, her determination to save her... it was like electricity through Antonia's body. She relived the sense memory of it over and over, reinterpreting it in her mind – Heather was pulling her towards a huge double bed laden with pillows, throwing her down, unfastening her jeans, the buttons deliciously stubborn. Pressing her face in close, tongue darting forward, finding its way into her mouth, her hand softly cupping Antonia's jaw.

But no, it was all just a pathetic fantasy. Heather sauntered now beside Rachel, hands deep in pockets, happy as the day she was born: barely aware of Antonia trudging a couple of steps behind, and talking about something in her usual unstoppable stream of consciousness. Antonia was too far inside her own head to keep track of what Heather was saying.

'Why do guys have to pee against things?' Heather said. 'You always see them pissing up a tree or a wall or a tractor tyre. Never just into the air. Why is that?'

'I don't know,' said Rachel.

'My Uncle Michael built a scarecrow at the bottom of his garden, just to piss against. Did I ever tell you that?'

'Your family is weird, though.'

'He called it Kevin, and he used to go out there when my auntie was in the shower, and he'd pee up its front. Sometimes when she wasn't in the shower. And it wasn't a secluded garden either, all the neighbours could see. Standing there peeing up the front of a scarecrow. Never the back.'

'I'm going to regret asking this, but why Kevin?'

'Kevin was the name of his best mate. Kevin Smith, they used to fly model planes together. He'd say, *I'm going outside to piss up Kevin.*'

'While his mate was there?'

'No, he never told Kevin about this, that'd be weird.'

'Yeah, perish the thought that your Uncle Michael would do something weird. Heather, I'm rapidly coming to the conclusion that you're actually the sane one in your family.'

'What are you talking about? I'm the most sane and boring person there is.'

'Of course you are.'

'I'm the definition of normal. You don't get more normal than me.'

'All right, name something normal that you do.'

'I have cereal for breakfast. I clean my teeth. I wear clothes. I do all the normal things!'

'You spent all last week with your face painted like a tiger.'

'It's fun to be a tiger.'

Antonia daydreamed of snow. She daydreamed of wet woollen gloves and cracked and bleeding knuckles, and of tracking footprints through a virgin field. Someone had been there since the previous night's snowfall. She daydreamed of Jack the snowman and his crown of gold, and of the police gathering in the scrubby woodland beyond, and of tracking small footprints through a virgin field. And of being a teenager building a snowman with a crown of gold pinecones and naming him Jack, and of wandering around the village early in the morning looking for someone random to choose. Someone random to lead out into a remote field at the crack of dawn, and…

No, that was ridiculous. She wouldn't hurt a fly. She wasn't Ellis Warren or Ed Kent, she was Antonia Coleridge. Gentle, vegetarian, peace-loving Antonia Coleridge.

Antonia daydreamed of snow. She daydreamed of wet woollen gloves and prickly heat and red-raw ears. She daydreamed of lying with Heather curled up beside her, lying in the frozen undergrowth and cradling Heather's head, comforting her, *there there*, *ssh now*, while she bled out.

34

The midday sun sat like a burden, hot and heavy, on the arched back of the sky. It pressed down on everything it touched – on the trees and the fields and the animals and the people. All except Heather, who seemed to have gained a renewed vigour, and raced around in increasingly elaborate Spirograph whorls.

They'd left the road a long way behind them now, and had instead picked up the trail of the River Coll, which cut its way through the countryside, green and slow and sulking beneath the heady humidity. Kingfishers and dragonflies patrolled the line of the river, flashing back and forth along its length, while clouds of gnats held court and mayflies danced their elegant up and down and up and down and up and down quadrille into eternity. Over on the left, beyond the sheep and ghosts and hedgerows, sat the spires and suntanned roofs of identical twins Collbeck and Collbrook, and then tiny Collford beyond that.

Heather ran circles around Rachel and Antonia, her grin bordering on manic. Rachel's frown twitched with irritation.

'It was Steven who taught me how to knit,' said Heather, barely out of breath. 'Everyone thinks I taught him. But he taught me.'

'Fascinating,' Rachel said.

'We knitted jumpers and socks for all the displaced people and the poor people. Every Sunday, down at the village hall with the old ladies. All the old cauliflower heads. I thought it'd be really boring, but actually it was fun. He used to organise raffles. And parcels. All sorts of crap like that, it was great. I've got an itchy leg.'

And again, she was off, curving out into the field and chortling at every random passing thought.

'Bloody hell,' said Rachel.

An official-looking sign, attached to the trunk of a large willow, read:

PRICK IT AND PAT IT
AND MARK IT WITH B
AND PUT IT IN THE OVEN
FOR BABY AND ME.

'And one time we were hanging out, and he drew this picture on my back in felt tip pen. A picture of his house. It was so hot, you guys. Like, the sexiest thing ever. Oh my god. We had sex four times that day. Four! And... and... ooh, he made the best cakes. Carrot cake. He put carrot in a cake! Isn't that crazy? But it totally worked. I suggested peas and runner beans, but he thought that was funny. Hey guys, what do you think 7 Penfold Lane is like? I bet Steven has made it all cosy with fairy lights and drapes and shit. I bet he's there right now with his feet up watching some weird film on TV, that one with the Japanese schoolgirls and the cat and the watermelons.'

And with that, she was off again, running loop-the-loop through the grass. And now she was gone, nowhere to be seen or heard.

'Are you all right?' Antonia said.

'Why wouldn't I be?' said Rachel.

'You just seem a bit… grumpy. It should be me who's in the bad mood.'

'I'm fine.'

'Are you sure? You look pale.'

'I'm fine. I'm really fine.' Rachel opened her mouth to continue when Heather exploded out of nowhere and attached herself to her back.

'Come on, Rach, do one of your tricks,' Heather said, chortling demonically.

'Heather, get down.'

'I'm not letting go till you do one.'

'I thought you hated them.'

'I want to see one. Just one. Please! Ow, fuck!'

Heather sprang off Rachel's back as if she'd been electrocuted, an expression of pain flashing across her face. 'I felt that!' she cried.

'You said you wanted to see one.'

'You got electric cables under there or something?'

'It's all in the wrist,' Rachel winked.

Heather glared at her a moment like a scolded child, then broke into a grin. 'Seriously, you have to tell me how they're done.'

Up ahead the riverbank flattened out into a small crescent beach, like a bite out of the earth. Heather ran on, scampering across the yellow sand.

'Day at the seaside!' She snapped off a bulrush and swung it at Rachel's head. 'Day at the seaside!' she reiterated, before hurling the bulrush javelin-style into the water. With a thump, she fell to the sand, too preoccupied with stripping off her socks and shoes to remember to balance. And then she was upright again, and wading out into crown-glass water, her pale legs all ripply and tinted green.

'Don't you just want to murder her?' said Rachel.

'What?' Antonia said, startled out of her Heather reverie.

'Look at her. Couldn't you snap her silly little neck?'

'No, of course not. I think she's cool.'

'I think you deserve her, just by dint of being the only person in the world who could put up with her for any length of time.'

'You know what would make this perfect?' Heather shouted over her shoulder.

'Ice cream?' Rachel muttered.

'Ice cream.'

'You don't say.'

'I had this Turkish delight ice cream once,' she said, as if about to embark on a lengthy anecdote, but tailed off into silence, then waved at a passing heron.

Rachel nudged Antonia and nodded towards the water. Antonia folded her arms and made her mouth small and tight. Rachel rolled her eyes.

'There are sticklebacks in here,' said Heather. 'Oh man, ice cream ice cream ice cream. Know what it's like to crave something so much you could just reach in through your chest and rip your own soul out?'

'I've got a fair idea.'

Rachel nudged Antonia again.

Antonia shook her head.

'Go on!'

'You guys should come in,' said Heather. 'It's all sandy on my toes. Come and commune with the fish!'

'Go on!'

Antonia exhaled unhappily.

'Go on! You're a fucking stand-up comic. If you can tell shit jokes to a room full of pensioners, you can walk into a bit of water.'

At last, Antonia hunched her shoulders and made her way awkwardly to the waterside, where she spent some time watching Heather.

'Nothing fancy,' said Heather. 'Just an ordinary cone. Just an ordinary soft-whip vanilla cone. Melting slightly at the bottom, turning the rim of the cone wet and milky. Perfect. And maybe... and maybe just a dash of strawberry sauce. Hey, Antonia, come in. Come on.'

Antonia glanced back at Rachel, who rolled her eyes a second time. Antonia rubbed the back of her head, pinched her nose, and then finally slipped off her shoes, rolled up her trousers, and waded into the water, one wobbly step at a time. Fronds of slippery green weed tickled her ankles. The water felt warm around her calves.

And Antonia realised that it'd all been worth it for this moment.

'It's nice, isn't it,' said Heather.

'Yeah,' Antonia said.

Antonia arced out towards Heather, out towards the middle of the river. There was something transgressive about leaving behind ground and walking out into a body of water. Especially flowing water. Being somewhere she shouldn't be, somewhere she wasn't designed to go. The tug of the currents, the buoyancy, the drag from the liquid made the pair of them stupid and clumsy. And it was *so much fun*.

As if on cue, Heather stumbled and grabbed onto Antonia's arm. Antonia steadied her.

'Thanks,' Heather said softly.

They held one another's forearms as they helped each other across a rocky part of the riverbed. A spiky piece of rusted farm machinery lay half-hidden among the reeds.

'Watch your foot,' said Antonia.

'Whoops.' Heather adjusted her course, and they picked their way around the reeds and into a deeper part of the river. The water was up over Heather's knees by now.

They paddled in silence for a bit, each holding the other's hand. Antonia felt giddy. Light-headed. She never wanted this moment to end. It was so casual, not a big deal, just two friends holding hands. Nice physical contact. She imagined them kissing in the middle of the river, the texture of Heather's tongue against her own, slipping repeatedly inside her mouth. But the thought made her go all wobbly; she had to concentrate, focus on the now. Enjoy it for what it was.

'How's your arm?' she said.

'Yeah, sore I guess.'

They'd reached the middle of the river now. The water was just below Heather's bottom and just above Antonia's knees. Here they stopped and just stood. Antonia was aware that her trousers were wet and almost suggested they leave the river, but stopped herself just in time.

She felt the weight of social awkwardness and almost let go of Heather's hand, but stopped herself just in time.

She felt suddenly bashful and self-conscious and all too aware of her own clammy palm, how ridiculous it was to be holding Heather's hand, how stupidly obvious her feelings must be, and she almost let go, she almost let go, she almost turned and headed for dry land, but stopped herself just in time.

Heather looked up at Antonia and was about to say something, when Rachel called from the bank: 'We'd better get going!'

They glanced up to see Rachel pointing across the field. A large collection of ghosts was rapidly tottering in their direction. Their dusty black clothing looked like holes in the sunshine.

'I guess we'd better get going,' said Heather. Still hand in hand, Heather and Antonia helped each other back to the riverbank.

'It's not fair!' said Heather. 'I remember when you could lie in your garden, close your eyes, and take a nap, and not have to worry about anything sneaking up on you and bashing your skull in. I just want to *be* somewhere. I just want to be somewhere and enjoy myself for as long as I want, and not have to rush off because dead people are chasing me. Is that too much to ask?'

'If the Spanish for dog is *el perro*,' said Antonia, 'then the Spanish for cat should definitely be *el purro*.'

35

On a ratty patch of wasteland they found an abandoned funfair. Most of it had been dismantled and lay semi-naked under tarpaulin, like the aftermath of an alien autopsy – the spray-painted superheroes, busty serving wenches and Clint Eastwoods, and the billion multicoloured light bulbs, they all sparkled happily in the afternoon sun on dismembered limbs and the trunks of once-mighty machines, now oblivious to their fate. But an equestrian carousel remained intact over in the far corner, an old-fashioned roundabout with garish, leering horses and layer upon layer of Edwardian grotesquery.

Antonia and Heather mounted a horse each, side by side, while Rachel slid into the booth and pressed every button she could find, till all the options were exhausted and they had to admit defeat. The carousel was as dead as the rest of it.

Someone was watching them. Not a ghost – a young man. A man whose presence was almost an absence, a gap in the surroundings. Over on the far side of the wasteland, too distant to make out a face or an expression. But he was definitely watching *them*.

'Look at that pervert,' said Heather.

'What do you reckon he wants?' Antonia said.

'A punch up the throat. Come on, let's bugger off,' said Heather with a shiver.

And then, fields. A whole Atlantic-Ocean-worth of fields, one after the other, all the same.

They walked instinctively. They'd ventured so far off the road that Rachel's directions were useless – but they didn't need them now anyhow. Each one of them could sense Almanby, a dark, heavy presence, a curled dragon, and it drew them ever onward.

They felt drunk. Or euphoric. Or stoned. Or a combination of the three. Or maybe they were all simply enjoying it at the same time at last, their buoyant moods finally synced up. They ran around, they giggled helplessly at nothing, they rode on each other's backs, they tumbled in the grass, they sang songs at the top of their lungs, they dashed out of the grasp of marauding ghosts even as they chortled like lunatics. Heather tried to grab the package from Rachel's hand while Rachel held it just out of reach and skipped and jumped and bounced, and Antonia bent double with laughter.

'I don't know why Sigourney Weaver didn't just use a really big jam jar and piece of card,' Antonia said out of nowhere, and they all fell about laughing again as if it was the funniest thing anyone had ever said.

Rachel stopped to get her breath back, worn out by all the running, while Heather and Antonia scampered on ahead.

She fell to her knees. Her legs shook too much to stand. She looked at her hands – they were ghastly pale and trembled too.

And all the while, Heather and Antonia chased and frolicked and tussled as they disappeared over the brow of the hill.

36

Heather spent hours of her life sitting on the deep windowsill of her bedroom and looking out over her garden and the fields beyond, watching the dead wander to and fro. Sometimes, to amuse herself, she'd give them names and imagine backstories. There was Carol who worked at the library and liked to peek at the dirty parts of romance novels when no one was around. Sometimes she'd even slip a hand down the front of her skirt. There was Ed, lollipop man by day, serial killer by night. There was Anne who owned a café which no one ever visited, so she passed her time dancing by herself to crackly old records on the jukebox. There was Susan, who collected toys with her husband, and who had more pieces than she could keep track of. There was Laura, who had an attic full of mysterious treasures she never looked at.

And there was Gabriel, Heather's boyfriend, just passing through to say goodbye. She hardly thought about Gabriel at all these days. She barely remembered that she'd dated him for those few weeks in March and April, five years ago. Steven had all but occluded Gabriel. *The Angel Gabriel*, she'd called him, and he rolled his eyes every time; 'I've never heard that one before.'

Heather and Gabriel had driven out to the seaside once. They had an inflatable lilo each, and they got swept out to sea. Just like in a storybook Heather had read when she was little. She couldn't remember anymore how they got rescued. Maybe they were still out there? Maybe this whole thing was a heat-and-thirst-induced mirage. That made more sense than it being real.

Heather, Rachel and Antonia pushed on through a copse of trees, so green it threatened to swallow them, to osmose them body and soul into the hot emerald air. They'd join the flies and the bacteria and they'd circulate in this place forever. Even the few arcs of sunlight which managed to penetrate the canopy became trapped and sticky like insects in a spider's web. The place reeked of sap and soil and heat. Heather cut her own eccentric path through the trees, jogging along fallen trunks and through gullies and over hummocks. Antonia followed wordlessly, a few feet behind, copying Heather's exact movements.

Rachel trailed further back. Her chest heaved from the effort of walking. Antonia noticed, and paused a moment to let her catch up.

'I've been here before,' she said.

'Mm?' Rachel seemed distracted.

'This place. I've been here before.'

'Yeah. We went on that school trip to the Iron Age fort at Cullby, and we managed to wander off and get lost, and we ended up here. Me, you and that other girl. Remember?'

'That was here?'

'Yeah. We ended up wandering around for hours. You both became convinced that we'd be here all night, and that we'd starve to death or freeze to death, and no one would ever find us. It was so funny. You both started hunting for food, picking the plants you thought were edible. You were going to eat mushrooms, but we didn't know which were poisonous and which were safe. And you found some old bits of corrugated iron and put them on top of some straw bales, and that was going to be our shelter so we wouldn't get hypothermia and die. You were being so serious about it all. I think you were trying to impress her.'

'I remember it being bigger.'

'We were smaller.'

'We were teenagers.'

'We were ten or eleven.'

'No, we were fifteen.'

'Or maybe it *was* bigger. Exactly the same size, but... bigger.'

'I liked her, she was fun.'

'Oh, I know you liked her. Half the class knew you liked her. What was her name? Laura? Lauren?'

'Laurel. Her name was Laurel Hardy.'

'Yes, of course. Hey, Heather, we went to school with this girl called Laurel Hardy. Antonia had the biggest crush on her, it was hilarious.'

'It was hilarious because she was called Laurel Hardy. My crush was not the hilarious part.'

'Right. We got lost for like three hours. Just the three of us. Three girls wandering around the woods on their own. It was Antonia's big chance, and she blew it, she completely bottled it.'

'She wasn't interested.'

'How do you know?'

'She was straight. She had a boyfriend.'

'I swear to God, she would've done anything. You can't write these things off.'

'Is there any point at which you stop talking?' Antonia sighed and wandered deeper into the green. 'Anyway, all that would've happened is she'd have said no, and then it'd have been all awkward and we'd be out in the woods all lost and crap and no one would've known what to say anymore.'

'And that's why you lose. You're more afraid of what might happen than what's already happening. You're more afraid of a moment of awkwardness than you are a lifetime of loneliness.'

'It's true,' said Heather. 'Gotta live life to the full.'

'You see? If you like someone, you have to tell them. You never know what might happen.'

'She had a boyfriend!' Antonia walked in uncomfortable circles, her hands deep in her pockets. 'She was sweet,' she said eventually. 'I wonder what happened to her.'

'She got killed,' Rachel shrugged.

'She got *killed*?'

'Yeah.'

'Fuck. I had no idea. Why did no one tell me?'

'Maybe they knew you'd be upset.'

'I am upset! Jesus. What happened?'

'A car accident, I think. Only a few years later. It was in the paper.'

'That's sad. She was fun, she was always laughing.'

Heather plucked a broad white mushroom from the base of a tree and waggled it in Rachel's face. 'So you didn't eat the poisoned mushrooms, then?'

'No, clearly not,' said Rachel.

'You could be tripping right now. This whole thing could've just been one big hallucination.'

'You would know about that, Heather.'

'I don't know anything about mushrooms.'

'No, but you probably only exist in someone else's hallucination. I've always thought that about you.'

'I can't believe she died,' Antonia said. 'She was so funny.'

'How is being funny going to prevent impact trauma?'

'For fuck's sake, Rachel. Can't you just let me have this moment? Why do you have to rationalise everything? Why does everything always have to be a smart comeback?'

'You said that you couldn't believe she died, she was so funny. I just don't get what's so unbelievable about a funny person dying.'

'It's a thing that humans say, Rachel. I know that people die. I know what happens when they get into car crashes. It's what people say when they're trying to process bad news. Heather – you know what I'm talking about, right? It's not just me.'

'Rachel's a dick,' said Heather. 'You should know that by now.'

Up ahead, a ghost meandered towards them – a girl in her late teens with hair down to her shoulders and mushroom-white flesh. Her black dress stood starkly against the wall of green. She carried a long, stout stick.

'Do you think they ever get lonely?' Heather said

'They're just things,' said Rachel. 'Things don't get lonely. Your shoes don't get lonely.'

'My shoes don't have faces. My shoes didn't used to be people.'

'They're still things.'

'Jesus, Rachel,' said Antonia. 'No one can say anything around you. Why do you have to argue every point?'

'Sarah had sex with one,' Heather said.

'No she didn't,' said Rachel.

'I swear, as Geoff is my witness…'

'You're such a liar!'

As the ghost neared, Heather and Rachel scattered, but Antonia remained where she stood, gazing at the young woman's mournful expression.

'It's her,' she said at last. 'It's Laurel.'

'How can it be?' Rachel said.

'Look at her face. It's her.'

'I can't remember what she looked like. Anyway, she died way out by Kelthorpe. What would she be doing back here?'

'She came to find me.'

A flicker of recognition seemed to cross the ghost's face. Its head tilted a little as it examined Antonia. It slowed to a halt till they were just a few feet apart.

'It is her,' Antonia breathed, then said, 'it's Laurel.'

The ghost's eyes were large and round, its brow a little furrowed.

'Laurel. It's me. It's Antonia. You remember me? I'm here, I came back.'

The ghost took a step forward, tilting its head the other way, its frown deepening.

'You do recognise me. I always liked you. Just so you know. I always liked you, Laurel. You were funny, you made me laugh. I'm glad we got lost together. It's one of my happiest memories. I'd do it all over if I could.' The ghost tilted its head again. 'You liked me too, didn't you? You liked getting lost, just the two of us together. It was fun, wasn't it? You should've told me. You should've told me how you felt. You weren't shy like I was. You should've said something.' Antonia let out a long, slow, sad sigh. 'Oh, Laurel. I wish I knew how to help you.'

The ghost raised its stick and struck Antonia as hard as it could across the temple.

37

'Let me see.'

'I don't want to look.'

'Then let me look.'

Heather prised Antonia's fingers away from the wad of tissue paper pressed to her forehead and peered underneath.

'Still bleeding?' said Antonia.

'Head injuries always bleed a lot. It's not as bad as it seems.'

'That was the funniest thing I've ever seen,' said Rachel, without much mirth, as she caught them up. Heather shot her a glare.

'Come on,' said Rachel. 'You've got to admit that was funny.'

'Can you tip your head back,' Heather said, as she dabbed at Antonia's injury.

Antonia pointed into the sky. 'Do you see that?' she said.

'Where?' said Heather.

'There. That flash.'

'I can't see anything.'

'That white dot. See it?'

'No.'

'It's a satellite.'

'I can't see it.'

They both peered into the mortar-blue bowl of the sky. Rachel rolled her eyes and carried on ahead.

'I can't see it,' Heather repeated. 'Whereabouts?'

'It's gone.'

'Jesus Christ, you two,' said Rachel. 'Just hurry up.'

Antonia climbed up from her cross-legged position. 'What's your problem, Rach? Why are you being like this? What happened to 'living for the moment'? You were getting at *me* earlier. I'm just doing what you said!'

Rachel said, quietly and carefully, 'You know, Antonia. Sometimes I wonder what it would've been like if it was you who'd died instead of Laurel.'

'What?'

'Would that have been better? Would she have made more of her life than you? Reading out puns to a dozen bored people in a village hall. I mean, what's the point of you? What are you *for*, Antonia?'

'Fuck's sake, Rachel,' said Heather.

'I don't know what you're saying, Rach.' Antonia rubbed the back of her head. She felt the edges of her eyeballs prickle.

Rachel leaned forward to peer at Antonia. Her eyes seemed clouded, like she was somewhere else. Antonia took a step back.

'What I'm saying is, why you? Why not Laurel? Imagine all the things she could've done. Would my life have been better with her as my friend instead of you?'

'All right, Rachel, that's enough,' said Heather.

'Would we have had better adventures? Would I have had a nicer time? Would she have wasted her life like you have?'

'That's not fair,' said Antonia, her voice cracking.

'Isn't it? What are you, what have you done? What's the purpose of you even being alive? What about Laurel? What about her opportunities? *That's* what's not fair.'

'Shut the fuck up, Rachel,' said Heather.

'That isn't how it works!' Antonia said. 'I had nothing to do with the car crash, I didn't even know about it. Why does it have to be one or the other? We could've both been alive.'

'But you're not, are you? You're not both alive. It's you.'

'You didn't even like her! *I* liked her!'

'I never had the chance. Maybe I'd have liked her more. Maybe if you'd died and Laurel was here now, I'd be thinking, "I'm glad that deadweight Antonia was killed, and not my wonderful pal Laurel."'

Antonia tried to formulate a reply but feared she might cry instead. She stood dumbstruck as Rachel carried on her way through the crackling grass.

38

With every step they became the landscape, and the landscape became them. More and more. Their violet shadows wriggled ahead of them, staining the earth like iodine. Antonia walked apart from the other two, sullen, lost in her own thoughts. Heather had acquired a daisy chain and wore it around her head.

'I had sex with Steven twenty-three times,' she said.

'That's nice,' said Rachel.

'Not in one go. Like, spread out over time. Four times in one go, though. Seven times outdoors and sixteen indoors. Once in the kitchen, twice in the bathroom. Actually, five times in the bathroom if you count the three times in the bath. But twice on the bathroom floor. Which I guess is pretty gross, but you don't think about that when you're horny. Um. Twice in the loft.'

'You're really doing this, aren't you.'

'Once in the living room on the sofa watching TV. It was a show about antiques, it was pretty boring. The sex wasn't boring though, and we got to learn about Regency vases. I had my back to the TV, so I didn't see any of them. But they sounded nice, from what the presenters were saying. Twice in the hallway. How many does that leave?'

'I wasn't keeping track.'

'Well, the rest in bed like normal, anyway. It's a boring thing to say, but I quite liked doing it in bed. Especially in Steven's bed. His wardrobe has a mirror on the front so we could see ourselves. I always thought it was cute how small I looked next to him. And I liked catching sight of the funny faces we'd pull. A couple of times his neighbour came round to complain because I was getting too excited. That was funny. Steven would talk to him at the front door and have to apologise, and I'd watch from the window and hope he'd look up and see me, the neighbour that is, so he could know what I looked like. Is this too much information? I don't know, that turned me on anyway. Oh, and Steven has this tattoo across his shoulder, *There's a goose asleep in the rain.* I can't remember why. He did tell me. He does this thing when he laughs. It's sort of like... Well, I can't really do it. But it's cute. I miss hearing him laugh. He always laughed a lot.'

'You don't think he seemed weird before he left?' said Rachel.

'What do you mean?'

'I don't know. It's probably nothing.'

'What? What sort of weird?'

'Well, just... It's hard to describe. Distracted. Scared.'

'Scared? No. He was fine. He was happy. He seemed happy. Yeah, he was happy.'

'That's not what he told me.'

'You spoke to him?'

'Yeah.'

'When?'

'The morning he left.'

'You didn't tell me that! What did he say?'

'He said he was scared. That he had business to attend to. That he didn't think he was coming back.'

'You didn't tell me this.'

'Didn't I? I'm sure I meant to.'

'What business? What did he mean?'

Rachel shrugged lazily. 'He just said business. I didn't ask. None of mine.'

'But... *I* didn't even see him the morning he left.' Heather had wrapped her arms around herself. Her knuckles were white.

'Huh. I did,' said Rachel, suddenly beaming with pure happiness. 'And the evening before.'

Heather stopped in her tracks. Rachel turned, walking backwards.

'You know, twenty-three times isn't even that much,' she said. 'Especially when it comes to Steven. And you're right about the mirror, that is fun.' Rachel turned back and marched on.

Antonia stopped beside Heather, who was motionless with horror.

'Your problem is,' Rachel called over her shoulder, 'you were always too busy playing hide-and-seek.'

39

The only shred of comfort Rachel could find was wrapped around the base of a sycamore tree; foetal, her jaw clenched with agony and nausea. Trying not to scream. Her mouth was full of bark chippings – she spat them out, but there always seemed to be more and she wondered vaguely through the pain and sickness whether they were even really there.

Her body burned with it. Every nerve, every square inch of her skin, every ounce of her flesh, her jigsaw of bones. Her stomach, her intestines, her lungs, her heart. Every atom of her body simultaneously threatened to turn to liquid and petrify into rock.

But she knew it would pass. She just needed a few minutes. Just a few minutes. And she hoped she was deep enough into the woods that the others wouldn't hear her screams.

Heather wanted to leave. Just go. Whatever Rachel was doing in the woods, fuck her. Heather would've been quite happy to walk away and abandon Rachel and her fucking stupid schemes for good. Never see her smug, self-satisfied face ever again.

Images of Rachel and Steven screwing each other senseless revolved through her mind like a zoetrope gone septic. All while Heather gambolled around the countryside picking flowers and identifying butterflies and inventing melodies, like a total idiot. Steven making excuses, distracting her, sending her on errands, insisting she hide, then sneaking Rachel in through the back door and fucking her. Not the happy sex he had with Heather, the cute, fun, playful sex – their sex was nasty, dark, violent. His hand clawed around Rachel's throat while her face purpled and her eyes bulged. Her head twisted backwards as he tore at her hair. Claw-marks down his back.

No. No, it couldn't be. That wasn't Steven, he wouldn't do that to her, that wasn't who he was.

Rachel was lying. She had to be lying.

Heather glanced across at Antonia, who sat with her arms wrapped around her lanky legs, staring straight ahead, as unreadable as ever. She always seemed distracted, like she'd rather be somewhere else. Except when Heather and Antonia were in the river, a couple of hours ago. That was the only time Antonia had ever seemed really present.

Heather had always been vaguely aware that Rachel's tall, mixed-race friend was a stand-up comedian, or some kind of performer, though she didn't catch her act till last night – a baffling stream of puns, wordplay and opaque references delivered by someone who looked like they wanted to cry, or at least go home and have a stiff cup of tea. The show wasn't *funny*, as such, but it'd been interesting, like a performance art version of stand-up. Someone imitating the rhythms of stand-up comedy. It was really clever, now she thought about it. Heather was glad she'd seen it.

Even having spent the best part of a day with her, though, Heather still had no idea who Antonia was. She was sad, but she wasn't morose – she seemed to have capacity for happiness, if only she could scratch some mysterious itch. She was probably either the kindest and most sensitive person Heather knew, or a serial killer – Heather couldn't decide which. Right now, the one thing she *was* sure of was that she liked Antonia a whole lot better than she liked Rachel. Rachel, as far as Heather was concerned, could go all the way to hell and stay there.

As if on cue, Rachel emerged from the tree line, a wobbly grin plastered across her face. She looked sweaty, and somehow simultaneously pallid and flushed.

'What's eating you two mopey-chopses?' she said.

Heather gazed off towards the horizon.

'You all right?' said Antonia. 'You were gone ages.'

'Of course I am,' Rachel said, unconvincingly. 'What are you sitting around for? Come on!'

40

Blossom and straw bales; lambs and rosehips; snowdrops and blackberries – perpetual summer had sent the natural world haywire. Every process happening simultaneously: blooming and fruiting and seeding and decaying all at once, standing on one another's shoulders. There were as many butterflies as there were caterpillars, and as many tadpoles as there were frogs. And as the human world waned, so the natural world flourished, bursting and overflowing like an overstuffed bag of presents on Christmas morning.

Heather, Antonia and Rachel wound their way down through the Vale of Branhurst, along tracks baked as hard and pale as china clay. Out past Banbridge Lock, Benington Heath, Bembrook, Branbrook, Bardbury, Blynerton and Basterton.

A dusty bridleway took them over a series of small humpbacked bridges and along a narrow footpath between paddocks of neatly shorn grass and restless horses. A farmhouse and its attendant broad-shouldered barn, black and corrugated, reared up to their left; but there were no people, just ghosts, spilling out from every door and archway like an infestation of ants.

The trio walked mostly in silence, Rachel trailing behind, her chest heaving from the effort. Occasionally, Heather or Antonia would point something out to the other – 'Look, a family of foxes,' or, 'That ghost's riding a bicycle!' – but most of the time they only spoke to confer over directions or avoid the wandering dead.

Still the presence of Almanby summoned them forward, dark as a blood clot, swelling behind the horizon as they inched nearer. The air felt heavier now, thicker, and their ears sang with tinnitus.

They crested the edge of an escarpment and set off down through cornfields towards the plain below. From their lofty position, they could spy the little clusters of Blennly, Ballerton, Benthorpe, Boxton and Billingholme, dotted like bacterial colonies across the landscape.

Partway down the escarpment, Heather and Antonia heard a snapping of stalks and turned to see that Rachel had collapsed. Antonia raced back to where she lay sprawled amid the stubble.

'I knew it!' she said.

'I'm fine. I'm just tired.'

'You look awful.'

Antonia helped Rachel into the shade of one of the large cotton-reel bales which lay strewn across the hillside.

'Just ten minutes,' Rachel murmured. 'That's all.'

But she seemed almost to sink into the ground with relief, as if she was ready now to be absorbed. She closed her eyes; her whole body appeared to expand and contract with the effort of breathing. Her face was so pale she looked like a ghost.

Unsure what else to do, Antonia and Heather sat next to her. They listened to the ticker tape burble of the blackbirds and a lone woodpigeon's repeated six-note Morse code call, an abandoned double-agent hoping desperately for rescue.

Heather flexed her fingers. 'It's gone numb,' she said.

'Have a look,' said Antonia.

'I don't want to.'

'You should look.'

Heather gingerly rolled up her sleeve. Where her arm had been purple, it was blackening, and the red was now a deep, sickly maroon. Since they'd last looked, the skin had become laced with microscopic cracks, peeling in places like wax shavings. Heather winced.

'We have to get you to a doctor,' Antonia said.

Rachel chortled. 'Where?'

'I don't know. But look at it! Both of you. You're both sick.'

Rachel laughed deliriously. Her eyes were still closed, but the raised indentations of her irises could be seen, thrashing back and forth.

'There's no doctors out here,' she said. 'There's nothing out here.'

'What's so funny?'

'You don't get it yet. It's Almanby. It's Almanby. This is all Almanby. Heather's arm, your car. Me. All of this. It's all Almanby. It's poison. We're past Banbridge Lock now. We're too close.'

'Then let's go. Let's get out of here.'

'Everyone ends up in Almanby eventually. Haven't you worked that out yet?'

'I don't know what you're talking about.'

'Hey, Toni, why don't you tell Heather a secret?'

'Leave me alone.'

'No, come on.' Rachel chuckled wickedly. 'What's the point of having a secret if you don't tell?'

'I'm not going to talk about it.'

'You do have emotions, right? You have feelings? You have hormones?'

'What are you doing?'

'Tell Heather. She wants to know.'

'No, I don't,' said Heather, who'd been sitting and quietly clenching and unclenching her hand.

'Sure you do. You love gossip.'

'Not if it's private. She doesn't want to say, and that's good enough for me.'

'Come on. You're curious, I know you are. Toni likes to keep secrets. There's something she's never told you.'

'Shut the fuck up, Rachel!' Antonia suddenly exploded, leaping upright and striding out into the field.

Rachel's rattling laugh echoed behind her. 'You people. You fucking people. I don't believe you. I don't believe all the things you keep bottled up. All the things you never say. Hey, Heth. Guess what. Guess what the big secret is. Toni has the hots for you. Pretty juicy stuff, yeah? She's in love with you. She talks about you all the time. You didn't know that, did you?'

Antonia slumped over a nearby bale. Heather continued to stare straight ahead.

'It's the only reason she came on this trip. To get close to you. In the hope that something might happen.'

'Please stop,' said Antonia.

'I'm right, though, aren't I?' Rachel sat up, opened her eyes, and squinted across towards Antonia. Antonia threw her hands up and walked to a further bale.

'Look at you,' said Rachel. 'Look at the pair of you. You never grew up, either of you.

You, stand-up comic, too arrested to form real adult connections. You, lost little girl, straining so hard to be spontaneous like the big exciting man who's already forgotten you. It's sad. It's really sad.'

'And what about you?' said Heather. 'Manipulative arsehole. Using everyone around you. You don't have friends, you have contacts.'

'At least I know what I am.'

Heather glared at her.

'What?' said Rachel.

'Are you going to blame Almanby for this, too?'

'I'm sick.'

'Of course you are.'

'I'm dying and you don't believe me!'

'Right,' said Heather, and then she too climbed to her feet and walked quickly away.

'You make it very hard for me to respect you!' Rachel called after her.

With pinpoint precision, Heather tweaked the tuning dial of her ORBITRAN radio, its silver-painted plastic flashing in the remorseless glare of the afternoon sun.

'Come on, Steven, where are you?' she whispered. 'Don't do this to me.'

But all she could find now was the ubiquitous whirl of Almanby white noise.

By the time she returned, Rachel was asleep. Antonia sat behind a different bale, head in hands.

'How long's she been asleep?' Heather asked, bending over Rachel. Antonia glanced up at her but didn't reply.

Heather scooped up the package from where it lay beside Rachel, then walked over to Antonia and sat down next to her.

'We should open it,' Heather said.

Antonia looked dubiously at Rachel.

'You want to know what's inside, don't you?' Heather turned the package over a couple of times in her hands, then picked a corner of the wrapping paper free and proceeded to tear it away. Underneath the wrapping paper she found an unmarked cardboard box, its lid held shut with a strip of sellotape.

'Intriguing,' she said. She split the tape with her thumbnail, then lifted the lid.

Inside a cocoon of bubble-wrap was a porcelain statuette. A long-legged, pink-cheeked shepherd boy with a crook in one hand and a lamb tucked under his arm. The sort of detritus that would wash up in charity shops across the land and see out the rest of its days there.

'Huh,' said Heather. She rotated it in her hands and examined it from every angle. 'This is what it's all about? This is what we've come all this way for? This is the big secret?'

'Sentimental value?' suggested Antonia.

'You mean, maybe it belonged to Oscar's grandmother or something?'

'Yeah. It's the only thing she left him in her will.'

'Could be something inside it.'

'Like drugs?'

'She said it wasn't drugs.'

'You believe her?'

'Or maybe money,' said Antonia. 'I don't know.'

Heather shook the statuette.

'It feels empty,' she said.

'So it is the statue.'

'Unless whatever it is, is taped to the inside. Something light. Maybe a key to a lock-up full of drugs.'

'Maybe it's a secret message? A code.'

'You reckon Oscar's a spy?' said Heather.

'Could be. Rachel too. That'd make sense.'

'Yeah, Rachel would totally be a spy. Probably an enemy agent.'

'Definitely,' said Antonia. 'She wouldn't be working for us.'

'She's probably KGB. I don't even know if there is a KGB anymore, but I still think Rachel works for them. Just out of spite.'

'Yeah. How would they get a message inside there?'

'They have ways,' said Heather. 'The KGB are very cunning.'

Antonia held out her hand for the statuette.

'I'll break it open,' she said.

Heather shook her head with sudden disinterest. She wrapped the statuette up, placed it back in its box, then walked over to Rachel and lay it on the ground beside her.

'We should go,' she said.

'Leave her?'

'Yeah.'

Antonia glanced towards Rachel.

'Come on,' said Heather. 'We don't owe her anything.'

'We can't just leave her here.'

'Why not?'

'She might die.'

'She might, mightn't she.' Heather stood and set off towards Almanby once more.

Antonia jogged over to Rachel and shook her by the shoulders.

'Rachel. Wake up.'

But Rachel couldn't be roused.

At the bottom of the field, the trail turned left into tangled countryside – hawthorn bushes, sloe bushes, hornbeam bushes and endless ranks of sticky goosegrass. Heather was already deep into the bewildering melange of greenery when Antonia caught up with her.

'Please. Just think about this.'

'I have thought about it,' said Heather. 'That's why I'm doing it.'

'Rachel's our friend.'

'Is she?'

'What if those things get her?'

'So go back.'

Heather continued blithely on her way till the chlorophyll vortex swallowed her up, greened her out of existence. Antonia hesitated a moment, then headed back up the hill the way she came.

* * *

But when she arrived at the bales, Rachel was gone.

And so was Heather, when Antonia returned to catch her up a few minutes later. Much of this countryside looked the same. In her panic, Antonia must've taken a wrong turning. She imagined herself lost out here forever, vainly searching for her missing friends till heatstroke took her, or dehydration, or an ambush by ghosts.

In the end, she discovered Heather further along the trail than she thought.

'Was she dead?' said Heather, without glancing back.

Antonia shook her head, though Heather didn't see. She didn't seem to care either way. They walked in silence for some time.

'Listen, about what she said...' Antonia ventured at last.

'It's fine, it's not important.'

'No, listen...'

'It doesn't bother me. Seriously. Whatever, it's cool.'

'I don't have the hots for you,' Antonia blurted. 'I—'

'Great. Then everything's all right.'

41

'What's your middle name?' said Heather.

Antonia thought for a moment, then said, 'Randolph.'

'Randolph?'

'Well, I don't have a middle name, but if I did, I'd like it to be Randolph. It has a certain sophistication. What's yours?'

'Sarah. Can you believe it?'

'What's wrong with Sarah?'

'Who calls their child Sarah?'

'Lots of people. It's a perfectly nice name.'

'It's a stupid name. Heather Sarah McLagan, it's ridiculous. I want to be a Randolph too.'

'Let's both be Randolph.' Antonia ducked around a patch of aggressively barbed briars encroaching onto their path and held them back for Heather to pass.

'If you could be any animal at all,' she said, 'what would it be?'

'A cat,' said Heather. 'Or a horse.'

'You have to pick one.'

'All right. A cat. Or a horse.'

'Why?'

'I don't know. I don't really want to be an animal, I'm happy as a human.'

'Fair enough. I want to be an axolotl.'

'I don't know what that is.'

'It's a type of amphibian. Its gills are on the outside.'

'All right. Why an axolotl?'

Antonia shrugged. 'I like the spelling.'

'Who was your celebrity crush growing up?'

'Hm.' Antonia thought for a moment. 'The bass player from The Bangles and the little guitarist from Fuzzbox.'

'I don't know what they look like.'

'Dark hair. Everyone else fancied the lead singer, but that seemed too obvious. How about you?'

'Chewbacca.'

'Chewbacca? Seriously?'

'Yeah.'

'But he's not even human!'

'I bet he gives great cuddles, though.'

Red kites and buzzards swirled overhead, drifting lazily on the thermal currents. Antonia watched them as she walked, her hand cupped over her eyes, and imagined them picking her up and carrying her to their nest to be fed to their young. Or maybe she was too big, but they could take Heather. She'd be a tasty morsel for a litter of raptor chicks.

'What's your earliest memory?' said Antonia.

'I remember this lime-green balloon tied to the handle of my pushchair,' Heather said. 'I don't think I even really knew what it was, it was just suddenly there, but I loved it. Sometimes it glowed from the sun shining through it. And I liked the way it bobbed along with me, just over my head, like a guardian angel. I thought it was magic. Like, the most magical thing in the world. I don't know what happened to it. I don't remember it bursting or getting smaller. I suppose I must've forgotten about it as soon as I got out of my pushchair. But I still think about it all the time. In my mind, it'll always be perfect... this perfect green balloon.'

Realising how hungry they were, Heather and Antonia stopped to pick blackberries, shovelling the little dark bundles into their faces by the handful, the juice staining their lips and fingers purple.

'All down the bramble-hatch!' Heather chortled.

A little further along, they found an apple tree and a greengage tree.

'What we need now,' said Antonia, 'is a packet-of-crisps tree.'

'Or a cheese-sandwich tree.'

'Yeah.'

'Or an ice-cream tree.'

'Well, that goes without saying.'

'Except maybe not – the ice cream would all be melted in this heat, wouldn't it?'

'No, the ice cream only starts to melt once you pick it,' said Antonia.

'Right, of course. You certainly know your botany.'

'We had this teacher,' said Heather, striding now through the long grass. 'Mrs Green. She told us she was a thousand years old.'

'Weird. Like, as a joke?'

'I don't know. She seemed like she really meant it. But you can't tell at that age – when grown-ups deadpan, you tend to take them seriously. She told us she was a thousand years old and lived in a hole in the ground and ate people to stay alive.'

'She sounds like a character.'

'Not really. We were a bit scared of her.'

'What subject did she teach?'

'This was at primary school. She was just our teacher, so she would've done all the subjects. I mean, Mr Collins was our *teacher* teacher, like our actual official teacher, but Mrs Green...' Heather scratched her curls. 'Actually, I can't remember. She was there in the classroom, anyway. Maybe she was the teaching assistant or something. She was there all the time, I suppose she must've been his helper, or... like a trainee teacher, though she seemed too old for that.'

'Maybe his mistress?'

'I like the way you think.'

'Thanks.'

'I'd completely forgotten about her till just now. Mrs Green. Huh. How could I forget something like that? I didn't like her, she was horrible.' Heather shuddered and pawed at the air as if batting away the memory; or maybe she was just batting away itinerant crane flies.

'We had a teacher called Mrs Green, too,' Antonia said, 'but she was nice. She was a really old lady, and she always said how smart we looked in our uniforms. She didn't yell at us like the other teachers did, I always liked her lessons the best.'

'Nice. You're lucky.'

'Her daughter was in our class, this girl called Rachel. Not our Rachel, a different one.'

'We have a Rachel?'

'We used to.'

Emerald green the boat that sails
The mouse will surely borrow
On shattered glass 'neath stars he cries
To guide this day to sorrow

42

Antonia didn't know what she was expecting.

All those years of dire whispered warnings, of school assemblies and safety pamphlets and photocopied flyers pushed through the letterbox:

STAY AWAY FROM ALMANBY.
Almanby is dangerous.
Go anywhere, but don't go to Almanby.

But no one ever specified why. No one thought to impress upon the children exactly what terrible fate would befall them if they did happen to venture across its threshold. It was likely no one actually had any idea. It was simply a fact: Almanby was dangerous. Everyone knew it, even if they couldn't remember how they knew. But there was certainly no need to question it or look into it any further. All anyone was really sure of was that if you went to Almanby, you'd never come back.

Curious children probably *would've* gone – they'd have dared each other, packed sandwiches and chocolate bars and cans of cola, and made a day of it. Except no one knew exactly where it was or how to get there. It wasn't within cycling distance, none of the bus routes went near, and there was certainly no one with a car who'd be willing to drive them, not even a tearaway older brother full of bravado and cheap lager. And so Almanby remained unexplored, at least by anyone Antonia knew.

Philip Swain, who was in their class at school, said his uncle lived in Almanby. He told them sometimes he would visit his uncle on weekends, and had to dodge 'whirlpools and quicksand', and was once chased all the way home from the sweet shop by a 'deranged wolf'. But this was the same boy who liked to boast of his father's derring-do as a flight lieutenant in the Royal Air Force, even though everyone knew full well Frank Swain was a milkman.

One rainy, overcast afternoon, while idly browsing her dad's A–Z roadmap, eleven-year-old Antonia Coleridge happened across Almanby. Right there, as plain as day, bang in the centre of page 44. She read the word a couple of times just to make sure.

ALMANBY.

She spent the rest of the afternoon cross-legged on the floorboards of the spare room, shivers running up and down her back, staring at the name, that innocent-looking black type – **ALMANBY** – and at the pale orange Rubik's cube of buildings, and at the twisty capillary B-roads radiating away on all four sides. She couldn't work out exactly how far away it was, just that it was two turns of the page distant from Headingham. Hardly close at all.

Antonia tried to imagine the terrible things that might go on there, but couldn't come up with anything which lived up to the place's reputation. And then she tried to picture what Almanby looked like. No one had ever said. She imagined a putrid medieval hellhole full of witches and gallows and plague. Then she imagined a petrified war zone of rotting concrete and broken windows, all piss and graffiti, with ragged people huddling in doorways and inside the carcasses of burnt-out tower blocks, like she sometimes saw in other countries on the news on TV. Then she imagined a dripping, sprawling black industrial wasteland which stretched as far as the eye could see, gobbling up unwary souls and spewing chemicals into the atmosphere.

It didn't look big enough for that, of course. On the map, it was barely larger than Headingham. Nonetheless, the mere idea of the place gave her the greyest and gloomiest nightmares she'd ever had. They woke her up at three a.m. and left her too rattled to even leave her bedroom for a wee.

The next time she searched in the A–Z, a few weeks later, she couldn't find Almanby at all. It was still listed in the index, right at the very top, but when she turned to page 44 and ran her finger along to square 5E, there was no sign of it.

As they grew older, the children thought less and less about Almanby, just as they thought less about exploring grain silos and train tracks and slurry pits, or drinking mysterious fluids from the garden shed. They were growing up – they were more interested in hormones and pop music and the latest movies. *Stay away from Almanby* was simply something they knew and didn't question, just like the adults knew it and didn't question it. They had no cause to seek the place out and discover whether the warnings held any truth.

Still, there were occasions, on long, lonely afternoons, when Antonia would let her mind wander back to Almanby. She wondered what it looked like and what really went on there, though she was never tempted to explore, even when she finally had a car of her own.

But once, just after her serial killer phase, she grew obsessed by the place. Only for a week or two, another of her hyperfixations. She realised she'd never seen a photo of it. She'd never even read anything of substance. Apart from that brief glimpse in the A–Z, Almanby was entirely word of mouth.

So she attempted to find pictures of it. She went to the library and looked in all the books she could lay her hands on. But there was nothing – no dire warnings, no scientific papers or historical documents enumerating its dangers. No geological surveys, no tourist brochures, no local newspaper articles, not even any photographs. Just maps – with Almanby always sitting at the dead centre of each. And if it wasn't for that, she could've quite believed the place didn't exist at all.

Antonia didn't hear anything more about Almanby for several years, or even really think much about it, until word came down that Heather's boyfriend, the famous Steven Cook, had gone there and not come back. She'd experienced a rush of joy, delight at his possible demise, followed by an equal and opposite rush of guilt… and then, oddly, a strange nostalgic thrill.

Almanby.

There was that name again. Like finding her childhood hamster in her parents' attic behind a stack of boxes, still running on its wheel.

Oh yes! Almanby!

It'd re-entered her life in the most oblique way. So much so that it felt like one of Heather's pranks at first, as if she'd told them that Steven was going off for a job with Santa at the North Pole, or that he'd been voted the new Man in the Moon.

But no, he really had gone to Almanby.

And that brought it all flooding back. The dank, festering pustule from the darkest recesses of her imagination. A place where it was always night, even in the middle of the day. The lurking bogeyman, forever hovering on the edge of her nightmares.

And then, a few months later, she'd found out that Heather was going, and Rachel as well.

The adults' warnings hadn't been enough.

Antonia, too, was finally going to Almanby.

As it turned out, from first appearances, Almanby was a village like any other.

Actually, that wasn't quite true – Almanby was *perfect*. It was those few degrees prettier and quainter than anywhere else Antonia had ever seen: a modest church with a neat symmetrical tower; clusters of salmon-pink roofs poking above the dark tree line like nests of hungry fledglings waiting to be fed. Crisscrossing bees; the random trajectories of butterflies; a sudden fox, gash-red against the green. Idyllic, by any definition of the word, but nothing to hint at its fearsome reputation.

Except for the way it felt. Antonia had sensed its presence this whole journey, but now Almanby was in sight, she found the sensation almost overwhelming. A hardness inside her body, like a magnet drawing her on and repelling her at the same time. A living thing – a looming tyrannosaur, a dragon curled around the hillside, a monstrous kraken from the deepest corners of the ocean, sitting on its hummock, brooding, breathing, watching, thinking, waiting.

The air pressure had been growing steadily during their approach to Almanby, too. She felt it around her eyes and in her eardrums. She pinched her nose in an attempt to make her ears pop. It didn't help. There was just the continued sense of being swallowed. A sense of going deeper, like a submariner travelling to the bottom of the ocean; a sense of walking down a long, dark tunnel, even as they strode through open fields during the brightest part of the day.

Heather and Antonia walked hand in hand now. Not romantically – at least, Antonia didn't think so – just two friends holding onto each other, facing the unknown. Ahead of them, the meadow of sun-cooked beige grass they'd been crossing suddenly became lush and green. The divide between Almanby and not-Almanby was millimetre-perfect. On the other side of the border, yellow flowers poked up through the emerald fronds. Dandelion seeds wafted like snow or the dislodged spirits of woodland sprites.

The two women came to a halt at the boundary. The stink of jasmine was almost overwhelming. Everything felt heavy. Antonia's tinnitus rose to the volume and intensity of a choir. She squeezed Heather's hand.

'Still want to do this?' said Heather.

'I never wanted to do this.'

'Oh yeah.'

'It's not too late to turn back.'

'Yeah it is,' said Heather.

She released Antonia's hand, sucked in a lungful of air…

…and stepped over the line into Almanby.

With a watchmaker's precision, she took five steps,

then six,

then seven,

the whole time staring intently at her feet.

'How is it?' said Antonia.

Heather stopped. Without turning, she threw her arms wide with fingers splayed, in a gesture Antonia couldn't read.

'Are you okay?' Antonia asked.

'Yeah,' said Heather. 'It's normal. It feels normal.' She turned and grinned. 'Come on in, the water's lovely and warm.'

'Are you sure?'

'Yeah, I'm sure. It's fine. It's all good. It feels…'

'What?'

'It feels okay.'

Antonia, too, inhaled.

'All right, if you say so.'

And then she took a step into Almanby.

Under her feet, solid ground. Ground as tangible as anywhere else. She could feel the pebbles and bumps and undulations, the little clods of soil. She crouched, ran her hand through the grass, touched its realness: the fine hairs of its topside, its shiny underside, the clover and dandelion stalks, the ragamuffin groundsel and the buttercups. Almanby grass, Almanby clover, Almanby dandelions and groundsel and buttercups. Tiny yellow flowers steeped in whatever dark enchantment ran through this place – grown from it, nourished by it. But every leaf of this meadow, every petal and grain of pollen and passing insect, looked as innocent as those anywhere else.

The atmosphere, though, was oppressive – like a storm was brewing overhead, even as the sky was bright and clear as glass. The air molecules themselves seemed to crackle with electricity. Antonia stood and, following Heather's footsteps as best she could, walked out to her, taking one step at a time, pausing to recalibrate after each of them, just in case – though just in case of what, she couldn't be entirely sure.

She came to a halt next to Heather amid a continent of clover. Each one had four leaves, she noticed.

'Almanby,' said Antonia.

'Yeah,' Heather said. 'Just like they always told us not to.'

Together, Antonia and Heather set off the rest of the way across the meadow, the fat grass stalks tickling their shins, the apparently permanent layer of dew soaking the hems of their trousers, despite the overpowering afternoon heat. Heather was breathing hard, and Antonia realised that she was too.

'You all right?' she heard herself say, and beside her Heather nodded.

* * *

'My legs feel heavy,' Heather said a little later. Antonia's legs felt heavy too. She reached out and took Heather's hand once more.

'I've been here before,' said Heather, later still, further into the meadow.

'You have?'

'Yeah. Oh man. It feels so familiar. I came here with my family.'

'When?'

'Years ago. We came on holiday. My mum and dad, and my grandparents, and my Uncle Tony. I…' She paused to think. 'I remember being on the beach. Searching in rock pools. I found a gold coin. It looked so old. A Spanish doubloon or something. That's what Uncle Tony said. I carried it around with me for the rest of the day, gripped in my hand, but by the time I got to bed it'd gone and I don't know how. I was so sad I'd lost it. I lost my special coin.'

'There's no beach here,' Antonia said. 'We're inland.'

She turned to look at Heather, to find her hand empty and Heather now two hundred yards away, on the far side of a rank of elder bushes.

Heather waved. 'How did you get over there?' she called.

They rushed to meet in the middle, and threw their arms around each other's necks. In that moment, hugging seemed like the right thing to do.

Ahead of them, Almanby reared up like a swollen insect bite on the landscape. They climbed a wooden stile at the bottom of the meadow and over onto a narrow lane with banks of wild grass on either side.

Somehow, they'd expected there to be no ghosts in Almanby, but they were everywhere: some on the verge, some loitering in the middle of the road, others in gardens and paddocks. Instantly, the ghosts began to amble in the direction of the two friends. Heather and Antonia walked away at speed till they came to a narrow footpath leading out and around in the direction of the church, damp and overhung with brooding horse chestnut trees. They ducked through the rusty iron kissing gate and scampered down the lane, kicking ripe green mace-heads and mahogany-dark conker eyeballs. Tiny wrens fluttered about their ears.

Antonia stopped and said to Heather, 'I found my uncle on the sofa. Uncle Warren. I can still see the bright red tracksuit top he was wearing. I thought he was sleeping, but...' She made a sad, vague gesture with her hands. 'I had to sit with him while we waited for the ambulance to come. Twenty minutes, maybe, but it felt longer. I kept waiting for him to sit up and laugh at his own prank, laugh at how stupid we all were for falling for it. But of course, he didn't. They put him in a black bag and took him away.'

'I convinced myself my dad had died,' said Heather. 'He was hours late from work, and Mum was walking round and round in circles, fretting and worrying. And I felt impossibly sick and helpless. And then the evening news came on TV, and I was sure I'd see a car crash as the lead story, with his picture behind the newsreader's head. Because that's how TV news works, right? And I got more and more worried as they ran through the headlines, expecting him to be one of the stories – *and next on the nine o'clock news, thirty-eight-year-old Terry McLagan has died in a car accident.* But of course, he was fine, he'd had a puncture and couldn't call home.'

Antonia glanced around. 'It's this place,' she said. 'It's dredging stuff up from the back of my brain.'

'I keep thinking about…' Heather folded her arms tightly. 'The day my grandfather died, I laughed. Because I was a teenager, I was too cool for all that stuff. I laughed at how hard my parents were crying, how silly it all was. I didn't want to get sucked into it, it was all so earnest and solemn. I don't know why I kicked back so hard. I was embarrassed, probably. I loved my grandad, he always gave me coins and toffees and interesting pebbles from the beach. And he taught me how to whistle with grass.'

'Come on,' said Antonia, continuing down the footpath.

'I just want to tell him I'm sorry.'

'It's Almanby. Come on.'

The footpath opened out onto a curving lane. Thatched cottages crowded in, with sentinel foxgloves and hollyhocks looming over quaint little painted gates. Sweet peas strung out along bamboo rigging, and big, broad rhubarb leaves turned to the sun. 'Merrydown Cottage' said the sign on one of the gates; 'Blacksmith's View' declared another. A ghost picked its way through an overgrown vegetable patch, nettles stinging its ankles in vain.

Heather glanced in both directions along the lane. 'What do you think?' she said.

'I guess we need to find Penfold Lane,' said Antonia.

'Yeah, but like, any ideas?'

Antonia glanced over to see that Heather was chewing her lip, arms wrapped around her torso. Antonia almost laughed. The pair of them were as nervous as each other. It'd only be a few minutes till they'd stumble upon the street sign proudly proclaiming 'PENFOLD LANE', and a few seconds after that that they'd locate house number 7. A knock on the door. Smiles, kisses, a grand reunion… and Antonia would be forgotten. She'd have to wait in the living room, hands clasped between knees, while Heather and Steven scampered upstairs to work through six months' worth of pent-up passions. Would Heather ever look in her direction again? They'd never hold hands again, Antonia was sure of that.

Heather and Antonia wound their way around the corkscrew streets of Almanby. Apart from the ghosts, the place seemed to be utterly deserted, like a museum reconstruction of a village. There were signs of life, but no one living: bunting, flags, streamers, a tea party laid out on a lawn – as if the populace had been pinched out of existence.

'Penfold Lane…' muttered Heather to herself, squinting at street signs as if the words would magically reveal themselves beneath Hawthorn Road or Jasper Avenue.

'If we see someone, we can ask,' said Antonia. 'It can't be too hard to find in a place this size.'

They forged on through the pretty labyrinth. Hanging baskets overflowed with every colour, like Greek fire. Chiffchaffs chattered, magpies rattled, and a song thrush, somewhere in a nearby hedgerow, made grand pronouncements.

'About what Rachel said,' said Antonia.

'Who?'

'Rachel.'

'Oh, Rachel. What did Rachel say?'

'You know. Back when we left her.'

'You might have to remind me.'

Antonia shifted uncomfortably. 'About me.'

Heather stopped and scratched her curls. 'Have we been here already?'

'I don't think so.'

'This bit feels familiar.' Heather walked away from Antonia with her arms held high in the air, as if feeling for clues.

'Déjà vu?'

'Did I what?'

'Déjà vu.'

'Oh. Maybe. My brain feels really weird. Like someone's turned it inside out. What were you saying just now?'

'What Rachel said. Back at the field.'

'She was being a shit.'

'Yeah. She was, wasn't she. Uh, anyway, the thing she was saying about me. Having feelings. You know. For...' She trailed off and gestured vaguely, hoping Heather would get the gist.

Heather looked at her blankly.

'Well.' Antonia blushed. 'Her exact words were... she said I had the hots for you.'

'Right. Which you don't.'

'No. Not the hots.'

'That's fine.'

'Not *exactly* that.'

'But something like that?'

Antonia shrugged lopsidedly. 'Something a bit similar, yeah.'

'I don't mind at all,' said Heather. 'It's all good. We've all got hormones.'

'Yeah. Hormones and feelings and all that.'

'Right. It's nothing to be embarrassed about. I'm always having a quick rub.'

'Uh. Right.' Antonia glanced around for something else to change the subject to before her brain called it a day and hit the eject button.

Three squirrels chased each other along the branch of an apple tree.

'So. Well, what I was thinking is, it's pretty quiet,' said Antonia. 'And so I wondered if you'd like to do something.'

'We are doing something, aren't we? Walking walking walking, speaking words.'

'I mean, like, find a private spot.' Antonia couldn't quite believe she was saying this. She felt warm and short of breath. Her neck was suddenly very uncomfortable and rather damp. 'Just hang out, you know? Or... you know. There are one or two things I'm quite good at.' She attempted a winning smile, but it came out all wobbly and upside down.

Heather beamed. 'A woman with a repertoire! That's what I like to hear.'

'Well. I've had a bit of practice. With other people and... um, on my own.'

'That's very nice of you,' Heather said. 'I'm very flattered. Genuinely.' And then with a happy wink, 'Come on, we'd better find Steven.'

While Antonia busied herself turning a weird shade of purple, Heather sauntered on ahead – then rotated, walking backwards, her hands stuffed in her pockets. 'Unless you want to dare me?' she said.

'I don't know if that'd be ethical,' said Antonia.

Heather chortled. 'Maybe not,' she said. 'Come on.'

Heather was saying something, but Antonia felt giddy. Her head was all thick and fizzy, and her ears were so hot they seemed totally unwilling to process sounds. She was at once insanely proud of herself and crushingly disappointed. Notions of kinky Almanby sex flashed periodically through her mind – having a fumble under a tree in that *forbidden place*, the exact village everyone said not to go to. That would've been quite something. That would've been *naughty*.

Luckily, Heather was the world's jauntiest person, and didn't allow a single iota of lingering awkwardness. She chatted away to Antonia, till all that stuff Antonia had said just a few minutes ago didn't seem to matter at all. It was all just conversation.

They didn't hold hands now, but that didn't matter. Still they wandered deeper into Almanby – and the deeper they wandered, the quainter and more bucolic it became. It was bigger than it'd seemed from the outside, and all too easy to become lost in its twisty-turny picture-book streets, like the pathways of a brain. Blossom drifted down onto the alleyways, big as fifty-pence coins, flaring in the sunlight. Pink and white and yellow. It mingled on the cobbles with confetti... a wedding? Or just ongoing celebrations? And clouds of orange-tip butterflies, moving from buddleia to rhododendron and back. And now a fox, red as flame, skittering down the middle of the street, checking the gutters for morsels of food. It passed within a few feet of Heather and Antonia, but didn't seem to notice them at all, except a cursory sniff of the air with its shiny black nose.

'I had a cat once,' Heather said. 'It was called Christopher. I buried it in my garden.'

'When it was dead?'

Heather laughed. 'Yeah.'

And still Penfold Lane stayed hidden.

'I always thought it was weird,' said Heather later, 'that our local butcher shop was called The Happy Pig. Like, wouldn't that put people off? It had a cartoon pig with a meat cleaver and a butcher's apron, and this big grin, like the happiest pig in the whole wide world. It was really fucked up. All the packets had the same illustrations on. To me it was really off-putting. And yet the grown-ups still went to the shop and bought their sausages and chops and burgers and chickens, and I couldn't work it out. If you were a butcher, why would you remind your customers that they were buying bits of animals you'd killed – animals with emotions, animals experiencing happiness? Surely you'd want to make out it's just disembodied food? *La la la*, just innocent food, nothing to see here. And this pig, this mascot – he's the worst kind of traitor. He's there helping chop up his own kind. Years later, it occurred to me: it's got nothing to do with distancing people from the animal. It's the illusion of consent. All these happy animals, they're into it. They're all friends, the animals and the farmers and the butcher. It's all fine, they *want* you to have the meat. *No problem, mate, take my flesh!* I've been a vegetarian ever since.'

'I'm vegetarian too,' said Antonia.

Later on, in a secluded side alley, they found a hopscotch board drawn in pink and green chalk, with a jam jar lid next to it.

'Fancy a game?' said Antonia.

'Can you remember how to play?'

'No.'

'Me neither.'

They took it in turns to hop and skip up the board and back, but it didn't jog their memories.

'What do you think of it so far?' said Antonia, as they traipsed along an aisle of emerald overgrowth, sticky willy plants soaking their clothes with dew. The freshness felt delicious, but they dried in moments. Heather picked cleavers from Antonia's sleeves. 'Does it feel like we shouldn't be here?'

'Sort of, yeah,' shrugged Heather. 'How long *have* we been here?'

'I don't know. A few hours?'

'I was thinking more like twenty minutes.'

'Yeah, maybe. I haven't really slept.'

The sun-baked tarmac of the lane was crumbling in places. Through the holes, Heather and Antonia could see a brook, under the lane, five or six feet below them. There were flowers down there in the half-light, and grass and butterflies and a family of ducks, like a second layer of Almanby.

'There are people down there,' said Heather, rubbing her eye with her forefinger.

'That's us,' Antonia said.

'Huh?'

'It's us. It's our reflections.'

Heather waved and Antonia waved too.

'I'm glad they waved back,' said Heather.

'Me too,' said Antonia.

'Come on.' Heather tugged Antonia's sleeve. 'Let's find Penfold Lane.'

But before long, Heather found she'd stopped again. It was hard to stay focused. Her brain felt murky, as if her head was full of pond water dampening the electrochemical impulses. She'd excused herself from Antonia, 'Just going for quick piss, mate,' and slunk away to a secluded paddock, a fenced-off square of grass and cloud-topped cow parsley no bigger than her own bedroom. Butterflies and bumblebees flitted around her head, drunk on nectar, bumping into one another. Snails with brightly coloured shells luxuriated in the dew.

But Heather didn't need a piss. She sat cross-legged on the grass and produced her ORBITRAN radio, twisting the on switch with a satisfying click. Shortwave noise like electronic sherbet fizzed and crackled and fizzled. Heather edged the dial, first one way and then the other, straining for any fragment of Steven's voice, any sign that he was still alive, that he was still somewhere in Almanby.

But there was nothing.

At what point would Heather allow herself to admit that he was dead – that she'd come all this way and missed him by a mere couple of hours? Never, she decided. Love means never giving up on someone. Not till she saw his body with her own eyes.

At last, after several minutes and in the narrowest band possible, she located a hushed voice whispering syllables into the void. But it wasn't Steven, it was a woman's voice, low and steady and inscrutable. A dark voice, almost guttural, barely human – like Mother Nature herself intoning balefully. Mostly, Heather couldn't make out what the voice was saying, although, occasionally, foreign-sounding words like *forgnage* and *acweorre* and *egesgrime* and *firas* would bob to the surface.

It was probably a European station drifting over on a summer breeze; or a passing weather satellite reading out the latest data for its waiting engineers. But there was something about the voice that made Heather's back prickle, something ancient, something from the deepest and darkest places of the earth. Like the time she stayed up too late reading tales of Spring-Heeled Jack and alien abduction and missing children, she became all a-shudder – till she couldn't stand it a moment longer and flicked the radio off again.

'Getting old is weird, isn't it?' said Heather sometime later.

'What makes you say that?'

'Like, you look exactly the same every day. Every time you wake up, you look exactly the same as you did yesterday. But one day you still get to be a really old lady, one of those crumpled-up old ladies you see on the news with a hundred candles. But, how does that work? Because I look exactly the same as I did yesterday, and I'm going to look exactly the same tomorrow.'

'I guess it's incremental. Like, the world is round, but it's so big that when you're down on the ground it looks flat because the curve is really gradual. So, you can't see it from day to day. You have to take a big step back, get really far away, so you're viewing it one year at a time rather than one day at a time.'

'It's still weird, though. There must be a point at which you cross over from looking like a young person to looking like a middle-aged person. You get up one morning and everyone says, heigh-ho, you're old now. Yesterday you were young but today you're old. Because you have to stop being young sometime, don't you. To get to being an old lady with a hundred candles, you have to one day stop being a sexy young thing that boys whistle at in the street.'

'I suppose.'

'You know I'm right. Anyway, it's all academic. I'm never getting old – me and Steven, we're going to be sexy young things forever. Even when we're a hundred, we're going to look like this.'

'How are you going to manage that?'

Heather shrugged. 'Willpower?'

'Is that all it takes?'

'Probably. I can't imagine there's much else to it.'

'So all the people who do get old just aren't concentrating hard enough?'

'Yeah. Or they just don't know. They haven't thought of it.'

'All right. Can I be a sexy young thing too?'

'If you want.'

'Can I be in your club?'

'It's not really a club, it's just us.'

'It should be a club. Sexy young people who live forever like vampires. That's worthy of a club.'

'Okay. But you can't live with us, you have to stay in your own house.'

'Okay.'

'Have you seen anyone at all?' said Heather later still, as they kicked along a dusty path running down the shadowy rear of a row of sandstone cottages. She wore a dandelion behind each ear.

'When we find Steven,' said Antonia, 'we should all buy some beers and lie around drinking in the park like teenagers. Just the three of us.'

Heather looked surprised. 'You don't drink,' she said.

'Yeah I do.'

'You do?'

'Yeah, of course.'

'Huh. You just seem like someone who wouldn't drink.'

'I'm a stand-up comedian.'

'I'd rather have ice cream anyway.'

'You can have both. One in each hand. Or, or, a rum and raisin ice cream. Gin and tonic ice cream.'

'Lager sorbet.'

'Hehe. A Special Brew Viennetta.'

'That sounds gross and I want one immediately.'

'Perfect. So let's find Penfold Lane and then we can pig out.'

* * *

'I'm thinking, if we walk for long enough, we'll bump into

Steven even if we don't find Penfold Lane. Like, he might be out for a walk or something. Posting a letter. Or… or maybe he's got a dog now.'

'Yeah,' said Antonia.

'He's here somewhere. I know he's here somewhere.' Heather pinched at the air with her fingertips. 'I know he's close, I just…' She trailed off and stuffed her hands deep into her pockets. She knew she was just pretending.

'How are you feeling? About Steven, I mean.'

Heather took Antonia by the wrist and placed her palm softly against her chest. Antonia could feel Heather's heart pumping, faster than she'd expected. Heather always seemed so confident and centred, even amid her hyperactivity.

'Wow. It's going really quickly.'

'Yeah.'

'It'll be all right.'

'I hope so.'

'Really. He'll be pleased to see you. It'll be like nothing ever happened. Everything will work out, you'll see.'

'Thanks, Toni.'

'I dare you,' said Antonia.

'What?'

'Hm.' Antonia thought for a few moments. 'What would you like to do?'

'No, you have to think of it, that's the point. Dare me something uncomfortable or dangerous. Or a bit sexy. Or all three.'

'All right.'

'Well?'

'I can't think of anything.'

'You have to. You can't start a dare and not finish it.'

'I was trying to distract you from thinking about Steven.'

'I know. You still have to finish the dare, though.'

'Am I allowed to see your bottom?'

'Is that the dare?'

'No, I just want to know what the parameters are.'

'It's up to you.'

'I was just thinking maybe you could moon some ghosts.'

'Then say it. Say the dare.'

'All right.' Antonia sucked down a lungful of air. 'I dare you to moon some ghosts. For twenty seconds. Those ones over there.' She indicated a knot of ghosts lurking somewhere over her shoulder.

'Fine. Challenge accepted.'

'Am I allowed to watch?'

'You're the adjudicator, you have to watch.'

'All right.'

Heather turned away from Antonia and unfastened her belt.

'Wait. I've changed my mind. Don't do it. I retract the dare.'

'Seriously?'

'Yeah, don't do it. I just wanted to see your bottom, and now I'm panicking about it. It's not right, I feel sick about it already and you haven't even done it yet.'

'I don't care. You can have a good old look, no skin off my nose.'

'I care. It's not what I want. Don't do it, I take it back.'

Heather shrugged and fastened her belt. 'Your loss, Tonio. I have a really nice arse. Everyone says so.'

'No. I'm sorry. It's Almanby, it's making me say things

I'd usually just think. I've gone all weird and uninhibited. Ignore me.'

'All right, if you say so. I would've done it, too.'

'I know you would.'

'I'll tell you something, though, Tonio,' said Heather with a chortle. 'That really did distract me from thinking about Steven.'

Later still, they arrived in the village square. A bakery, a little shop, and a higgledy-piggledy black-and-white Tudor pub called The Green Anne. A wooden sign above the door depicted a nocturnal scene, with owls and the full moon and an oak tree, and a pair of glowering green eyes beneath the ground. Pink, yellow and Easter-green bunting was strung from the tip of the war memorial in the centre of the square and stretched spider-like out to the eaves of the surrounding buildings. The list of names on the memorial was too worn – or blurred? – to make out, but a larger inscription read: THAT IT ALONE IS HIGH FANTASTICAL. Teardrop-shaped and star-shaped confetti littered the cobbles.

But there was still no one around.

Heather sat on the steps of the pub, her head in her hands.

'How are you feeling?' said Antonia.

'Tired,' said Heather. 'You?'

'Yeah, tired. It's been a long day, and we've only eaten fruit.'

'I feel tired to my bones. Old and tired.'

Antonia cupped her face to the window of the pub, but found that the curtains were drawn.

'Maybe everyone's in here,' she said. 'I bet they're watching a film. *Bridge on the River Kwai.*'

'That's not a film.'

'Sure it's a film! Hey, we should go in.' She tried the door. It was stiff, but opened after a bit of a tug. The interior was dark, and impossible make out through the glare of their surroundings, but it sounded empty. 'Hey, Heather, we should go in. They'll have a kitchen.'

Heather looked blankly at her.

'A kitchen. Food. Sandwiches and stuff. Ice cream!'

Heather's eyebrows rapidly ascended her forehead. With a yelp, she sprang to her feet, barged past Antonia, and plunged into the hot black inside.

43

The Green Anne was dark as a coffin and thick with a cacophony of smells – stale beer and even staler cigarette smoke and drinkers who were long dead, long passed into memory, the cadaverous old men who propped up the bar like corpses sharing one last round, *one for the road, lads*.

And it was sticky. Carpet, walls, tabletops, air. The whole melee was foul, but Antonia found it oddly nostalgic. She sucked in a lungful of this grubby atmosphere, feeling like a wine connoisseur savouring a particularly heady bouquet. Notes of misspent childhood, of tailing her father around Headingham social club like a wriggly little shadow, entertaining herself while he downed pints, threw darts, laughed with the other men and fed shiny silver coins into the fruit machine in the corner, with its flashing cherries and watermelons, like an ice-cream dispenser gone wild. Sometimes she was allowed a glass of lemonade or a packet of smoky bacon crisps or a lollipop, the type which changed colour as she sucked it. If her father was in a particularly good mood, he'd toss her a couple of those endless big ten-pence pieces and she'd take a few turns on the Space Invader.

5,740. She still remembered her high score.

Heather's small, pretty face, though, was screwed up with revulsion. Antonia had long suspected that Heather's childhood was more delicate than her own – one of ice-cream cones and daisy chains and flowery summer dresses and daydreams of ponies. *That's a lovely picture, darling, why don't you stick it on the fridge.* Antonia had spent hers memorising the names of beers, fetching packs of cigarettes from the bar, writing darts scores on the chalk board, and setting up balls in the plastic triangle on the pool table while the men chalked their cues. And she'd loved every moment of it. At least, that's how she remembered it. She had few mates her own age, and certainly didn't count her father or the club patrons as friends either (she was far too shy to engage with them, and they in turn mostly ignored her), but she'd relished playing the part of pub urchin, reclining on the beer-stained seating like it was her own home, or scouring the floor for stray twenty-pence coins. And she enjoyed eavesdropping on grown-up conversations, hearing the men say rude things about their wives, or enumerating the horrors they'd seen on the previous evening's news, or just telling jokes to make the others laugh. Antonia had wished she could tell jokes and make grown-ups laugh too.

The Green Anne was a pub much like that one – far removed from the sanitised chain pubs of the new cities, or the upmarket country pubs for middle-class folk which had insinuated their way like grey squirrels into the villages these last couple of decades. This was a red squirrel pub, a native pub – a properly grotty, grimy, gummy-floored pub, everything stained yellow from years of nicotine, farts and disappointment. It was horrible, and Antonia adored it.

The place was empty, of course. They knew it would be. Not just deserted, but actively abandoned: a trio of darts still protruded from the dartboard; dominoes snaked across a table in the far corner of the room; beer glasses, wine glasses and dinner plates remained uncollected in almost every place at every table.

Heather plucked a dog-eared paperback from one of the stools. Its cover depicted a big-nosed cartoon man squinting over a fence at partially clad picnicking women, with the title, *The Idea of Limb Bowlerpiece*, in big pink letters. A strip of paper, folded into a bookmark, lolled like a salacious tongue from the midway point.

'Looks like they left in a hurry,' said Antonia.

Heather pulled open a pair of curtains and gazed around the filthy lounge with increased dismay. 'I'd leave in a hurry too,' she said. 'What a shithole.'

'It's supposed to be like this.'

'Why?'

'It's cosy.'

'Cosy? It's depraved. And I know a thing or two about depravity. What sort of disgusting creature spends their time in a place like this?'

Antonia shrugged. 'Beats me.'

'I'll check the kitchen,' Heather said. She tossed the book onto the floor and disappeared through a door behind the bar.

Antonia made an anxious lap of the pool table, then peered down into the guts of the jukebox. She wanted to see if she recognised any of the songs, whether they were the same ones from her childhood. She couldn't quite shake the feeling that this was the very same lounge bar as the one in Headingham social club, down to the beer mats and the single coil of flypaper suspended from the ceiling, before they'd bulldozed it to make way for the shiny new King's Arms. But the titles of the songs were somehow out of focus, as if they'd all been printed blurred and no one had bothered to replace them.

For a moment, Antonia felt there was someone watching her, a face cupped to the window where her own had been minutes before.

But when she looked up, there was no one there.

Heather returned to the main lounge, affecting a dejected lope.

'Nothing?'

'Yep. Everything's empty. Not even a packet of peanuts. Not even a packet of those horrible bits of destroyed pig.'

Antonia slipped behind the bar and tried each of the beer taps in turn. They were all empty apart from one bearing the name 'Mr Coincido'. The sign on the front depicted a spiral-eyed hypnotist with green skin and a huge black moustache which corkscrewed at the tips. When Antonia pumped the handle, the tap coughed out two thirds of a pint of thick brown ale into a glass tankard. Heather and Antonia shared it between them, too hungry and thirsty to worry how old it might be.

'Maybe there's a map of the village,' said Heather. 'You know, so drunk people can find their way home.'

'Do you feel drunk?'

'I mean, for Penfold Lane.'

'Right, of course. I dunno... I think if you're too drunk to find your way home, you're too drunk to use a map.'

'I guess. Still, we can look.'

'All right.'

So Heather and Antonia rummaged behind the bar, in the kitchen drawers and all through the back office where the landlord kept his leaky pens and used raffle tickets. They found a flight of stairs leading up to a half-dozen sunlit guest rooms, all of which remained unused and immaculate. There were no maps here either, just 'The Green Anne' headed notepaper, more folded cotton napkins than anyone might conceivably need, as well as an occasional Gideon's Bible.

On the wall of the landing, screwed to the dark oak panels, was a framed picture: a reproduction of a seventeenth-century engraving, its paper yellowing and itself now part of long ago. The image depicted the Green Anne pub, instantly recognisable, but surrounded by trees and bushes. Outside the pub, in the village square, a crowd had gathered. They wore capes and pantaloons and tall seventeenth-century hats. Some carried mugs of ale.

Hanging from a makeshift scaffold were two surprised-looking women.

Antonia read aloud a small brass plaque attached to the bottom part of the frame. '*The Green Anne pub has stood on this site since 1614,*' she said. '*It was named after Green Anne.*'

'Helpful,' said Heather.

'Right? Who needs a tourist office?'

'Do you reckon one of those is Green Anne?'

'No. Their names are down here. Mary Manly and Elizabeth Cooper. It doesn't say what they were supposed to have done.'

'So which one's Green Anne?'

'I don't know. Maybe she's in the crowd.'

Heather jabbed a happy finger towards the two victims. 'Hey, Tonio – they look like you and me!' she chortled.

Antonia emerged from the hot treacle darkness of the pub into a wall of sunlight – and for a few moments she could see nothing but the bones in her own fingers. But soon her eyes adjusted to the glare, and she was met by the sight of Heather walking in a glum figure-of-eight.

'Are you all right?'

'We're getting nowhere, Tonio,' Heather said. 'This is all pointless.'

'We'll find Penfold Lane soon,' said Antonia.

'I know, but…' Heather swivelled on her heel a few times. 'Well, what if he's not here? There's no one else here. What if he's gone too?'

'You said you could feel him.'

'Maybe I'm wrong. Maybe I can feel where he used to be. Or, or,' she waved her arms around her head, 'maybe it's all this.'

'Steven's only been here a few months, right? I bet all the people disappeared years ago, and he's been wandering round all that time, same as us, wondering where everyone's got to.'

Heather shrugged. 'Yeah, maybe.' And then she said, 'I feel a bit sick.'

'From the beer?'

'Everything.' She waggled the fingers of her right hand and pulled a face. 'Everything,' she repeated, and for a fleeting moment all her spirit and drive and enthusiasm seemed to abandon her.

Antonia squinted as she approached the war memorial. Now she was closer, she *could* make out some of the names.

Paul Atkinson
Lizzie Wells
Simon Hunter
Paul Howard
Paulette Lake
John Parr
Sandy McInnes
Christie McNamara
Paul Doolan
Jess Holmes
Greg Hargreaves
Helen Doolan
Prithpal Gala
Helen Moore
Lucy Warren
Jack Peterson
Eric Peterson
Suzanne Peterson
Michael Peterson
Simon Thorpe
April Pennymonger
Marcy Ziegler

And then, at the very bottom:

Antonia Coleridge
Heather McLagan

Antonia straightened.

'Heather,' she said.

Heather was over on the other side of the square by now, face pressed to the window of the bakery, her glum interlude forgotten already.

'Heather,' said Antonia. 'Come and see this.'

But Heather was too busy studying something inside the bakery, or maybe just wondering why there were no cakes.

Antonia was about to call for her again, when the jangle of chimes split the air.

Shrill, high-pitched, distorted chimes.

Ice-cream van chimes.

> *Did you ever see a lassie,*
> *A lassie, a lassie?*
> *Did you ever see a lassie,*
> *Go this way and that?*

Joy exploded onto Heather's face. A sluice-gate of untempered, unfiltered, unrestrained delight.

'Ice cream!' she cried. 'Ice cream ice cream ice cream!'

She rotated her head, desperately trying to pinpoint the direction of the sound as the chimes reverberated off buildings and cobblestones and the war memorial. They pealed from tinny speakers and filled the air with a giddying cacophony.

Go this way and that way,
Go this way and that way.
Did you ever see a lassie,
Go this way and that?

'Tonio! Ice cream!'

'Heather, wait, listen,' said Antonia. 'Look at this. The names.'

But a moment later Heather was gone, running full tilt down Marchbread Lane and out of sight.

'Heather, stop!' Antonia called after her. 'There's something important I need to show you!'

'Ice cream! Come on!' came Heather's receding voice from around the corner. 'This is the most important thing in the world!'

44

Long and alive, Almanby spun on a plate. Tall, elliptical, peppered with froth and greening in the ears, rowing and roiling in the concrete flowers elasticated and blooming blueberries hovering behind the picnic on the seashore. In Alaskan deserts of peppercorn fancies, end over end, hopeless and without traction, still it became a forthright leaderboard of putrefied hope.

Heather's feet stopped running before she did, and she paused for the ground to catch up. Antonia was somewhere behind her. A big black banner, coastal and ripped, and tipped in gold, pulled and mangled and cobwebby with doubt. Castanets and crystal sets. There was an ice-cream van inside her skull and also outside her skull, somewhere in these rangly old tangled Almanby lanes. A funnelled, cacophonous cylinder of music. Petrified music, notes turned to tin, clattering together on their staves. They tasted of vanilla, of chocolate flake and neon-red spirals of strawberry sauce and blood-red spirals of raspberry sauce. And banana sauce the colour of a ladybird's poison.

Where was the van?

Where was the van?

Where was that growling, thrumbling minotaur van with its shiver of cola-coloured exhaust, its shuddering breath?

Except she was the minotaur, she was hunting the van with its virgin cargo. And her bull head huffed and puffed as she tried to suck in enough of this claggy wet summer air to keep her conscious, keep her upright. Everything in Almanby was so *heavy*.

And a big rod of pain she held in her hand, a lightning conductor, with trams of electrochemical badness, *choo-choo*, locomotives up her arm. People disembarking on the platform and into her flesh, with their Everest flags and their spiky Everest boots. The muscle felt hard as glacier.

Now there's a corner shop, a newsagent, lights as bright as sun refracting through a lens. And at the back of the shop, among the dust and expired cans and cereals no one eats anymore, an enormous chest freezer, chugging like a traction engine.

Heather leans over the lip of the chest freezer. It's full of ice lollies.

Each of the wrappers bears the name EGESGRIME.

There's something among the ice lollies. Something white. A severed arm, a diseased right forearm, veined in red like raspberry ripple ice cream.

Sucking a strawberry rocket, which stains her lips and chin and the front of her pretty pear-green summer dress that her mother bought her especially for today, Heather climbs into the cabinet freezer and begins to bury herself under the ice lollies, piling them on top of herself till she's all gone, all gone, all gone.

Heather woke. She felt very hot. Grilled chicken hot. She'd been hoping this whole thing was a dream and that she'd wake up in bed at home cuddled up next to Steven, their legs threaded together in a fleshy pigtail, but no – she was still in Almanby, stretched out on a grassy bank by the side of a small stream. Antonia sat a few feet away, long brown arms wrapped around her high knees.

'I must've fallen asleep,' Heather heard herself say, her voice sounding distant and woolly. Antonia helped her sit up. 'Did we catch the ice-cream van?'

'We didn't see it,' said Antonia. 'We ran, but we never saw it.'

'Shame.'

'Heather. Our names were on the war memorial. Not just us, everyone. Paul and Lizzie and Prithpal and Paulette. And John and Sandy from the Chicken Club. Everyone. How is that even possible?'

Heather looked at her sleepily. 'What about Rachel?' she said.

'No.'

'What about Steven?'

'No, I don't think so, I didn't see Steven. But everyone else. Everyone who disappeared. Greg, Christie, April. Marcy. How is that possible?'

'I don't know.'

'Do you think they came to Almanby and never went back?'

Heather blinked hard and rubbed her foggy head. 'Maybe,' she said.

'Why would they go to Almanby? No one goes to Almanby.'

'We came to Almanby.'

'We were on the war memorial too. Antonia Coleridge and Heather McLagan, right at the bottom. But it was all worn, like we'd been on there for years. What do you think it means?'

'I don't know.' Heather glanced around, still blinking, like a kitten that had been roused from a particularly deep slumber. 'What are we talking about?'

'The war memorial.'

'What war memorial?'

'The one in the village square. Didn't you see it? It had our names on it.'

'Why did it have our names on it?' said Heather. She tried to focus on Antonia's face, but the sun was too bright and her own head was too cloudy. 'We haven't been in a war.'

'No, Heather, but… we came to Almanby, and…'

'Maybe it's coincidence,' Heather said sleepily.

'Our names and all our friends' names?'

'Yeah. These things happen.' She glanced at Antonia. 'What are we talking about?'

'Heather, we have to get you out of here. We have to leave.'

'No. I've got to find Steven. He's here somewhere.'

'This whole village is deserted. There's no one around.'

'Except the ice-cream van.'

'Right, except the ice-cream van, which we haven't seen.'

Carefully, Heather rolled up her sleeve as if she was peeling an overripe fruit. Her arm was bad – mottled a dark purple, with glistening red cracks.

'Jesus,' said Antonia.

Heather flexed her fingers. They felt slow, sluggish, like the mechanism was damaged.

'I'll get help,' said Antonia, standing to go. 'I'll find a doctor, or, or someone. Look at you!'

'Don't. Tonio. Don't leave me.'

Heather found she was sitting on a small wooden bridge now, her legs dangling over the whisky waters of the village brook. She didn't remember moving.

Antonia walked over and sat next to her.

Heather chuckled. 'Now you're stuck in mousey rooms,' she said.

Antonia frowned, asked her to repeat it. But Heather couldn't remember what she just said, or what she'd really been intending to say.

Her left shoe became dislodged. It tumbled off and splashed into the water, and she watched in dismay as it was gulped down into the beckoning green weed. Now she'd have to walk around Almanby with one shoe off and one shoe on, like the diddle diddle dumpling boy.

But when she looked again, both shoes were still in place.

'Do you remember an old cartoon show called *Sock Draw?*' she said. 'What was funny about it was that they were sock puppets, but it was all was all hand-drawn animation...'

'I'm worried about you,' said Antonia. 'Your arm looks really bad.'

'We'll find Steven. He'll know what to do.'

'What if that's too late?'

'Too late for what?'

'For...' Antonia trailed off. 'I think we should find someone as soon as possible. Just to be safe.'

'Steven is someone. Let's find him.'

'We'll ask. The first person we see, we'll ask.'

Nearby, crows like bits of charcoal offered their hoarse opinions to the breeze. Heather swung her legs – at first both together, and then alternating left and right – back and forth.

'We have to find Penfold Lane,' said Heather with a yawn.

'I know.'

'That's where Steven is.'

'I know.'

'So that's why we have to find it.'

'Once you've rested a bit. You want to be nice and strong when you see him, don't you?'

'What shall I say to him?' she said.

'Just show him your arm. He'll see what's wrong.'

'I mean, generally. When I meet him. Help me think of something to say.'

'I thought you were great mates.'

'I know, but… it's been so long. It feels weird now. I'm nervous.'

'How can *you* be nervous?'

'I don't know what he'll be like. I don't know…' She shrugged. 'I don't know whether he'll want to see me.'

'What do you want to say?'

'I don't know.'

'Well… what have you been wanting to say to him? Like, all these weeks. Whenever you think about him, what do you want to say?'

'Just that I miss him, really. That I'm worried.'

'Then say that. Tell him how you feel. You don't need to ask him anything.'

'What if…?'

'What?'

45

An inrush of lavender and blossom and searing hot daytime.

Heather blinked awake. Her arm was numb now, a coldness which reached deep into the muscle, all the way to the bone. She opened her fingers then clenched them. It felt as if she was operating someone else's hand by remote control.

A familiar figure sat close by.

'I thought I *was* awake,' Heather said, her voice feeling woolly in her mouth.

'We should keep on the move,' said the figure.

'What time is it?'

'Afternoon sometime, I guess. I'm not sure, I don't have a watch.'

'Why do I keep falling asleep?'

'Come on, let's find you a doctor. Can you walk?'

Heather seemed not to recognise Antonia for a while. She kept peering quizzically at her as they continued through the lanes of Almanby, as if trying to fathom whether they'd met before.

'Thank you,' she said at last.

'What for?' said Antonia.

'Helping me. I'd have baked to death if you hadn't found me. It's kind of you.'

'I've been here the whole time.'

'Have you?'

'It's me. Antonia.'

Heather scrutinised her again. 'Antonia.'

'We drove here together. Me, you and Rachel.'

A light switched on behind Heather's eyes. 'Sorry, Tonio. I knew that.' She grinned unconvincingly. 'It was just a little joke. See, I'm a comedian too.'

A cloud of midges thronged around Heather's head as if to illustrate her confusion. She wafted at them, still grinning. She seemed to have forgotten why she was smiling and as a result didn't know when she should stop.

'How do you think of your jokes?' she said, at last.

'You want to talk about this now?'

'Yeah. Speak to me. Tell me things. Tell me anything. Tell me how you get your jokes.'

'I don't know, really. They just come to me. I'm always thinking anyway – like, instead of sleeping or enjoying the moment or any of that good stuff – and sometimes daft things pop into my head. It's like being given little presents.'

'Like Christmas presents.'

'Yeah.'

'So you don't sit down with a pen to write jokes?'

'No, not really. I don't have a formula or anything, I just wait for them to arrive.'

'Think of a joke about Almanby.'

'Now?'

'Yeah. Make one up for me.'

'Well, they don't really work like that.'

'Go on. For me.'

'All right. Um. Okay. Hey, Heather – if you think Alman-bee is bad, at least it's not Alman-wasp.'

'Yeah, I see what you mean.'

'Right? They're better when they come naturally. Like, the other day I thought of this. I've been trying to word it so I can fit it into my set. Hey, Heather – running your fingers through a girl's hair is fun, isn't it? If it's still attached to her head, anyway. Less so if you've just pulled it up from the plughole in the bath.'

'Because she's dead.'

'What?'

'You're a serial killer, and you disposed of the body in the bath, and you found some of her hair down the plughole.'

'I'm not a serial killer. Why did you say I'm a serial killer?'

'In the joke. You're running your fingers through the corpse's hair.'

'*No.* That's not it at all. It's just a joke about context. Hair is romantic when it's on someone's head, but the same hair when it's in the sink is gross. Because that's where hair goes, it gets tangled up in the plughole. It's nothing to do with murder.'

'Oh. Right. Yes, I get it now. Sorry, Tonio.'

Antonia shrugged her big lanky shoulders. 'It's all right. It'll be better when it's part of a set. You know, momentum and all that. It'll make more sense.'

Heather glanced up into the blue velodrome of the sky, shielding her eyes against the glare. Overhead, a team of gulls whirled in ragged circuits, flashing white. And then, out of nowhere, she let out a long, deep sigh. 'I feel like I'm being sucked empty,' she said, in a voice so weary it startled Antonia. She suddenly looked very pale, almost translucent. Even her irises were drained of colour.

Only now that she said the words aloud did the notion really coalesce: for the last few hours, or minutes, or however long they'd been wandering through this place, Antonia too had felt like she was being sucked empty. The sickly, creeping sensation that her life essence was draining down her legs and out through her feet. Into the ground. Into Almanby.

And it wasn't that she was growing *weaker* so much as *lesser*, as if she was 98.5 per cent of the Antonia that she'd been when she arrived: too little lost to make a practical difference – *yet* – but just enough to notice. Just enough to render her queasy, for it to feel like a violation. And that missing 1.5 per cent… it wasn't emptiness, it wasn't a hole. There was something else there instead, like she'd been 1.5 per cent replaced. 1.6 per cent replaced. 1.7 per cent replaced. Rising every few minutes. The longer they remained in Almanby, the less of them remained.

'Let's get out of here,' she said. 'As far away from Almanby as we can.'

'He needs me. I have to find him.'

'Who'll find *us*?'

'When we're all together, we'll be okay.'

All together. Heather didn't say 'together', just her and Steven, the reunited couple, facing the world hand-in-hand, shoulder-to-shoulder. She said, '*all* together'. The three of them, the team. Best buds.

Nonetheless, Antonia felt increasingly panicky. Heather wasn't going to let this one go. Even if Steven was long gone, migrated to another village or simply lost to the soil, they'd still be circling Almanby, searching in vain, waiting for their turn to slip down the drain along with the congealed soap and matted hair.

Antonia nonchalantly hooked her arm through Heather's. Not a romantic gesture, just something to prevent them both tumbling off into the void. 'Running your fingers through a woman's hair is fun, isn't it?' she said. 'Except when you've just pulled it from the plughole.'

'Yeah, that works better.'

Up ahead, tied around a lamppost on the far side of the street, was a piece of red fabric. Heather unlinked arms and rushed across the street to tug at the fabric till it came free. It was a man's T-shirt, with a big white Space Invader alien screen-printed on the front.

'This is Steven's T-shirt,' she said, as Antonia joined her.

'How do you know?'

'He has one just like it.'

'I bet lots of people have T-shirts like this.'

'Don't be daft, no one's as cool as Steven. Anyway, his has a moth-hole in the shoulder.' Heather pressed her fingertip against a small, ragged hole in the shoulder of the T-shirt. 'He left it for me to find so I'd know he was here.'

'It could mean anything.'

'What? No it couldn't. It was a birthday present. I bought it for his twenty-sixth birthday. He knew I'd recognise it. He put it here so I'd see it.'

Antonia was about to speak when Heather spotted something else a little further along the lane: a bright yellow baseball cap hooked over an iron fence paling. On the front was the red-and-black logo of the Chicken Club. She plucked the hat from the paling, placed it over her face, and inhaled deeply.

Fuck, thought Heather, *he's here. He's really here.*

Like her childhood hamster, still running on its wheel in her parents' attic, behind the cardboard boxes and old schoolbooks. She'd spent so much time thinking about Steven these last few months, he'd almost become a myth of Steven. A shadow, slipping out of reach whenever she tried to grab hold of it. Or a false memory, an anthropomorphic composite of all her happiest moments – a Steven-shaped simulacrum that'd split into all its component parts, like wriggling spooks, the moment she touched it.

But no… he was here in Almanby. Maybe just a few feet away from where she stood at that very moment. Lying on his bed, oblivious to her presence.

With a frantic edge, she said, 'You've been keeping your eyes open for Penfold Lane, right? You didn't notice it?'

'No. No, I didn't see anything.'

'Are you sure? Think, Tonio – are you sure?'

'I'm sure. I promise, I'm sure.'

'It can't be far. *He* can't be far.' She glanced feverishly around, looking ready to tear off her own skin. 'What we need is one of those maps.'

'Well, yeah.'

'I mean, one of those big metal maps on posts.'

'Right. Or just any kind of map.'

'Yeah.'

'We should do this methodically,' Antonia said. 'Start at the edge and work our way in towards the centre. In a spiral.'

'All right. Which bit's the edge?'

Now that they were inside the borders of Almanby, it was hard to get a sense of the place, to assemble a mental picture of the layout. Trees, cottages, leylandii and banks of pink and yellow blossom, like cumulonimbus clouds, reared up on every side. There seemed to be no vantage points in the whole village – it was a jigsaw puzzle of cosy nooks and secluded avenues. An inside-out Rubik's cube.

'Well, let's start here,' said Antonia, 'and head clockwise.'

Heather was quiet for a long time, trailing a few steps behind Antonia, eyes cast to the sun-bleached tarmac. Knowing what was probably on her mind, Antonia didn't disturb her. They were sufficiently comfortable in each other's presence now just to walk and think, and not always have to be filling an awkward silence.

For her part, Antonia tasked herself with keeping track of the street names, making sure they didn't wander blithely past Penfold Lane.

Cardinal Road, Gorse Road, Rosehip Lane, Farthing Crescent, Candlestick Lane, Green Lane, Huntsman's Street, Clove's End, Shilling Court, Honeybee Lane, Tuppence Lane, Pond Street...

'When I was at school,' Heather said eventually, 'I had this friend called Rachel. We sat on the same table. I liked her, we used to talk all the time. But she used to get these weird… I don't know what they were. Fainting fits. We'd all be out on the playground, then suddenly the teachers would call us back inside, and she'd still be out there lying on the grass.'

'That was me.'

'You had fainting fits?'

'No, *I* had the friend. My friend Rachel, she had the fainting fits, I told you about it earlier. She was in my class, with me and Rachel.'

'No, it was me. I can still see her out on the grass in her red shoes. They looked so bright in the sunlight.'

'How can we both have had a friend with red shoes called Rachel who had fainting fits?'

'I don't know. It was definitely me, though. I can see her face, clear as day. We used to chat in class all the time, so much we got in trouble. But every time she had one of her fits, I'd get really awkward around her and wouldn't talk to her. I felt really bad about it later. I wish I knew where she was so I could find her and apologise.'

'I said all this!'

'When?'

'Earlier. How come you didn't mention it when I was telling you then?'

'I don't remember you saying anything like that. I think you heard me say it, and it felt so real that now you think you remember it.'

'No. I said it first. Her name was Rachel – I can't remember her second name. She always wore bright red shoes like Dorothy, she was really funny, she was always saying funny things. But she used to have fits.'

'Right. That was my friend.'

'No, it was my friend. She sat across from me.'

'No, she sat across from *me*. She had these really blue eyes. Like, impossibly blue. Almost like glass.'

'Yes.'

'And she had this weird older brother. If I went round to her house, he wouldn't come inside, he'd just stand in the garden watching, till it got creepy. Rachel said he was just shy, but... I don't know, I didn't like it.'

'Right,' said Antonia. 'That was my friend. Rachel. Rachel Red Shoes.'

'Exactly. Rachel Red Shoes.'

'All right. If she was your friend, what was her surname?'

'Red Shoes. You just said it.'

'Her real surname. What was it?'

Heather frowned, and her mouth went very small. 'I can't remember,' she said.

> *Did you ever see a lassie,*
> *A lassie, a lassie?*
> *Did you ever see a lassie,*
> *Go this way and that?*

Heather instantly became rigid, as if a bolt of electricity had passed through her. Her lethargy evaporated, replaced by a gargoyle grin which spanned the width of her face.

'There it is!' she cried. 'There it is!' She scampered away, zigzagging wildly back and forth across the street.

'What about Steven?' Antonia called after her. 'We're supposed to be finding Penfold Lane.'

'I need an ice cream *now*! This is killing me!' She stopped, craned her neck, rotated her head, squinted her eyes.

> *Go this way and that way,*
> *Go this way and that way.*
> *Did you ever see a lassie,*
> *Go this way and that?*

'Over here!' she called at last, sprinting up Tuppence Lane towards the heart of the village.

'This isn't... we're supposed to be doing it methodically.'

'It's over here! It's so close!'

They funnelled up through Tuppence Lane, between great rearing sycamore trees and sappy chestnut trees, then veered left at the crossroads and down Old Road in a helter-skelter spiral, past the post office and past the duck pond with its bulrushes and lily pads, and past a bright red telephone box – till suddenly, the sound seemed to change direction, jump to a different location altogether.

> *Did you ever see a lassie,*
> *A lassie, a lassie?*
> *Did you ever see a lassie,*
> *Go this way and that?*

'Here!'

They took a sharp left along a footpath between the backs of houses and out onto a grassy track. Fenced-off gardens on one side, a brick wall shiny with snail trails on the other. Two ghosts blocked their route, both young women – one with a saw and the other with a snapped-off length of bicycle handlebar.

'We can make it!' said Heather.

'Don't be silly.'

'If we run fast enough, we can make it.'

'It's ice cream, Heather. It's not worth dying for!'

'It's *ice cream!*'

And then she was off once more, haring full-tilt towards the two ghosts. Antonia groaned – she had no choice but to slipstream Heather.

Despite being smaller than both ghosts, Heather somehow managed to barge through the pair of them. Antonia, though, impacted against the two hard, cold bodies, barely managing to keep her footing as she shoved and struggled through them. The handlebar ghost took a swing at her as she passed, and only missed her skull by millimetres.

> *Go this way and that way,*
> *Go this way and that way.*
> *Did you ever see a lassie,*
> *Go this way and that?*

And then they burst back onto Marchbread Lane, hurtling downhill once more, their shoes clattering on the tarmac. The chimes were louder here, fuller, reverberating through the space. The van should surely be visible by now – but no, it was still just out of sight, just around the next corner, just behind one more row of houses.

It was *somewhere*. Tantalisingly close.

* * *

And then, without warning –

> *Did you ever see a lassie,*
> *A lassie, a lass—*

– the chimes stopped.

'No!' Heather jogged to a halt. 'Where is it? *Where is it?*'

They listened. Close by, a diesel engine sputtered, coughed, grumbled away into a different part of Almanby, fading from earshot.

'Where is it?' cried Heather. 'Where is it? Make it come back!'

'Heather...'

'Shut up!'

They stood absolutely still. The six-note hoots of woodpigeons rang through the trees, answered by a sarcastic mock-offended cuckoo, *oo-oo, oo-oo*.

'Heather...'

'Be *quiet*!' Heather's intensity was almost feral now, almost wolf-like as she crouched forward, head cocked to the air. The occasional twitch, the occasional readjustment of her stereo field, utter concentration.

> *Did you ever see a lassie,*
> *A lassie, a lassie?*
> *Did you ever see a lassie,*
> *Go this way and that?*

'Over here!' she cried, and was gone again, her legs and arms pumping ludicrously as she darted off, deeper into the village.

'This way!' Antonia called after her.

Heather came to a halt at the side of a house, her hand resting on its gatepost as her ribcage heaved.

'It's this way!' she yelled.

'It's over here! It's behind us!'

Both women listened, their heads turning as they tried to pinpoint the music. It saturated the humid air, seemed to fill every nook, every corner, every cubic millimetre of Almanby. It was all around them, on every side. Outside them, inside them. Inside their heads. And it grew louder, louder, louder, till it hurt Antonia's ears.

> *Go this way and that way,*
> *Go this way and that way.*
> *Did you ever see a lassie,*
> *Go this way and that?*

Heather set off running once more.

'You're going the wrong way! Heather!' Antonia shook her head and followed on behind. With her longer legs, she quickly caught up to Heather and pulled her to a halt.

'What are you doing?' Heather's eyes flashed with genuine fury as she yanked herself free. Her knuckles whitened – she looked ready to strike Antonia.

'We're not going to catch it.'

'Don't you want me to be happy?'

'What?'

'That's it, isn't it. You don't want me to be happy. You want to fuck this up for me, this one thing I really need. You're trying to sabotage it.'

'No, of course not. Heather, listen. *It's* moving and *we're* moving. We're just chasing it round and round. We haven't even seen it yet! Look, if we stand still, it'll probably drive right past us eventually, we can flag it down. We just have to be patient.'

Heather's eyes were huge and round. 'That's crazy! *You're* crazy! You're fucked up! I know what you're trying to do – you can't ruin this for me, I won't let you!'

'What are you talking about? Heather, please, listen!'

But Heather was running again.

46

'Hey, Prithpal. You can drive, right?'

'You know I can, I took you swimming last week.'

'Right, of course. Well, with that in mind, I was wondering whether there was any chance you'd fancy doing me a favour?'

'Like taking you swimming, you mean?'

'Yeah, a bit like that. But maybe... maybe a slightly bigger favour.'

'It's probably about time for you to do me a favour, don't you think?'

'After this one. I promise. Anything at all. Just name it.'

'Fine, all right, I'll do it. You're going to wear me down anyway, I may as well save us both a headache. What is it?'

'Okay, so, I have this friend. You know Oscar?'

'No.'

'Well, my friend Oscar really needs a parcel taking to him.'

'So post it.'

'You know what the post is like these days. Anyway, he needs it tomorrow.'

'Then get the bus.'

'Well, you see, that's the thing – the buses don't go where he lives.'

'Why, where does he live?'

287

47

Did you ever see a lassie,
A lassie, a lassie?
Did you ever see a lassie,
Go this way and that?

– sang an ice-cream van's horrible metallic chimes somewhere in the distance, their blaring clarion stretched and diluted by the trees.

Rachel's strength had failed her again. It came in waves – sometimes she felt well enough to stumble onwards, one foot dully in front of the other; other times she could only lay face down in the grass, its blades tickling the inside of her open mouth.

One of these times, she was going to fall down and never get up.

Maybe this time.

She fumbled for the package, the box with the porcelain shepherd inside, then realised she'd dropped it a mile or two back. It'd slipped from her fingers and she hadn't even noticed.

Ah well. She didn't need it now anyway. It was just for show.

* * *

There was probably an irony in the fact that she was going to die in Almanby. It seemed ironic anyway, though she didn't have the wherewithal to quite work out why. She felt cold, despite the heat, but she was comfortable now stretched out on the turf, as if her body could sink into the pores of the soil, as if it could break down into fertiliser there and then. She'd be fine with that. She'd be fine with turning into goo and disappearing into the earth if it meant an end to her pain.

'I'm melting!' cried the Wicked Witch of the West.
'Actually, you're dissolving,' said Pedantic Dorothy.

The sun shone very bright. Hot as a griddle. Rachel could almost smell her skin cooking.

One of these times, I'm going to fall down and never get up.
Maybe this time.
Maybe this time.

And with that, Rachel closed her eyes.

48

'Marcy Ziegler – my most excellent friend! What are you up to?'

'Eating dinner, what does it look like?'

'After that?'

'I dunno. I was thinking of watching a video.'

'You have a video?'

'I found it. There was a tape inside – it seems to be old episodes of M*A*S*H*.'

'What would you say to an adventure instead?'

'What sort of adventure?'

'Remember my friend Oscar?'

'Oscar... I don't think I know an Oscar.'

'You maybe didn't meet him. Well, I have a package I need to take to Oscar...'

'Right.'

'April's coming, too. I wondered if you fancied tagging along?'

'I guess so, if it won't take all night. Where does he live?'

'Well, that's the thing with Oscar's house...'

'Here we go.'

'It's not... it's not very close. Not close to where we are, anyway.'

'Rachel, where does he live?'

49

Rachel was in the woodgrain.

She *was* the woodgrain.

She was the raindrops waiting in the clouds, high overhead. She was the impurities in the air and the minerals in the soil. She was the woodlice and the worms, every spider spinning its web and every tangled insect waiting to die. She was the mountains. She was the oceans and the ice caps and the endless deserts. She was the consciousness of the great forests, their every creature: the mighty gestalt. She wafted to and fro on the breezes of time – swirling around the leathered ankles of warring roundheads, or visiting glittering silver futures, staying for the day as she surveyed each of the untapped possibilities. She was the protozoa and the dragonflies and the dinosaurs and the moa birds; she was the last pigeon, slate-grey against the snow at the end of the world. Her long fingers stretched around the planet like the fingers of a bat, and she held the rocky sphere against her belly. And now it was inside her, part of her gut, its hardness weighing her down, turning her inside out, even now as she was almost formless, almost beyond the boundaries of what used to be Rachel. She was the clouds of Venus and the canyons of Mars; she was the icy rings of Saturn and Jupiter's tempests and the raging volcanoes of Io.

And throughout everything, throughout all of existence and time, three large rectangular obelisks of light watched over her. They watched over the whole span of creation: all the obscure, hidden nooks into which she'd seeped; all the jungles and rivers which she smothered with the infinite vastness of her body. The rectangles seemed familiar somehow, though she couldn't place them. She'd come back to them once she'd had time to think. Once she'd had time to really understand her place in the universe.

And so she spent millennia in contemplation. Silently stretching out between stars, infusing into the phosphorescent candyfloss nebulae. Surveying each one, weighing them in the collection of atoms that she used to call her hand. Turning them over, studying them from every side. Cataloguing them in her brain.

But she couldn't concentrate. She couldn't settle. All the while those three rectangles of light still watched her, side by side and inscrutable through all eternity. And they seemed *so* familiar. Distractingly familiar. Like they meant something important, they signified something she couldn't put her finger on. The whole of the universe and the whole of time was her playground, and she couldn't enjoy it, not really, because she couldn't solve that one final puzzle. The hair in her mouth, the fly in her amber.

For all her freedom, Rachel was unable to move. She tried to flex a finger, she tried to mouth a word, but nothing came. She was a haunted wax museum replica of herself, a Rachelshaped mannequin stretched out on a sofa. And the light from the three big rectangular windows, white like obelisks, hurt her eyes, but she couldn't screw them up, she couldn't squint.

It was a fat, brown-leather walrus of a sofa. She'd lain here before, though it wasn't her own sofa, she wasn't at home. She didn't know where she was, though every part of it felt achingly familiar. The room was dark, overpowered by the light from outside. Her ears sang with tinnitus, a whole choir of frequencies clamouring for her attention.

She felt at once heavy and pathetically insubstantial, as if all her atoms were too far apart, but they'd become lead atoms. She was a translucent lead golem, sinking deeper into the sofa. Into its mites and biscuit crumbs and nicotine-yellow stuffing.

But at least she didn't hurt anymore. At least there was that. And because she didn't hurt anymore, she knew exactly where she was: she was right at the heart of Almanby. The only place she felt safe, the only place she was no longer dying quite so rapidly. And this room protected her. There were no ghosts here, she could lie for as long as she liked without fear.

Rachel was able to discern some of the details of the room now. It was wide and modern, with a high, sloped ceiling and bare polished floorboards. Lights behind frosted-glass discs were set into the ceiling. There was a grand piano in one corner, black and shiny as a beetle. She'd played that piano – how long ago? A thousand years? Eighty million years, when dinosaurs roamed the Earth, the ankylosaurus and the nedoceratops?

Outside the three big obelisk windows, the trees of Almanby swayed in a non-existent breeze.

She tried to sit up but her muscles were still useless, even if she could blink now, move her eyeballs, look around. A chromium lamp, as tall as a person; a black-framed portrait of sunflowers and poppies; a sleek black cabinet; an office chair; a desk.

And a figure. A silhouetted shape by the door, to the left of the windows. How long had he been waiting there, silently watching? A thousand years? A hundred and fifty million years, when dinosaurs roamed the Earth, the kentrosaurus and the diplodocus?

No. 5 Tourmaline Crescent, Almanby.

She knew this place intimately. She knew this sofa intimately – she'd slept on its broad, thick folds often enough, curled up soundly under the electric Almanby night. That forbidden village, the place where everyone was scared to go except her. And sleep she did – never so deeply or peacefully as when she was in Almanby, there in the stone-and-mortar womb of 5 Tourmaline Crescent.

'Where's Sam?' said Oscar's silhouette.

'Sam's dead,' Rachel said with the last smidgen of energy she possessed, though she could feel more returning drip by drip, edging its way tentatively back along her capillaries, back out into her extremities.

'You brought the package?' said Oscar.

'Of course I did.'

'And?'

'I already told you. I'm not going to do it.'

'You don't really have a choice, do you?'

'I can't. They're my friends.'

'That hasn't stopped you before.'

'Why? Why's it so important?'

'You know why, Rachel. It has to be a sacrifice.'

'It's a sacrifice. Trust me, it's already a fucking sacrifice.'

'Would you like a drink?'

'Water.'

Oscar's silhouette drifted from the room. Rachel heard his footsteps recede into the kitchen.

With a groan, she swung her legs down off the sofa and sat up. Her head was murky and filled with stagnant ditch water, daphnia and protozoa flitting around her brain.

She paced around the floor, trying to coax feeling back into her limbs. She'd almost died out there among the moist green grass on the edge of Almanby – like Sam, she'd very nearly left it too late. But now she was back in the nurturing bosom of Oscar's house. Right in the heart of Almanby. The place where everyone else felt wrong, the place at the core of all this toxic, creeping, insidious wrongness. The epicentre. And Rachel, like some incandescent little demon, couldn't survive for long anywhere else. It was the one place left in the world where she felt *right*.

Oscar was… actually, now she thought of it, Rachel wasn't sure of their relationship. They weren't friends – she had so few actual friends, especially now. She and Oscar had an *understanding*… that was about as far as it went. She provided for him and he in turn provided for her. Oscar *was* Almanby. He was an extension of Almanby, a protuberance, a pseudopod.

When Rachel first heard – through a friend of a friend, naturally – that this *thing*, this disease which had corrupted reality and brought sombre, violent versions of the dead back to life, was somehow connected with the village of Almanby, her curiosity had got the better of her. The place they'd been warned against since they were children, the place most of them hadn't thought about in a decade or more. It was at the heart of this malaise.

As far as anyone else was concerned, it was just a conspiracy theory. There were enough of those about. But Rachel was a woman with sources. People knew, if you knew the right people to ask.

She took the bus out to Branbrook – while there were buses still running – and hiked the rest of the way, feeling ever more peculiar the closer she came to Almanby, but with every strange tingle in her nerve endings and uncomfortable increase of pressure in her eardrums, she grew ever more determined to see this thing through.

Almanby was the eye of the storm. Utterly peaceful, utterly quiet compared to the turmoil of the approach – she could think clearly now, she could breathe – but she knew it was also toxic to its smallest atom. Rachel could feel it through her pores.

She met Oscar there. They went back to his place and they fucked. She couldn't really remember how it'd happened, how they'd met or what spurred them to strike up a conversation. That whole first visit was hazy at best. In fact, every visit became hazy once she was no longer inside Almanby, as if she could only clearly think about the place so long as she was there.

After the fuckery, she felt good, like she'd never felt before. She was in a state of euphoria – euphoria cubed, like a minor deity crashed to earth. She felt magic. She *was* magic: she could perform acts of telekinesis, project little nuggets of that strange Almanby enchantment, do party tricks no one could fathom. But it was killing her too: from her second day home, when Almanby's energy started to ebb away, she knew she was doomed.

They said that people who went to Almanby never returned. Rachel had been, and true enough, she hadn't returned. Not fully. A half-empty version of Rachel came home. She'd left some important part of herself there, something which kept calling her back. And each time she went, it chipped a little more of her away, and a little more, until there was hardly anything left.

She was only complete when she was in Almanby.

Around her friends, she could pretend she was okay. Put on a front, act through it. She could make sure no one suspected she was ill. But that took energy, it wore down her precious reserves. It was dangerous to pretend for too long.

She wanted to stay, she wanted to live there. But after a day or two, she'd always start to feel prohibitively nauseous. Almanby was rejecting her – she was a toxin, she didn't belong there. So she had to return to Headingham and wait it out, till she really needed to go back.

She met other people in the same position as her. Sam and Glen and Other Antonia. Often they'd travel together. They all had the same story – they'd visited out of curiosity and became hooked. They'd slept with a local in a tryst they could no longer really remember, they'd felt more euphoric and more alive than they'd ever felt before; then they started dying the moment they left. If they tried to stay in Almanby they always got sick; but they got sick, too, if they stayed away too long.

One by one the others died. They found Glen in his bathtub, up to his neck in water; and Other Antonia by the side of the road in the exact spot where they'd arranged to meet her; and Sam in that squalid farmhouse of his. A few more hours and they'd have been okay.

By that time, things had become even more complicated. They soon discovered that visiting Almanby wasn't free.

Almanby demanded payment.

Rachel wandered around the room, sliding a little on the polished wooden floor in her socks. At the piano, she stepped on the sustain pedal and played a dramatic chord, enjoying the sound of it reverberating through the heavy midsummer air. At the mantelpiece, she plucked a tall, electric-green catlike figurine from a parade of figurines and idly turned it over in her hand. Oscar had been a real person once, back when he spent his days holed up in his glass-ceilinged workshop, beavering away at those weird kitsch little figurines of his, sculpting them from anything he could lay his hands on. His studio still stood at the back of the house in the conservatory, untouched these last few years. Now he was a silhouette of a man. Even when she could see his face clearly, she couldn't see his face, as if he was never quite fully present. Nondescript features, nondescript short dark hair.

Nondescript black trousers and dark pullover. A transparent man. She'd never seen him smile, she'd never known him to crack a joke. He was all but a manifestation of the village.

Oscar was back in the room now, and there was a large glass of water on the coffee table behind her. He was too far away to have placed it there, but that was Almanby. Even here, even in Oscar's living room, geography wasn't what it used to be.

Rachel drank deeply. She could've managed three times the amount – she'd sweated that much out – but it'd do for now. She stood by the large window at the rear of the room, which looked out onto the back yard and the long sweep of the garden down to Almanby brook. In the concrete yard were gathered a fresh collection of a dozen or so larger statues, most of them around three feet tall. Some were shapeless and abstract, others looked a little like people: struggling human shapes who seemed, vaguely, to be trying to escape some kind of perilously sticky quagmire.

'Did you make these?' she said, amazed at the idea of Oscar still absorbed in his hobby when no one was around.

'Mostly.'

'Mostly?'

'I had help.'

'Almanby?'

She glanced back at him and he nodded. 'Some of them I didn't even touch,' he said. 'I woke up in the morning and they were there, waiting for me in my workshop.'

Almanby figuring out what humans did, trying its best to join in, to replicate their actions, to see what all the fuss was about, but managing only to replicate its own nightmares.

* * *

Rachel's legs suddenly buckled under her and she sat down on the floor. There were snakes in her belly and her blood felt like milk. She leaned her forehead against her knees. Almanby wasn't doing so much for her this time. It wasn't keeping her as strong as it normally did.

'More water?' said Oscar.

She looked up at him. 'I could do with something a little stronger.'

'Water. Till the job's done.'

50

'Have you seen anyone?' Antonia said. 'Anyone at all?'

'Lots of villages are quiet.' Heather drew her sleeve across her brow and removed a layer of perspiration.

Antonia sauntered over to a nearby parked car – a silver-grey thing with a Volkswagen logo on the grille. She bent to examine it, brushing a fingertip where its wheels met the tarmac. Moss.

'It hasn't been driven in years,' she said.

'Maybe…' Heather scratched her curls. She had no idea why she was still trying to rationalise this, but she felt compelled. Just to stave off the fear. Just to stave off the thought that Steven might already be long gone. 'Maybe they like it here.'

'Right.'

'I don't know.'

The elm and sycamore along Topaz Avenue formed a heavy canopy pierced by harpoons of sunlight. With each overgrown, overflowing garden they passed through bands of fragrance: jasmine, sweet pea, lavender, gardenia, honeysuckle, and little impatient huddles of dark mint plants, brooding and plotting. Lawns grew three feet high, swaying their seeded tips in unkempt bravado. Orange-tip butterflies and yellow brimstones and Adonis blues chased through the hot currents. Somewhere, the church clock struck a time of its own devising – but the bells sounded muffled somehow and came in heavy, sluggish waves.

Heather studied the objects in her hands: a black digital watch, a gold-plated ring with a sliver of hexagonal jade, a string necklace whose pendant was made from a thick plastic bass guitar plectrum, a tie patterned with moons and planets, a blue-and-white striped sock. All Steven's, all left around the village for her to find. Now they were her talismans, as if their presence in her pocket would somehow draw her to him. And maybe it would.

A large black dog trotted up the pathway of a nearby cottage. A sign on the gate read: GOODBYE, SHILLINGS! The dog's glossy coat glistened in the afternoon glare.

'Hey, fellah,' said Heather. 'Where's your owners?'

The dog barked – twice, three times, four times. But the sound of the bark echoed from the other side of the village, diffuse among the buildings and trees.

'There's someone watching us,' Heather said later, glancing furtively over her shoulder.

'Who?' Antonia turned to follow Heather's eyeline.

'Don't.'

'Who is it?'

'That boy over there. A teenager, I think.'

'I can't see anyone.'

'Behind those bushes. Look.'

'You told me not to look.'

'He's been watching us for a while. Ever since the pub.'

'He's following us?'

'No. Just watching.'

'But we've been walking all over the place. How can he be watching us without following us?'

'You can't see him?'

Antonia squinted in the direction of Heather's surreptitious nod. 'Yeah. I think so. There's someone there. I can't make him out. Maybe it's a ghost?'

Heather shook her head. 'He's watching us. He knows we're here.'

'Are you sure it's not just a shadow?' said Antonia, shielding her eyes against the glare of the sun. 'The leaves of a bush or something. Or… or… it's just one of those electrical junction boxes, isn't it?'

'It's a person. I can see his face.'

'We could ask him for directions?'

'No.'

'Why not? He might know where Penfold Lane is.'

'No. Come on. We should keep walking.'

Turning left onto the narrow strip of Green Lane, they threaded between two columns of painted terraced cottages, garlanded with bunting and hanging baskets, and then out onto a short backstreet of happy thatched cottages and apple trees in full bloom. Whatever time of day this was now, the humidity seemed to be growing more oppressive by the moment. Heather sat down to rest, towelling off her face and neck with Steven's red T-shirt.

'This is crazy!' she said. 'How can we have been walking around a village this small and not be able to find an entire *street*? What the fuck's going on, Tonio?'

But then Antonia was laughing. Laughing, and pointing between Heather's legs. Laughing so hard she was doubled over.

Heather looked down. She was sitting on a metal street sign atop two stubby wooden posts. A black street sign with two words in raised white capitals.

And now she was laughing, too.

Penfold Lane.

51

Steven had been there once, for a time. Heather recognised his traces throughout 7 Penfold Lane: one of his shirts, draped over the banister; a pair of socks next to the bed; a dinosaur museum souvenir pen she knew he treasured; a couple of cans of cherryade in the fridge; a doodle of a smiling, curly-haired woman on a pad of paper beside the sofa. Relics of Steven which made him feel even more absent, like a lost civilisation.

There was no forwarding address, no clues as to his new whereabouts. Either he'd left in a hurry, or he'd now decided he wanted to remain elusive. Heather wondered if it was her fault... Steven had expected her to follow in a couple of weeks. After all, she was Heather McLagan – the woman who was obsessed by him, the woman who found it impossible to sit still. She'd last two, maybe three days, then she'd be cadging a ride from some poor sucker, and turn up at his house ringing on his doorbell before he'd even unpacked his underpants. And maybe at one point she'd intended to do exactly that. But time had slipped away from her, life had settled back down into its usual rhythm, and before she knew it, she'd neglected him for a whole six months. In the intervening weeks, Steven must've given up waiting. Or worse. Maybe, by the time she'd started hearing his voice over the radio, it was already too late to save him.

Either way, he wasn't here, and hadn't been for quite some time. No. 7 Penfold Lane was a dead end.

All the nervous energy, all the adrenaline which had flooded her system as she'd approached the front door, tentatively knocked, opened it a crack and called inside, '*Steven*,' was starting to dissipate. Her legs didn't feel too strong. She perched on the sofa and had a little cry.

Antonia sat next to her and put her long arm around her shoulders.

52

There was a man in one of the beds.

In a magnolia spare room at the back of 7 Penfold Lane, with sunlight streaming in between dusty orange curtains, she found him. It was a room she hadn't noticed on her first or second inspection of the house. She hadn't even realised there was anyone else there until now.

It wasn't Steven – or at least, she didn't think it was. A man in a bed with the covers pulled up to his middle. A teenager, or a young man. A man with no skin, or... no, it wasn't that. She couldn't look at him directly. This was the problem. Whenever she tried, he was gone... it was just an empty bed. An empty bed, clean and bright and unsullied. But she could see him from the corner of her eye, lying on his back, staring at the ceiling, arms by his sides. He was dark red, silhouetted by the brightness of the sunlight. No features that she could discern, but she could tell he was young. Shy, mild-mannered. Wouldn't hurt a fly.

She called out to him, asked him his name. His head turned in her direction but he didn't answer. He made no sound at all.

'Are you Steven?' she said, because although she knew he wasn't, there was no harm in asking.

The man didn't reply. His head was still tilted in her direction. Could he see her? Could he see anything?

Heather decided not to tell Antonia about the man. It'd be her secret. She didn't want a fuss, and she was too worn out to discuss it. And… and if she was really honest with herself, she didn't want to share. *She* had found this man, and that surely meant something. Finders keepers, losers weepers.

'My name's Heather,' she said slowly, as if introducing herself to an alien being, and feeling foolish even as she did so.

The man didn't respond. Heather gazed towards the far corner of the room, taking in as much detail as she could from her periphery. Neat hair or… or maybe no hair at all. Was he naked or just dressed in very neutral clothes? No, she was sure he was naked, at least the portion of him that was above the covers. She could sort of make out features now – he had a pleasant face, kind. Or maybe it was just her imagination.

Heather suddenly felt very tired. A big adrenaline comedown. She found she could hardly stand. Just a quick nap. Five minutes. Ten minutes, tops. Then she'd be back looking for Steven.

But in the meantime.

But in the meantime.

* * *

But in the meantime, she rolled back the sheets and climbed in next to the young man.

Forty winks, that was all. Just till this godawful fatigue went away.

'Forty winks, that's all,' she said. 'Just till I feel better.'

She linked fingers with the man. They lay side by side, gazing up at the magnolia ceiling till the sound of birdsong from outside drowned out all Heather's thoughts.

Heather stayed with the man for twenty years in that little house. His name was Christopher, though she wasn't sure how she knew, as he never spoke and they barely interacted. She must've seen his mail on top of the cabinet – the unpaid bills and unanswered chain letters, the Christmas card which arrived every year from the wild teenage girl he met long ago. He was a very old man, but also a very young man, but also… well, it was hard to explain, but Heather knew, and that was all that mattered.

They mostly lived separate lives, as they really had nothing in common. But that didn't seem to matter, it was enough that they were together. They still made time to have dinner together every evening, in that little bedroom at the back of the house, Christopher under the blankets and Heather on top, twiddling her toes while they watched TV. At least for the first few years. Then it became every two days, then every Friday; then they mostly forgot. But that didn't seem to matter either.

Heather was happy there. Or at least, she was content. Her own little cottage in a peaceful little village. The craziness of her youth, all that untapped potential, all those myriad possibilities, had funnelled down to this one outcome. A woman in a house with a man. But she was fine with that. She could've easily spent her life adrift, searching for something she'd never find – instead, she'd found something she'd never searched for. And that was okay. It was okay.

Eventually, Heather and Christopher married, and they stayed together for twenty years more, and twenty years after that. Heather grew old and Christopher remained exactly the same, a young-old man, a shadow in the corner of her eye like a flaw in her retina. But they never fell out of love.

Or…

Had they ever really been in love? Heather wasn't sure if she could even remember what love was. She knew she'd been in love with a boy once – a terribly tall and terribly handsome boy called Steven, who swamped her every conscious thought and made her body tingle when she thought about him. But that seemed so very long ago. Heather was an old lady now. She wore slippers and drank tea from delicate china cups and smelled of lavender. Her brown curly hair had gone white and flat: she put spiky pastel-coloured curlers in at night to make it keep its proper shape. And lipstick on her lips and rouge on her cheeks and a splash of perfume on her thin, wrinkled neck in the morning. Not that she ever saw anyone, but she liked to do it for herself.

Heather had been the name of a young person once. A wild young girl who did stupid things and never stopped talking. It was funny how, bit by bit, Heather had become a little old lady's name – one who'd forgotten how to be wild, once who hardly ever spoke at all. She never talked to Christopher and he never said anything back. She wasn't even sure if he was still in the house, or whether the occasional glimpses of him were now just her imagination. For all she knew, she was all alone, and had been for years.

The clock on the mantelpiece ticked day after day after day. Heather knew she would die soon. She felt it in her very core, like an egg in her middle preparing to hatch. It might not be this year or even next year. But she was certain she wouldn't see another twenty years inside this dusty old cottage. One day, after tidying up, she'd lie down on the living room carpet, close her eyes, and that would be that.

She put the kettle on and prepared another cup of tea.

There weren't many visitors to that little cottage, but one day a girl came to the door. She was maybe ten or eleven, and had dark brown hair, bright red shoes and the bluest eyes Heather had ever seen. As blue as glass. She handed Heather a piece of paper, which read: *The Mother, the Daughter and the Holy Ghost*. Heather folded in half with laughter at this very clever joke. She laughed until tears came from her eyes – although later, when she tried to remember, she couldn't think of what was funny about it. It was hardly a joke at all.

The girl said that Heather was very welcome to the village and everyone was happy she was there, and that they would like to give her a present. It was a ring, set with three sparkly stones – one green, one red and one clear white. As she didn't have a wedding ring, she was very pleased to receive this gift.

Heather hoped she would see more of the little girl, and maybe her family too – she was such a polite young thing.

But she never returned, and no one else came to visit in all the years she lived there.

Heather sat in a chair by her bedroom window and looked out over her garden and the fields beyond, watching the dead wander to and fro. She had a cushion for her back, a tartan shawl for her knees, and a cup of tea by her slippered feet.

Her garden was so overgrown these days. The lawn hadn't been mown in years, and the flower beds were a jungle of creepers and blooms, the whole cavalcade glowing brilliantly beneath the furnace sun. A smattering of ghosts lurked at the bottom of the garden, beneath the twin apple trees – one tree blossoming and the other fruiting – but the foliage was too dense for them to venture much further in than that.

Nothing had changed inside the cottage for sixty years, though. Her bedroom was exactly the same as the day she first saw it, all browns and olive greens and muted pastel shades. That floral wallpaper, bluebells repeating into infinity like a Victorian's fever dream. There were photographs of children in school uniform all along the shelf, and a portrait of Jesus with his neatly trimmed beard and long, silky mane. Were they her children and her grandchildren, or…? No, those pictures too were here when she'd arrived. Why had she never thought to change them, to take them down? All that time to fill, sixty long years, and it'd never occurred to her. Well, they were nice-looking kids, and anyway, they were the only company she had these days.

There had been a time when she'd found it impossible to sit still. She'd burst with energy from every pore. She was never going to grow up, she would stay young forever. She and Steven would spend their lives travelling the globe, causing mischief, outrunning everything. And she'd nearly found him, nearly caught up with him. But not quite; and she'd become distracted by the man in the house, by Christopher. Right in the middle of an adventure. And that was that, she'd spent the rest of her life there in that little cottage. It wasn't really what she'd hoped for, but it was what it was.

Sometimes she thought of Steven. Maybe she still loved him, somewhere deep down, in a way that she'd never loved Christopher. Where was Steven now? Had he outrun old age after all, and still roamed the globe exactly as she remembered him, or was he a little old man, bent in half and complaining about the weather and the youth of today? She couldn't imagine that at all. Perhaps he was dead and had gone to dust with the bugs and the mites and the spores.

Ah well, there was no way to know. And maybe it didn't matter anymore.

She'd watch TV later. She liked to watch TV. The gameshows were her favourite – she enjoyed seeing people younger and more energetic than herself, it reminded her of how she used to be. Popping balloons, getting covered in slime. So much chaos and mischief.

And then bed. Maybe Christopher would be there with her, on the other pillow, eyes fixed on the ceiling the way they always were, or maybe he was long gone. It was hard to be sure anymore.

It was hard to be certain if he had ever existed.

* * *

Footsteps creaked downstairs.

There was someone else in the house.

An intruder. Heather's heart raced – the first time she'd felt any real emotion, any real excitement, in decades. Maybe she wouldn't die peacefully and alone after all, maybe *this* was her moment – bludgeoned to death by some ne'er-do-well with a stocking pulled down over his face. A serial killer with a wickedly serrated blade. She watched the white slab of the bedroom door as the footsteps slowly ascended the stairs, creak by creak. There was a table lamp nearby that she could grab, use it to defend herself…

But no. She didn't have the energy or even the inclination. If this was the end, then let it be the end. Quickly, please, and without too much fuss.

The footsteps made their way along the landing and stopped outside her door. The sound of someone breathing.

A turn of the handle, and the door drifted open.

It wasn't a man after all, but a young woman. She was tall and broad-shouldered, with a brown face and big round eyes.

'Are you here to kill me?' said Heather. She realised it was the first time she'd spoken aloud in… months, probably. Maybe years. Her voice sounded so old, so dry and crackly. Even now it was easy to forget she was more than eighty.

The young woman seemed startled. 'No,' she said.

'Why are you here?'

'I've been looking all over for you.'

Heather recognised the woman. Really, *really* recognised her. She was so familiar that Heather should've instantly known who she was, but she couldn't *quite* place her. But this was the first time she'd seen a real, living person in more than half a century. Her memory was filled with the faces of the ghosts and the children in the photographs and the Jesus on her wall.

'Heather, are you okay?' the woman said.

So, this girl knows my name. A serial killer with a list, perhaps, bumping off all the old ladies around town (whichever town this was – the name had slipped from her memory). No, she had gentle eyes. Despite her height, she was hardly a threatening presence. Maybe she was an apparition? An angel come to guide her into the next life?

The angel grimaced awkwardly. 'Why are you acting so weird?' she said.

'I'm all right.' Heather shrugged noncommittally, staring blankly.

'I keep getting lost. This house is all wrong. Doors don't lead where you think they'll lead. It's built wrong. You can't get back to the room you just came from, you have to go the long way round. Even then, it doesn't make any sense.'

'It's a small house,' said Heather.

'Yeah, but it's like a maze.'

'What are you doing in my room?'

'Seriously, Heather, what's up with you today? You keep acting like we've never met before.'

'I know we've met, but… I can't remember you. I've been here sixty years.'

'*Sixty years?* That's it, I'm making an executive decision. We haven't found Steven, he's not here, we don't even know if he's still alive. I'm getting you out of Almanby while I still can.'

'Almanby?'

'You know we're still in Almanby, right?'

That was a word she hadn't heard since she was young. She hadn't even thought about it in so long that she almost doubted it was a real thing. The sound of it, the feel of it on her tongue, made her think of rainy autumn afternoons, colouring pictures on the floor of her childhood bedroom while her dusty wardrobe towered over her like an inscrutable alien guardian. *Why would I be in Almanby?* Everybody knew you weren't supposed to go there. Even children knew that. It didn't seem likely that she would be in Almanby, especially since she couldn't recall travelling there.

Except...

Except, maybe she could. A big bright stripe in her memory, a road trip. Three friends in a champagne car. Heather and Antonia and one other. And, for a little while, there was someone else in the car too. A bearded man, very angry. Spiky. With claws. Or... not claws, but a gun. But he was gone now, so that was all fixed.

There was a reason she'd come to Almanby. A pressing, urgent reason... one which made her sad when she thought about it. Utterly, hopelessly, irredeemably, awfully, achingly sad.

Steven.

Big tall beautiful Steven.

He was in Almanby. That's why they were here – to find Steven.

'Steven,' she said.

'Yeah,' Antonia replied.

'Where is he?'

'That's what I'm saying – we don't know. Heather, are you *sure* you're all right?'

Heather rubbed her bouncy brown curls. 'Of course I am. Sorry, Tonio. I don't know what came over me. It's a weird day.'

'You can say that again. Come on. Stay with me, don't wander off.'

53

'That's a nice ring,' said Antonia. 'It's new, isn't it? Where did you get it?'

The three gems sparkled in the magnesium sunlight – red, green and white, the colours of Christmas.

'I can't remember,' Heather shrugged. 'I suppose I must've found it.'

Antonia was all for dragging Heather home there and then, but Heather begged her for one last chance to find Steven. They'd come this far, they were so close, she could *feel* him nearby. Just five more minutes. Ten more minutes. A half hour. That's all. Then they could go. *Please, Tonio.*

She couldn't feel him, of course. She hadn't been aware of his presence for a while. As far as she knew, he really might be dead. If only they'd arrived a couple of hours sooner – if only they hadn't pulled over to help Daniel, if only she hadn't nagged them into stopping at the café, if only the car had lasted those final few miles into Almanby.

It was what it was, though, and there was nothing she could do now to change anything. But at what point would she admit defeat? At what point *could* she admit defeat? She was like a dog with a bone, after all – if she had her way, she'd be searching for

Steven forever, like the tragic heroine from some nineteenth-century novel. And Heather was very good at getting her way.

Besides… would Almanby even let them leave?

With their one clue to his whereabouts now exhausted, it was time for a more direct approach. Almost spontaneously, they began knocking on doors, hollering through letterboxes, Heather taking the even side of Penfold Lane and Antonia the odds. If they weren't going to bump into anyone in the street, they'd root out someone to ask.

By the time they'd turned onto Green Lane and tried a further eight, ten, fifteen houses each, they petered out. Not a single person had opened their door, not a solitary human had emerged to see what all the racket was about. There were no dogs roused nor children calling for a parent to come. The place was as still as when they'd started.

'Maybe they're all at church?' said Antonia.

'It's not Sunday.'

'Isn't it? What day is it?'

'I can't remember. But I'm pretty sure it's not Sunday.'

They wandered up the path of the nearest cottage, 48 Green Lane, between the rose bushes and hollyhocks. Heather cupped her face to the living room window.

'No one home,' she said.

Antonia tried the door handle. 'It's open.'

'Antonia Coleridge! That's trespassing!'

'Only if we're caught,' Antonia shrugged.

Heather winked at her. 'I like your style. I should make you an honorary Chicken Club member.'

* * *

The smell of garlic, tomato, balsamic vinegar, olive oil and cucumber wafted through on the hot air, like the salad Antonia's middle-class Aunt Carole used to make whenever they'd visit. White wine for the grown-ups, unpalatable elderflower cordial for the kids. And that same rose potpourri Antonia would sometimes nibble, as if *this time* it would taste how it smelled and not bitter like soap. And just through there, in the living room – that's where she'd found Uncle Warren in his bright red tracksuit, stretched out on the sofa, the veins in his neck and the backs of his hands all purple and distended.

But, of course, it was a different house with a different living room and a different sofa.

Somewhere, a grandfather clock said *tock – tock – tock – tock – tock*.

The cottage was deserted, that much was certain. Just like, they suspected, all the other cottages in the street, and all the other cottages in all the other streets of Almanby. But it was like the people had simply upped and left. The drawers were still full of clothes. Two rows of shoes sat, like expectant puppies, in the hallway by the door. On the dining room table, cutlery and dishes were set out for dinner – two places, waiting for a husband and wife who were no longer there and a meal that was never cooked. An empty vase sat in between.

On the wall of the living room was a framed photograph from Victorian times. It showed Almanby village square, just outside the Green Anne pub, with lots of men in hats and barefoot urchins gathering for a spectacle. As Heather and Antonia leaned closer, they were able to make out a rough wooden scaffold on the far side of the square. Three bodies hung from the scaffold, silhouetted black against an ocean-white sky.

'Oh fuck,' said Heather, backing away. 'What kind of sick fucko has something like *that* on their wall?'

'It's certainly a statement.'

'It's fucked up.'

Antonia studied the bottom of the photograph. Inscribed into the right-hand corner in tiny lettering were three names: *Archibald Swain, Harry Robinson and Lily Lewis.*

And below that: *GREEN ANNE DAY, MAY 2, 1884.*

Together, Antonia and Heather explored 48 Green Lane. They moved from room to room – the kitchen, the living room, the dining room, the end room, the hallway, the spare room. Just like 7 Penfold Lane, nothing was where it ought to be. Doors led to different rooms than they had on previous occasions… the living room connected to the kitchen which connected to the spare room which connected to the dining room which connected back to the kitchen through the door which had just been the living room door only moments before. Either the place was changing around them, continuously shuffling like pack of cards, or… it was just too damn hard to think straight. Like Almanby was inside their heads, nestled between their brains and their skulls. Were they just forgetting, getting confused, losing themselves?

'Come on, we should get out of here before we get stuck forever,' said Antonia at last, her voice hushed.

'Wait, before we go,' Heather said, 'let's check the freezer for ice cream.' And then, for good measure, she chanted under her breath, 'Ice cream! Ice cream! Ice cream! Ice cream!'

Having found the kitchen again, they discovered that the freezer door was iced shut. A sudden intensity overtook Heather and she tugged and tugged and tugged at the door, till it popped open and she fell backwards onto the tiles. Inside, the freezer looked like a smoker's arteries, clogged and furred with years' worth of ice – but right in the middle of the top cabinet sat a carton of Victor Pendry's Luxury Vanilla Ice Cream.

'Ice cream!' cried Heather, and set about freeing the carton, her face stretched into a determined scowl which grew ruddier by the second. 'Ice cream!' she repeated as the carton finally began to work loose.

When at last the carton popped free of the ice, she tumbled back onto the floor for a second time, then hungrily prised off the lid – only to find the container completely, mockingly empty.

'Fuck!' she said, throwing it across the kitchen. 'What kind of shit garbage bollock weasel washes out an empty carton and puts it back in the freezer? Fuck! Fuck it all to hell! Bollocks!'

She retreated to the corner of the room and sat on the tiles with her face in her hands.

Antonia opened the refrigerator door. Inside were three empty milk bottles, several empty sauce bottles, an empty jar of olives, an empty jar of mango chutney, two empty jam jars, an empty bottle of Stout's Authentic Dandelion

& Burdock, two empty egg boxes and an empty tub of Best Margarine.

She crossed to the pantry on the opposite side of the room, in which were empty cereal packets, empty boxes of rice and pasta, empty bags of sugar, flour and cocoa, and a whole array of empty spice jars. She shook a can of chopped tomatoes – it too was light and contained nothing but air.

'The food's gone,' she said. 'It wasn't eaten. No one opened any of the cans. These boxes are still sealed. It all disappeared. From inside the packets. The people have disappeared and the food's disappeared.'

54

A sign outside the little brick building said: ALMANBY PRIMARY SCHOOL.

Tied to the railings outside the school, a yellow scarf fluttered limply in the soupy summer breezes.

'He's here!' Heather cried, grabbing Antonia's wrists. 'He's in here! Of course he is! I'm such a fuckwit!'

'This is something we always talked about,' said Heather breathlessly, as they climbed in through a half-open window and plopped down into the main school corridor. 'Setting up a base in an abandoned primary school. Like, as Chicken Club HQ, or just as a stronghold if the dead people got too much.'

'Why?'

Heather shrugged. 'It'd be cool. We liked the aesthetics of it, disused school, brilliant. *Steven!*' she called. '*Steven! I'm here! I found you!*'

They searched the kitchen, the offices, the little assembly hall and the solitary classroom, but Steven wasn't here either.

He *had* been here – a pair of his favourite trainers sat by the wastepaper basket – but there was no sign of him now.

'Bollocks to it,' Heather said, slumping down in one of the tiny plywood chairs. 'Bollocks to all of it.'

'He's got to be in Almanby somewhere,' said Antonia.

'Does he?'

'I mean… we haven't looked everywhere yet. I'm sure he'll turn up.'

On the blackboard, in big chalk letters, was written: THE BEAUTIFUL DRUMMER BOY. It was underlined twice, but beneath that there was a blank space, as if everyone had deserted mid-lesson.

A trapped peacock butterfly flapped at the glass. Heather pulled the window down halfway till it bobbed out into the sunshine. But Heather and Antonia liked it where they were. They enjoyed the coolness of the classroom – Heather pulled up her shirt and lay on the floor to absorb as much of it as she could.

'Maybe we *should* just go home,' she said.

'I'd be down with that.'

'We don't need boys to make us happy. *You've* got the right idea. Whatever Steven's doing here, he doesn't need me chasing round after him like a lost puppy.'

'Right.'

'I sat over there,' said Heather, lazily extending an arm towards the back right-hand corner of the room.

'You didn't go to school in Almanby,' Antonia said.

'Yeah, but in my classroom. I sat over there. With the cool kids, of course, because I was a cool kid.'

'I sat here.' Antonia perched her lanky frame on a chair towards the middle of the front row.

'Teacher's pet?'

'I just didn't want to be in among all the other kids. I didn't like them and they didn't like me, so it suited everyone.' Antonia levered the desk open. Inside was a faded yellow exercise book. She reached in and opened it to the first page.

'*Helen Crowther. Mathematics. Spring term, 1972.*'

'Wow.' Heather sat up. 'That's how long this place has been abandoned?'

'Wait,' said Antonia, opening a neighbouring desk and producing two more exercise books. '*Simon Harris. Geography. Autumn term, 1983. Simon Harris. Mathematics. Autumn term, 1984.*'

Heather climbed to her feet and wandered over to the nearest desk. Inside she found a battered pink exercise book, which she also flipped open. '*Spring term, 1958. Almanby School. Jill Cooper. History. King Henry was a bad king called Henry the Eighth. He had six wives and killed two of them, although the other four were all right. He also had one daughter, who he named Elizabeth. She was Elizabeth the first, Queen of England, although not when she was a baby. When she was a baby, she was just a baby.*'

'There are books from all over,' said Antonia. 'Like all the lessons were happening all at once.' She selected a desk at random and plucked out the exercise book. '*Karen Hills. Summer term, 1977. English. The story of Green Anne. Green Anne has been a part of our village for a long time, from back when she was called Green Annis. Sometimes she was just called Annis the Egesgrime* – the teacher has crossed that sentence out. *Green Annis lives under the ground. She comes out at night and looks for children to steal away from their beds. Once she stole my friend Kevin, though my mummy said he just died. Some people say Annis isn't real, but I think she is. She has lived here since medieval times. People used to be sacrificed to fill up her tummy, but this stopped for World War One because the young men had to go off to fight in the Great War, and there have been no sacrifices for sixty-three years. Steven says that she must be very hungry and he made a scary face, but Sally says that Steven is a liar.'*

'This village is fucked up,' said Heather.

'Yeah.'

'What is all this Green Anne shit? Hanging people and eating children and all that crap – what a load of creepy old wank.'

'My sentiments exactly.'

'Come on – one last look for Steven, then we'll bugger off home.'

55

'If we were Holmes and Watson,' said Antonia, kicking a little white pebble down the street, 'who would be who?'

'Which of us is cleverer?' said Heather.

'I don't know, that's not something I've ever really thought about.'

'Which of us is more likely to spend the day off our face on opium, giggling at nothing?' said Heather.

'Definitely you.'

'All right, I'll be Holmes, you can be Watson.'

'Great,' said Antonia, 'I've always wanted to be a sidekick.'

'The Adventure of the Missing Steven. How hard can it be to solve a mystery?'

'You just need the right attitude,' said Antonia. 'Go at it with confidence, it'll be a doddle.'

'Right. How would Sherlock Holmes do this?'

'You tell me, you're Sherlock Holmes.'

'Good point,' said Heather. 'Right, well, I'd… I'd look for clues. But not obvious ones, like fingerprints and shit, and I don't know, secret tape recordings. I'd look for traces of Steven. Evidence that he'd been there.'

'Like, fingerprints?'

'No. *Not* like fingerprints. I don't have any powder for a start.'

'So, footprints?'

'I don't know what his footprints look like, I haven't memorised Steven's shoes. But, something unique to Steven.'

'Like fingerprints.'

'Something *else* unique to him. Jeez, Tonio, no wonder you're single.'

'Like a jumper? Or a scarf.'

'He wouldn't be wearing those, would he?'

'Good point – this is why you're Sherlock Holmes.'

'And his other clothes are probably still on him, unless he's naked.' She paused for a moment to picture Steven naked, striding across the Almanby countryside. 'No, listen, we're thinking about this the wrong way. We have to, like, you know, use… I don't know what to call it.'

'Magnets?'

'No… Like, deductive reasoning. We don't follow clues, we don't waste time *looking* for him, we work out where he is and then just go there. Make sense?'

'All right, I think so.'

'So, if all the people who live here are gone but Steven's still here, where would he be?'

'I don't know.'

'Think about it. If everyone disappeared, but he didn't, he was the only one, where would he be?'

'Somewhere the other people weren't when they disappeared,' said Antonia.

'Right. So, not in any of the houses. Not in the shops, not in the pub, not in the school. Somewhere else.'

They wandered along Green Lane until it became Parson's Lane, which turned left into Foxhunter Drive, which became

Gorsefield Road, which then veered right onto Elderborn Lane. They crunched through fallen acorns.

'Actually,' said Heather, 'Steven would be Sherlock Holmes. I'd be Watson, you'd be Lestrade.'

'Thanks.'

'Rachel would be Moriarty, for sure.'

'How can Steven be Sherlock Holmes, if that's who we're looking for?'

Heather shrugged. 'I don't make the rules.'

'Right, that settles it, it's my turn to be Sherlock Holmes. If you've declared yourself Watson, then I claim Holmes.'

'Fine, I don't care. You solve it.'

'All right. If it's somewhere that's not a house or a pub or a shop, I think we're looking at a phone box or a bus shelter.'

'You reckon Steven might be in a phone box?'

'Yeah. Or a bus shelter.'

'Except, they all disappeared before he got here.'

'Probably.'

'Yeah, probably. I guess we don't even know that for sure.'

Almanby wound round now like a cowlick, and they found themselves in a part of the village they hadn't been yet, a series of intertwining black tarmac footpaths that ran between overgrown privet bushes and overhanging laburnum trees, somehow still damp with dew under the blazing afternoon sun. The wetness refreshed them as they pushed their way through the foliage, and Heather sucked it off the backs of her wrists and hands, despite the greenfly. The pair could occasionally glimpse the church above them now on the top of the hill, and they tried to work their way towards it whenever the paths allowed.

'*A weird world, twisted and curled, and never a nugget of sound,*' Heather sang to her own invented tune, skipping slightly on a lilt.

Something disturbed a peppering of crows, and they took off, lazy and directionless. Every now and then, a crow would blip huge in the sky, just for a moment, filling the whole span of the firmament as if magnified by an invisible lens. Thunder rumbled in the near-cloudless sky... or was it the sound of the molecules in Antonia's body shifting? Was she gradually becoming something else? Some post-Antonia thing? She wouldn't die here, just evolve into something new: a dinosaur or a Dracula, or the thing which lived behind her childhood wardrobe with its imagined tentacles and spider-legs. That'd be something to look forward to: watching over her younger self while she slept, keeping her safe from harm. That timid, anxious, depressive child, nails and long hair chewed. Antonia was suddenly overwhelmed by a feeling of protectiveness towards child-Antonia. She wanted desperately to go back, steer her in a different direction, save her from all this. Keep her in a bubble, keep her seven forever. But how would that be possible? How can you stay seven forever?

'Can we walk arm in arm?' said Antonia. 'Just for a bit.'

'All right.'

'I don't mean in a romantic way, just...'

'I don't mind, whatever you want.'

Antonia and Heather walked arm in arm. Just for a bit.

'You know,' said Heather, a bit later, her face turning suddenly serious, 'we're still being watched.'

Antonia turned to scrutinise the swaying poplars and imperious meadow grass. 'I can't see anyone.'

They stopped and stood shoulder to shoulder, gazing back along the lane.

'Same person?' said Antonia.

'Yeah,' Heather said. 'There he is.' She pointed off to the side, where a man peered at them from behind the trunk of a tree, half hidden. The sun was behind him and his face was obscured.

It was a young man with a kindly face, or... maybe it was an old man. It was difficult to tell at this distance.

'He's creeping me out.'

'I think I know him,' said Heather.

'Seriously?'

'Yeah. I know him, I'm sure I know him.'

'Who is he?'

Heather shook her head. 'Ever forgotten a close friend? Like, your best friend in the whole world. You're walking along, and suddenly you realise there's someone you're really close to, someone you know well enough that they're practically the other half of you – you can say anything to them, be yourself completely around them. And I'm racking my brains, and I just can't remember them.'

'No. No, I never have.'

'Fuck, who is it?' Heather waved, but the man didn't wave back.

'He's creeping me out,' said Antonia.

'Yeah, me too.'

Heather took Antonia's hand and led her on down the street.

At the bottom of Elderborn Lane they turned right onto a narrow footpath between green-stained rose trellises. Heather broke into a run here, forcing Antonia to sprint to catch up. And then – unexpectedly – they were back on Tuppence Lane with its burly sycamore and chestnut trees stinking sweetly in the hot air.

Glancing over her shoulder, Heather jogged to a halt.

'Have we lost him?' said Antonia.

Heather shook her head.

'How can he still be there?'

'Look.'

Antonia followed the line of Heather's pointing finger – and right there, watching them from behind the trunk of a tree, was the same man.

'*How can he still be there?*'

'His name's Christopher,' said Heather. 'I knew him a long time ago. And...' She trailed off. Like the hamster still running on its wheel in her parents' attic, there he was, exactly the same as he'd always been.

Or had she dreamed him?

The time she snuck into his house and climbed into bed with him, and neither of them said a word.

Or—

No, she'd snuck into his house and slept in his spare room while he made tea and toast downstairs, completely unaware of her presence.

Or—

No, it wasn't that. It wasn't that at all. He was her special friend. They did dares and kissed secretly in the woods and ran home for sex when it all got too much.

Or—

Or was that someone else?

And now everything was still and quiet. Just the singing of the birds and the discontented shuffling of the phantoms in their black suits.

Leaning close to Heather's ear, Antonia said sleepily, as if imparting a great secret, 'I'm Porthos, you're Aramis and Rachel is Athos.' Then she repeated a second later, 'I'm Porthos, you're Aramis and Rachel is Athos. We're the three musketeers. We're a team. You know? We're tight.' She glanced around with a frown. 'Where is Rachel?'

'Let's keep moving, yeah?' said Heather.

'Steven is the King of France. We're on a secret mission to rescue him from the clutches of… who's the bad guy?'

'Keep walking.'

'He has an arm made of gold,' said Antonia, 'and he's been kidnapped by bandits led by the wicked count… I can't remember the count's name. It's a French name. They're holding the king prisoner, tied to a chair, and we have to rescue him, before… well, as soon as we can. Sooner, if we can.'

All of sudden, Antonia's legs gave way, as if the verve and glucose had drained right out of her blood and down into Almanby's soil. Her energy, her spirit, her life force. She slumped against the trunk of the nearest tree. 'The air's so thick,' she said. 'It's hard to breathe it in.'

'Keep moving, Tone!'

'In out, in out, in out, all the time, all day. It's so much work. I need to rest.'

Heather returned to her and took both her hands. 'Keep going, Toni. Good girl.' She prised Antonia off the tree and ushered her on down Tuppence Lane. The road was strewn with acorns, browning under a turquoise sky, and they crunched underfoot.

Something bright issued from a side track and onto Tuppence Lane, a hundred yards ahead. A red car, flaring like sodium. It parked across the road, its flank to the two women.

Heather shielded her eyes but couldn't make out anyone inside. She wondered whether to run. She could make it back to the footpath and lose herself among all the overgrown gardens of Almanby, providing the ghosts didn't get her. But Antonia couldn't run, and now that she thought about it, Heather felt pretty bad herself. She was too hot, too thirsty, her blood sugar was low (ice cream). Her injured right arm was cramping up. She didn't dare look at it.

The shell of the car cracked a little, then the driver's-side door opened and a small wiry figure stepped out.

'Hello Daniel,' said Heather.

56

'What happens to me?' said Rachel as Oscar hunted through his cluttered wardrobe. Shirts and trousers and jackets in muted colours. Bric-a-brac. A glimpse of a colourful mask, like a harlequin mask. Rachel briefly imagined an annual Almanby fancy dress ball, with its empty-eyed occupants glumly going through the motions, no idea what they were supposed to be feeling or why, indeed, any of this was happening. The scant few remaining citizens milling aimlessly, those that Almanby had allowed to continue as people-shaped beings, trying to fill their days from the vaguest of memories. Birthdays, Christmases, the occasional vestigial wedding, its clueless participants lined up and going through some approximation of the ceremony.

No, Oscar knew what was going on. Whatever he was now, he hadn't lost that much of his humanity. She studied his back as he rummaged with unwavering concentration.

'After this, what happens?' she repeated.

'You go home.'

'You know what I mean. When I need it again.'

Oscar found what he was looking for. He pulled a long gun from the back of the wardrobe – more sophisticated than Daniel's, but still obviously homemade. A backboard which looked like it'd been fashioned from the body of an electric guitar whittled down into a gun shape, several lengths of copper piping, two large sticky batteries, all manner of fiddly circuitry and soldering.

A sick feeling began to well up from the base of Rachel's belly. She'd held this nasty thing before – too many times before. Paulette, Prithpal, Sandy, John, April, Greg, Helen, Jess... she'd lost count of how many. An entire fifty per cent of the fucking Chicken Club. They'd survived every one of those stupid stunts, every one of Heather's outrageous dares, every foolhardy close encounter with the ghosts, inches from death – but they couldn't survive Rachel's innocent little trips to Almanby. No one had suspected a thing, not a single one of the poor bastards. None of them had cottoned on to Rachel's increasingly nervous behaviour, questioned why they'd come all the way to Almanby just to deliver a box with some random piece of tat in it. They'd simply gone along with whatever she said, such were her powers of persuasion. She'd waited for a quiet moment when their backs were turned, and—

Most of them had no idea. Most of them. She could still hear Sandy's howls. It took a second shot to finish her off – then Rachel emptied her guts behind a tree while Sandy's body was absorbed into the sod.

She hated it, she hated herself, and she hated Almanby for making her do it. It was perfectly capable of absorbing living people; but that was a slow process, it took a long time, and there was something about the trauma of a violent death it thrived on, the sacrifice. And she was sure it feasted on her own misery, too.

Rachel knew, of course, that if she had any honour she'd give up her own life before murdering so many of her friends. She'd hang herself from the rafters, or just go cold turkey and fade away like Sam had. But she had no honour. She had no spine and no moral fibre. And so she was locked into this grim ritual, ferrying her pals one by one – or in groups of twos and threes, depending on who Almanby demanded – to meet their final end, till all she had left were two friends.

The last two. The two best friends she'd ever had. Heather and Antonia. Two of the only friends she actually cared about, beyond what she could get from them. Beyond all the wheeler-dealing and reciprocated favours. Heather and Antonia were her actual *mates*.

This time would be the hardest.

'I want proof,' she said, at last.

Oscar closed and locked the wardrobe door and headed for the landing.

She followed him out. 'I want proof. I want to see for myself.'

'You don't normally ask for proof.'

'Well, this time I am. I need to know for sure that it's Heather and Toni that Almanby has asked for. I need to see their names.'

'Why do you doubt it?'

'They're the last friends I have.'

'Then who else is it going to be?'

'I can't do it,' Rachel said to Oscar's back. He stood in the middle of the living room now, his stance completely neutral. Was he looking at something on the far wall, or was he just… standing?

'I can't do it,' she repeated. 'I don't have the strength. I'm too ill.'

'You're not ill.'

'You know what I mean. I'm weak. I won't last long enough. Oscar.' She took him by the shoulders, spun him around and pushed him against the wall. 'Please.' She began to unbutton his shirt. He batted her hands away.

'When the job's done,' he said.

'I'm tired, Oscar. My bones feel like chalk.' She'd crumble to dust before the day was out. The pain, the sickness, the awful, desperate longing would be dust and she would be dust and all her problems and worries and preoccupations would be dust.

Oscar made an attempt to push past her but she forced him back against the wall and once more began to unbutton his shirt. Again he pushed her hands away.

'Fuck you, Oscar! What do you expect from me?'

He stared at her with his big unblinking, unnerving eyes.

'I'll die before I can do a single thing,' she said. 'I have to find them. I won't get a hundred yards. Then what? Tell me. Then what?'

Oscar thought for a moment, his eyes staring right through her.

Then he started to unbutton his shirt.

57

'*Where is it?*'

Heather crashed to the tarmac, Daniel's hand around her throat, his knife pressed against the soft triangle under her chin.

'Where's what?'

'You know what.'

'I threw it in a lake.' Heather shrugged with a contented smile, as if this was a perfectly normal conversation on a completely normal day.

'Why the fuck did you do that?'

'Because you wanted it. You looked so earnest rummaging through that stack of hay bales, I couldn't bear it. So I threw it in a lake and watched it go all the way to the bottom.'

'Who sent you?'

'I'm not telling you that.'

'You want me to slice you open?'

'Fine. It was Robert.'

'Robert?'

'Yeah. Robert sent me. I'm working for Robert, okay? Happy now?'

Daniel looked baffled. 'Who's Robert?'

'Robert Watson. Tall, curly hair, nice smile. Very cool guy, you wouldn't know him. Sagittarius. Keeps chickens.'

'Are you fucking with me?'

'Of course I'm fucking with you.' She reached into her jacket pocket and produced the small green rectangle of circuitry. Daniel snatched it from her fingertips and released her.

'I could've killed you.'

'Nah,' Heather chortled, dusting herself off and clambering to her feet. 'You wouldn't hurt me.'

'Don't count on it, I still might.'

'Anyway, if you must know, Steven sent us. Steven Cook.'

'That's not possible,' said Daniel.

'How do *you* know?'

'Because Steven Cook sent me.'

'*You know Steven?*' Her pain and sickness suddenly relegated to a distant consideration, she jumped and skipped. 'Why didn't you tell me?'

'Because it's none of your business.'

'It's Steven, of course it's my business. Hey, this might mean we're on the same side.'

'I doubt it.'

'Come on, what's the deal? Tell me all about it. You know where Steven is, right? How is he? Did he mention me? What's the circuit for? Come on, Daniel, tell me. I need you to tell me everything you know. What did he say? Where is he? Is he okay? Did he mention me? What did he say?' Heather suddenly wrapped her arms around Daniel and gave him the biggest squeeze she could muster. An involuntary gasp escaped into the sweltering afternoon.

'I'm not going to tell you anything.' He prised her off.

'Well, in that case I shall make it my mission to find out.'

'If you really want to get yourself killed, that's an excellent idea.'

'I'm so happy to see you again!'

'Don't be.'

'How did you end up with the car?'

'Stop with the questions! Jesus. I'd forgotten how irritating you are.'

'I'm endearing. Irritating is a different thing. So, how did you end up with the car, Dan?'

'I killed the people and took it.'

Heather stopped and squinted at him. 'No you didn't.'

'They wanted to stop me reaching Almanby, so I killed them.'

'I don't believe you.'

'How else do you think I got it?'

'I don't know. You punched them?'

'I punched them?'

'Why would you kill them?'

'Why would I punch them?'

'Because you're really a puppy dog. Anyway,' she said, poking a finger towards the homemade gun in his hand, 'I still don't think that thing even really works.'

58

Antonia dragged her heels till Heather and Daniel were a little way ahead…

…and then a long way ahead…

…and then around the next corner…

…and then gone.

Not once did Heather look back. She probably wouldn't realise Antonia was missing for hours, if she noticed at all.

Just like that, Antonia was all alone in Almanby. She came to a stop in the middle of the street and gazed around at the blank-eyed cottages and blank-eyed ghosts.

She put her hands in her pockets. She peered down at her shoes and studied the billion tiny pebbles encrusted into the tarmac, like seeing detail in a dream. Exactly the same tiny black pebbles and exactly the same worn grey tarmac as anywhere else. The same dust motes, the same microscopic spiders, the same purpling dandelion stalks and misshapen discs of lichen – but this was Almanby. And now she was here too. The Almanby version of Antonia. She was becoming her own reflection.

Unlike Heather or Rachel, she had no real reason to be here – no one to visit and nowhere in particular to go. Her lack of assertiveness had come back to bite her: glorified chauffeur, all because she was too much of a pushover to say no.

At least while she was spending quality one-on-one time with Heather, this whole ordeal had been worth it, and she could actually say she was having a good time. They'd built up a rapport, an actual friendship. But now Heather had abandoned her in favour of the local homicidal maniac, all that remained was a heavy, sick feeling in the bottom of her stomach; plus the general sense of mounting doom which Heather's company had been quietly staving off for the last few hours.

This, she realised, was the Heather she'd spent all these years pining after – one moment absolutely and positively done with the gun-toting lunatic, the next all over him again; then the next moment appalled and horrified by his actions, and the next clinging to his every word like a groupie. It was all very well falling in love with a wild, quirky girl, but then you had to put up with the wild, quirky girl. Antonia had never wanted to *tame* Heather, but neither had she expected her to be quite so rudderless. Quite so inconsistent. Every time she thought she'd found the lucid and reasonable Heather under all her impetuous, impulsive, crazy-eyed layers, the Heather with whom she could hold a deep and sensitive conversation – *bang*, the silly version was off again, larking around with all the self-control of a toddler undergoing an out-of-body experience. Maybe Rachel was right, maybe Antonia would eventually find Heather annoying. Maybe everyone else found Heather annoying too, and Antonia was the one cow-eyed sucker still mooning after her, obliviously worshipping the resident pillock.

That wasn't how things were supposed to pan out at all.

* * *

There was a handful of loose change in Antonia's pocket. On the off chance she found a shop, she could at least treat herself to an ice cream or a lemonade. Wouldn't that be ironic if she reached ice cream before Heather did? And doubly ironic if she then bought the last ice cream in the shop. Frankly, it'd serve Heather right. Right now, though, Antonia would give all the teeth she had for a can of ice-cold ginger beer and a packet of smoky bacon crisps (one of the few remaining vestiges of her meat-eating days). She opened her palm and counted coins as bright as stars: £4.57. White giant fifty-pence coins and little red dwarf pennies and a solitary pound as yellow as the sun, all flickering and flashing and winking in the glare.

She strolled along Cavershaw Road and down onto higgledy-piggledy Chancel Lane, where cedars stretched their yawning limbs across the road. Despite everything, despite the stress of her situation, Antonia actually hadn't felt this relaxed in a long time. She was normally so possessed with things to do: booking and publicising her stand-up shows; writing new material; working on the little monthly black-and-white satirical comic book, *The Rhubarb Times*, which she handmade and secretly distributed around the area; daydreaming about Heather and cooking up schemes to interact with her, most of which came to nothing. And then there were her neighbours – the dog on one side and Mr McKinnon drilling and hammering and mowing on the other – teaming up to subject her to constant sleep deprivation... to the extent that sometimes she really did believe she might be a prisoner undergoing some form of advanced psychological torture. One day, she'd find Mr McKinnon in her bedroom, dressed in a black uniform with black leather gloves, threatening to do something unspeakable with a length of rubber hose.

Now, though, she had nothing to do and nowhere to go, and she felt pleasantly drowsy, despite the danger she knew she must be in. She'd find a patch of lawn to lie down on and treat herself to a nap in a welcoming pool of sunlight – except there were still ghosts dotted around, milling discontentedly and looking for a fight: several behind the cedars, one or two visible in gardens along the street, and a couple out in the open hovering by the big red hexagonal pillar box as if waiting to accost the postman. And then there was Almanby itself. She felt so sluggish. It was having an effect on her for sure, like radiation poisoning. If she stopped moving for too long, who knew what might happen?

So she circled around the village, idly trying to orient herself. No matter which way she turned, she kept ending up back on Chancel Lane with its cedar trees and its hexagonal pillar box. This place was more intricate than she'd imagined, like a bucolic Escher labyrinth. Like 7 Penfold Lane and 48 Green Lane. She briefly considered leaving a trail of pebbles, but her brain was foggy and she couldn't quite pinpoint what that would achieve – but she did find a piece of sapphire-blue bottle glass in the gutter, washed smooth by some distant ocean. She licked saliva onto her thumb, wiped away the dullness from the glass, and gazed through it at the clouds, all blue and crinkled.

* * *

She encountered the same streets, time and again, but couldn't make them connect in her mind. Lavender Lane was memorable for the maypole in someone's garden (as well as all the lavender), and she knew that a narrow shortcut at the bottom of Lavender Lane led through to Lyon Avenue which in turn led back onto Green Lane. But the third time she ended up on Lavender Lane, she couldn't find either Lyon Avenue or Green Lane at all. So maybe she was wrong, maybe there was another step before that, but she had no idea now what it might be. And each time she thought she was making progress, each time she seemed to be about to stumble upon a new part of the village, there she was back on Lavender Lane or issuing down a side-alley and onto Lyon Avenue. Almanby was much bigger than it'd seemed from the outside – for a start, she hadn't been able to find the village square with the war memorial a second time, and she was damned if she could fathom out how to get there.

On Gorsefield Road, she spotted a secluded footpath between the walls of two houses. At the bottom of the footpath there appeared to be a wide meadow of tall grass. Tied to the gate at the far end of the footpath with a length of twine bobbed a perfect lime-green balloon.

Just like the childhood balloon Heather had described. The rays of the sun caught it side-on and illuminated it like a beacon.

Antonia pictured herself presenting the balloon to Heather. She imagined Heather skipping round in circles, her face exploding with joy, all smiles and delighted chortles. This, she decided, would be her mission. She would collect the balloon, find Heather, and distract her from Daniel's toxic presence. Win her back with something beautiful.

As she approached the gate at the far end of the footpath, she realised the balloon wasn't tied to it at all, but was floating a little way beyond, its twine trailing in the grass. And just as this thought crossed her mind, a hot breeze took the balloon and carried it further into the ocean of green.

Antonia clambered over the gate and waded out after the balloon. Poppies came up to her middle. The balloon skipped and danced across the surface, and Antonia ploughed on undeterred, swinging her arms as she trudged through the grass, leaving it flattened in her wake.

The meadow stretched out on every side, as far as the eye could see, until Antonia's entire field of vision was grass and sky and poppies and the solitary balloon and a creosoted-black tumbledown barn lying along the top of the hill like an ancient reptile's dried-out husk.

On

and on

the balloon led her

until it brushed against a protruding teasel

and popped.

So that was that. Once again, Antonia was left all alone. She was nearly at the barn now, at the top of the incline. Behind her, at the foot of the meadow, she could see the whole of Almanby. From this vantage point, it all made perfect sense: there was the maypole and the red pillar box and a red telephone box and the duck pond and the village square with the war memorial. Just like the map in the front of those twee Milly Molly Mandy books she'd loved as a child. And there, right in the centre, like a spider in a web, was Almanby church.

Antonia realised she wasn't alone. A half-dozen ghosts were already making their way across the meadow towards her. One carried a silver golf club which glinted like a lightsaber in the sun. She backed towards the barn, wondering whether to hide and wait till the ghosts dispersed again, or make a run for it and duck around them. Theoretically, she should be able to outrun them, but many people had discovered to their cost how easy it was to become hemmed in, or simply grabbed or struck on the way past. Like crocodiles, ghosts could occasionally muster surprising bursts of speed when they wanted to.

She circled around to the back of the barn in search of an entrance, or at least a gap in the wall large enough for her to squeeze through. All around its base grew pineapple weed and ragwort and ribwort and nettly yellow archangel, and acres of groundsel and dock plants. The terrain here was thick with grasshoppers, and they fizzed and chirruped and exploded away from her with every step.

'Toni!' called a voice from inside the barn. It sounded a little like Heather and a little like Rachel and a little like someone else achingly familiar, yet she couldn't put her finger on who.

'Who is it?' she called back.

'Quickly!' the voice replied.

On the far side of the barn, in the blue-brown rectangle of its shadow, another couple of ghosts were lurking, much closer than the rest. Two very prim-looking middle-aged women. One carried a stout length of branch and the other a rusty butcher's hook. And here too was a door, standing open a crack – just enough for Antonia to squeeze through sideways before the ghosts could reach her. She pulled it closed behind her.

The barn was dark and hot inside and smelled of fermenting soil and old straw. Far from the cavernous space she'd been expecting, the place was poky and seemed to comprise a series of small rooms built on several levels. She wound her way through the rooms: here a rat-eaten old armchair; here an abandoned motorbike leaning against the wall and half-swallowed by creepers; here a rack of rusted-up old farm machinery, all chains and prongs and struts and vicious teeth, like the bones of an alien fallen to Earth.

'Hey!' Antonia called. 'Where are you?'

There was no reply, just a deep, throaty snoring coming from somewhere she couldn't pinpoint. And still she wound her way through the rooms of the barn – over straw and grass and loose dusty soil, through doorways, through doorways, through doorways. And all the time she could hear the snoring – sometimes behind her, sometimes over to her left, sometimes up ahead and just to the right.

In one room, nettles and yellow sow thistles had grown out of control and were nearly as tall as Antonia herself, and she had to stamp down a pathway before she could cross. In another room she found an old Victorian cabinet riddled with woodworm holes. When she opened the doors of the cabinet, she discovered glass jars full of murky yellow-green liquid and curled organic shapes she couldn't properly make out in the gloom, some with eyes and nostrils and vestigial limbs.

The next two rooms were empty. Still she could hear the snoring.

'Hello?' she said. 'Who called for me? I'm here – where are you?'

Still no reply.

Maybe the snoring was coming from overhead now? She found a room with a rickety wooden ladder leading upwards to the next floor and clambered up, weighing each step as she went, checking each rung for rot. The floorboards up here were warped with age and creaked underfoot, but they too seemed sturdy enough to hold her weight.

She explored the first floor, moving from room to room. Most of the rooms were empty. One contained piled-up trestle tables. Bright bits of sunlight poked in through the wood like grubs. Big spiders inhabited all the corners, which they'd painted grey with their arachnid candyfloss. And still she could hear the snoring, though it seemed to be slowing, growing gradually weaker by the moment.

'Who's there?' she called. 'It's me, it's Antonia.'

And then she found herself back at the room with the rusty farm machinery, and she noticed the ground underfoot was once more compacted soil and marooned clumps of grass. She hadn't gone upstairs at all. Except she had, only a few minutes ago. With rising panic, she continued on through the barn, through the different rooms, some new, some she recognised – there was the cabinet full of jars again, and the disused, vine-clad motorcycle – and up a ladder onto the first floor, and then up another ladder onto the second floor. And she could see through the cracks in the wood that she was up high: the sweep of the meadow, and Almanby at the bottom of the hill in its tree-lined nest.

She continued on, treading ever more carefully across the rickety boards, which seemed to bow ever so slightly under her weight. The whole barn seemed to lean under her weight.

Here is a hay-feeder, and here is an empty crumpled cardboard box.

And here is the motorbike and here is the rusted farm machinery.

And just like that she was on ground level again, soil beneath her, as if she hadn't just climbed two ladders and peered out at the panorama. And she was breathing quickly and the sides of her head hurt from a sudden pressure just above her ears.

She felt trapped. Claustrophobic. She pictured herself wandering through ever-tightening circles for the rest of eternity, or at least till thirst overtook her and she ended her days as a dried-up husk in one of the rooms, like a dead mountaineer high on the slopes of Everest, hand reaching out for some imagined saviour.

But in the next room she found a sofa – a threadbare and maddeningly familiar sofa of brown and fawn checks. And on the sofa lay a man. She could see his round head and his thinning hair and his bright red tracksuit. His snoring had faded to a faint, slow purr.

'Uncle Warren?' she said as she walked over to the man.

The faintest aroma of rose potpourri. Of salad and balsamic vinegar.

Uncle Warren's mass took up the whole of the sofa, which seemed about to buckle in the middle. The thing was half-rotten. His snoring had stopped now, as had his breathing. For a moment she considered shaking him to wake him up, but she knew it was too late. Uncle Warren had died.

Warren was not a nice uncle. Uncle Peter and Uncle Stefan she liked, but Uncle Warren was mean. He pretended to be nice till no one else was around, then he said bad things about her skin, about her colour, about how he didn't like her brownness or her thick black hair. And it hurt Antonia so much that one day she put poison in his tea and Uncle Warren lay down on the sofa and he died. She'd only wanted to make him sick, to teach him a lesson, but he'd closed his eyes and didn't open them again.

For a while she felt panic, but afterwards she was calm. Very calm. Somehow she knew that the grown-ups would assume he'd had a heart attack after jogging and that would be that. No need for an autopsy, no need for any kind of investigation. An open-and-shut case, as they said on TV. They wouldn't suspect her, the quiet little girl who spent her days drawing and writing silly stories and racking up the pool balls for her father at the pub... she wouldn't get in trouble, and life would go on as normal except without horrible Uncle Warren. But for now, she had to pretend to have discovered him. She had to act shocked and confused and upset. But she could do that. She would tug her mother's sleeve and say, 'Mum, Uncle Warren isn't moving.' And after that, everyone would be too upset to notice her, too distraught to contemplate her as the culprit.

Or...

Or had he simply died of a jogging-induced heart attack after all? Antonia couldn't remember. She couldn't be sure now what was a real memory and what was Almanby. Almanby was inside her head, rummaging through her files, moving things around, adding memories of its own.

It was important to know, though. For her own sanity. For her identity. What age would she have been? Eight or nine, no older than that. Would nine-year-old Antonia have thought of poisoning an adult, no matter how unpleasant he was? Was that why she'd later developed a fascination with serial killer books, to scratch a lingering psychological itch? To see if there was something innate in her which could be stirred into action? Because maybe Uncle Warren was just the start. The more she thought about it, the more it rang true. It wasn't *normal* for a teenage girl to foster an obsession with murderers, was it?

More to the point, would nine-year-old Antonia even know how to poison a grown-up? Where would she find the poison? From the garden shed, probably. Was it just coincidence that she'd hit upon the very chemical which would make Uncle Warren lie down and quietly die, as if he'd had a heart attack, rather than writhe and scream and foam on the living room carpet, spewing green stuff?

Had she researched it?

Long ago, there was a snowman called Jack, and police gathering at the bottom of the field. And small footprints which weren't her own.

Here was Uncle Warren before her, solid and real, as if today was the day he'd died. But she knew it was just an illusion. Something excavated from her brain and manifested before her. She'd suppressed the memory all these years. She'd suppressed the memory of wandering around the village early in the morning, aged seventeen, looking for someone random to choose.

Someone to lead out into a remote field at the crack of dawn, and...

She'd suppressed the memory, or Almanby had given her a new one which didn't belong to her. She couldn't see the faces of any of her victims. She couldn't hear their final screams or feel their heartbeat growing weaker, or smell the rusty tang of their blood as it pooled onto the ground and darkened the soil. She couldn't think where she might've buried them. How many was she supposed to have killed? Three or four... or dozens? Was she as prolific as she was brutal?

The sun was vibrating now, its wavelengths jostling as they speared in through the slats of the barn. All the colours, siphoned out into bands; plus new colours either side of the spectrum, invisible to normal people. She was becoming something else, something beyond normal.

She had to get out of there.

And now she was back on the move, past the motorbike, past the farm machinery, past the Victorian cabinet, through the room overgrown with nettles, past the farm machinery, past the rat-eaten armchair, past the farm machinery,

past the rat-eaten armchair,

past the farm machinery,

past the rat-eaten armchair,

past the farm machinery...

And that was it. No matter which door she went through, she was trapped between the same two rooms. Past the rat-eaten armchair, past the farm machinery, past the rat-eaten armchair, past the farm machinery, past the rat-eaten armchair, past the farm machinery.

Past the rat-eaten armchair.

Past the farm machinery.

Past the rat-eaten armchair.

Past the farm machinery.

Antonia knew now that she would die here. All for the want of a green balloon. All for the want of a smidgen of Heather's attention.

She sat down in the rat-eaten armchair and wondered what to do next. Whether there was any reasonable plan that might occur to her. She thought of Heather and wondered if she'd noticed she was missing yet; whether she was now hunting round frantically for Antonia, or if she'd just shrugged it off and continued on with her ridiculous flirting. If they weren't already in a deserted cottage somewhere screwing, her ankles up around his ears. Maybe if Antonia confessed that she'd killed her abusive Uncle Warren, Heather would be impressed. Maybe Heather would see her in a whole new light. She'd address Antonia as 'Killer', and she'd skip excitedly around her demanding to know what kind of poison she'd used and what it felt like to see a dead body and whether anyone in her family had ever suspected, and whether she'd ever felt like killing again. And Antonia could let slip hints that maybe she had, one snowy morning; that maybe she ought to have a book of her own written about her – *A Lady Murders: The Gruesome Crimes of Antonia Coleridge.*

Heather would be turned on by the danger of it all and suddenly Daniel would be history and all Antonia's dreams would come true.

But she'd never know, because she was going to die here.

Antonia must've dropped off for a moment. When she reopened her eyes, she found a schoolgirl standing before her like a mirage, hands behind her back and head cocked to one side. The girl must've been around ten years old, perhaps a little older. Her brown hair was braided into a ponytail, and she wore a conifer-green school cardigan, long white socks up to her knees, and bright red shoes like Dorothy.

'Why are you sleeping?' said the little girl. She had the bluest eyes Antonia had ever seen.

Antonia blinked. 'I was just resting.'

'Who are you looking for?' said the little girl. 'I heard you calling.'

'I'm not looking for anyone. I'm trying to find my way out,' Antonia said, still not sure whether she was talking to a real person or some kind of hypnopompic after-dream apparition.

'That's easy.' The little girl held her hand out to Antonia.

Feeling big and old, Antonia levered herself upright and towered over the child. After a moment's hesitation, she took the little girl's hand and allowed herself to be led through the rooms in the barn, like the rooms of a doll's house.

'What are you doing in here?' asked the little girl.

'I'm hiding.'

'Who from?'

'From the ghosts.'

The girl gave a non-committal shrug, pushing her shoulders up to her ears, as if she didn't really care to hear such a disappointing answer; as if she considered hiding from ghosts the most self-indulgent and unimaginative thing possible.

'I'm trying to find a friend,' said Antonia. 'Well, a friend of a friend. And a friend too, I suppose. I'm trying to find anyone I know.'

'Why?'

'Why? Well... I've lost them, I want to find them again. And one of them is very sick.'

'My mother is sick too.'

'Oh no. I'm sorry to hear that. What's wrong with her?'

'I don't know,' the girl said. 'She's been sick for a long time. She's very sad.'

'Have you spoken to a doctor?'

The girl squinted at Antonia as if she'd asked the stupidest question known to man.

'What about your father?' said Antonia.

'I don't have a father. Just an older brother. I think she's sick because she's old, but she doesn't want to admit it.'

'How old is she?'

'She's very old.'

When Antonia exited the barn, she was unable to see for several seconds. The brightest green and the brightest blue rushed in through her corneas and straight to her brain, and she clamped her eyelids tight shut.

'Come on,' the little girl urged, tugging at Antonia's fingers.

As Antonia's vision began to clear, she saw that the ghosts at least seemed to have dispersed, and the pair of them were alone on the hillside.

'Do you go to school in Almanby?' Antonia asked the girl, as they began to meander back down the hill towards the village.

The girl thought for a moment. 'Yes,' she said at last.

'Are there many other children there?'

'Yes, of course, it's a school. It's all children. Apart from the teachers. They're grown-ups.'

'I mean… is it full of children, or empty?'

'About medium.'

'I haven't seen anyone in Almanby yet. You're the first one.'

Again, the girl shrugged.

'Where is everyone?'

'They're here. They're…' She gestured broadly with her arms.

The little girl led Antonia with great confidence and long strides through the outer layers of the village: the ditches and footpaths and the raggedy remains of a playground. A climbing frame protruded above the nettles like the rigging of a half-sunk galleon; a few feet away reared the Loch Ness Monster arc of the slide.

'What's your name?' Antonia asked.

'Rachel,' said the little girl. 'I'm not supposed to tell my name to strangers, but I've said it now anyway. As long as you're not a murderer.'

'Or a serial killer,' chuckled Antonia. And then, changing the subject, she said, 'I had a friend called Rachel.'

'Different people can have the same name.'

'I know. I wasn't suggesting you were lying.'

'What happened to her?'

'I'm not sure. I haven't seen her in a while. Maybe she died.'

'People die sometimes.'

'I suppose.'

'Your friend is at the church,' said the little girl, turning briefly and fixing Antonia with an inscrutable stare.

'Which friend?'

'I don't know his name.'

'Steven?'

'I don't know his name.'

'It must be Steven. That's the friend we're looking for.'

'Well, he's in the church.'

'Can you take me there?'

'All right.' The girl did a little skip.

But she didn't take Antonia to the church. Instead, they ended up in a small, overgrown field behind a row of houses at the eastern end of the village. The girl tugged harder on Antonia's fingers as she led her towards the middle of the field. There they found a perfectly circular hole in the ground surrounded by a crumbling wall, six bricks high.

'Why have you brought me here?' Antonia asked.

'This is where my mother is.'

Antonia felt a sudden tightness in her stomach. 'Your mother fell down the well?' She leaned over and called into the darkness, '*Hello?*'

'She *lives* down the well.'

Antonia squinted at her. 'Are you telling me porkies?'

'I don't know what that means.'

'Are you telling me a story? A joke?'

'Cross my heart.'

'How can your mother live down the well?'

'Because.'

'Because what?'

'Because that's where she lives. Well, she lives under the well. Under the village.'

Antonia stepped away from the well. 'How long has your mother lived down the well?'

'Eight hundred years. Well, a bit longer, but I can't remember exactly. She gets very hungry.'

'All right, eight hundred years. That's normal.'

'It's normal for her.'

'Is she sick from living down the well?'

The girl shrugged. 'She didn't say. She's been sick for six years, so probably she can't remember.'

'I think you're spinning me a yarn.'

'I promise.'

'How can someone be alive for eight hundred years?'

'You keep asking me questions!'

'Not everyone has an eight-hundred-year-old mother who lives down a well. I have lots of questions!'

'Well, I don't want to answer any more.'

'Fine.'

Antonia stepped forward again and peered down into the blackness, but she could see nothing.

'I want to show you something,' said the girl.

'I thought you just did.'

'I want to show you something else.'

'All right.'

The girl took Antonia by the hand and led her to a tumbledown chapel half-hidden in a nearby unruly copse of ash, beech and sycamore. The girl pushed open the door with her shoulder and beckoned for Antonia to follow her inside.

Maybe I'm not the serial killer, thought Antonia with a lurch, *maybe I'm the victim*. Murdered by a child serial killer, how embarrassing. How could she ever live it down? *Still, in for a penny, in for a pound*, she thought, whatever that meant. She followed Little Rachel inside.

The chapel smelled of dust and cobwebs. Parts of the walls had collapsed over the centuries, but the tiled floor was mostly intact, bar the occasional impudent nettle or blade of grass peeping through. A big brown dragonfly lazily flew laps of the room, before flitting out through a hole in the ceiling.

'Over here,' said the girl.

At the rear of the chapel, a big unsightly rectangle of chipboard had been fastened to the wall like a sticking plaster.

'Help me with this,' the girl said.

They hooked their fingertips behind the chipboard and prised it off the wall. Underneath was an image crudely carved into the stonework: a row of houses and three simple human figures. Two of the figures were normal size, but the third towered above the houses, barefoot and broad-shouldered, three times the height of them. The carving looked hundreds of years old.

The little girl beamed with satisfaction. 'There she is,' she said, pointing at the big figure.

'That's your mother?'

'Yes. And that one's me, and that one's my brother Christopher. We're a family.'

'You're a weird family.'

'What do you mean?'

'Never mind. Why are you showing me this?'

'I want you to see it.'

'Why?'

The girl pointed to the carving. 'Don't you like it?'

'It's fascinating. But why do you want me to see it?'

Unexpectedly, the girl reached up and pressed her hand against Antonia's chest. 'You have a sad heart,' she said.

Taken aback, Antonia shrugged. 'I'm all right,' she said.

'No, you have a sad heart. I can tell. Your soul is sad. What's wrong?'

'Oh, just grown-up things. It's nothing, it's just stuff I have to work out myself.'

'Tell me about it.'

'You're too young, it'd feel weird.'

'No it wouldn't. It's all right, I want you to tell me. Why is your soul so sad?'

Antonia sighed. 'Fine, if you must know, I'm just lonely, that's all. I never seem to fit in anywhere, I always feel different from everyone else. I'm here with my friend Heather, and… most of the time we have a really nice time. We get along really well. But she doesn't focus very well, and… I don't know. I think she forgets about me easily. I don't know if we're really friends or if she just talks to me because I'm there. She's probably already forgotten about me.'

'What would make you happy?'

'Wow, this is like a proper therapy session!'

'Tell me what would make you happy.'

'I don't know. I'm not sure anything would anymore. A proper friend? It could be Heather, it'd be nice if it was Heather. But just someone I can be around... you know, be myself around. And it'd be nice to fit in somewhere. Everyone I know is different to me, everywhere I go I feel like a weirdo. People are mostly nice, but I look different and I think differently, and... and I know that shouldn't matter, but it seems to. I don't think they know what to do with me, even though I've lived in Headingham all my life. So, I guess I'd like to feel like I really belong.'

Without warning, the girl threw her arms around Antonia and squeezed her tight. 'I'm glad you came to Almanby,' she said. 'This is the happiest day.'

The girl took Antonia's hand and led her back through the long grass, back to the well.

'Oh, is it like a wishing well?' Antonia couldn't resist leaning over and peering down into the blackness again. 'Like, if I throw a coin in, I can ask your mother a question and she'll grant me my wishes?' She didn't really believe any of it, but she took a shiny bright five-pence coin from her pocket, laid it on her thumbnail, and flicked it into the well. 'I guess it'd be nice not to be so lonely. Do I have to say 'I wish' at the start?'

But when Antonia turned around, the little girl was

lying in the grass, her shiny red shoes glistening in the sunlight.

'Rachel!' cried Antonia, and rushed over to her.

The girl's eyes were rolled back in her head, so far they were almost entirely white. Her limbs and her face muscles twitched like a sleeping cat.

'Rachel, can you hear me?'

But the girl was unresponsive. Antonia picked her up and set off across the field – but quickly realised she had no idea where to take her. Rachel was the first and only real person Antonia had met since they'd arrived in Almanby – it would do her no good to carry her all over a deserted village. Antonia laid her gently back down in the grass while she pondered the best course of action.

But when she looked back, the little girl had gone.

Now there was music.

Antonia wasn't sure how much time had passed, how long she'd been sitting there in the long grass by the well. It couldn't have been long, no more than a few minutes, but it felt as if Almanby had simply put time on pause for its own amusement.

But now there was music.

At first, just a diffuse wash of skirling harmonics that Antonia recognised as being in a major key, too spread out across the landscape to identify any kind of structure or rhythm or melody, or even any kind of specific instrumentation.

She rose and walked to the edge of the field.

It was accordion music: some kind of an English folk reel burbling round and round in multicoloured waltz-time cartwheels, *one two three, one two three*, but still too distant to make out a tune. It seemed to be everywhere at once, and nowhere in particular, a big omniscient blur, quiet and loud, swelling and receding, discordant and melodic and melancholic and bright.

'It's a party,' said the little girl, suddenly there beside Antonia.

'Whose party?'

'Mine.'

'Is it your birthday?'

'No. Better than that.'

'Then what?'

The girl grinned up at Rachel, then took hold of her hand once more. She wasn't going to say.

'Well, I think you're very lucky,' Antonia said. 'No one ever threw a party like that for me. But why aren't you down there enjoying it?'

'I was looking for you.'

'Me?'

'I want you to come to my party. You're my special guest.'

'But you don't even know me.'

'Yes I do. We've always been friends. Don't you remember?'

And as the little girl led her back along the ridge towards Almanby, Antonia saw that it wasn't uninhabited at all. Out on the green, on the far side of the village, beyond the square and the pub and the war memorial, people had gathered, each one a microscopic speck, fizzing like TV snowstorm. There were stalls and bunting and sideshows: a ducking stool, big wooden skittles, a hoopla, a tombola, the stocks, beanbag games of every description. The maypole had been moved from Lavender Lane to the green too, and was making its pulsating jellyfish shapes in time to the music.

One two three
One two three
One two three
One two three

59

Heather was running, helter skelter, stumbling blindly through trees and tensed for the moment that a flash of gunfire would strike her dead. Like accidentally catching the setting sun in your eyeline. And then she'd be on the ground amid the moss and twigs, twisting and crying as the last of her life ebbed away.

It'd all happened so quickly. She'd been strolling with Daniel down a dusty, tyre-grooved track, hot air drifting from adjacent farm buildings and stinking of manure and silage and all things stagnant. Horseflies bothered them and diced in mid-air tussles with fat metallic green-bottles like escaped flecks of rainbow.

'Where are you taking me?' she'd asked, buzzing around Daniel.

'I'm not taking you anywhere, you're following me. Go away.'

'Seriously, though, where are you taking me?'

'Ssh.' He seemed to be listening to the air.

'What is it?'

'Ssh.'

They both stopped where they were and listened intently. Heather could hear nothing but birdsong. Somewhere a peacock meowed.

'We're being followed,' said Daniel

'No, that was you. You were following us, remember?'

'We're being followed now.'

He peered back along the track, back towards Gorsehill Lane, which sat as still as a postcard.

'Keep walking.' Daniel ushered her along the track. He seemed so tense, so alert – almost scared – that Heather's heartrate eked up a notch or two. Little squirts of adrenaline made her twitchy. She wanted to giggle or run around, just to take the edge off the weird atmosphere which had suddenly descended, but even she sensed this wasn't the moment.

They were approaching a small patch of woodland on the rim of Almanby, overgrown and unkempt, and encircled by half-hearted barbed wire which had mostly been trampled down years ago.

'There must've been a second car,' Daniel said at last, under his breath. Heather wasn't sure if he was addressing her or simply thinking aloud.

'When?'

'On the road. On the way here. I don't get it. I don't get it. How could they know?'

'How could they know what?'

'About me. They shouldn't have known. I had it all under control. I took every precaution possible. There's no way they could've known. Unless...'

'What?'

Daniel suddenly turned to face her. 'Unless it *was* one of you.'

'What are you talking about?'

'They couldn't have followed me unless someone tipped them off. And there's no one else it could've been except one of you. Or all three of you.'

'That's stupid. We've never met you before, we don't know who you are.'

'Don't you?'

'No, of course not. We were just out for a drive and you hijacked us. How is that our fault? Wait… you don't think it was *me*, do you?'

Daniel narrowed his eyes. 'No,' he said at last, with a shake of his head. 'You're too much of a pillock. I don't think it was your driver, either.'

'Right, then.'

'Right.'

'Wait… are you saying Rachel did this?'

Daniel picked up his pace and Heather jogged to catch him up. 'I've known Rachel half my life,' she said. 'We're like best mates. We've done everything together.'

'Then you know why she brought you to Almanby?'

Frowning, Heather said, 'See, you're not so smart. She didn't bring me, I nagged her into letting me come.'

'Right.'

'I came to find Steven. I came of my own free will.'

'Of course you did.'

He was just opening his mouth to say more when he was interrupted by a weird dry popping sound, like balloons bursting, or light bulbs falling to the floor, but much louder. And flashes. And a bottle-green car somewhere behind them, shimmering in the heat haze radiating up from the stones of Gorsehill Lane. And they were running. Daniel bolted first. It took Heather a second to register that they were being shot at. No one had ever fired a gun at her before. It all felt unreal. The idea that she could be snuffed out at any moment, even before she realised. *Are you really dead if you don't realise you're dead?* And then she'd spend the rest of eternity gloomily wandering the streets of Almanby, vaguely aware there was something she was supposed to be doing, someone she was supposed to be finding, but frustrated like a toddler at the fact that she was unable to cohere the thoughts in her own brain.

Somehow, though, they both made it to the woods. It was dense with brambles and ferns and all sorts of foliage grown wild. Within a few moments, Daniel was gone and Heather was left stumbling through the whirling centrifuge of tree trunks and undergrowth, with no idea where she was going, or where she should be going, or what was happening. Occasionally, the *blap blap* of gunfire would reverberate through the woods – two slightly different tones, one of which she imagined was Daniel's homemade gun. Sometimes it was close, but mostly it was distant and stretched out by echoes.

Heather stumbled and fell to the woodland floor. She decided to stay down, at least for a while, and pressed herself as flat as she could, hoping the *blap blaps* would sail harmlessly overhead, and whoever the hell this was would recognise her as a non-participant. The smell of moss filled her nostrils.

But after only a few seconds she'd grown too twitchy to lie still and was on her feet again and running to nowhere.

There were people asleep in the woods. Two men in khaki-green outfits lying at weird angles taking a nap in the sunlight, their eyes closed, their faces upturned and with oddly satisfied expressions, like they'd just enjoyed a really good meal. *How can they sleep with all this noise going on?* Heather wondered giddily – then realised with a lurch that the men were dead. Freshly killed. That silly-looking thing Daniel carried around with him had done its job.

A few paces further on, there was a woman too. Not much older than Heather, her frizzy auburn hair tied up with a blue hairband. Chipped green nail varnish. A piercing on the side of her nostril, a glittery stud. She too wore the khaki outfit – jacket, T-shirt, loose-fitting trousers – and she also had a similarly peaceful expression. An almost-smile on her chubby cheeks. There was faint smoke or steam rising from her corpse.

Heather felt like vomiting. She was used to seeing ghosts, of course; and she'd even, on numerous occasions, seen people who'd been killed by ghosts. But she'd never seen a dead person who'd been alive mere seconds before, the body of someone who was deliberately killed by another person – someone she half-considered a friend. She'd convinced herself that Daniel was all bluster: underneath all that hard-man bravado was a big softie. Not a cold-blooded killer. How naïve and stupid she was.

An unsettling silence had fallen; just the twittering of a lone blackbird. Heather was working on automatic pilot now, placing one foot in front of the other, wandering blindly, feeling as if she was floating above her own body – aware of the rhythm of her shoes crunching against twigs, and a smoky tang which reminded her of fireworks, the smell of scorched air, the smell of some mysterious chemical discharge.

And then a figure stumbled out of the woods to her left. A woman in her forties, dark hair tucked beneath a black baseball cap. Blood stained the side of her green uniform purple. She carried a gun not unlike Daniel's, all pipes and tubes and soldered components, but more manufactured, less of a cobbled-together homemade affair.

The pair startled each other. Heather froze to the spot; the woman raised her gun. Heather closed her eyes, raised her hands, and braced for her final moment. But the woman exhaled and lowered her gun.

'Are you okay?' she said. 'Did he hurt you?'

Heather was too scared to reply.

'Daniel. Did he hurt you?'

Heather shook her head.

'Are you sure? You're sure you're okay?'

'Yeah.'

With a groan, the woman slumped against a tree and ventured a look at her injury. Heather took a step or two towards her and crouched as if to help, though she had no idea what she might be able to do.

'Does he have something with him?' said the woman, through her grimace. She opened her thumb and forefinger a little way. 'About this size? He might've collected it along the way.'

'You're bleeding,' said Heather. 'Let me help you.'

'Tell me. It's important. Does he have it?'

'Yeah.'

The woman glanced into the woods, her attention momentarily distracted, then she turned back to Heather. 'What's your name?'

'Heather. What's yours?'

'I'm Heather too.'

'Seriously?'

'Yeah.'

'Heather McLagan.'

'Heather Long. Pleased to meet you, Heather McLagan.'

'I'm looking for Steven.'

'Steven Cook?'

'You know him?' said Heather.

'Yeah, I know him. I know who he is, anyway. I'm here to kill him.'

Heather looked at the woman a moment, then suddenly lunged for her and attempted to wrestle the gun from her grasp. But even though the woman was wounded, she was too strong, Heather was too weak, and she quickly found herself flat on her back amid the ferns, clutching her injured arm, the woman's gun now pointed in her face.

'Don't kill me!' cried Heather. 'I'm sorry! Don't kill me!'

'Get as far away from here as you can,' said Heather Long. 'This isn't your fight.'

'Please. Don't hurt Steven. He's not a bad person. Whatever you've heard about him, he's a good person. I know him.'

'Listen to me. They're building… I don't know what it is. Something big. Something to destroy Almanby.'

'Like a bomb?'

'Yeah. Like a bomb.'

'Why Almanby?'

Heather Long gestured broadly, as if to say, *all this*. 'He wants to stop the decay,' she said. 'The entropy. The ghosts. The sickness.'

'That's good, isn't it?'

'It's catastrophic. If that component reaches Steven, if the bomb goes off, that's it. All over. Not just Almanby – everything for miles around. Countless people. Animals. Everything. It'll be like a nuclear blast. The soil sterilised, the air and water poisoned. Just ash. That's all there'll be. Just moon dust. He's dangerous. They're both dangerous. They're fanatics.'

'Steven helps people. He wouldn't harm anyone. He's the most caring person I've ever met.'

'Look how young you are. Just a baby. You shouldn't be chasing after men like these. You can't save him, you'll only get hurt. Go home. Leave him to us.' Heather Long eased herself upright and hauled Heather McLagan to her feet. 'Are you all right, Heather McLagan?'

Heather nodded.

With a final, 'Go home,' the woman peered through the trees then headed off out of sight.

Heather was rooted to the spot for a moment. And then, plaintively, she called after her: 'Please. Heather Long.'

After a few moments she followed gingerly, doing her best to trace the other Heather's trajectory. If she achieved nothing else today, she had to prevent this woman from murdering Steven. She had it all wrong, there was no way Steven was who she said he was – he was here to help, not destroy. If Heather Long could just be persuaded to sit down with them and talk it through, Heather was sure she would see sense.

A single *blap* echoed through the impassive trunks.

A few metres later, Heather found Heather Long's corpse bent awkwardly on the sod, mouth gaping, eyes rolled up till they were nearly blank.

Startled by Heather's arrival, a big white barn owl took off from a branch overhead like Heather Long's escaping soul, and flapped through the trees with its impossibly long wings: a wraith so white and so perfect against the dirty browns and greens and greys that it looked almost artificial, a thing spun from silk and cotton.

Among the grass, just next to the woman, was a small collection of coins. About £1.50 in change. It must've slipped from her pocket as she fell. Almost in a trance, Heather crouched and retrieved the money one coin at a time. She didn't know yet what she'd do with it – maybe tuck it back in the woman's pocket as her own pathetically small mark of respect. Or spend it; buy something in Heather Long's name, a can of sickly blue bubblegum-flavour pop, and drink to her memory. The best way Heather knew.

At that moment, Daniel emerged ahead of her, his face split in half with a big ugly grin.

'Only one left,' he chuckled, breathing hard. 'These poor dumb fuckers don't know who they're messing with.'

Heather looked at him, her eyes hollow. 'You killed her,' she said.

Daniel nodded towards the coins in her hand. 'Always rob the dead. You're learning fast.'

Heather wasn't even thinking now – she was too numb to do anything except follow Daniel, stick close behind like a gosling. She didn't want to be around him anymore. She wanted to be as far away from him as possible. But she had nothing left. Her arm hurt. Her whole left side hurt. She hadn't slept, she hadn't drunk, she hadn't eaten. And despite everything else that had happened, thoughts of ice cream still clamoured around her brain, occupying every square inch. She couldn't chase away the image of herself, seven or eight years old, in her favourite white and pear-green floral dress and her favourite sky-blue cardigan, standing in a park not far from Grandma's house, amid the endless constellations of daisies and hot dandelion suns, clutching a 99 cone with both hands, her grin a giant capital D. Feeling like a big girl for buying the ice cream all by herself. She wanted to go back there. She wanted to live in that world, before all of this. Before Daniel, before Rachel, before Steven, before Almanby and the ghosts and the entropy and the decay. Before adulthood. She'd made a poor job of being an adult, she decided, and she'd made a poor job of remaining a child. All at once, she felt like a grotesque museum piece trapped in perpetual adolescence, a miniature kiddified Miss Haversham, never maturing, never growing into herself, never becoming the 'real' Heather.

Or was that just Almanby? Getting into her head, playing tricks on her, undermining her.

They were in a farmyard now. Baked white concrete. The stench of slurry made it hard to breathe, and the shoals of flies.

Heather and Daniel pinballed between staggering ghosts. Still grinning like Satan, Daniel unloosed his gun – *blap* – at a ghost which wandered too close, a green flash, the report of the shot resounding around the walls like cannon fire. Heather stumbled in fright, landed painfully on her left side. The ghost was down too, wriggling like an upended tortoise.

'Get up!' Daniel mouthed through the dullness in her ears. 'There's still one more.'

He hauled her back to her feet. The next thing she knew, she was pressed against a sheet of dirty corrugated iron propped up on an outhouse wall, Daniel beside her. His eyes scanned every window, every doorway, every opening, with a fevered intensity.

'Am I dreaming or is it just my imagination waking up?' he muttered, apparently to himself, apparently apropos of nothing. Talking himself into a degree of extra lucidity perhaps, fighting off Almanby's influence.

A moment later, the corrugated sheet spasmed and rattled with a great juddering boom. Daniel returned fire – *blap! Blap! Blap!* – his gun illuminating green each time – aiming randomly at an unseen target.

Heather was on the ground, curled into a ball, her hands over her head. A reflex action – she was surprised to find herself there and thought for a moment she'd already been shot. But she hadn't, not yet, and she wondered, with each new thought, whether this new thought would be her last.

Neither Heather nor Daniel had moved for several minutes. Maybe they were both dead now, and this was how it felt: an eternity of suspended animation, the final moment stretched out forever. But then Daniel was off, scampering across the courtyard to the open door of the farmhouse – gun held in front of him – and inside.

A minute or so later he reappeared, his beaming grin back in place, his shoulders squared with exhilaration.

'Got him,' he announced, and strutted back towards the track.

Heather followed on behind. Till she could reorient herself, recalibrate her senses, shake this sick feeling and pounding headache, she could think of few other options. 'What happens now?' she said grimly.

'You can do what you want. I'm going to the church.'

'To save your soul?'

'It's too late for that.'

60

In the corner of the room, Oscar's television sprang to life and flicked through several channels, oversaturated with colour like the fevered scribblings of a napalm crayon set.

The living room door drifted open, pulled by invisible fingers, then slammed shut with a bang.

Rachel lay on the rug, her lower half bared, her head thrown back, screaming with laughter, howling with laughter, uncontrollably whooping and cheering and hollering, spine arched off the floor. For half a second she was out on the patio, still horizontal, still laughing, then she blipped back indoors, back to her original spot on the living room floor.

The ceiling lights flashed on and off.

Rachel's dark red shirt was now a dark blue shirt, and now a dark green shirt. Her blue jeans – on the other side of the floor – were green jeans, were red jeans, were yellow jeans, were blue jeans.

'*Ohhhh yes!*' she cried hoarsely. '*I'm back! I'm back!*'

She laughed and wept and punched the air and kicked her feet, unable to adequately contain the energy now coursing through her. Almanby energy.

In a swell of orgasmic shortwave static, the radio burst into life with a boisterous brass band rendition of 'The Floral Dance'.

I thought I could hear the curious tone
Of cornet, clarinet and big trombone,
Fiddle, cello, big bass drum,
Bassoon, flute and euphonium,
Far away as in a trance
I heard the sound of the floral dance.

Rachel was invisible now.

And now she was back.

And now she was upstairs.

And now she was downstairs again, back on the living room rug, big exuberant tears flooding down her cheeks, her fingers stretched so far apart it almost seemed like they might snap from her hands.

And now, just for the briefest moment, there were three Rachels side by side on the living room floor.

And still she laughed, and she thought she would never stop, not until her larynx broke free from the confines of her throat and scuttled away across the floorboards all by itself. Every part of her felt alive, every cell in her body was a little yellow Pacman, each of them chasing the others round and round, snapping snapping snapping, and she giggled, and the Pacmen grew arms and then hands with tickly fingers, and they tickled every iota of her, every nanometre, every subatomic particle, and she was rolled out thin like dough beneath a cosmic rolling pin, and it was the best feeling she'd ever experienced, and she never wanted it to stop, even as she knew it soon would. In a few minutes, the best of it would wear off. In a day or two, she'd be back to normal: that fragile, precarious, membrane-thin equilibrium that she appreciated so much while it lasted, but knew it only bore her weight by the slimmest of margins. And sure enough, a week or two after that, she'd start to feel bad again, she'd feel her cells gradually dismantling themselves, atom by atom… and she'd yearn beyond anything reasonable – beyond the death of distant suns and the formation of black holes and the collapse of the galaxy – for her next taste of Almanby.

Please.

I'll give anything.

And she did. She gave everything.

But she'd have to wait. She'd have to be patient. A phone call would come when Almanby was good and ready: on the other end of the line would be Oscar, his welcome deep voice giving her the go-ahead and letting her know who Almanby had chosen this time.

Except this time there would be no next time, because last time it'd chosen Antonia and Heather, just as Rachel knew it would.

And now there was no one else left to choose.

After Antonia and Heather were gone, absorbed into the soil, that would be that.

She was down to her last two sacrificial lambs.

And then, Rachel would die slowly and painfully, just as Sam had, just as Other Antonia and Glen had. Her only hope was to find new friends, ones that she genuinely, truly cared about. And that would be a difficult thing to do when all she wanted them for was to kill them.

Later, when Rachel was sitting on that big leather walrus of a sofa, drinking tea, feeling herself coming down from that highest of all peaks and normalising once more, Oscar handed her the gun.

'It's time,' he said.

61

Did you ever see a lassie,
A lassie, a lassie?
Did you ever see a lassie,
Go this way and that?

The ice-cream van was back. Chiming somewhere close by. Heather ran to catch it, desperate to find it, even for a single glimpse of it coughing its brown diesel fumes into the sauna air. Vanilla ice cream always tasted better amid a cloud of combusted lead and petroleum.

Go this way and that way,
Go this way and that way.
Did you ever see a lassie,
Go this way and that?

The image of Heather Long filled Heather McLagan's head, twisted and smoking in the grass.

And small Heather McLagan in her white and pear-green dress and sky-blue cardigan, tiny hands wrapped around an oversize wafer cone. She saw herself perched on Heather Long's lap, the pair of them licking their 99-flake soft-whip ice-cream cones and gazing out across a sandy beach bustling with holidaymakers. A magical past where ice-cream cones cost 75p each, paid for with the £1.50 in Heather Long's pocket, which Heather Long had placed in tiny Heather McLagan's palm to carefully hand over to the ice-cream man.

What do you say?

Thank you.

And the dust got into her mouth as she ran, and collected in her curls and gathered under her fingernails. And dust and grit crunched underneath her shoes. And Rosehip Lane turned right into Tuppence Lane turned left onto Old Road, past the closed-down post office and past the duck pond. The ice-cream van was somewhere close – she was sure that at any moment she'd round the corner and spy it parked up on the corner, enticing children from their homes.

But no – Old Road turned right onto the naggingly deserted Mason's Avenue, which turned left onto Rosehip Lane.

All without a glimpse of the ice-cream van.

Heather ran to a halt. Dust was in her ears and up her nostrils. She turned as the van's cacophony encircled her. For a few seconds, the chimes seemed to emanate from the treetops, then the roar of the engine cut through and she knew the van was immediately up ahead.

And then, ducking past a couple of ghosts which had emerged from someone's garden and were looming in her direction, she was off again.

Heather could feel every element in her body, every individual O and C and N and Ca and Na, rattling and grinding against one another like colourful plastic building bricks out of whack. The air was heavy. *Everything* was heavy, and growing heavier by the second. The sky, absolutely still, whirled as fast as a carousel. Flickering tungsten bulbs, red, blue, green, pink. Lowering, growling, hollow-faced night-time; inky depths of midnight, disguised as a burning-hot afternoon. Time had stretched out – it must surely be tomorrow by now. It *felt* like tomorrow. It felt like the early hours: the purple hessian scrubbed-throated first blades of dawn, all dew-pocked and weighted down. Pale as a drowned man with stones in his pockets. A hallucination overlapping with reality: an exact match, nothing to choose between the two.

Heather ran, wondering all the time when she might die. Wondering what it'd be like to die, and how people usually went about it. Should she keep running till it happened, or sit down on the grass and wait for it to arrive? Or get it over with – jump off something high, or go have a chat with a ghost. Maybe find a spike to impale herself on. She felt resigned to the whole idea of it. No, more than resigned – detached. A floating speck in her own reality, a translucent dot in the fluid of her own eye. Only the crunch of gravel and the whoosh of grass beneath her shoes prevented her from drifting away into space.

Later she realised she was chanting softly to herself, under her breath: '...*Vanilla Killer, Chocolate Lobster, Rosalind the Robot, Raspberry Blastberry, Betelgeuse Orange Treat, The Colosseum, The Big White, Mr Jones the Janitor, Applecadabra, Bananacadabra, Ugly-Wugly, Apple & Blackberry Utopia, Blue Versus Green, Apricot Dracula...*'

She was very hot and very thirsty. Coming to a halt, she walked over and sat down cross-legged on the grass verge, staring straight ahead like someone whose soul had been plucked out through the top of their head, just a porcelain garden gnome now.

And here she would wait. Surely it wouldn't be long.

Emma Green is boldly hale
Her house is warm but narrow
On scattered grass until she dies
She's wide awake in sorrow

62

A shoal of butterflies passed all around Heather. At least a thousand, maybe two, their orange tips tickling her face and arms. A horizontal snowstorm. They bobbed and whirled and fluttered, and then were gone, off on their happy way to another part of Almanby.

Heather wondered if that was it, that was death: a threshold of butterflies, through which every mortal soul would pass at the moment of dying. And now here she was, stuck in limbo forever, her own personal purgatory, as punishment for all the mischief she'd caused over the years. All the pranks and smells and funny noises, and for all the lies she'd told: the spacesuits for married couples and the dehydrated water. And now, for the rest of time, her existence would pan out like that black-and-white film she saw once at the Triscutine Picture Palace, about the woman who got into a car accident and ended up roaming the world, invisible and inaudible to everyone but herself.

Or maybe she would be judged Good after all, and Jesus would turn up shortly and lead her by the hand into some better place, all harps and clouds and shit. She wasn't even a Christian, but right now it was as nice a thought as any other.

Adam S. Leslie

* * *

As if on cue, a tall figure coalesced from the heat haze, striding towards her. But it wasn't Jesus; it was Antonia, her loping gait instantly familiar.

Heather sprang to her feet and ran to meet her. She wrapped her arms around Antonia's torso and squeezed as hard as she could.

'I missed you,' said Heather. 'I thought I was going to die here. I've never been so glad to see anyone.'

'Come with me,' Antonia said with unexpected urgency, tugging Heather's fingers. 'There's something I need to show you.'

'What is it?'

'Come and see.' She tugged harder at Heather's hand. 'Heather, quickly.'

'Where are you taking me?'

'It's a surprise.'

'I don't want a surprise. Just tell me.'

'I…' Antonia hesitated. She looked lost somehow, as if she'd forgotten something, as if there was a half-buried thought nagging at the back of her subconscious.

'Seriously, Tonio, what is it?'

'It's ice cream. I found ice cream.'

'*What?*'

'I didn't want to ruin the surprise. But we have to hurry while there's still some left. This is the happiest day.'

Heather was about to follow, about to break out into a desperate, delirious run, when she caught herself and pulled back, stepping away from Antonia.

Something was wrong.

Something was ever so subtly wrong, and for a moment she couldn't pinpoint exactly what it was.

Squinting through the afternoon glare, she realised that Antonia was different somehow. Her eyes were different. They *looked* the same, but there was someone new behind them, as if a different soul had moved into Antonia's body and set up residence. A chill ran down Heather's back.

'What do you mean, 'this is the happiest day'?'

Antonia gazed through her. 'Heather, just come. Please, before it all gets eaten. There's… there's banana, strawberry, watermelon, bubblegum. Bright blue bubblegum. And vanilla twist! You wanted vanilla twist.'

It'd only been a few minutes since Heather had last seen Antonia. An hour or two at the most. It was difficult to tell in Almanby – time felt all stretched out here and all squished up at the same time, like childhood fevers. It should've been tomorrow by now, or the next day, but somehow it was still mid-afternoon. Grimly, stubbornly mid-afternoon.

But even so, they hadn't been apart for long. And yet something had happened in the meantime, something had changed Antonia.

'Is that really you, Toni?'

'Of course it's me.'

'I mean, really really you. Not some fucked-up Almanby thing come to mess with my head?'

'It's me. Feel my hand. I'm real.'

'You seem weird, though.'

'No, I'm normal. I'm just excited for you on this happy day. There's ice cream at the village green!'

'Antonia wouldn't say *on this happy day*. You sound all creepy and wrong.'

'But it *is* a happy day. Please, Heather, come on.'

'Why is there ice cream at the village green?'

'Because that's where it is.'

'Your shoes are red,' said Heather. She bent to examine Antonia's feet. 'They've been painted.'

'Yeah.'

'Why are your shoes painted red, Antonia? What's going on?'

Antonia scratched her head and let out a conflicted sigh. 'I'm… Heather, something special's happened. I'm Green Anne's Daughter.'

'You're what?'

'I'm Green Anne's Daughter.'

'I don't know what that means.'

'I've been to this party. A sort of celebration. It's like a village fête. But not a normal one. Like, a really magical one. There's tombolas and skittles and a maypole and cake stalls and… and a ducking stool.'

'That sounds normal.'

'I'm not describing it very well. It's… it's like all the village fêtes there have ever been, all at once. Not because it's big, it's mostly normal size, but just the way it feels. Just intense. But in a good way. All the ones you went to when you were five and six and seven, all the ones you can only just remember, right at the back of your memory, and all the ones you missed because you had to stay in and do homework, or you didn't even know about till afterwards. All squished together. And it's like all your friends are there, and your mum and dad how they used to be, and your gran and grandpa, and your other gran and grandpa. They're *not* there, but that's how it feels, like they were there. And there's an ice-cream van on the green, I think it's the one we've been chasing.' Antonia's eyes darted around as she tried to articulate her jumble of thoughts; but the essential Antonia-ness of them had yet to return. 'And *that's* where everyone is. That's why Almanby is deserted. They haven't disappeared. They're at the festival on the green. And Heather, listen, they're really nice, they're really friendly and welcoming. It's not what you think. I mean, this place, Almanby, it's not what you think. It's not what they've been telling us all these years. It isn't dangerous, it isn't sinister. It's... Heather, it's beautiful. This is the happiest day of all the days.'

'But why are your shoes red?'

'What?'

'I asked why your shoes are red.'

'I already said. They've made me Green Anne's Daughter. It's a ceremonial position. They made me Green Anne's Daughter for the party. They choose one every Green Anne Day, and this time they chose me. It's a great honour.' An ecstatic smile blossomed across Antonia's face. 'Green Anne's Daughter has to wear red shoes, but they didn't have any my size because I'm so tall, so they painted the ones I'm wearing. And look, I have a ring like yours.' She held out her hand as if freshly engaged. The ring flashed in the sunlight. 'Green, red and see-through. The Mother, the Daughter and the Holy Ghost. The colours of Christmas. Isn't this fantastic?'

'Tonio, I don't understand any of this.'

'This is the first time I've felt like I've belonged. Anywhere. I feel like I'm part of a family at last. I'm always the shadow at the back, the one no one ever notices, except as the tall freak with brown skin. No one's ever made me queen of a festival before. I'm not blonde, I'm not pretty, but they chose me! I get to be Green Anne's Daughter, I get to wear the red shoes. Me – not anyone else. This is the most wonderful Green Anne Day ever.'

Without warning, she wrapped Heather in a beatific embrace. Heather disengaged herself and took another step back. 'Green Anne Day like in those pictures? Where they hang people?'

'Oh, they don't do that anymore, they stopped that years ago. It's all symbolic now. They dance and they sing songs, and there's a special feast after it gets dark. A special feast for me – I'm guest of honour. Come on, Heather, let's hurry! I really want to share this with you. It would mean everything to me if you were there,' said someone who looked like Antonia. 'There's a crowning ceremony and all sorts.'

'It sounds weird. *You* sound weird.'

'You'll get it when you see it. It's five minutes away. Heather, there's ice cream!'

'You said.'

'Well?'

'You go on ahead, mate. I'll catch you up.'

'You won't find it without me.'

'I'll find it. You go be belle of the ball.'

'It's fine. I promise. It's great fun, you'll have the best time. You're not scared, are you?'

'Why would I be scared?' said Heather, feeling suddenly scared.

'You wouldn't.'

'Then why did you say it?'

'Because… because there's nothing to worry about. So you should come. We ought to be there already. And don't forget about the ice cream! Why won't you come?'

'Because you're not talking like you anymore, you're talking like some weird robot or TV evangelist or something.'

'All right, maybe I am different. Maybe this has changed me. Why should I always be awkward and depressed? I can be happy, can't I?'

'Mate, I want you to be happy, but it doesn't sound like you.'

'If I've changed, I've changed for the better. This is a better me. But it's still me, it's still Antonia. Green Anne Day is the happiest day, that's all. It's like Christmas but a billion times better. I'm excited. You should be excited too.' Antonia wore a smile that didn't belong to Antonia. 'Rachel's there.'

'Rachel?'

'Yeah. She's there already. She's happy for me. And she said she's sorry for all the stupid things she said, none of them were true. She really wants to see you. She really wants us all to be friends again.'

63

But when they got there the field was bare.

Just grass and bees and butterflies, and daisies making constellations, and dandelion clocks telling the time to anyone who cared to look.

'Where is it?' said Heather. 'Where's the fête?'

Antonia gestured vaguely. She seemed lost, as if she too had been expecting to see it.

'It *was* here,' she said. 'Just before I found you.'

'It's not here now,' said Heather. 'I guess it all got cleared away in the last ten minutes?'

'It's always here. It's always Green Anne Day in Almanby. Last year, and the year before that, and twenty years ago, and a hundred years ago, and a hundred and fifty years ago. Nineteen fifty-eight, nineteen seventy-seven, nineteen eighty-three. And next year, and the year after that. But all at the same time. All together at the same time.' She scratched her head. 'All the people and all the things.'

'The ice cream and the tombolas?' Heather squinted sceptically.

'Yeah.'

'But it's not here now.'

'It's here all the time,' said Antonia, without much conviction, 'we just can't always see it. It used to be once a year. But she got sick.'

'Who got sick?'

'Green Anne. She was too hungry so she got sick.'

'Right. Green Anne.'

'Green Anne's real. The Great Mother. The Egesgrime. She lives under the village.'

'Like, buried in the cemetery, you mean?'

'No, of course not. You shouldn't say things like that.'

'Then where?'

'I already told you. She lives under the earth, under the village.'

'Of course she does.'

'And I'm her daughter.'

Cross-legged in the middle of the field, Heather suddenly noticed, sat Rachel.

Upon seeing the pair, Rachel rose to her feet. She cut a dejected figure, as if all the worries of the world had bent her in half like an old person. It took Heather a moment to recognise her.

'Hey, Rachel,' Heather said, without smiling.

Rachel didn't reply.

In her hand, she held something large. A strange-looking object built from wood, copper pipes and batteries.

64

When it came to the moment of execution, Rachel always experienced a weird thrill. Yes, there was that horrible sick feeling right to her core, but also a strange frisson she could never quite put her finger on. Execution as seduction, seduction as execution. She'd led these people on, brought them out to a secluded spot – and here was where her true motives would be revealed. A coy brush of her hand through their hair, leaning a little closer, suddenly earnest, breathing hard, her lips inching towards theirs. Or... distracting them with some random thing, maybe a pretty patch of flowers or a frolicking squirrel, ensuring their backs would be turned long enough for her to raise the gun. Slowly and carefully pointing it at the back of their head.

Pulling the trigger.

Snuffing them out.

And not some poor stranger she'd only met that morning, but a long-term friend, someone with whom she had a history. All those evenings watching the sunset, or lying under the stars, or drinking beer together till they collapsed in the grass giggling too hard to stand, or sitting in the back row of the cinema in the thrall of its zoetrope of emotions. The sorts of shared experiences most people would want to treasure, to preserve forever, Rachel would extinguish as casually as stepping on a bug, or wringing the neck of a chicken up at the disused Gedby weather station. A single quick action: gone forever, never to come back. Bye bye Sandy, bye bye Prithpal, bye bye John and April and Marcy.

Bye bye Heather and Antonia.

Once the deed was done, she mostly felt terrible. Killing her friends didn't make her happy – she wasn't *that* much of a maniac. But there was always the same tell-tale tingle as the moment approached. A little sparkle of glee which made her wonder whether she was evil. Not just cowardly and selfish and corrupted beyond help, but actually an evil person. In a way, the thought that she might be was oddly reassuring.

It's not my fault. I'm evil, I can't help it.

A note from her doctor: 'Please excuse Rachel Harrison's horrible crimes, she has been diagnosed as evil.'

A large part of her hoped Heather and Antonia would never show up, and she'd be left waiting on the village green all afternoon. Then maybe she could finally admit defeat. Turn the gun on herself, if she was able to pluck up enough courage, end this miserable existence once and for all. Or wait for the ghosts to come along and bludgeon her to death.

Antonia had seemed weird, as if in a trance, or half her brain was elsewhere. Rachel had made up some flimsy story about wanting to make amends with Heather, and that Antonia should fetch her as quickly as possible.

'You're going to kill her, right?' Antonia had said.

A lurch in Rachel's stomach. 'No, of course not, I just want to talk to her.'

'I don't believe you.'

'I want to talk to her, I want to make things right.'

'That's why you came.' Antonia had pointed towards the gun. 'You're going to kill her.' It wasn't a question, and Rachel didn't try to argue against the certainty in her voice. 'She's the sacrifice, isn't she. That's why you brought her here. For Almanby. For Green Anne. For the Egesgrime.'

How did she know all this? None of the others ever realised, none of the others worked it out. No one suspected Rachel for a moment. And yet somehow Antonia – big, trusting Antonia, of all people – was two steps ahead of her.

At last, Rachel said, 'Yes.'

Antonia paused, thought for a moment, then said, 'I'll go and fetch her.'

When is Antonia not Antonia? thought Rachel, as her friend made her way back towards the far corner of the village green, her pace picking up speed the more she receded. Antonia's demeanour had chilled Rachel; she seemed to have been stripped of her personality, of everything that made her who she was.

Just like Oscar.

Rachel hoped it was all a ruse, that Antonia would find Heather and breathlessly entreat her to flee the area. '*Rachel wants to kill you, we have to get as far away from here as we can!*'

But no – a few minutes later, Antonia returned, leading Heather across the village green. Heather was hesitant, hanging back, clearly sensing that something was badly wrong. She'd have been an idiot if she didn't.

'Hey, Rachel,' Heather said, without smiling.

Rachel didn't reply.

'Where've you been?' Heather demanded. 'What are you guys up to?' And then, gesturing towards the gun, 'What's that?'

'I'm sorry,' said Rachel.

'You were being a shit, but it's fine,' Heather said. 'I don't believe you actually did any of that stuff anyway. You and Steven have zero chemistry.'

'I always liked you two the best. You were my favourites. You understand that, don't you?'

'What are you talking about?' said Heather. 'What's going on?'

Rachel raised her gun arm. She directed the brass muzzle towards Heather's face. Once more that tingle, that vicious twinge of excitement. The feeling of power, of ending two and a half decades of existence with one motion of a forefinger against the smooth brass trigger. All those hopes, all those dreams, all those memories and emotions, all that personality – right there in the palm of her hand for her to crush. Once. Twice. Two more people gone because of her. The two people remaining in this shitty world for whom she had any love, any real affection at all. For all her misery and self-loathing, something in her middle felt horribly *good*.

'Rachel, it's me,' said Heather. 'What the fuck is this?'

'It's nothing,' said Rachel. 'It's nothing to worry about.'

'It looks like something.'

'Did you have a nice day out?'

'What?'

'You had your ice cream, right? Heather, you had your ice cream?'

'No.'

'Come on, Heth. You must've. You had your ice cream?'

'I never found the van,' Heather said flatly.

'Ant. You told her how you feel, didn't you? You had a nice time? I mean, this is a dream come true for you, isn't it? A day with Heather – I wasn't even there to fuck things up.'

Rachel was gabbling now. Flushed, trying to smile. 'You enjoyed paddling in the river. You were having a great time. I could see it, you have such a connection. A really natural connection. I love seeing you two together.'

'Just get it over with,' said Antonia.

Heather glanced at Antonia. 'Get what over with?'

Rachel rotated the gun so that it pointed at Antonia. 'Sorry, Toni, it's you too.'

'I know.'

'You know?'

'I know. Just get it over with.'

Rachel cried out and turned away, pacing with agitation. 'Why don't you run? Why don't you do *something*? Don't just stand there gawping at me! *You* know what's going on, Toni – you understand why I have to do this, right?'

'Yes.'

'I don't want to do it, any of this. You get that, don't you? It's Almanby.'

'Yes. I know all about Almanby.'

In horror, Heather glanced between Antonia and Rachel. 'You two set all this up? You brought me here to kill me? *I'm* the package?'

'It wasn't her,' said Rachel. 'It was all me. I set it up, I brought you both here. I don't know… I don't know what's happened to Toni, I don't know why she's acting like this.'

'I'm Green Anne's Daughter,' said Antonia, with a smile. 'My shoes are red.'

'I'm sorry, guys,' said Rachel. 'I really am. I have to do it. I love you both, but I have to do it.'

With renewed determination, Rachel raised the gun.

'Rachel, don't!' said Heather.

Rachel screwed up her eyes and pulled the trigger.

65

And nothing happened.

Nothing happened, the gun didn't work. There was no green flash; no hot, dry popping sound. Heather remained upright.

Fuck.

'I'm sorry, Rachel,' said Antonia. 'That was a mean trick to play.'

'What are you talking about?'

'I didn't fetch Heather here so you could kill her. I brought her so she could be part of this. It's the happiest of days. It's Green Anne Day. Do you know what that means?'

'No,' said Rachel.

'There's been a change of plan. You're all used up, Rachel. You have no more friends. You're half-dead anyway. You're no use to anyone. She doesn't think it's worth keeping you around anymore.'

'Who doesn't?'

'Green Anne. Almanby. The Egesgrime. Whatever you want to call her.'

'Tonio, wait, listen. This doesn't sound like you, you sound weird...'

'Happy Green Anne Day, Rachel.'

Antonia took out the knife she'd been given at the party and slid the blade between Rachel's ribs.

That was easy, she thought.

Over on the far side of the green, Christopher had been watching them the whole time.

Everything was right now.

He held hands with his sister Rachel. Her eyes shone blue like glass. They turned and walked away.

66

Heather ran.

She didn't know where and she didn't know how long. She ran till the hot air burned her lungs; till her legs gave way and deposited her onto a grass verge among the bluebells and grasshoppers.

Only now did she register the six words Antonia had called after her as she ran.

'*It's safe, Heather. It's all over.*'

Safe? Nothing was safe, not anymore. Heather had just watched her oldest friend try to kill her. She'd watched the woman she'd grown to like and trust casually murder that friend in front of her, as if it was nothing at all, as if she was posting a letter into a letterbox.

Heather didn't understand. She didn't understand any of it.

She was certain Rachel was dead. She'd stuck around long enough to see the blade go all the way in, and the blood start to drench Rachel's clothing. She doubted she'd ever scrub the image of Rachel's final surprised expression from her memory. It'd dangle in front of her eyes at night as she tried to sleep; it'd flash up like an advertising hoarding in moments of joy, in moments of ecstasy.

It was Almanby. It had to be. Heather finally understood how dangerous it really was, why the grown-ups warned against visiting, why she never should've come. Had Rachel really brought her here to kill her, as a sacrifice to... well, to whatever bollocks the pair of them were talking about – Green Anne, the spirit of Almanby?

Antonia had changed. Almanby had done something to her mind. But this had been Rachel's plan all along, Heather was sure of it. Delivering packages to Almanby every few months, neatly tied up with a bow. All their friends. The Chicken Club, John and Sandy and Paulette, all murdered. Almost everyone she knew, murdered by Rachel.

Heather felt she should cry, break down and sob uncontrollably, but it was impossible to take in. The notion was just too ridiculous to be anything but an abstract concept, a silly story someone had made up. *Hey, wouldn't it be weird if all your friends were systematically murdered by one of your other friends?*

Pictures of the fun times she'd had with Rachel these last couple of years flashed through her mind – eating pizza in the cinema, inventing cocktails in Rachel's kitchen, prank-calling Harkington police station, peeping through a crack in the pavilion roof at showering cricketers, painting the Bramble Lane mural, baking gooseberry pies, their epic game of drunk football that spanned the best part of a week, the nettle wine they brewed, the boxes of abandoned gumballs they discovered behind a bush. This whole day out today.

For every single one, Rachel was already a murderer. Heather had spent many of her happiest times laughing and joking with a mass-murderer.

Heather wasn't sorry that Rachel was dead, but she was sorry she'd had to see it. She was sorry that something, some aspect of Almanby, had made Antonia do it. She deserved better than that.

'Are you all right?' said Daniel, who happened to be passing.

'Of course.' Heather sprang to her feet and affected a jaunty pose. But it all felt rather tired now, this ridiculous Calamity Jane shtick – for who? Who was she even trying to impress anymore? She felt like a stupid little girl, too busy looking back to ever remember to look forward. One day she'd wake up and she would no longer be a delightfully eccentric young woman, she'd be a weird middle-aged lady with unkempt grey hair and a house full of cats – still desperately aping her childhood self, but coming off now as ghoulish, as cloying, as someone that people would avoid.

'You look like shit,' said Daniel.

Heather shrugged and thrust her hands into her pockets. 'Yeah. I feel like shit,' she said.

'Well? Are you coming or not?'

'Where are we going?'

'To the church. To meet Steven.'

67

The church maintained a constant presence now, squatting above them amid its attendant yew trees like a sleeping grey dragon, conqueror of the village, stony scales curled around its interred pile of corpses. It seemed to move, rolling its shoulders, exhaling, settling deeper into the hillside.

The closer they drew to the church, the more enlivened Daniel became, as if a poltergeist had taken hold of him, some genie had worked its way into his body – as if, indeed, he'd been possessed by Heather herself. By the time they reached the lip of the hill, he was scampering this way and that across the grass and dandelions, laughing and bounding and even occasionally twirling.

'This is it!' he called back across the turf to Heather. 'Can't you feel it? There's a storm coming. Tell me you can feel it!' He flung his arms skyward. 'It's almost time. Heather, it's almost time. It's almost three.'

Heather *could* feel it. Still the air grew heavier, till it threatened to crush the buildings to dust and squeeze the two humans into jammy smears on the grass. Choirs of tinnitus sang in her eardrums; red fireworks prickled around the edges of her eyeballs. Her fingers felt swollen. It was becoming difficult to swallow, to think straight, to maintain a train of thought… as if the hill wasn't a hill at all, it was really a hollow, and all of Almanby – all the shops and houses and the pub and the school and the war memorial and the duck pond and the maypole and all the trees and ghosts – were tumbling down onto her. The whole weight of Almanby on her shoulders, on her back, in her blood, in her skull where her brain should be; in her ears, behind her eyes, in her throat. Heather felt sick. And she felt a great sickness all around her.

Ghosts swarmed in the cemetery like a biblical plague, and Heather shuddered with revulsion; but they seemed for the moment to only be interested in the higgledy-piggledy dentistry of the gravestones. Maybe these were their own graves, and they were wondering how to get their bodies out. One woman-ghost, in a long black dress, seemed to be crying.

Oak and sycamore branches thrashed, groaned, swayed, creaked, even though there wasn't even a breeze. *Something* was buffeting Daniel too, making it hard for him to walk.

'Over here,' he called, leading Heather to a shady spot at the rear of the church – '*the devil's side*' as Heather's primary school teacher had informed her, long ago, as if imparting some profound canonical secret – and parked her beneath a low, wide yew with its plastic red berries.

'Wait here,' he said. 'I'll see what mood Steven's in.'

'Steven's always in a good mood. That's one of the things I love about him.'

'*Right*,' said Daniel, as if she'd just said the stupidest thing in the world. 'Look, I'm just saying he might not want to see you. Don't get your hopes up.'

'He'll want to see me.'

'Don't get your hopes up.'

'All right.' Heather had wrapped her arms tightly around herself, despite the heat.

'I like your shoes, by the way.'

'Thank you.'

'*Mood mood mood mood mood*,' Daniel sang happily as he trundled off to a small wooden side door of the church, and disappeared inside. '*Daniel's in a mood. Steven's in a mood. Heather's in a mood. We're all in a mood.*'

Heather sat on the grass, crossed her legs, then stood up again and paced in a figure of eight.

Steven was here. Really here this time. Just inside the church, just the other side of that big stone wall. Only a few feet away. And… and she wasn't excited. In fact, she felt quite nauseous. This wasn't how it was supposed to be – waiting for permission to see him, held at arm's length. Like one of Rachel's secrets, Steven had become a dark whisper, something clandestine. He should've been scampering across the turf to embrace her, arms splayed, primary colours bursting from every pore. Sweeping her off her feet into a joyous twirl like anime teenagers.

Instead, she felt herself prickling with anxiety. Not excitement, not even a nervous anticipation, just something hollow and unpleasant tugging at her guts. Antonia was a killer. Daniel was a killer. Rachel was a killer, and now she was dead too. And Heather Long and all those other mercenaries, or whoever they were. Even if there was a grand, joyful reunion with Steven, it was all ruined anyway.

And that possibility was feeling more and more remote by the second as it was.

I'm an idiot, she thought. Chasing pathetically after some man just because he was impressive. That wasn't who she was. She'd taken her eye off the ball, become enamoured and lost track of herself. The real Heather McLagan was back in Headingham, concocting all sorts of mischief and chortling at the memory of their sexy exploits. She shouldn't be here alone in a graveyard, chewing her nails. Made to stand outside like a naughty schoolgirl waiting for the headmaster to cane her. *Know your place, little girl.* Was Steven really so busy, or was this deliberate?

Fuck you, Steven. I'm Heather McLagan.

Heather perched on the edge of an upturned tin bath, nettles poking through holes rusted in its side. She could feel her own body trembling.

A thrush hopped across the grass looking for itinerant snails. Ghosts wandered to and fro over on the bright side of the church, oblivious to Heather. She pulled her shoe off, rattled it around, and tipped out a piece of grit.

And then, suddenly, a spear of intense pain, as if lightning had struck her on the top of her head and travelled all the way down her right arm, out to the fingertips.

She pulled her top all the way off. Underneath, her left arm and much of her left side were translucent and as white as alabaster, as white as a ghost's skin. Black and purple veins plotted a course through her flesh deep below the surface like a pirate's treasure map.

Fuck.

Lost in the Garden

More than anything, Heather wanted Antonia to be here. The real Antonia, the normal Antonia. She'd nag at Heather about finding a doctor, about getting as far away from Almanby as they could and seeking urgent medical attention. And this time, Heather felt, she would've listened.

A side door opened in the church, and Daniel emerged.

'He's ready to see you,' he said. 'You can come inside.'

Heather looked up, her eyes big. She felt her stomach tighten and her heartrate accelerate. She rose to her feet.

'What's he like?' she said.

Anna Green is old and frail
Her house a warmer barrow
Her scattered ashes, unbidden eyes
Still wide awake and hollow

68

In the nave of the church, darkness. Total and impenetrable, like the eternity before the dawn of time. And yet... and yet, Heather could see herself. She could see her own hands, her own arms, her own body, bright and tungsten-yellow, suspended in the void. Only a shallow pool of light on the tiles at her feet grounded her.

Above her head, she saw, was a dazzling spotlight, a yellow diorama sun. She suddenly felt like a contestant in a quiz show. The final round, seconds from the big prize. The tie-breaker question: *Does Steven still love you?*

No, the tie-breaker question: *Did Steven ever love you?*

This place certainly didn't feel like the Steven she remembered. Steven was light and life and energy and joy, not this. Not darkness. Not dusty, stuffy masonry. Not fear and anxiety.

Heather called out, 'Steven?'

Somewhere, off to one side, a smattering of footsteps, which stopped as abruptly as they began. The footsteps didn't approach; it was someone shifting position.

'Steven?' Heather rotated, peering into the black. Now her eyes were beginning to adjust, she could make out a drape or curtain. The shadow of a lectern. She half expected to see Steven's distinctive silhouette behind it, gripping it firmly with both hands, pantomiming a sermon for her amusement; but no.

More footsteps, a shuffle, a scrape.

'Is that you?' she said, hand shielding her eyes. 'Steven. I came to find you.'

'*I don't think you counted to a hundred,*' said a voice from somewhere overhead. Higher up than she'd imagined. It sounded a little like Steven. But too frail, too insubstantial. Not familiar. A Steven strained of all his colour – a Steven boiled in water overnight, left to soak till he was all but gone.

'I counted to a hundred million.' She looked around, trying to spot him.

'*Well, then it's your turn to hide.*'

'I don't want to play this game anymore. Come out, let's talk.' There was no reply. Heather circled, her footsteps fluttering up into the rafters. 'I can't see you.'

'*I told you not to come.*' Was that really *Steven*? It could've been Steven's grandfather for all Heather could tell. An old man with a cracked, brittle voice.

'Yeah, but when have I ever done what I'm told?'

'*It's dangerous.*'

'That's why I'm here.'

'*Fuck's sake, Heather. Just for once. Just for once, can't you listen?*'

'It's a bit late for scolding me, isn't it? I'm here now. I thought you'd be happy to see me.'

'*No.*'

Wow. Heather heard her own sharp intake of breath, like a punch in the stomach. 'Beat about the bush, why don't you? Jesus.'

'*Why do you think I didn't want to tell you in the first place?*'

'You were calling for help.'

'*No, I wasn't.*'

'You left notes for me. You asked me to come and find you.'

'*I don't know what you're talking about, Heth.*'

'The note in your car. Your red Space Invader T-shirt.'

'*What about it?*'

'I found it tied to a lamppost. You left it for me to see so I'd know you were here.'

'*That old thing? I didn't even bring it with me. I threw it away months ago.*'

'But… I bought that for your birthday.'

'*The moths got to it. There was a hole in the shoulder. What do you want me to do, keep every moth-eaten rag anyone ever buys for me? I'd have a wardrobe full of shit.*'

'I thought it might have sentimental value.'

'*Thank you. It was a nice T-shirt. I liked the T-shirt, I enjoyed wearing it, I was grateful you bought it for me. But then it got a hole in. What can I say? Anyway, it's long gone – I didn't leave it out for you to find.*'

'And there was an address. 7 Penfold Lane.'

'*Yeah, I lived there. Ages ago. I haven't been back in weeks. I live here now. Almanby can't get me in here, I'm safe in the church.*'

'Steven, I saw the T-shirt with my own eyes. The notes were in your handwriting. I heard your voice.'

'*Almanby's been messing with you, mate. That's what happens here, or hadn't you noticed? Fuck's sake… why did you have to come, Heather? I told you, you shouldn't come. Seriously, it's not safe here.*'

'No shit.'

Heather waited for Steven to speak. To say something, anything. Just to prove he still cared to strike up conversation.

When the silence became too awkward, like a rubber band stretching tighter and tighter till it threatened to snap, Heather called, 'Why don't you come down?'

'*I'm fine up here.*'

'This is silly. I'm shouting, you're shouting. Come down. Let's talk properly.'

'*I'm comfortable.*'

'Then let me come up there.'

'*You wouldn't like it.*'

'Who says I wouldn't like it?'

'*I says you wouldn't like it. It's not your thing.*'

'How do you know it's not my thing?'

'*Close your eyes. Close your eyes and I'll come down.*'

'I want to see you.'

'*No. Close your eyes. Otherwise I won't come.*'

Heather closed her eyes as tightly as she could.

'*Are they closed?*'

'Yes.'

The sound of someone descending a ladder, slowly and carefully. Breathing hard, making an unnatural effort. The creaks of feet on wooden rungs like the creaks of old bones.

And then footsteps on stone. A faltering gait, approaching from behind.

A presence leaned close to Heather's face, a presence she didn't recognise. Cold breath on her neck.

She kept her eyes tight shut.

'Heather,' said a voice in her ear.

'Can I open my eyes?'

'No. I don't want you to see me.'

A palm passed across her eyes, just briefly, brushing her lashes.

'Your hand's cold.'

'You're warm.'

'It's a hot day.'

'I haven't been outside. Not in a long time.'

He stroked her face with the back of his hand. It felt withered. Bony. Like an old man's hand.

'You shouldn't have followed me. I said not to follow me.'

'You really expected me just to give up on you?'

'Yeah.' He stepped away from her.

'How could I not follow?'

'I didn't think you were that stupid.'

'I loved you.'

'Did you?'

'Of course I did.'

'Seriously?'

'I didn't think you were that stupid.'

'Sorry, Heth. I didn't realise.'

A single tear rolled down Heather's cheek.

'I reckon you wanted to be found really,' she said. 'I think you were waiting for me to come and tell you how silly all this is, and everything would be all right again. I think you're just pretending not to have loved me so I don't feel too bad about what's happened.'

'How's the cinema?'

'It got sick. Like everything else gets sick.'

'That's a shame. I really enjoyed seeing films with you. Remember that time we watched *London After Midnight*, and we couldn't stop giggling?'

'I think we were drunk.'

'We were pissed out of our heads. We drank three bottles of red wine between us.'

'That was so much fun.'

'Yeah.'

'Steven. Why didn't you come home?'

'I am home. How about you?'

Heather sensed movement on the other side of the room. Instinctively, she opened her eyes. Half-hidden behind the big wine-red velvet drapes skulked Daniel.

Startled by Heather's eyes opening, Steven retreated back into the shadows. Heather spun round to catch sight of him, but too late. And then he was climbing again, like an animal from the deep parts of the ocean, pale and translucent. Even in this darkness, she could make out the whiteness of his skin.

'Didn't I tell you not to go to Almanby, Steven? I mean – everyone's been telling us our whole lives. Don't go to Almanby. Whatever you do, kids, don't go to Almanby. Don't play in the farmyard, don't fly your kite near the pylons, look both ways when you cross the road, stay away from Almanby. And what did you go and do?'

'*You came too.*'

'I had to.'

'*Well, I had to, too.*'

'Why?'

'*Rachel. I found out what she was doing. I found out where John and Sandy and Paulette and all the others went.*'

'Yeah, me too.'

'*Shit, isn't it.*'

'It really, really is. Why didn't you just stop her instead?'

'*I came to see if they could be saved. I came to see if there was anything I could do. But it was too late – she brought them here to die.*'

'You didn't warn me. You could've warned me.'

'*I know what you're like, Heth. I didn't want you following me. I didn't want you muscling in on the action. And you're such a blabbermouth. Rachel would've found out sooner or later, the whole thing would've been fucked. Honestly, Heather, I really thought I'd be coming back. I really expected to be home in a few days, and I could warn you then. And do something about Rachel, too.*'

'So why didn't you?'

Unexpectedly, Steven laughed. '*It turns out they were right. Coming to Almanby is a really, really bad idea. You must've realised that by now.*'

'Yeah, I did get an inkling.'

'*When I found out they were all dead, and there was no chance to help them, I had to think of something else. If I couldn't save the people who'd already come here, then I had to stop this. Put an end to the whole thing. And the only way to do that was to destroy Almanby. Take it off the map. And by chance, I had a friend. Our*'

Daniel here. A sort of a friend-of-a-friend, really. A bit of a shady character, as I'm sure you'll agree. Somehow, for some reason, he's not affected by Almanby like other people. Most people either get stuck here, like me, or they're like Rachel – Almanby lets them come and go providing they bring sacrifices. But Dan's different, Dan's an anomaly. He can come and go as he pleases… Almanby can't touch him, we don't know why. So I got him to help me, I got him to bring stuff in. And… and together we've built something.'

'The bomb?'

Steven hesitated. *'Yeah. It's… it's sort of a bomb, I suppose. How did you know?'*

'I met someone. I made a friend too.'

'Congratulations.'

'But Daniel killed her.'

'Oh. I'm sorry. He does that.'

'But listen, Steven. This is really important. What you're doing… this thing you're planning… destroying Almanby is a bad idea. Like – not just bad, but… catastrophic. Disastrous. You wouldn't just be destroying this one village. But, y'know, lots. Like a nuclear bomb. That's what she said – like a nuclear bomb. Everything dead, everything turned to ash.'

'I know.'

'You *know?*'

'Yeah. You can't take out something like Almanby without making a bit of a splash. You heard the stories of something living under the village?'

'Yeah. A woman or something.'

'Right. And I think they might be true. Or nearly true. Approximately true. And she's powerful. Powerful and sick. There's a lot of sickness and bad energy in this place.'

'Then…'

'You're going to try and talk me out of this, aren't you. You're going to ask me to reconsider, to think about my moral duty.'

'Well, yeah…'

'I know it sounds extreme. But sometimes sacrifices have to be made.'

'You sound like Rachel. You're the one to make those sacrifices, are you?'

'It looks like it. What's your alternative?'

'Well… now we know it's Almanby causing all this, we can do something. We can tell people. We can work out some way to stop it.'

'I have worked out a way to stop it.'

'Some other way. Some way that doesn't involve killing everything for miles around.'

'Heather. We're not getting out of here. No one ever does. Who are we going to tell even if we could?'

'Daniel could tell someone.'

'Who would he tell?'

'All right – what happens to us? What happens to *me*? You really want to kill me?'

'Yeah, that's a bit shit. No, I don't want to kill you. But honestly, it's your own fault. I warned you not to come here. I warned you not to come and you came anyway. You probably would've been safe if you'd stayed in Headingham.'

'Probably?'

'Well, you know. This has never been tried before.'

'Almanby has damaged you, Steven. This isn't you. You're someone who creates and nurtures and loves, not destroys. You're not well, you need help.'

'*That hurts my feelings, Heth. You always tell me how well I look.*'

'Yeah. Because you did used to look well. You were always such a beacon of light. You never got sick, you never even had a bad day.'

'*Everyone has bad days, Heather.*'

'Yeah, but you never let it affect you. You were always so cheerful. That's one of the things I loved most about you. You were about positivity and hope and… and humanity. Not destroying, not making 'necessary sacrifices'. All the world would be crumbling around you, and there you were – always the same. Always smiling, making the best of things, keeping us all going.'

'*Things change, Heth. People change.*'

'Not you. You don't change.'

'*Everyone changes. Everyone gets old and sick eventually.*'

Movement above her head. A glimpse of scrawny baby-bird arms. Shaggy, unkempt hair. She strained to see his face, but he was gone, back into the shadows like something nocturnal. His silhouette was bent over now, moving something large, heavy. He seemed to be on a platform built into the church wall, with a long, wooden ladder leaning precariously against it. As he shifted position, he knocked the ladder. Heather jumped to one side as it crashed to the floor, the boom echoing like a gunshot.

'*Bollocks,*' he said.

Heather rushed over to Daniel, who flinched at the suddenness of her approach. He'd been quietly lurking all this time, subdued, placid, drained of personality. A transparent version of himself.

'Dan. Give me the thing. The component. You heard what he said. We'll be killed if we don't do something. We can still stop him.'

Steven's frail voice echoed into the nave. '*I already have it, Heather. It was the first thing he did when he got here.*'

Heather returned to the yellow disc of the spotlight.

'How about we just talk? Let's go for ice cream and talk, like we used to. You remember?'

'*Yeah, I remember. We used to talk about what it'd be like to have a fresh start, to go back before all this, all the corruption and decay.*'

'I meant like old TV shows and shit. Remember *Pod and the Beans*? Steven. Remember *Star Force*? That show was such a load of old crap. Remember *Sock Draw*? Those hand-drawn sock puppets? And it was funny because they could've used real—'

'*Sock draw, sock draw, living in a sock drawer,*' Steven sang, cutting across her, his voice light and wobbly. '*Sock draw, sock draw, living in a sock drawer.*'

'*There's Pete and Posy and Peppermint too,*' sang Heather. '*There's Sam and Sandy and Bobby and Sue. Sock draw, sock draw, socks are clever. Sock draw, sock draw, friends forever. Join us, join us, we all love socks.*'

Steven was already laughing by the time Heather finished the song, marching around in a little circle on the faded red and white tiles.

They fell silent. The final traces of their song dissipated into cobwebby nooks and corners. Big spiders that had died twenty years ago, fifty years ago, too dry to rot.

She heard Steven sniff.

'Come down, Steven. Come give me a hug.'

'I'd love to, but it's nearly three o'clock. It's nearly time.'

'People are still doing stuff. People are living their lives. I know it's an imperfect present, Steven, but it's the only one we've got. Who are you to take that away from us?'

'Someone has to make that decision.'

'Do they?'

'Yeah. Ordinary men accept their situation, great men decide to change it.'

'So that's what this is about? Your ego? You proving you're a great man?'

'It's my chance to do something great. To really make a difference.'

'Don't I count for anything? You always said I was the most alive person in the whole world.'

'That was our thing, wasn't it? You and me against the universe. Whatever happened, nothing could get to us. But look at us now. Look at your arm. You're decaying too, Heather.'

'Four minutes,' said Daniel from the corner of the room.

'Four minutes, Heather. What are you going to do with your final four minutes?'

'Steven, stop this and come down,' said Heather. 'I'm not asking now, I'm telling you. Switch that thing off and come here.'

'It's too late, Heather. It's too late to change anything now. I couldn't stop it even if I wanted to. That's how I designed it – so I couldn't change my mind. This is too important for my human fallibility to get in the way. And I wouldn't be human if I didn't get spooked or have second thoughts, would I? I've factored that in, Heth. I can't switch it off. At three o'clock, this ends. The

decision's out of my hands. No regrets, eh? It's too late for regrets anyway. It's too late for words. It's too late for tears or apologies. It is what it is.'

'It's not too late for the damned to repent.'

'Yes it is. Yes it is, Heth. Can't you feel it? It's so close. Less than four minutes. Probably nearly three minutes by now. It's so close you can almost taste it. Tick tock tick tock. Every time your heart beats, your time grows shorter still…'

'Three minutes,' said Daniel.

A stream of water sprang from the ceiling, a leak, and spattered on the tiles close to where Daniel stood. At the same moment, a trickle of blood wound its way down Heather's forearm and dripped from her fingertips.

Daniel cupped his hand into the stream of water, let it splash through his fingers.

'Each moment a melting snowflake,' he said.

'Hey, Steven,' said Heather. 'Remember how we used to do dares? You took your trousers off all day. We climbed over into that woman's garden. And we kissed. Right there in the garden, you in your underpants, while the old lady watched from the window. We spent an hour just standing there kissing, we didn't care that people saw us. I thought I loved you. I really thought I loved you. I guess I was just impressed. You were weird and interesting. I was lonely. You did all this cool stuff. And you didn't treat me like a novelty. You didn't talk down to me or treat me like a silly little girl.'

'Two minutes,' said Daniel.

'At the end of the day, after we went back to your house, you didn't put your trousers back on, we just took the rest of our clothes off. You must still think about that.'

A boom in the darkness to Heather's right and a muffled cry. Too high pitched to be Daniel, but it was Daniel. Then another boom. He was throwing chairs, swinging them against the wall. He shrieked like an animal caught in a trap.

'Daniel!' cried Heather. She took a step towards him, almost instinctively, and then ducked to one side as a wooden chair sailed past her ear, inches from striking her full in the face. It splintered into three pieces on the tiled floor behind her. 'Daniel, stop! What are you doing?'

But still Daniel screamed his inhuman scream. Desperate, agonised. As if the full import of what was happening had finally come crashing down. As if all the sickness from all his trips to Almanby had finally caught up with him.

'Daniel, it's me!'

This time, a chair-back made contact with Heather, colliding with the side of her head. She tumbled to the floor, too shocked to react.

For less than a moment – a micro-moment – the church was illuminated lime green, so bright it rendered Heather's eyesight pink for a time afterwards, a bubblegum-pink replica of the nave. And, simultaneous to that, another boom, louder than wood on stone.

Then all was silent, except for the dying echoes, and Heather knew at once what had happened. Daniel lay on the floor, his gun beside him. His head was blackened and scorched and elongated.

'Fuck,' Heather said.

'Fuck,' she repeated.

'*Poor Daniel*,' said Steven. '*He only meant harm.*'

'Stop this, Steven!' Heather said. 'For god's sake, please stop it. For me. Look, it's me. I'm right here. Good old Heather. How about that ice cream? Raspberry ripple, yeah? That's your favourite. We'll eat ice cream and we'll just... we'll just hang out, exactly like it used to be. Right?'

'*One minute,*' said Steven.

'I came to find you. I could've stayed at home, but I came for you. I came because you matter to me. I came because our friendship, or whatever it was we had... it's important. It's more important than a bomb or a village, or any of this. It's real. I know you know that. I know you felt it too.'

'*Yeah. I felt it too.*'

'Steven. I want to go home. I'm scared.'

'*I'm scared too, Heather.*'

But now there was nothing else to say, for the church bells had begun to peal. Great rolling, roiling, tumbling cascades, drowning out everything else.

All Heather could do now was stare up into the darkness and assume Steven was staring back down at her.

And then the noise stopped.

And the minute hand of the clock clicked into place.

And the church bell struck once,

then twice,

then a third time.

69

Nothing happened.

Nothing exploded.

Almanby was still there, the church was still there, Heather was still there, her chest heaving – she'd forgotten to breathe for the last minute or so.

'*It didn't work!*' cried Steven. '*It didn't work!*' Heather could hear the bangs and clangs as he kicked his painstaking assembly of bomb components. '*What's* wrong *with you? What the fuck went* wrong*? You were supposed to work! You were supposed to do something! I had it all figured out!*'

'It's Almanby, Steven. It's Almanby.'

'*No! That's not possible. Almanby can't get me in the church. Everybody knows that. Everybody knows that, Heather! This was supposed to work!*'

'I'm Almanby.'

'*What are you talking about?*'

'I'm Almanby.'

'*You're Heather.*'

'I'm Heather and I'm Almanby. I lived here for sixty years. In your old house, in Penfold Lane. A whole lifetime, till I couldn't remember anything else, just that one small cottage in this one small village. I thought I was going to die there, all alone, an old lady. Then Antonia came and pulled me back. Don't you see? I could've been swallowed up like everyone else. But Almanby let me stay. Almanby let me become part of it. It was Almanby who called me here, not you. It was Almanby I could hear asking for help. *Help me, help me.* Not you. I made the bomb fail. Me being here. I should've understood sooner. But I realise now. I'm Almanby.'

A thump as Steven sat down on the platform. She could hear him breathing heavily in the darkness. Sobbing.

'*I want to go home now, Heather.*'

'You are home.'

'*Really home. Take me home.*'

'You *are* home.'

'*Help me down. Come on, Heather, help me down. Fetch the ladder, I can't get down on my own. Heather. I don't want to do this anymore. I want to go home. Heth, help me down.*'

But Heather was already gone.

70

Brightness and greenness overwhelmed Heather as she emerged from the church, like her days at the cinema when she'd exit blinking and troglodyte-pale from matinee screenings.

Her job was done. A job she hadn't realised she had until after it was completed. And she didn't know how to feel. Almanby still stood because of her. It still festered, septic and diseased, in the heart of the countryside because of her. Steven had failed. However noble his intentions, he had failed.

Somewhere, far in the distance, ice-cream van chimes tinkled.

> *Oh dear, what can the matter be?*
> *Oh dear, what can the matter be?*
> *Oh dear, what can the matter be?*
> *Johnny's so long at the fair.*

> *He promised he'd book me a place at the table,*
> *And all summer long he would kiss and he'd tease me,*
> *He promised he'd come home and bring his long fingers,*
> *To run through my bonnie brown hair.*

Heather didn't have the energy to chase after it anymore. She only made it a few yards from the porch of the church before she collapsed onto a grassy bank by the side of the lane, amid a horoscope of daisies.

Did she ever really believe she'd make it out of Almanby? Did she really imagine herself strolling back to the main road, flagging down a passing motorist and hitchhiking all the way home to Headingham? Maybe. Not now, though. This would be as far as she went.

She was spent. Her job was done. Almanby had no use for her now.

Three ghosts had seen her and were ambling in her direction. Two women and a man. Two of them were unarmed, but one of the women carried a vicious-looking length of iron, a snapped-off piece of a fence.

This wasn't how Heather wanted to go. Maybe if she concentrated hard enough, she could die before they reached her. Her arm and her whole left side were totally numb, as if they belonged to somebody else. As if they belonged to Almanby. And now that she was stretched out on the verge, the last of her energy was rapidly ebbing away, out through her back and down into the soil.

This was it. This was where it'd end. She couldn't help but feel a little cheated. She was still so young. She still had so much to look forward to. And now that she'd spent sixty years married to the invisible man in the bed, in that one small cottage in this one small village, she wanted to do *everything*.

But despite the approaching ghosts, she felt oddly peaceful.

Whatever happened, happened. It'd all be over soon.

* * *

Somewhere, far in the distance, a car engine reverberated, sounding like a broken trombone.

71

A bottle-green car pulled up opposite the churchyard.

The driver's-side window rolled down, and Antonia Coleridge leaned out.

'Come on if you're coming,' she said with a grin.

Anne Green so old and frail
Her house is waiting below
And at her wishes, two children rise
By night and day they follow

72

Morning burst through the curtains like an incendiary device. Birdsong and church bells clamoured for Heather's attention, and, somewhere not too far away, the modest tinkle of wind chimes.

The dregs of Heather's dream dissipated. She felt rested and peaceful... even a little content. It took her a moment to orient herself back to her present reality – to realise that she wasn't dead, to remember where she was.

Pastel-coloured floral wallpaper.

A watercolour of a young girl in a field of long grass and poppies, holding a wide-brimmed straw hat on her head.

A small portable television set.

A teddy bear with a tartan bow around its neck.

A circular mirror with a ridiculously ornate gold-painted frame.

A red alarm clock.

An empty glass.

A pair of slippers, stowed neatly by the door.

Heather's arm was red and still a little blotchy, but the feeling was back now and most of the pain had subsided. She hoped it'd return to normal soon. She hoped life in general would return to normal soon, too – at least as normal as was possible.

Which actually probably wasn't very normal.

Antonia poked her head into the room.

'How are you feeling?' she said.

Heather stretched and smiled. 'Good,' she said. 'Thank you. I can't believe how much I've been sleeping.'

'Looks like you needed the rest.' Antonia edged into the room sideways like a space invader, her hands thrust awkwardly into her trouser pockets. 'Is there anything I can get you?'

'Just water, if that's okay. I can't seem to shake this thirst. Thank you, Toni.'

'Coming right up!'

Foxgloves outside the window nodded patiently in the breeze. Bumblebees visited each of the flowers in turn, ferreting around for their gold dust, then flying away giddy with triumph.

Antonia filled a tall glass with water and set it on the counter. She went to the freezer, pulled open the door, took out an ice cube tray, then bent the plastic back till the last two blocks plopped out into the glass. Behind her, the freezer door swung closed of its own accord. She tossed the empty tray into the sink. She'd refill it later.

Two of the pine kitchen chairs sat at unruly angles away from the table. Antonia frowned, and they shuffled obediently back into place. The glass of water scooted an inch or two along the counter into easy reaching distance. Antonia plucked it up, then headed for the kitchen door.

* * *

Heather and Antonia lived in that little cottage in Almanby for a hundred years, and a hundred years more.

Sometimes, Antonia thought about her old life in Headingham – her increasingly desperate comedy shows, her thoughtless neighbours, her dwindling coterie of friends – but it was all so distant, as if it had happened to someone else. And maybe it had. Antonia was part of Almanby now, and so was Heather; and Almanby was part of them.

Occasionally, strangers would drift through the village, intrigued by the hushed warnings and enticed by the sense of danger. It was Heather's job to seduce them. She was very good at that – Heather was extremely cute, and people instinctively trusted her. Antonia heard their sex upstairs, but she didn't mind. It was what had to be done.

And then, when these strangers were in the thrall of Almanby's special power, granted to them by Green Anne, they would bring friends for sacrifice, just as Rachel had. It was Antonia's task to supervise the sacrifice, make sure it was done correctly. She was a bit of a soft touch, though – often she'd just end up doing it herself. It came so naturally she barely even had to think about it. Usually stabbing, that seemed to be best.

She'd finally found a job she was good at. She finally felt like she belonged.

As the years passed, Antonia saw less and less of Heather. Often she was aware of her presence, a feeling of being watched, of being followed without moving. Heather was *somewhere*, even if Antonia wasn't always sure where – in the birdsong and the gentle summer breezes and the chimes of the ice-cream van, or just suspended between air particles. But that was okay, Antonia felt safe knowing she was there and that she was looking out for her.

After three hundred years, Antonia couldn't remember whether Heather had ever been real, or whether she was just a friend she'd invented once. She liked inventing friends, she was very imaginative. A memory of a crush from long ago extrapolated into a lifelong companion for her own amusement. A silly hyperactive girl with curly brown hair and an infectious giggle. Was that Heather, or was she getting her mixed up with someone else?

It was so hard to remember much of anything anymore.

But that was okay. She was Green Anne's Daughter now, and that was very special indeed.

ACKNOWLEDGEMENTS

Thank you to everyone who's supported me over the years, read my stuff and just generally put up with me, including (but not limited to): Ace, Vanessa, Amanda, Peter, Shannon, Hilary, Annika Ester, Evelyn, Emily, Colin, and shipwrecked Pirate Sophia – ahoy there, wherever ye be.

A big thank you to everyone at UA and Dead Ink involved in making this book a reality: Eli, Becky, Harriet, Dan, Luke, Nate, Bekkii, Michael and Nathan. Thank you to Sophie from FMcM. Special early *Lost in the Garden* gestation thanks to Richard Tunstall and Sarah Fiern.

Hats off to my super compatriots at Blackwell's Oxford over the years, and hello to everyone at no. 7 and no. 20.

And an off-topic thank you to Christina for sticking with this particular screenwriter above and beyond the call of duty – you've been a life-saver.

ABOUT THE AUTHOR

Adam grew up in rural Lincolnshire during the 1980s, in a tiny remote village called Carlton Scroop not far from *Moondial*, spending his days among the pylons daydreaming of Beatles records and *Star Wars* figures. He now lives in Oxford, where he pretends to be a grownup but still mostly daydreams of Beatles records.

As well as an author, Adam is a screenwriter, songwriter and musician. He makes psychedelic pop-rock records under the name Berlin Horse, and has been working on his most recent album *Light Omitting Diode* for far longer than he'd like to admit.

Adam isn't married and has no children, but did once have a box of snails.

About Dead Ink

Dead Ink is a publisher of bold new fiction based in Liverpool. We're an Arts Council England National Portfolio Organisation.

If you would like to keep up to date with what we're up to, check out our website and join our mailing list.

www.deadinkbooks.com | @deadinkbooks